WICKED LITTLE ISLAND

Rhea Ryan

For those who rise from the ashes.

TRIGGER WARNINGS

Gore
Violence
Mental Health
BDSM
Murder
Open Door Sex Scenes
Bullying
Death

PROLOGUE

MICAH

My adult life started like a shattered mirror—fractured, with the sharp pieces scattering and digging into my flesh. Day by day, I tried to pull each out to heal, only for them to cause more pain. The more I pulled them out, the more I realized the internal wounds within me were embedded in my veins, spreading like cancer. They would never go away, and trying to find a cure hurt.

So, eventually, I turned it all off. *Feeling anything.* Until I met London King, who is the sole person who made me come alive again. And now my darkness has spread to her to the point where I barely recognize the girl I fell for. She breathed in my poison, causing my sickness to take root in her, too.

Not giving a shit was certainly easier than this.

Love is highly overrated.

Do it, motherfucker, pull the trigger.

I'm holding the cold metal flare gun in my hand, sitting alone, surrounded by charred trees and mud in the northern wilderness, wondering what it would be like if I blew my brains out. I kept the flare gun hidden from the others, knowing it was my final escape if needed. Flames surround me, threatening to engulf me, and I've resorted to talking to myself. I'd promised myself if I ever got to that point, it would be the day I'd end this. However, it's my twin standing in front of me who mouthed the words I spoke.

He emerges from the ashes wearing the same hooded sweater and gray sweatpants as me, as if I'm looking in that fractured mirror reflecting my version of hell. The threatening flames creep closer, and I welcome the heat on my face after nearly a year of icy inferno. If I stay here any longer, the acrid smoke will suffocate me, which makes me contemplate surrendering to the flames. But death by fire is a horrible way to go, and I always appreciate efficiency, even if I deserve to be burned at the stake.

Because I never thought I'd watch my twin die before me—the possibility never played out in my mind. Maison was supposed to live, and I was supposed to die first. I was supposed to protect him. Ever since I witnessed him bleed out on the snow, I've been convinced in my heart that the wrong twin perished that day.

"What are you waiting for, Micah?" he says, his words dripping with an uncharacteristic edge. I shoot him a piercing glare, and he calmly mirrors my every move as I itch my forehead with the barrel of my flare gun. My emotions are reflected in his eyes. "Come join me, then, fucker."

I scoff and drop the gun to my side. "You're pretty cocky for a dead guy. Why don't you go haunt someone else?"

His lips curl into a smug smile—the same smile he used to give me whenever he beat me at something, which didn't happen often. My smile. "There is no one else left to haunt, Micah."

No one else.

No one left.

Just me and Maison.

"You're chickenshit, aren't you? You can't kill yourself, but you can't live with yourself, either." He gives me a look of pity. "That's quite the predicament."

"Go. Away."

I close my eyes and drown him out, breathing slowly. A tight grip clutches my stomach, thinking of how close I am to joining him. I have no fear because I'm incapable of the emotion.

I've always had an innate fascination with death because I wasn't supposed to be born. I should have died when I was eleven, and then again in the accident with Olivia. I should have died in the plane crash and sliced up by that fucked-up prick Nigel.

I've watched countless people take their last breath in my lifetime. I hand-bombed a mass grave of teenagers. A girl I freshly fucked took her last breath in the seat next to me in a car that I then crashed. I watched my twin die in the arms of the girl I love.

I always thought I'd die young, which is why I live the way I live. Reckless. Like I don't matter and don't give a shit. Hurting people, shoving most people out of my life, beating the ever-loving hell out of them on the hockey rink, or torturing them behind my parents' back because I could. No one ever stopped me from digging my elbow into their neck to see how long it would take for them to pass out.

One. Two. Three...

Number ten was usually when their eyes would roll to the back of their head, and I would ease off just enough so I wouldn't kill them. Only Maison could bring me back from the darkest places my mind brought me to. He's the only person who brought light into my otherwise dead soul. Just like he's doing now, and like London did for four months until she experienced the worst of me.

I'm exactly who she thinks I am.

Destroyer, hunter, killer.

I am everything *he* is. The one who hunted me.

If I had died like I was supposed to, then she wouldn't have fallen for me, and she'd still be whole. I let her down in the worst possible way, and I can't even begin to comprehend the extent of the damage I've done to the one girl who means the world to me.

When I open my eyes, Maison is gone, and the metal trigger slips through my fingers as I revel in the danger of it. The only thing keeping me from pulling the trigger is that every time I blink, I see her gorgeous dark eyes, her full rosy lips, and the innocence that exudes from her stunning pale face, which utterly melts my heart.

I keep thinking of everything she's been through, of everything I put her through because I wanted her so badly and couldn't deal with *any* other emotion but loving her. How I fell so fucking hard for her that it felt like my skin was burning. And how I could ever need someone this fucking much.

She is the embodiment of everything I am not.

I think of those auburn eyes as she peered up at me for months—mainly on her knees because that's how I liked her—willing to do anything for me.

Blind love was pouring out of her.

Her precious life was in my hands, and I used that power and her body to fulfill every one of my dark desires. She gave herself to me—body and soul—loving me unconditionally because I promised to keep her alive and protect her. When ultimately, I was the one she needed protection from.

My hands don't tremble as I turn the gun to my face. I don't waver in my resolve as I click the safety off and spare one last glance at the bone weapon sitting in the grass beside me.

The symbol of the primitive creature I've become.

I take a deep breath of smoky air, enjoying the burning sensation in my lungs while the forest hums around me. I don't hesitate to pull the trigger and—

Blow.

CHAPTER ONE

MICAH

Four Months Earlier

There is an unexpected serenity in betrayal.

At least, that seems to be the case for the six other people sleeping soundly around me in the cold Arctic night, warming themselves from the relentless winter we are about to endure. Or should I say, *they* are about to endure. I've given them everything they need to survive and taught them everything I could, yet they've still managed to take the one thing from me they shouldn't have: my trust in humanity. This place was once a peaceful haven, but unfortunately, the rest of the group has now infiltrated it and ruined that. By aiding my enemy, they became my enemy.

All of them.

I'm dead quiet as I make my way through the darkened campsite. The moonlight snakes around the branches of the trees that blend together as I navigate through them, like I am part of the forest itself. My heart rate is calm—too calm—as I use the rushing water of the nearby creek as my guide through the night.

Silent. Tranquil. Beautiful.

Pleasant thoughts I shouldn't be having given our circumstances, which shows just how fucked up I am to be so at peace after what we went through. The untouched landscape reminds me we are alone out here, and I can make the rules on this island, bending and changing them as I see fit. And I enjoy having that kind of power.

Peaceful is also how I would describe the gorgeous brunette sleeping in the shelter in front of me, even though she is anything but. Maison's death has taken a toll on her. Her eyes have lost their brightness, her body is deteriorating, and each breath is a painful effort. I can't lose her, and I can't take care of her here, where I don't trust anyone, so I need to get her the fuck away from the others.

She doesn't stir as I approach the shelter, nor when I crouch in front of it and gaze at her. She makes this bed of prickly fir tree branches seem comfortable, even though I can see her icy breath in the air around her.

How the hell I'm still alive is beyond me. How either of us are still breathing is a fucking miracle, and one I'm not taking for granted anymore.

I pause for a moment to take her in, appreciating the slow rise and fall of her perky breasts and the dull ache it causes in my chest. This girl slid into my life two months ago with all her awkwardness and slowly planted herself inside my heart, then twisted it with a butter knife.

A week has passed since my brother was murdered. And I've only had that gripping panic once, but it was so consuming it nearly broke me. A twisted sense of urgency that had nothing to do with this island, the lack of food, or the ridiculously cold season we are about to endure. None of it felt real, almost like it was happening to somebody else.

So I shut it down and decided to focus on what's real, what's important.

The obsessive need I now have to protect this girl I don't deserve in the way I should have protected my brother and couldn't.

Hunger, thirst, and sex are all that really matter to me anymore. And she is quite necessary for the third piece of my trinity—the foundation of my new existence.

So I put Maison out of my mind and give her my undivided attention… She's my only priority from this point forward.

I crawl over the bed in our shelter, running my knuckles over her face, shifting her hair out of her eyes, which spring open as soon as I touch her. She's never that far from consciousness—she's always paying attention and alert.

"Is it time to go, Micah?" she whispers, shifting her body closer. She must have heard me prepping earlier because I never told her we were leaving tonight. Either that, or she sensed it as I couldn't sit down all day and left the campsite—left her side—for the first time since I came back to her after Maison died. She keeps her voice low because she doesn't want anyone else to hear, and the others are close—too fucking close.

"Yeah, baby, it's time."

A wolf howls in the distance, and she shudders.

I lie down with her for a moment and squeeze her frail body against mine, pressing my lips to her forehead. "We have to leave now, okay? If we wait even a day, the temperature will drop." More snow is coming; I can smell it. And heavy snowfall is usually followed by a prolonged deep freeze. I'm not risking getting stuck here all winter with them, not when I can have London all to myself—completely devoid of anyone else. No more distractions for her. Just me, her, and the island… like it's supposed to be.

Her breath lengthens, and her tiny fingers grasp the fabric of my shirt. She raises her head to gaze at me, then grabs me harder and lays her head in the crook of my arm. Her eyes are glassy, like she's been crying. I understand what she's thinking; I've left her too many times, and as a result, she doesn't fully trust me. The thought of being alone out here terrifies her, and being here without Maison scares her even more. And in the back of her mind, she is petrified of who is out there… the one wearing a bow tie.

I arch my brows, sensing her hesitation to leave with me. "I won't let anything bad happen to you, London." I keep my voice low and even. "You need to trust me. I'll take care of you."

I love her like I've never loved anyone. And even though she knows I struggle to say the words, she must feel it. I won't let anyone near her again. And when I'm done with her—not that I plan on ever being done with her—she won't have the capacity to think about anyone else, let alone cry about anyone else.

That seems to settle her. She nods, her eyes hooded, and gives me a faint smile. She looks broken, her pale skin blending in with the fresh snow I packed around this shelter.

Hold on a little longer, sweetheart. I've got you.

It's dumped at least a foot of snow already, which is a perfect framework for a liveable shelter the others can use to survive. I have a small sense of relief knowing I'm abandoning them to it. Snow is a natural insulator, so it's as if they have a thermal blanket... if they choose to see it that way.

I grab London's hand, and she winces. She will need major rehab from what that fucker did to her a week ago when he stepped on it, twisting her wrist and shattering her fragile bones and veins before stabbing her in the hip. When I finally have time to focus on her, I plan to put her back together. She can't walk long distances yet, and I won't push her—at least, not this time. I've pushed her enough on this island. I'm going to carry her every step of the way if I can.

The place is ready; I've spent the last three days making sure it's fucking perfect for her. I have no intention of leaving, and I have no intention of letting her leave, either.

With her head resting on me, her shallow breaths tease my chest. She may have fallen back asleep. "Are you sure we shouldn't at least tell Thomas and Jade where we are going?" She yawns, keeping her eyes closed. "They won't be happy we're leaving," she adds, a tinge of guilt in her voice, "especially since we're fleeing in the dead of night."

That makes me chuckle. "We're not fleeing, London. I don't run." However, fleeing might be accurate. Thomas has been watching me; he knows I'm up to something. But he won't speak to me... We haven't uttered a word to each other since I cut off his hand. And other than saying I was sorry to him when he regained consciousness, what else was I supposed to fucking say about it?

"Whatever you say, Micah," London murmurs, her lips on my neck. "But it seems like we're fleeing." I shift beneath her as I suppress the jolt in my groin from her lips touching me like that—it happens every time those beautiful lips touch my skin. But there will be ample opportunity to focus on that once she's fully healed.

"I don't trust any of them anymore," I tell her softly. "It's better for everyone if we leave."

A week ago, her fury matched mine, but now that her energy has depleted, all that's left within her is all-consuming grief. And all that's left within me is a primal need to claim her, to make her pain go away and pull it inside me.

Her body is like an ice cube next to me, so I rub her arms and back, pulling her wolf blanket around her. As I gaze at the midnight sky, I can feel the gentle rhythm of her breathing next to me. The stars are the main reason why I don't sleep at night—they fill the void of nothingness within me. I much prefer nocturnal life when I don't have to talk to anyone.

I see the way they all look at me now. Every single one of them fears me. I chopped Ezra's fingers off with zero hesitation, and I would have done it to Nigel, too, if he hadn't scuttled away from me like a fucking mouse. They believe I'm unhinged because Maison died. They barely bring up his name when I'm around, like it's some dirty, taboo topic. They all moved on, gathering wood, hunting, and fishing, and I helped them stock up for winter. It makes me feel less guilty knowing they at least have some food to keep them going. If they run out, it's their problem. Maybe they shouldn't have given a third of our supplies away.

I rest my eyes, and after a few minutes, soft snores fill the shelter. That's my signal. With London so drained, she will hopefully sleep most of the way. So I gather her in my arms and wrap her wolf blanket around her head. She's going to need the comfort and warmth since the trek won't be fun for either of us, but the payoff will be worth it.

She lets me lift her without any complaint and leans her head against my chest as I cradle her. Her eyes are barely open, her lashes fluttering. She's wearing Maison's hockey sweater, which she hasn't taken off since he died. My body tenses at the sight of it, but I quickly push him out of my mind. She isn't his anymore. And it doesn't matter that she won't let him go because she'll learn who she belongs to soon enough.

I walk through the dark camp with my hood over my head, past the pile of food I left them along with some hunting wire. I've already made this walk twice tonight, counting when I took London's pack and all her belongings. This will be my third and last trip, and by the hint of light in the sky, I can tell it's nearly morning. I took what I deemed mine, including the girl in my arms, away from here. The only other item I have on me is my hunting knife, which is secured and sheathed on my back.

I think about the knife often... more often than I should. What the sensation would be like having it slice into my side instead of his. I swear, Maison's pain fused with my own, creating an indistinguishable blend of anguish between us.

London is light as a feather in my arms as I glide through the soft snow, but her face betrays her. Every step I take hurts her. She whimpers, even though I take careful steps through the planned route to the abandoned hunting cabin I found a few days ago, sequestered among the trees. She isn't well, but I couldn't keep her here any longer knowing I have a place much better for her. Somewhere she can actually heal and forget all the shit she's been through. Where I can keep her alive while preserving our sanity.

The cold wind bites through the fabric of my hoodie, and the snow seeps through my shoes to the point where I can no longer feel my toes. Since I only have shoes, not boots like any sane person should have given we are in Alaska, my feet are fucking frozen. I have a clear understanding of the route despite the snow reaching up to my calf. I've done it a few times prepping for this, and I'm not making London walk in the snow. Not that she can even walk yet since her wound is still fresh. And I can handle the cold, probably better than I should.

Everything is still so fresh... white and crisp. After a while, her whimpers stop, and I'm certain she's asleep. How this girl can sleep while being carried like this is beyond me, but she seems to have no issue anytime she's in my arms. She passes out within minutes.

I've always wanted her... I was certain the day after the plane crash—when she was wearing the wrong number on her back and looking at me with utter disdain—that we belonged together.

So I took her, just as I'm taking her now. Over the course of a month and a half, I carefully and gradually separated her from my brother. At first, I resisted it, but eventually, my desire seeped into my subconscious. Despite my efforts to despise her, I now realize that every action I took—every touch, gaze, or avoidance—was an attempt to make her fall in love with me. Unlike Olivia, who was wrong for me from the beginning, London should have been mine from the start. Maison had his chance at love, but he killed his last girlfriend.

He didn't deserve London.

My body nearly gives out after an hour of walking. The only light is the moon reflecting off the snow, but I learned a long time ago that on a clear night during winter, snow acts as a flashlight. I can see perfectly in the dark.

London shifts in my arms as I sit for a rest, keeping her cradled on my lap. The passenger princess finally wakes up. "Micah, are we almost there?" Her lips tickle my stubble. Her soft angel-like cheek is cold as it presses against my face.

"Yeah, London. We're close. I just need a break."

Her body shivers. "Good. I'm so cold, and I just want to sleep for a year."

Her eyes are glued to me now. She's awake—alert and pondering—but her eyelids are heavy and she's missing the spark I love so much about her.

The tip of her nose is red, so are her ears, and her hair is frozen, but bringing her out here is a risk I'm willing to take. I lean down and kiss her brow, pulling the blanket around her again.

"Come on. Let's keep moving." The frost is here to stay now. Within days, we probably won't be going outside for months.

I continue on and finally see the trail marker I left for myself, indicating that the cabin is nearby. Behind me is a deep trail of footprints I left... The others could easily find us if they wanted, but if they follow me, I will kill them. They must be aware of that and, hopefully, will concentrate on their own survival without worrying about us. Eventually, the snow will hide my tracks, and this hunting cabin is so well-hidden that not even the spawn of Satan would be able to find it.

I carry her through the thick forest of fir trees and ignore the burning sensation on my ears and nose until I see it, hidden among the trees and brush, the roof covered in snow. When I arrive, I push open the wooden door and step inside. The room is sparsely furnished, with just a double bed tucked in the corner and one small table and chair, and the kitchen is comprised of a small wood-burning stove. The air inside smells of aged timber and musty earth. I place her on the foam mattress someone left here, next to the stone fireplace that takes over an entire wall, which is blackened from soot from the countless fires lit by whoever was here before us.

Earlier, I put four blankets down on top of the bed. She lies down and curls her knees to her chest, pulling her wolf blanket over her. I already prepared as much wood as I could, and I smile as I light the fire while she makes herself comfortable.

"Why is this place here?" she finally asks after countless minutes of watching me work. "Is this a dream?"

I see that gleam in her eyes as I crawl in and lie down, curling myself behind her, the day finally catching up with me. "No, it's not a dream. It's where we're going to live now, baby. They won't find us here. I promise." Nobody will ever find this place. Whoever built it clearly didn't want to be found.

She lifts her head, and the edges of my lips quirk at the look she's giving me—the same look she's been giving me from the beginning, her eyes bright with curiosity. It's how I eventually suspected she felt the same.

She turns her attention to the cabin itself as if inspecting every inch of it. Eventually, she crinkles her nose and rests her head down. "It's small and dirty in here, and it smells funny," she says.

I kiss the back of her head, suppressing a smile, and press my warm hands over her freezing ears. "Sorry I can't provide you with more luxury, sweetheart, but this is home now. It has a stocked fridge, a woodstove, and a bed, so you're welcome."

The stove even has some cast-iron pots and pans which, along with the supplies I brought here, should sustain us for a while. Fuel, fire starter, a knife, the canned beans she loves so much, lard, pasta, spam, canned fish, sauces, and a bunch of frozen meat from small game I hunted and smoked over the past week to prepare for this. The freshwater creek that leads into the lake is close by, so we will be able to catch fish even during winter.

It has everything we need for long-term survival. It's as if someone wrapped it up like a present, just for me.

"It's perfect," she finally says. "But... what if whoever lives here comes back?"

I tuck her into my arms. "The person who built this place hasn't been here for a long time, baby. They won't come back; it's ours now."

She turns to face me, placing her good hand over my face and cupping my cheek as the morning light shines through our one tiny window. I think she does that to prove to herself it's me she's with, and not Maison. I've never seen her do that to Maison. It's like she has to touch my jawline to determine which brother she's fucking. It probably doesn't help that I'm being all gushy and calling her *baby*, either. It must be confusing for her.

She kisses me, pressing her lips to mine. It's missing the luster it usually has, so I peel away. She's tired... When I fuck her again, I want to unleash. I can't hold back, so it's easier and better for both of us if we wait. Especially for what I have planned for her. Because then, she'll never question who's inside her anymore.

"Not yet, London," I whisper. "You're not ready. I want you to focus on getting better. Just sleep now."

I haven't fucked her since Maison died; I haven't even tried since the night I hurt her at the cove and called her the wrong name. Every day I spend with her is torturous. I want her so fucking badly that she's consuming every single one of my thoughts.

She purses her lips but rests her head down, and her eyes grow heavy as her body finally warms. "I am ready for you, Micah," she whispers before sleep takes her. "I want to make you feel good now."

That makes two of us.

But she isn't ready for me, for what I really need from her. I'll be patient.

I run my hand over her forehead. "When you're better, I plan on fucking you in every position, in every square inch of this shack. Be careful what you wish for, sweetheart, because once I start, I won't stop."

She pulls away and runs her hand through my hair. Then she lays her head down again, but the flash in her eyes pains me. It betrays her because I can see the anguish in them, even if she's putting on a brave face for me.

She's thinking about him.

That's what she says she wants—to satisfy me—but to satisfy me, it will only be me. And she will have to explore her own limits and expose a side of me I haven't shared with anyone. Even Olivia didn't get the full breadth of what I'm capable of.

"I love you, Micah," London breathes as I slide my hand over her stomach and let my eyes hang heavy. I love hearing my name from her lips. Heat fills my core at her blind trust in me. "I'm sorry about Maison."

I bristle at her ruining the moment.

"Go to sleep, London. It's going to be a long winter." I yawn, shifting to get into a comfortable position, resting one hand behind my head and one on her hip.

I don't want to share her with him, even in grief. She doesn't seem to pick up on my annoyance and nestles in for the night. As I watch her lips part, I wonder for a moment if I've made the right decision to bring her here.

As perfect as this situation is for me right now, it's only a matter of time before I truly wreck this girl... more than I already have. Because I'm fucked up, I've always been fucked up, and I doubt that will ever change. I'm selfish... and I want her completely and utterly to myself.

I draw circles on her stomach and move my fingers to her back, where she melts even further into my body. The wind kicks up outside, pushing cold air through the poorly insulated, splintered walls. We barely made it before the snow hit. To the final place she will ever call home, with the last person she will ever see. Because I've found my new obsession, and there is no one here to stop me. What I have planned for her will erase Maison from her mind. I will make her forget the existence of everyone in this world but me.

CHAPTER TWO

MICAH

I always suspected I was different. Tragedy or no tragedy... it doesn't matter. I was aware before I turned eleven that something was off about me. Before I almost lost Maison in the ice, before Olivia ruined my life, before the island happened. It's a primal part of me, hidden in my inner psyche. I've fought it down for as long as I can remember, but it drives my need to control, to conquer, and to obsess over things until I master them. Whatever I choose to focus on in the moment so I don't self-depreciate become my addictions.

I am driven by a relentless need for control, and I assert my dominance over anything I can manipulate. I suspect Maison knew... His instincts were never wrong. He let me be despite my demons. But when things slip out of control, that's when I spiral.

It's my vulnerability.

That realization this morning solidified how different I actually am. I spent the day shoveling snow and tending to the property. I don't mind the hard work; I grew up in these hunting lodges. I appreciate them as much as the fancy houses—the simplicity of them—because deep down, beneath my complex personality, I have pretty basic fucking needs.

I decided we needed space around our door so we could at least get it open if we needed to leave. And by shoveling snow, I mean scraping it with a pot and moving it with my bare hands. My fingers registered the cold, knowing it should have hurt, but I didn't move them. I kept my hands in the snow for as long as I could because the pain was a temporary relief from the emotions swirling inside me.

Before I head inside, I see London is awake through the singular window of the weathered shelter. She's sitting up for the first time after sleeping for almost two full days and nights following our three-hour trek in the cold. She spent most of that time in a feverish state, moaning Maison's name. She sits cross-legged on the bed, staring with her wolf blanket over her lap and wearing nothing but a spaghetti-strap tank top.

Damn, she looks delicious.

I can't help but admire the swell of her breasts as she plays with the bandage of her broken hand. Her hair is matted and long, and she desperately needs a bath, but her pretty dark eyes are more full of life than I've seen in days.

Watching her, I pause for a moment, questioning whether she'll be disappointed it's me after dreaming about him for two nights. My insides clam up, knowing how fragile she is. Knowing if she breaks, it will be my fault. I hate how utterly pissed off I was watching her almost die, knowing I wasn't the guy she was dreaming about.

I lift my hood and kick the snow off my shoes before creaking the door open and making my presence known. The moment our eyes meet, a flash hits her eyes. She can't hide it—

She's scared of me.

Or disappointed...

One is just as bad as the other.

We are in the most impossible situation—we are likely both going to die—yet my thoughts are wholly consumed by all the ways I can make this broken girl mine as she sits trembling like a kitten.

Like I said... I'm different.

It's a part of me I'm sick of suppressing.

It's also the part of me she fell in love with. Because London King sees me, too, and this girl is staring right at me like I'm a puzzle she's trying to figure out.

Don't bother, sweetheart. Even I haven't sorted myself out.

She recovers quickly. "How long was I asleep?" she asks, giving me only a hint of a smile, even though she knows exactly how I'm looking at her. It's not the smile I so desperately want to see; it's sadness that still lingers in her eyes. I don't make girls smile—it's just not an emotion I bring out in them, apparently. But I'm determined to fucking change that.

"We've been here for a couple of days. You had a fever." I fall on the bed beside her. "How's your hand?"

She places her hand over her bandaged wrist. "It still hurts when I move it. Will it get better?"

I grab it and inspect it, moving her wrist around, trying to keep my fingers soft knowing it hurts her. "Now that you're awake, we will have to start working on therapy, among other things..."

She smirks and pulls her hand away. "I suppose you know how to do that, too?"

I shrug and move a piece of matted hair from her forehead. "Not really, but I'm good at pretending."

She slumps her shoulders and stares at the small door I just walked through—her only escape to the outside world. I underestimated her strength or how close I was to losing her entirely. I've already decided that when I see Nigel again, I will cut off both his fucking hands for what he did to her, or maybe his leg. Then I'll keep him alive for a couple of days before killing him in the worst way possible so he can experience what it's like to lose an appendage before his miserable life ends.

"How far away are we from the others?" she asks, looking around the cabin again as if seeing it for the first time. I get it; she hasn't been lucid since we've been here, and it's dark. It will be dark here moving forward, the closer we push to December.

"Far enough that they won't bother us," I tell her as I rise and light a fire on our wooden stove, turning my back to her. "Don't worry. They won't find you."

A pause.

"Won't they come looking for us, Micah?"

"They better fucking not." I turn and pull my shirt off. "They will have to figure things out for themselves now. They have everything they need to survive. I left them plenty of food, and they can take over my old shelter. I winterized it for them, so if they are smart and careful, they should be okay. The snow built up around the shelter will keep them warm enough, even through the worst parts of the season. People survive up here, London."

She arches a brow, her eyes trailing down my abs to the waistband of my fitted sweats. "Do you believe they will live through this?"

I step toward her, grabbing a spare shirt and throwing it on before cupping her in my arms. "I don't care. I told you, baby. I only care about you and me now."

She frowns. "Micah, what about Thomas, Jade, Serena..." she pauses, "or Naomi? You don't care about them?"

The other name we don't talk about. London knows I have a sexual history with Naomi—one I will have to explain sooner or later. I'd be curious if I were in her shoes. The problem is that I can't explain who Naomi was to me, no more than I can explain Olivia. The difference, however, is that neither of them were really mine. Not like London is... or will be.

"No, not even them." I don't blink as I say it.

They are dead to me.

Once the water boils, I grab the pot and sit on the bed. I pull off her blanket and stare down at her beautiful ivory thighs as she leans her head back. My groin starts to ache, watching her as she assesses me—like she's been doing since day one.

This girl...

I haven't been this turned on since I started fucking Olivia. I never expected a girl would turn me on like this again, but here we are... She has no clue how beautiful she is, which makes her even more endearing.

Her eyes soften, and she runs her hand down my arm. "Do you want to talk about him?"

I lean forward and press my hands on either side of her. "No."

"Micah—"

I slide my tongue into her mouth, and I don't let her finish her sentence. She returns my kiss, but I sense her hesitation. If I keep kissing her, she can't talk, and if I move my hand between her legs, her moaning will take over.

Keeping my mouth on hers, I slide the blanket off entirely, pull off her tank top, and slide her underwear down her legs. She gives me that sound I was waiting for, so I deepen my kiss and slide my right hand off her. Finding the pot of warm water I placed near the bed, I grab the shirt I put inside and place it right between her legs, cleaning her.

She flinches just a little, and it reminds me of the day I cleaned her wound—the day I realized I loved her. "You can't avoid talking about him forever, Micah. We need to talk about him eventually... about what happened."

I run the wet shirt down her thighs and each calf muscle, taking my time before placing it back in the hot water and dousing her belly with it.

"Not today, sweetheart."

Her pupils flash, and she hisses. I suppress a smile when her body jolts from the hot water as it hits her skin. She hates it when I call her *sweetheart*, and she bristles every time.

She kicks at me. "Don't, Micah. That hurts."

That's the point.

"Yeah, well, at least you don't smell like a corpse."

Her mouth gapes and her eyes narrow before her lips slide into a small grin. However, her anger is short-lived when the hot water becomes warm, and I soak her skin, massaging her belly and thighs.

Her body loosens, and she sinks into the bed, closing her eyes while I wash her. "When can we talk about him?" she finally asks as I scrub dirt off her. This island fucked her up, and now it's up to me to make it better. London is completely at my mercy, but I'm not stupid enough to believe she doesn't have little claws that scratch—I've been on the receiving end of them a couple of times.

I take my time, admiring every curve, not wanting to take any moment I have with her for granted. I remain silent as I clean every inch of her, making her roll on her belly so I can check her wound and clean her back, and I pointedly ignore her question. She doesn't bring up Maison again, and I forget him as she distracts me enough with her tight little ass, focusing solely on how much I want to fuck it.

When I finish cleaning her, I pick her up and position her back toward me. Her deep brown eyes blink at me a few times, and she runs her hands through my hair before tickling the stubble on my chin. "What do you need from me right now, Micah?" she asks, and I tense.

She has no clue what I need yet... but she will.

I pull my bottom lip between my teeth, moving my hands to play with each of her breasts before taking one into my mouth. I playfully bite her nipple, then suck on the fleshy part of her breast. "I need you to show me how much you want me, London," I tell her, raising my eyebrows as she squirms from the jolt of pain from my teeth.

"Micah, I want you so bad," she whispers. "You are the center of my universe. How have you not comprehended that by now?"

I pause my sucking before I kiss her cheek, then her ear, then work my way to her neck. "No, baby... but I need you to fully understand something. I don't want to be the center of your universe; I want to be *your universe*. When I'm finished with you, you won't be able to occupy your mind with anyone else. I'm going to train you, baby. You will understand exactly what I need; you won't have to ask."

She bites her bottom lip as her eyes widen, and her breath hitches.

It's time to show her.

I run my tongue down her belly to the soft part of her leg, and finally, to the apex of her thigh and start to suck...

She giggles at first. I'm sure it tickles, and I make it pleasurable, kissing her softly, caressing her with my tongue. Her giggles stop when I keep sucking harder.

"You like that?" I murmur, keeping my lips tight on her skin.

"*Micah...*" She grips the sides of the bed.

I grip her thighs harder, hinting for her to quiet down.

She doesn't. She wiggles, squirms, and digs her fingers into my back. "Micah, what are you doing?"

I keep going harder... harder... and harder. The more she wiggles and cries out, the harder I suck. I release, licking and kissing her, and she visibly relaxes. She arches her back and starts to moan, and I keep my attention on the place she likes to touch when she gets herself off.

"Micah, please..." she moans, gripping my hair and practically pulling it out, which only turns me on more.

I arch my brows at her, and slowly, my kissing turns to sucking again.

"Micah..."

Eventually, she relaxes and her whole body goes limp. After a few extra seconds of trying to embed myself into her forever, I pull off.

She got the hint that fighting it would only make it worse. I peer down to the spots on her ivory skin and admire my handiwork. She's practically bleeding—already a black bruise forming on that spot by the time I'm done with her.

Once I'm done admiring her body, I check to see her reaction. Her eyes are wide—no fear. Surprise maybe, but no fear. She's frowning, looking at me quizzically. "Is that what you need, Micah? To mark me? To make sure everyone—who are not even here right now—knows I'm yours?"

I pull myself up so I'm flush with her pussy and slip my fingers inside, rubbing her clit. It's no surprise that she's dripping like a faucet.

She parts her lips to say something, but I run my lips down her body and my teeth along her clit. She cries out at the suddenness of it. "Fuck, Micah," she moans as I run my tongue up and down the length of her, enjoying the fresh taste of her juices.

I smile and pull back. "Not yet, baby. You're not strong enough for that yet. But we have all winter, sweetheart. And as you've probably noticed, I can fuck for hours. I need you to get your strength back."

Her eyes reflect a hint of hesitation, as they rightfully should. However, I persist in teasing and pleasuring her until her body quivers, signaling she has reached her limit. After the moan that accompanies her third orgasm, her fingers grip my shoulders. She leans her head back on the bed in exhaustion, her breaths full and heavy. I can't get enough of how full her tits are as they bounce. I get why Maison jumped on her the first day of school—he always moved quickly on the super hot ones.

Her body is perfection.

Her cheeks are flushed, and I resist the urge to fuck her silly. I don't want to break her yet. She needs at least one more night.

It's only the early evening, but I lie down beside her as the light of the fire simmers. The early December solstice is nearly upon us, the woods around us shrouded in darkness. I rub her forehead until her breathing evens out, and she falls asleep in my arms as shadows dance across the room. I lift her head and place it in the crook of my arm. I warned her that I would dominate every aspect of her life, and despite that, she's still so trusting.

She doesn't understand yet...

She murmurs something incoherent against my shoulder in that weak voice. Her body is warm beneath me before she passes out. I tease her freshly washed hair with my fingers, staring out the window, listening to the wind and the shuttering cabin door. As the light dwindles, I'm acutely aware that it is just the two of us now.

I pull her closer as I get more comfortable, and a deep tightness forms in my stomach. Her skin shines in the snow-glazed moonlight, and I watch her slender throat as she swallows. I can sense the pitter of her heartbeat under the arm I have wrapped around her as her breakable body conforms to mine.

She's so fucking delicate.

I admire the little bruise I gave her, and I hate to admit how much it turns me on. My finger wipes away a single tear as it falls down my cheek. Ignoring the burning in my eyes, I press my lips to her head. "I'll try not to kill you, London King," I whisper as a fresh wave of panic tightens my core.

Losing her.

It's a very real fear, especially now that Pandora's box has been opened and there is nothing stopping me from marking every inch of her. And worse, knowing I won't be able to stop now that I've started.

CHAPTER THREE

LONDON

Day unknown

Sometime in December

This is my first entry since Maison died. I haven't been able to write about it because that makes it real. Nigel killed him in cold blood, and now Micah has lost his twin. And I've lost a piece of Micah.

Micah took me away to an abandoned hunting cabin a few days ago. It's small, quaint, and it's been here for a long time. It's half-broken, weather-beaten, and weary... kind of like us. The front door creaks and shutters in the wind, almost as if the place is alive and telling us to go away. Like we are disturbing its peace. I still don't know exactly where we are, only that it's a frozen wooded landscape and we are hidden within a denser part of it.

Almost like I'm a prisoner within it...

I understand why we left the others, why he can't take care of them like he did before. I can see his guilt, shame, and grief, and it consumes him, even if he won't admit it. I can only imagine how much worse it is for him than it is for me. He's turning off his emotions. He's so cold and distant about Maison dying, even if he's warm with me. He will never understand how much I love him, yet it's Maison who still brings me to the calmer part of my mind.

I'm scared... I'm scared to be alone out here—of who else is lurking out there, still alive, waiting in the shadows. And *most of all, I'm terrified of who Micah is transforming into. I have to do everything I can to keep him with me, even if that means giving in to him entirely.*

Life is a collection of moments, many of which are so mundane that you forget them. Like daily commuting, walking the dog, or in our case, fishing. It's funny to me, looking back on my life, how little I actually remember. It's the extreme moments that really etch themselves into my brain—my parents divorcing, fucking my teacher, and the plane crashing.

None of them I care to remember.

Now it's the tiny moments I cling to because they are simply easier.

"London, focus on what I'm telling you. Quit gazing at the sky."

My head whips up, and I wrap my arms around Micah's waist. Leaning my head against his muscular back, I shove my hands into his pockets to warm myself as he stands near the edge of the water, over the tiny hole he dug through the ice with the knife.

There is only a minute during a sunset when you can catch a glimpse of the true beauty of the sky. The clouds are the pinkest, the sky is still a shade of blue, and the trees are silky black against it. I learned to take in these moments from Maison, so when I see the sunset at the peak of its beauty, I stop to take it in, no matter what I'm doing.

Sunrises and sunsets will always belong to Maison.

"I'm watching." I stare at my icy breath, mesmerized by the sky and the memories the sunsets bring. I repeat his instructions back to him, "Loop the wire twice, hook the bait, and jig the wire while in the water to attract the fish."

His body stills as if not believing me and knowing I was just repeating his words back to him like a parrot. I was listening, just not paying attention. And I am focusing... just not on what he wants me to.

He drops the wire and turns to face me. He frowns as he cups my cheeks in his hands. "We're done; you're freezing. Let's go back."

I blow out a breath and stare at his amazing dark eyes blazing into me. "Micah, why? I'm listening."

"No, you're not, London. I know what you're doing. You're trying to figure out where we are. And I told you; I'm not telling you. It's better if you don't know."

Better for who?

North. He brought me north. I can tell by the position of the sun as it seems to sit farther away when I stare at the sunset. I want to ask him why he won't tell me, but I don't dare. His temperament is so fragile—just as fragile as my physical state. Earlier, we walked for about five minutes till we hit the stream... I suspect that if I follow the stream south, I will find our camp. From there, it's twenty minutes to the lake site where Maison died, a place I never want to set foot in again.

It warmed up today. And by warming up, I mean it went from unbearable to slightly bearable, almost balmy, and Micah wanted to teach me how to ice fish. The sun came out after days of dreary gray, and now the frozen landscape is blinding white. So I bundled up with four layers and followed him outside. It's the first time I've left the hunting cabin in the eight days we've been here, but if he hadn't allowed it, I was going to go crazy.

I've been keeping track of the number of days—even in my state. I've etched a mark on the wall by our bed every day. This morning, I carved my eighth line. Micah got sick of my huffing and moaning, and I kept reading my book out loud, forcing him to listen. He busied himself with his wood carving, but he was listening, even if he was pretending that he wasn't.

The line pulls, which distracts him, and my body relaxes as he jumps into action. I love watching him work, watching him move, watching him exist.

He's been waiting patiently for an hour, pulling on the line in various ways, trying to attract the fish with the bit of bait we have hooked on the end of it. "Come on, London. We're doing this so you can learn, then we can go warm up. We need food, baby. And you need to learn to do these things in case I'm not with you one day."

I break into a cold sweat and close my eyes, refusing to respond. He grabs my chin and forces me to look at him, raising his eyebrows and jerking his head toward the line in his hand. "Grab this and tug like I showed you."

"Okay," I whisper, resigning myself to following his instructions. My fingers are frozen, so he wraps his hands around them to keep them warm.

He looms over me, pressing himself against me as my gaze keeps darting toward the sunset and the forest beyond. "Focus on me, baby. Don't worry about what's out there. Turn off what's going on in that little head of yours and do what I say," he whispers, and I lean my head into his chest, exposing my neck to him.

He's controlling, and I'm starting to like it. He enjoys telling me what to do, and I enjoy listening to him. The praise he gives me makes my heart swell, as it has from the beginning—even when I was in denial about it. And right now, that's much easier for me because his happiness keeps me alive and losing myself in him is effortless. Just by existing, he makes me feel safe, so I'm willing to do anything for him. This island terrifies me now more than it ever has.

"Take this line; do it quick before the fish gets away," he says as I pull my hands from his warmth and grab the line. He rests one hand on my hip and the other over my bandaged hand to make sure I don't use it.

Not that I would, considering I can barely move it—it's hideous, deformed, and bruised. The bones are cracked and in pieces beneath the skin, and the throbbing pain is relentless.

"Pull it up slowly." His breath tickles the hairs on my neck as I yank the line up too quickly for his liking. "It takes finesse; don't be such a brute," he teases. I smile and let him pull on my hand, following his lead, moving slowly and keeping my focus steady, and enjoying this softer side of him.

My breath stalls as he presses himself against me in the way I love, making me feel small and insignificant beneath him as if he can protect me from this island by merely covering me. His lips tease my neck, giving me what my body has been craving from him all day.

"That's my girl," he whispers. I nearly crumble at those words as I twist to face him, pressing my lips to his before he can stop me.

I woke up crying today, as I have every morning since we arrived—the mornings are always the hardest for me. I was shaking from the cold that had seeped into my bones, as if my blood itself was freezing despite Micah making the lodge as comfortable as he could while preserving our limited fuel supply. He didn't speak as he held me and let me grieve. He didn't tell me it would be okay or kiss me like he usually does because he sensed I wasn't crying over him.

The line pulls easily enough, and a small gray fish is tethered on the other end when I finally get it through the hole in the ice. He leans down and grabs the slimy, wiggly fish, severing its neck with his bone weapon and killing it. He then leans into the water and washes his hands.

With his attention entirely focused elsewhere, I place my hands on his back, turn him to face me, and bite my bottom lip. I might have been crying over Maison earlier, but Micah has all my attention now.

He holds my gaze for a moment, his eyes flashing, looking... haunted. The pain is so evident in them. He wants this. He wants to give in to me, but after our first night here—when he bruised me—he hasn't touched me again. He keeps saying I'm too weak, too helpless, and that I need my strength back before we do anything again. So all that sucking for what? Giving me that dark bruise just to treat me like glass for three days.

He gives me a weak smile and merely shakes his head. "Don't look at me like that. It's not happening," he says as he grabs the fish, rejecting me once again. Sometimes, I believe he's punishing me for something.

I lock myself in place, refusing to move a single step as he calls over his shoulder, "Come on, London."

I reach down and grab a handful of snow, much softer than the rock I once hurled at him. It forms in my fist, and

I throw the ice at him, snickering when it explodes on his back.

He turns to face me and tilts his head. A silent, icy pause as he looks at my guilty hand, still dripping wet with ice crystals on it. He cocks a brow, and my heart jolts at the dark gaze he gives me, knowing I'm fucked.

He drops the fish into the snow. "Oh, you did not just do that."

I drop to my knees, curling on the ground, giggling, as he closes the distance between us. Leaning down and cupping snow in his hands, he's on me in a second, his face full of smiles.

"You think you're so tough, sweetheart?" He reaches down and pulls me into his arms. I grab more snow and press it into his face, taking him by surprise.

"Yeah, you are tough, aren't you?" He coughs and wipes the snow from his eyes, then tickles my sides as he grabs some snow and rubs it up my back before stuffing some into the waistband of my pants.

"Micah, stop." I laugh as his fingers tease me relentlessly. I'm so ticklish that I'm quickly out of breath, but mainly, I'm happy I was able to get a rise out of him. I haven't giggled like this since being on the island... or ever, really. It's been a week of sitting in near silence, grieving—even if we're not admitting that's what we were doing. It's nice to laugh, even for a moment.

And he smiled. I saw it. It's something I so rarely get to see from him.

He gives me no choice now; he picks me up and carries me home. "Now we're both frozen," he mutters. His face is growing hard again, but I can tell by the way he's carrying me that he's loosened up a bit. The sticky snow is stuck to my clothes, wetness dripping down my skin. I'm so frozen that I have no sensation in my fingers. There is still a hint of a small smile on his lips as I wrap my hands around his neck to warm myself up and let him carry me, keeping a big smirk on my face.

"Yeah, keep laughing," he teases, trudging through a thicker part of the snowbank, and I decide now is a good time to nibble on his earlobe as he tries to keep us balanced. I still marvel at how strong he is.

Once inside, we shake off the snow from our shoes and clothing, and Micah immediately plops me onto the bed, signaling for me to stay put. He then fires up the wood heater and gets to work, popping in and out of the cabin and tending to the fish. I shed my wet clothes, throw on one of his oversized T-shirts, and pull the wolf blanket over me to warm up. Lying curled up in my spot, I watch him as he heads outside to gut the fish.

I'm strictly forbidden from leaving the cabin without his permission... He's made it perfectly clear I am not to cross that boundary under any circumstances.

I don't dare disobey him...

He comes back in and cleans his hands, then works in the kitchen area in his sexy sweatpants, his arm muscles rippling even when he isn't trying to flex. I admire the long, smooth lines of his body.

Tired, I rest my head, unravel the bandage on my hand, and try to wiggle my fingers. I wince at the burning sensation shooting up my wrist and into my arm.

Nigel really did a number on me. Micah promises he will get my hand back to normal, but I don't see how that's possible. The bones were shattered, and I will probably never have proper use of my hand again.

Micah steps to the side of the bed and crouches, giving me a few bites of fish. It's very unlike him to spoon-feed me, but then again, he hasn't been himself since Maison died. Subtle things, but some big ones, like how much he dotes on me now. Almost as if he's emulating his brother... giving me what he thinks I want in this moment. But in actuality, I need *him* more than anything—the version he gave me the first night we were at this cabin. Right now, I want more of that version.

But I'll take the sweet side of Micah if that's the side he wants to show me right now. I'll let him do whatever he wants, as long as he heals and I don't lose him to the darkness that lingers so close to the surface.

He runs his fingers along my shattered hand. "Ball your fist for me, London."

I can move my fingers, but squeezing my hand is excruciating. "I can't..."

"Do it, baby, please. You'll lose the ability to use your hand if you don't try."

My hand shakes as I try my best to squeeze it, but it's literally impossible. Tears threaten to fall from my eyes as he takes me in, watching my wincing face rather than the hand he's trying to rehabilitate.

His eyes are etched in concern as he shakes his head. "It needs more time. You have to rest it. Which means you have to rest more."

Another reason why he won't touch me.

I bite my lip to shake off the tears, both from the pain and the overwhelming sense of longing for someone so close. He checks the wound on my hip while I run my good hand through his hair, playing with it and tugging it. "I'm healing, Micah. I promise you that I'm not going anywhere." My lungs tighten, which happens anytime I think about him leaving, or me leaving, or about either of us dying.

But I'm better, almost back to whatever normal is these days, and I want his hands on me. I daydream about it when I'm not shaking during my nightmares.

I shift beneath him, pulling my shirt up, and bare everything to him.

"London," he warns, but he can't take his eyes off me. I'm tired of waiting for him; I reject the notion that I should feel guilty for desiring happiness amidst my sorrow. I need to take in the pain I see in his eyes and absorb it into me. I shift my hips, spreading my legs for him, splaying myself out like a platter.

The bruise he gave me the other night is now yellow. He's staring at it and furrowing his brows, as if regretting giving it to me to begin with and fighting some internal battle while I run my finger over it.

"Is this what you need?" I ask curiously, intertwining his fingers with mine over the sensitive spot. The pressure on it hurts. It hurt a lot while he was giving it to me, but I didn't hate it.

I forgot everything else—my hurt, anger, suffering—my mind occupied with how hard he was sucking. I didn't realize at first that he was punishing me as I enjoyed the sensation of his soft lips on my body since he's held back so much with me.

He tilts his head as if considering. His lips part, and his dark eyes are back to their regular brooding expression. I bite my tongue before saying what I want to say, bringing up Maison again. That's what will make him snap and let out all his pent-up emotions. Otherwise, he seems too content, nothing like a person who just lost his twin should appear.

I swallow a lump in my throat. How do I ask for this? How do I articulate that I want him to bruise me? To hurt me?

I'm fucked up even thinking about it.

He licks his lips like a dog about to devour a bone. He pulls off his shirt, his muscles rippling, and he looks as sexy as ever. The long strands of his hair are tousled and fall over his eyes, the shadows dancing behind him making him glow. He's always been ethereal to me, but right now, he looks like a god. Deadly.

I run my hand down his cheek. "Please, Micah. You want to do this to me, don't you? You want to hurt me?"

Still, he does nothing, just stares at my skin. The vein in his neck pulses, his pupils dilating, the demons fighting within him.

Suddenly ashamed of begging, I pull my wolf blanket over me, dragging my eyes away from him, blocking any further view of my body as a draft blows through the door. I purse my lips, my body shaking as he sits in silence.

I flinch away from him. "Why won't you? Is it because you think I'm going to die or something? Or do you believe I still love him more than you?"

He scoffs, flexing his jaw.

"What the fuck is it?" I snap at him.

His dark eyes flicker dangerously, all signs of playfulness gone, replaced by the dark, cold stare I'm used to. He flexes his jaw as he beholds me in the way he used to when he hated me—or when he wanted to tear my clothes off.

His voice comes out dark and dangerous, the intensity making my insides weep. "I told you. When I start, I won't stop. I'll hurt you, London, and I'll fucking enjoy it. Trust me, sweetheart, it's not what you want."

I hold his heavy stare, my heart a pitter-pattering mess. Gathering every ounce of courage, I finally ask, "Why won't you talk about him?"

This garners a reaction. He can't hide the pain in his face as he rips the blanket off me and leans over me menacingly. "I don't want to talk about him, London."

Maison said those same words to me once...

My legs instinctively wrap around him. I can tell how hard he is; I can *feel* him. Apparently, Maison is the only topic that will get him into the headspace I need him to be in so I can have the physical side of him I want so desperately.

"Please," I whisper, so hungry for him that my skin is burning.

He pulls up, looking at me as his dark pupils flare. "Do that again."

My eyebrows draw together. "Do what?"

"Beg."

My stomach swirls, and I can't help but smile. "Please," I whisper, running my fingers through his hair again. "Please. Please. Please."

For someone so strong, his ego really is so fragile.

He presses his lips to my belly this time. "Are you sure?" he whispers. "It's going to hurt."

My breath hitches, and I give him a nod of consent, although I'm not sure exactly what I'm consenting to.

He starts sucking right near my belly button. I let out a moan as he scrapes his teeth down my stomach. I'm so thin that I barely have any fat for him to suck, but that doesn't seem to stop him.

His lips tickle me at first, and I flinch when he bites me, puncturing my skin only slightly. He hesitates, looking up at me, so I buck into his torso, his contact making me desperate for more attention to release the deep pressure between my legs.

"Keep going," I breathe.

He intensifies the pressure, then eases off. And during that moment of respite, I grab his fingers and place them on the sensitive part of my clit. He sucks harder, and I moan as the pressure mounts and an orgasm rolls through me. I can't help but dig my fingers into his back. Instead of stopping, he just moves to another spot, and I let him, knowing he'll give me another awful bruise, but that's what he needs.

By the time he's done, I have bruises on my belly, each hip bone, and one on my inner thigh. Each time, it gets progressively more painful, but my orgasms more intense. His fingers are deep inside me, pleasuring me during the worst part of it, blurring the line between pleasure and pain.

He's so focused on me while he's doing it. It's just us, the deafening silence of the woods that besieges us, and the creaking door of the cabin reminding me that I am, indeed, still on earth.

I am breathless and glistening with sweat when he finally gives me relief. I have no idea how long he was doing that, but the sun is now setting. I guess it doesn't matter because time as I understand it doesn't exist.

Our eyes connect, and I smile at him. He didn't speak the entire time, but he seems lighter now, even if I can't properly breathe. The fact that I'm the reason for it makes my heart burst. "Do that again, too," he says, cupping his skilled hands over each breast. His hands feel like silk as he rubs them over me.

I suck in a breath, my body on fire. I lean up to see him, to understand the look in his eyes. "Do what? What do you want me to do?"

He licks his bottom lip. "Smile. I want you to smile, baby."

A big grin spreads over my face. He really has no idea how happy he makes me. Even in this impossible situation, I'm exactly where I belong.

He continues kissing my stomach, moving his way to my breasts, taking his time kissing every inch of them with his skilled tongue. He's soft now, only giving me pleasure as an icy breeze pushes in a draft that painfully hardens each nipple. I giggle as he captures one between his teeth.

A smile tugs at his lips. "Fuck, I love you," he says, and I melt. If those words were the last I ever heard, I would die in peace.

I remember the moment I first saw him, the explosions in my belly in the lunchroom at school. Which, at this point, seems like a lifetime ago, even though it was only in August. The explosions I have now are from enjoying the pain—his pain—as I pull it into me.

My eyes roam over to the window as large snowflakes drift to the ground like on a holiday card.

"Micah?" I whisper as the evening settles, the sharp wind outside subsiding and the snow blanketing the world around us.

"London," he murmurs, not really listening.

"Who was Olivia to you? Please tell me now. All of it."

He pauses his kisses, and I wince, worrying he might stop entirely. He doesn't; he continues worshiping me. "She was a fuck. I needed a release, so Maison let me screw her pretending I was him. She suspected what we were doing and blackmailed me to keep fucking her. So I did, until shit turned ugly, and well... you know the rest."

There you have it: a pointed explanation after months of half-truths and lies and years of deceit. He just lays it all out like it's no big deal. I suppress my jealousy, the stinging twinge in my belly, considering the possibility he enjoyed having sex with her more than he does with me. I'm sick of being jealous of a ghost.

She doesn't matter anymore.

"What about Naomi? Who was she to you?"

A beat of silence this time, and his body goes rigid. A response I dislike but don't show. "She was a mediocre fuck," he says. "And I screwed her for the same reasons I did Olivia."

I burst out laughing, even though I don't want to laugh about Naomi and Micah, or any blonde for that matter. Watching them together for those few weeks on the island never sat right with me, even before I fell in love with him.

Naomi always seemed like a cardboard cut-out, like she was just a shell of a person.

Micah manages a small smile as I meet his eyes, and I stop laughing. He pokes at my ribs, making me squirm. "Naomi was never anything to me," he reassures me. "But I do feel bad for how I treated her. I was nothing but a bad habit for her, and I fed her addiction every time it suited me."

This makes my stomach fill with acid.

"And what about me? Who am I to you?" I ask, pressing my lips together as heat rises to my face. I move his tousled dark hair out of his eyes so I can truly see them.

He says he loves me, but sometimes I wonder if it's the forced proximity. Like, maybe, if we were never in this scenario, he would have continued ignoring me at school. I would have graduated, he would have gone off to do whatever it was he was meant to do, and I would have never seen him again. I hate having that vile thought when I feel like he is my soulmate. And there was a high likelihood we never would have found each other.

He lowers his lips to mine and kisses me, soft and sensual. "You are fucking precious to me, and you're mine in a way they never were. You're my cure, London. Is that what you want to hear?"

All the tension in my body releases, but I still dig my nails into his back. "It is what I want to hear," I mutter, "but I want you to mean it."

He keeps his laser-focused eyes on me. "Words are hollow, sweetheart."

My breath becomes jagged, my eyes mischievous. I'm nowhere near done, and we have all the time in the world. "Well, show me, then, Micah," I tease.

He pulls off me and nudges me up to my knees, pulling out his cock, which has been fully erect since he started sucking on my stomach. He wraps his hand around the back of my head, sliding his fingers through my hair, and gently pulls me to his muscled body.

"No, baby," he grips me harder, "you are going to show me. Are you sure you're ready for me, London?"

I open my eyes wide and give him a nod as heat pools in the innermost parts of me. This is what I live for now, making Micah happy. I'm blindly in love with him, even though he isn't stable. He's been through too much to ever be normal. And it excites me to experience him this way. My body, heart, and soul are completely at his mercy.

It helps me forget, too.

He arches both eyebrows and gazes down at me, and the predatory expression sends shivers down my spine. "Now, open your mouth, sweetheart, and suck."

CHAPTER FOUR

LONDON

*C***hristmas**

The paradox of experiencing immense pleasure and excruciating pain simultaneously is beyond comprehension—almost as if they are two sides of the same coin. I've become numb to the pain from being on this island; my body fails to register it. My grief from losing Maison is so real, yet the fire I have for Micah burns so strongly that it overwhelms it. I'm still alive because of Micah, and I only remain alive because he chooses to let me live. And there is something so incredibly sexy about the power he has over me.

I'm happy for the first time in a long time. And it pains me beyond belief to admit that. It kills me inside because I miss Maison so much and shouldn't feel this way. Micah managed to find us a home out here—even through all odds. He found a place for us. And for the first time in a long time, I have a home. It's like the person who built this place never wanted to truly leave it. The land around it is so isolated and cold. Their energy is still here, whoever they are—they saved us. I hope the person who owns it won't come back. But then I picture the three feet of snow trapping us in, and I remember we don't have to leave yet. No one is coming for us.

I constantly worry about the others—Jade, especially. I doubt they are as warm and comfortable as we are, although Micah assures me that he left them with everything they need to survive. In the rare times of my day when I'm not fully consumed with the boy whose lips are constantly on me, I think about them, and a tiny wave of guilt breezes over me. For the first time since being on this island, I can truly relax.

I'm not sure how long Micah has been kissing me as I slowly slip into consciousness. His lips are most certainly on my neck, his hands around my waist, and his hard body pressed firmly against mine, my wolf blanket covering me. The scent of snow I've come to cherish over these past couple of weeks seeps through the cracks of the roof, reminding me that it's still falling out there, only the whistle of the wind in an otherwise silent, dark void that is the wilderness of Alaska.

Even the wolves, it seems, do not howl as much in the winter.

The fire is out, but the heat lingers.

"Wakey, wakey, sweetheart." Micah's deep whisper tickles my ear.

I turn to him and touch his face as I always do, and although I can't see him in the veil of the night, I can picture his expression as I've now memorized every part of him. His dark eyes, his tousled hair I keep threatening to cut, his lips I can't get enough of, his shadowed face under his black hood. Somehow, he inches closer to me on our small bed, and any chance of sleep is now gone until he's had enough and merely falls asleep himself.

I've come to learn he can never get enough of me. It's simply a pause for him... To eat, to sleep the bare minimum, before he's ravishing me once more. So I wait for his approval by being the good girl he wants me to be.

"Again?" I murmur in a drowsy state. Unlike Micah, I enjoy sleep and need it. However, I'd never tell him the true reasons why I sometimes prefer my state of unconsciousness, and it has nothing to do with my lack of senses. If anything, my senses are heightened. I remember things in a way I can't when I'm awake and with him.

Because when I'm awake, it's only him.

And when I sleep... I get Maison.

"Yeah, sweetheart. Again." He grabs a bottle of water from the floor by our bed. He must have filled it with melted snow before we passed out earlier. "Here, baby, drink this."

I grab it from him and take a big gulp, then another before wiping the hair out of my eyes. Pushing myself under the covers, I pull down the band of his sweats, taking him into my mouth.

Never in my life did I think I would ever give this many blow jobs or be as skilled at it as I am. I've mastered every trick to get Micah off; I've memorized every twitch, every hair tug. I'm well acquainted with how he reacts when I go fast or slow or cup my hands around him and pull while I do it. And even then, it's never quite enough for him.

Since being here, alone and secluded, our relationship has turned into something I can't describe. I'm sure there is a word for it, and it's nothing I thought I'd ever willingly be into.

The bruising was just the start.

He completely controls me now.

He even controls my thoughts.

While I lack a proper diet, Micah takes care of me. He feeds and cleans me, forces me to exercise, rations food, and makes sure I sleep enough and drink water. He listens to me while I chatter, as I realized I enjoy talking after years of thinking I didn't. Perhaps because I've never had anyone I can talk to the way I can talk to him. Even though he barely speaks, he listens to me while he works away in his corner, usually carving something.

When we fuck, he takes over, giving me various amounts of pain, knowing it intensifies my pleasure. He makes me beg and say his name over and over. Although we haven't explicitly discussed it, I've found myself assuming a submissive role because I enjoy being nurtured by him and it seems to make him happy.

I realize this is toxic, and it's all very confusing, but it's what we both need right now to survive—mentally, at least.

I'm trapped in Alaskan winter, in the middle of nowhere, with an athlete in peak physical condition during his sexual prime. And he is slightly, if not overtly, unhinged on so many levels and, potentially, the horniest person on the planet.

I take my time licking and playing with his cock before he reaches down and pulls me up. I crawl over him, sink onto his cock, and start grinding. "Fuck, baby. I can never get enough of you." He grips my hips and matches my motions while I clench around him. His fingers dig into the bruises on either side of my pelvis. He created these buttons on my body and only presses them when I do something he likes, usually intensifying his pressure right before I climax. He's able to control when that happens, too.

Despite our circumstances, we're healthy and thriving. I constantly wonder if he had an option of leaving, if he would even take it, or if I would, either. He's in his version of heaven here.

Hunting, fucking, wilderness, and isolation.

Me.

He flips me around so he's on top, taking no time to press inside me, grabbing my good wrist and holding it over my head so I can't move as he finishes in his usual aggressive way.

Considering this is the fifth time we've had sex in twenty-four hours, I'm hoping he's tired enough to let me rest after this. He finally pulls out of me, lying beside me and pulling me close. His breath is heavy against me.

"Micah," I whisper after a few moments, calming myself down from the euphoric high he just brought me to. The soft sound of his breathing tells me he's still awake. "I think it's Christmas."

He plays with a strand of my hair, which usually lulls me to sleep, but I'm too wired for sleep right now, even though it's still dark outside.

It's always dark in Alaska.

"What makes you say that?"

"The notches on the wall and my estimation of how long we've been on this island. It's close, it must be."

He chuckles. "Sorry, sweetheart, I didn't get you anything."

I clear my throat. "Well, there is one thing..."

There's a moment of silence before he groans.

"Please, Micah, it's Christmas. And it's all I really want."

He nibbles my ear. "So, it's suddenly Christmas morning, is it?"

I wrap myself around his waist. "Yes... and I love Christmas. Don't be like that," I say as I press my lips to his cheek. "Please, Micah."

I beg because that usually works. I plead when I need to, and often.

He softens beside me. "Please, don't tell me you're the kind of person who decorates for Christmas on November 1st? Because I fucking *hate* those people."

I scoff and bristle beside him. "Well, I am, so deal with it."

He slides out of bed, leaving a cold draft behind. I can hear him fussing with the fireplace for light, and smug satisfaction hits my lips. I've won this battle. We don't run the fire all the time because, just like with the food, our resources are limited. It's dark this far north. It's night more often than it's daytime. We only have four hours of sunlight right now, and we cherish that time when we have it.

I often have no idea at all when the sun will rise. We're not living like normal people, and winter has really settled in. The deep freeze started a week ago, and we couldn't go out there, even if we wanted to. We usually just sit in the dark; we talk, eat, sleep, wake up, and fuck.

The fire blasts to life, and Micah's tall, lean frame hovers in front of it. There's enough light for me to grab my backpack and pull out *The Great Gatsby* as I wait for him, but not before I admire him for a moment. I rarely get to see him.

He runs his hand over the back of his neck before he looks at me. Sometimes, in the right light, in the right moment, he looks like Maison, and I catch my breath, remembering he's not. I toss on an old sweater, making sure it's not the one with the wrong number on it—even though Maison's sweater is my favorite and probably always will be.

Micah brings me a bit of dried meat from some small animal. I hardly care which one anymore since they all taste the same to me now. He comes and snuggles in next to me as I take small bites. He barely eats, letting me have most of it.

Finally, it seems I've satiated him for the moment, and now I get to have the softer side of him I love just as much. When he chooses to show me this side, it's my favorite side of him.

He watches me, and I notice his throat bobs as if he's nervous about something. "Close your eyes," he tells me when I'm done chewing.

I smirk. "What for?"

He arches a brow, indicating that he isn't messing around. "Do it... Please."

Did Micah just say please?

I snap my eyes shut, realizing he's being serious. This must be important if he said please. He places something small and wooden in my hand. "Okay, open them," he whispers.

My mouth gapes open when I take in what he just gave me. A wooden carving of a flower, so expertly done that it looks real, the petals so intricate. I have no idea how or when he did this, especially since he only has that big knife. He looks at me awkwardly, almost blushing.

I'm speechless. It's unsurprising since he is talented at basically everything, but this?

"Micah," I whisper, more breathless from this gift than anything he has ever done. It's his love language, I realize, doing these small gestures. He's done it from the beginning—the wolf blanket, the spears, the music he managed to find when it should have been impossible to have music in the wilderness.

He leans his head on his elbow, watching me with an amused expression as I inspect it. "I guess, since you're my girlfriend now, I am supposed to buy you flowers, and since I can't do that, I made this for you instead."

I look at him, and my eyes widen, figuring out that he's just admitted he's never been in a relationship before. I just assumed with the number of women he's fucked...

My eyes draw down to the carving, still marveling at how expertly crafted it is. My lips burst into a smile. "Micah Matei... Am I your first?"

His moment of vulnerability is over. He looks at me with a cool expression and merely shrugs. "It's not a big deal."

Tilting my body toward him, I press my lips against his, pouring all my love into him. "It is a big deal. I'm your first girlfriend." I say those words out loud with pride, but a slice of guilt cuts through me. I said those words recently—to Maison.

Girlfriend.

I can't pretend Micah is my first. He isn't... not even close.

He runs his muscled arm over my chest, and I swallow a lump in my throat. "Do you like it?"

I turn away from him as tears burn the back of my eyes, and hopefully, I can hide the hint of emotion on my face so he doesn't catch it. We still have a zero-Maison policy in this relationship, and if he guesses I was thinking of him...

"I love it, Micah. When did you make this?"

He cuddles in next to me, placing his hand over my injured one—a protective gesture I don't think he realizes he does. "You tend to sleep a lot, baby," he jokes.

And he rarely does.

He grabs the book, hands it to me, and sighs. "Alright, London. Where did we leave off?"

I turn to face him and smile. "Oh no, we are starting from the very beginning again." I pick up the book and open it to the first page. "*Chapter one...*"

CHAPTER FIVE

LONDON

*W*inter

I've let the days get away from me, but we estimate from the position of the sun that it's February. That, and the notches on the wall when I bother to make them. The days are getting longer, but the nights are excruciating. I'm starting to forget things, like details of my life. I keep wondering... Is that all? Is this my life forever now? Maybe it's not a bad thing, being here forever... But what if this isn't how it's supposed to end? We haven't seen anyone, and there is no sign of life anywhere. No one is around but us.

Micah is quieter than he has ever been. His silence mirrors the world around us. He disappears for hours at a time, even though he's right beside me. He's running out of wood to carve, and I'm not sure what he will do with himself then. There are only so many bruises I can endure. We often lie in a still silence, drowning in our own thoughts. We don't talk about Maison, even though weeks have gone by. We seem to lack the ability to mourn, and the isolation of winter... it's starting to get to us.

I can usually bring Micah back to me by kneeling in front of him and forcing him to feel me. It usually works, and when I wake up that part of him, we fuck for hours, if not days. Then we slip back into our eerie silence. But we are still here, and we are still breathing, so I suppose that means something. And in the short moments when Micah isn't looking, I swear I see Maison watching me from the window.

As I pull my hood over my head and run, I can't help but feel a shortage of oxygen in the air—as if Alaska doesn't have enough of it. Unseen enemies chase me, lurking and laughing, while I navigate through the thick mist and snow. The air is suffocating, and my lungs feel as if they are full of blood and ash, crushing my heart as I seek out anything to help me decipher where I am. The bones of my hand are breaking into pieces beneath my skin.

Breathe. Breathe. Breathe.

"Maison?" I sputter, calling out in the forest.

Concealed among the branches and leaves, he silently waits for me, his whispers calling for me through the wind and pushing me forward.

"Where are you going, London?" A hooded monster blocks my path, the tip of his crooked bow tie sticking out from under his neck. I stop dead in my tracks, catching my breath as I behold him smirking at me, a silent scream on the tip of my tongue.

"Away from you," I spit, and my spear appears in my hand, or perhaps I was holding it the entire time. My knuckles are white as I grip it.

A dark chuckle. "There's no getting away from me. I'm coming for you, *London King*." He says my name as if he's a serpent.

The pain in my hand intensifies, and I fall to my knees. Black spirals form in my veins as I watch in horror as the sepsis begins to take over, like shadows eating my hand. Nigel steps toward me, my heart beating violently in my chest.

"Go away," I beg him. I repeat those words as the wind picks up and the ash falls all around me, grasping my hand as I watch the flesh further decay every second.

When I peer up, he's gone, and a new hooded figure replaces him.

"Maison," I whisper, and his smile instantly warms me.

"I'll protect you, baby," he says, kneeling. His eyes shift in the night as he blinks at me, his sexy hair falling in his face. A calm and steady aura surrounds him. "Don't worry about your hand, I'll fix it." A flash in his hand gives me pause, striking terror deep within my core. He's holding a knife, I realize. For a moment, I meet his steady, dark gaze, and my hand finds his face.

It can't be Maison.

"Micah." I let out a shaky breath. "Don't do this."

His smile turns into a pained frown. "I have to, London. You'll die if I don't."

"Micah... no!" I scream, although no sound comes out, as he grabs my wrist and pushes it to the cold, hard ground, his eyes bound and set on his mission.

I suffocate on my breath, and he begins sawing metal on flesh, giving me no reprieve.

Wake up!

My eyes shoot open, and I wake up from one hell, only to be met with the inky darkness of another. Still stranded, still hungry, still broken. Micah's wrapped around me, pulling me into him, and his hand goes directly to my heart, trying to calm my shaking body, which is drenched in sweat.

"Calm down, London," he whispers, his breath grounding me to this dimension. "I'm right here, baby."

As I regain my composure, I realize he was the center of my nightmare, not the hero I know him to be. I turn to him, straining to see his dark features, and he gently takes hold of my injured hand, the one he's been tirelessly trying to rehabilitate. He places our hands against his chest, reassuring me.

Overwhelmed with emotion, I can only sob, unable to find the words to express my anguish, bile hitting my throat.

"You need to distract yourself. Try to think about something else," he whispers in a soothing voice. His thumb finds its way to my brow, and he wipes the pool of sweat and tears from my cheeks with his fingers. "It's all in your mind. You need to master it, or it's what's going to end up killing you. Turn it off, baby. Focus on me."

"I can't," I sob between jagged breaths. I still feel the knife slide through my skin. I still taste the copper of blood as it stings my mouth from when I bit my tongue in my sleep.

His lips eventually find mine, and I resist his kiss by hitching a breath.

"Open your mouth, baby. Let me in."

His lips are like silk and instantly make me feel better. I moan as I open my mouth and lose myself in him as he teases my tongue with his. Eventually, I give in and deepen the kiss, pouring all my agony into him.

My heart slows, and I find my breath, but I still can't seem to find my voice.

"What did you dream about?" he asks, pulling his lips from mine.

How can I possibly answer?

"I dreamt about you." I manage a whisper. It's not exactly a lie...

His fingers find the hem of my pants, teasing my skin and causing me to press my body against his. The distance between us feels like an eternity. I want him... and I need him to know how badly.

My lips find his neck, and I kiss him softly for a few seconds before my hand finds his hard bulge pressing against my abdomen. I pull it out and wrap my fingers around the length of it.

This will help me forget. I moisten my lips and lower myself beneath the covers, where I spend the remainder of the night letting go of everything.

The laughter wakes me again.

The same laughter I've heard the last few weeks in my dreams. Micah's breath is heavy beside me, which tells me I may not even be awake, although my hand painfully throbs. My hand is better, much better than before, and Micah says the throbbing is a good thing.

I nudge him slightly, but he doesn't move. Micah barely sleeps, but when he does, he's impenetrable, which means I am fully conscious and aware of him. If I were dreaming, would I have such practical thoughts?

This means the laughter is real.

Micah doesn't stir as I slip out of bed, throw on an extra sweater, and grab my spear. I tiptoe to the door and step outside into the frigid temperatures, which now slap me in the face. The thin layer of clouds deep in the sky parts, allowing the Artic moon and stars to shine their light on the snow, providing me with the light I need to see.

I'm so aware of my surroundings that my senses are fired up. And somehow, despite the air burning my face and numbing my fingers and toes, I don't consider myself truly conscious. Because this is the laughter I only hear in my nightmares.

And right now, I hear it clear as day.

I drag my fingers up my sleeve, giving me access to my exposed skin, and pinch myself, digging my long nails into my arm until three little drops of blood seep out. The pain is real, very real. I smear the blood to make sure that it's real, too.

Someone's out there. And they are taunting me.

I curl my toes and step into the deep snow, dragging myself toward the thick woods that surround our cabin. I instantly regret my decision as my foot sinks at least two feet. I trudge through it anyway, willing myself through it, ignoring the dull ache in my legs and the numbness in my toes. I pull my hood over my eyes to block the icy wind from penetrating my skull, and the laughter continues. I follow it, pausing a moment to listen... to truly listen.

It shifts from male to female. A dull ache simmers inside me. I dig my nails into my palms and continue. I need to end this before it begins.

I look back at the cabin, knowing Micah is there and I've broken his rule. I have two options. Tell him I hear voices and have him freak out and possibly kill someone tonight. Or admit to myself that the laughter probably isn't real, and therefore, I should go back inside. I don't want Micah worrying that I'm going crazy.

The laughter doesn't stop. Someone is there just beyond the tree line; I can sense them.

I scan the woods, waiting for someone to show themselves. Gripping my spear tightly, I cautiously decide to explore, just to be safe. If it is the others, I can scream, and Micah will come running immediately. There's a good chance it's nothing and that I am sleepwalking. I'm probably not even really outside. My dreams are so vivid that I often cannot tell them apart from reality.

As I take each step, the laughter dissipates, replaced by the comforting stillness of the snow I have grown accustomed to. In certain areas where the snow is too heavy, the occasional crack of a branch breaks the silence. A gentle wind teases the bare branches as if calling me, trying to suck me deeper into the depths of the forest.

It is as if I'm not in control, and my feet root into the icy ground. In my stillness, I hear it again... the dark laughter. Images of sharp knives and bow ties flash through my mind. The laughter surrounds me now, their laughter... Naomi, Ezra, and Nigel. It has to be them.

However, what catches my attention is a figure in a dark hoodie standing completely still in the trees beyond. A dark hoodie with argyle sticking out of it.

I breathe. I calm my trembling heart and close my eyes. When I open them, Nigel's gone. I still can't shake the laughter, and now I'm positive I must be losing my mind. I pull up my spear and inspect it. Micah's kept it sharp, although I haven't needed to use it over these past few icy weeks.

Wiping frozen tears from my face, I press it into my injured hand to feel something again.

"*Fuck*," I cry out as pain radiates from my hand to my arm and up to my shoulder. Pain to acknowledge I'm alive, to keep me grounded, to keep me from dying in these dark woods. The pain I've come so dependent on to feel anything, as mundane and critical as the air I breathe.

I should go back; the cold wind is biting my exposed skin. I am utterly insane for following laughter out into these dense woods. I snap my head around, and the darkness has now completely taken over. The laughter returns—Naomi's laugh this time, I realize—and I have no idea where to go from there. With the moon now behind a cloud, the direction back to the cabin isn't clear. Panic settles into my chest as I realize I'm lost.

Naomi's laughter echoes in my ears, mocking and relentless. My despair is humorous to her and has been since the moment we met. I remember that moment with her and Micah in the woods, the moment I stole from her.

It sickens me to think that there might be some unresolved emotions between them. What if she comes back for him?

A tiny whimper escapes me as I hunch down and sit in the snow, placing my head in my hands as tears flow from my eyes. I try to scream out for Micah, but no words—no sounds—come out of me.

Another shadow... another dark hood snaps me out of my thoughts.

A gray one shimmers in the night, but this time, the tension in my body immediately ceases.

"Maison," I whisper, knowing how crazy I sound, but I've been waiting for this moment to see him again. He's the real reason I came out here. I knew he'd appear to me. In the darkest part of my mind, that hallucinogenic part of my brain is so soothing. These visions have happened over the past few weeks, and I figured the isolation must be getting to me. I haven't told Micah, although I wonder if he sees him, too.

The easier twin.

Maison peers over me, his cute, crooked smile instantly putting me at ease. I reach up to touch him. He isn't too far away from me, only a few short feet, and he could be mine.

I sit in the snow and peer up at him. "Maison," I call out to him again.

"London... what are you doing?"

His eyebrows pinch together in a very un-Maison-like manner. It's the brooding face I love so much. I blink at him a few times and realize it is Micah. I'm not dreaming, and I'm cold, very, *very* cold.

I snap back to reality. What the fuck *am* I doing?

He kneels in front of me, his face as stone cold as the snow surrounding us, but his hands still so warm. "It's me, baby, it's Micah."

I blow out a breath. It's Micah. Of course, it's Micah.

"Micah..." I whisper his name as I gather myself, still confused about which twin I'm seeing.

Maison is fucking dead, London. Pull it together.

He pulls me out of the snow, and I lean into his warm arms and finally start shivering, as if my body only now registers how fucking cold it is outside. My fingers are blue, and I have no sensation in them. I touch his face, cupping his cheek, running my finger over the face I've now memorized.

He isn't cold; he's so warm, concerned, and perfect. What is wrong with me?

"Micah, I'm sorry..."

"Fucking hell, London." He immediately grabs my hands in an attempt to warm me with his body heat. He pulls my hands to his lips. "You're frozen, baby. You could have died out here." He glides his hands over my entire body, making sure I'm not broken. His eyes are wild, panicked and scared in a way I've never seen before. I can't respond; my teeth are chattering too hard, and my body is shaking. I am fully conscious now, and the laughter is gone.

And I just called him Maison. This won't be good.

Finally, I find my voice. "Micah, I didn't mean to leave. I thought..." I have to explain myself. Explain why I would leave the cabin at night like that, why I would leave him. I can't find the words. I don't know what I thought.

"Let's get you home, baby," he says without any anger in his voice.

Baby. Why does he have to call me that? It reminds me so much of Maison.

He carries me back to the cabin, but I keep my eyes planted on the space where I was sitting. My eyes catch onto something in the woods a short distance away, something I can't seem to rip my gaze from. Something that makes my skin crawl... like a million tiny insects scuttling all over me. Something that terrifies me to the core.

I close my eyes and drown it out, hoping what I saw was nothing but a trick of the light and more of my hallucinations.

Once back in the cabin, Micah places me on the bed, rubbing his hands over each finger to warm them first. Then he takes off my snow-covered sweater and the tank top I'm wearing beneath until I am naked. He stokes the fire and crawls in with me, warming me with his hands. Skin-to-skin contact is best for warming, or so he says. Eventually, he takes off his sweater, and I lay my head on his bare, muscled chest.

After a few minutes, and as my body begins to defrost, he finally whispers, "Are you going to explain yourself?"

I turn my head away from him. I don't want him to see the guilt riddled on my face. "I... I heard something."

His body goes rigid. "There's nothing out there, London. It's just a forest, and a really fucking cold one at that. What the hell did you hear that would make you go out there without me?"

He sounds so desperate and scared, and all I want to do is alleviate that. He doesn't deserve what I just did. "You fucking scared me, London. When I saw you weren't in the cabin..." He's shaking in a way I haven't seen him do before.

The beat of my heart is all I can focus on at this moment. My words get choked up in my throat as I try to explain myself. He's interrogating me, as he should. The guilt overwhelms me for desperately wanting it to be Maison instead of Micah in the woods. I just wanted one fucking minute with Maison.

I finally find the will to face him. Micah's so perfect in every way, and he's alive, taking care of me, making sure I live through this. And all I'm doing is fantasizing about his dead brother.

His face is hard and concerned, and his eyes have a hint of something in them. That hint of emotion I can never quite grasp in him. Despite the many hours I've spent with him, I don't truly understand him yet. I've spent more time with Micah now than I ever have with Maison, and yet there's still a mystery to Micah I have not pieced together, a layer of him I still have not experienced. It lingers so close to the surface that sometimes I get a glimpse, and even then, it's only when he *chooses* to show me. I can never guess how he will react to me.

Anger... He's seething and trying to control it. I did something he had no control over. I snap my eyes shut. If it were Maison right now, his features would be soft. He wouldn't push me for answers; he'd let me rest.

His voice comes out hard as steel. "Maison's not here, London, if that is who you went out looking for."

He always does that... reads my mind.

I slide my hand to my mouth, a gesture only a guilty person would do. "I wasn't. I mean..." My voice sputters. "That's not what I heard."

He arches a brow, seeing right through me. "Don't lie to me, sweetheart. You called me *Maison*. You've never done that before."

A pit forms in my stomach, and I lay my head down on him and let a few minutes pass, listening to the rhythm of his heart. He's quiet, letting me rest, and the heat begins to return to my body, although the chilliness lingers, and a blush hits my cheeks before it shifts to a bit of anger.

How dare he not let me grieve?

All these weeks, and he won't even let me utter his name.

"I... I didn't mean to," I finally respond, hoping he will let this go. "I love you, Micah." I lie rigid in his arm, a sign I'm not happy and not caring about the consequences. He wraps his arm around my head and pulls my chin toward him. His hands are soft, but his grip is firm, and a tightness forms in my chest.

"You could have died, London," he says, his fingers and body softening as he runs his fingers down my arm and rests them on my shattered hand. "I can't let you die. Because I love you too fucking much to let you die, especially like that. Do you understand what you just did to me?"

I pause as the weight of him crashes into me.

"Do you?" He can't control the tremble of his lips.

I turn to face him, press my lips to his, and close my eyes. A swell of emotions pours through me. "I'm sorry," I utter again, running my hands through his hair, then over his face. I'm angry with him, but I truly mean my apology. How would I feel if he suddenly left me? If I woke up, and he was gone? I'd be broken. My mind would shatter before my body.

His intense energy softens, but I can sense how hard he is against my torso, turned on as usual. Luckily, he shifts and pulls the wolf blanket tighter over me. I simply do not have the energy to please him right now, even though my body reacts to him as it always does.

"Get some sleep," he whispers, tucking me in tight before pressing his lips to my forehead. He runs his fingers down my arm to my shattered hand. He pauses for a moment, and I think back to the woods, how easily those woods could have consumed me. Right before I drift off to sleep, I hear him. "If you leave like that again, London, I will have to tie you up at night. Do you understand that, baby?"

My eyes pop open, but I barely register the threat coming out of his mouth. I love him. I've never wavered in my love for him, and I'll spend the next few days making sure he remembers that. I have to do better at hiding the fact that I might be slowly losing my mind. I need to do better at controlling whatever urge I have to put myself in jeopardy like that. And I have to explain to him that perhaps, this isolation and the way we are dealing with our pain and grief by completely ignoring it might be slowly killing us. It might be impacting us in ways we don't understand yet.

But right now... right now, my thoughts are consumed by what I saw in the forest. The set of footprints I saw in the snow... because they weren't mine.

And I think they belonged to Nigel.

CHAPTER SIX

MICAH

"*How many girls do you think I can screw before I graduate?*" *Maison jokes and takes a swig of whatever dark liquor he poured into his flask before we left for fishing. "I figure that if I shoot for a girl a week, I can probably sleep with the entire class by the end of our senior year and maybe even some of the younger ones."*

I roll my eyes, even though I can't help but smirk, wishing I had such simplistic thoughts and life goals. I also laugh because, while he's joking, it's possible he might achieve it. I wouldn't put it past him. Most of the cheer squad has fallen for his charm at one point or another, and somehow, none of them are aware he slept with their best friend the week before. They all just sit back, bat their eyes, and wait for their turn.

A tug on my line has me ignoring Maison, his stupid grin, and his adolescent obsession with sex. Not that I'm much better. I just haven't had the energy to actually talk to any of them.

"What about you?" he asks. "Naomi Wilson seems super into you."

I shrug, keeping my focus on the glass-like water of the lake and the three ripples where my line sits a few feet away, the sun slowly setting in the distance. "Yeah, she's alright, I guess. I may wait until Ezra fucks her first, though, then just take her from him. I don't need any clingy bullshit right now. Virgins are the worst after they finally get fucked... I learned that the hard way last year."

"Hold on, I've got something." I pull the reel nice and slow, and it comes up empty... I lost my fucking fish. "Damn it." Tensing my jaw, I immediately bait the hook and try again.

Maison senses my frustration.

"Micah, it's almost dusk, man. We should head home." Maison pulls out his fishing line and starts packing up. "The fish aren't biting, and I want to be good for our game tomorrow. You should rest up, too. It's really your game."

The sun. That determines when we have to leave. Our mom always threatens that if we aren't back before dark and she has to send a search and rescue party out for us, she will chain us in our bedrooms until we graduate high school.

The regional finals are tomorrow, and the scouts are coming... My future could be determined this week if I play to win. I have an opportunity to play for an NHL field team, which is the only outcome I will be okay with for my life.

"Ten more minutes," I say without looking at him. Catching a fish is the only thing that matters at this moment. "I don't want to go home and fight with Mom again about my medication." I overheard her and my dad talking about my mental health issues, and it triggered me. Maison overheard them fighting about it, too. He gave me a knowing stare and started packing to come out here.

He shrugs and casts his line deep into the lake, then sits down and cracks open another beer from our cooler without a fucking care in the world. "Fine," he says, staring off into the sunset, "but you can deal with Mom's wrath. I'll tell her it was your idea."

Usually, Mom couldn't give two shits about where I am, but if the two of us are at the lake alone, she has an absolute meltdown. She relives the trauma of almost losing us when we were eleven, but it's not my problem. It certainly won't stop me from living my life.

Because I relive it every minute of every day anyway.

Despite my trauma, I still love fishing. Unlike normal people who probably would avoid the place or activity that fucked them up, I attacked it, and fishing became one of my favorite activities. It must take a special kind of fucked-up person to cope with trauma by learning to master it. Because

I have a weird fascination with death, like how close to it I can get before I tip over the edge.

Maison only comes fishing with me because he doesn't want me to go alone. He worries about me constantly—he understands the depth of the thoughts I have, even if he won't admit it. And I usually only go fishing when something shitty is happening in my life. I don't invite him—he invites himself—and I suppose it's become our thing over the years, even if I would prefer to do it alone. I swear, he talks too damn much and scares the fish away.

Like now.

Maison presses his lips together as his fishing line goes buck wild. He looks at me, arches his eyebrows, and smiles. "I got something."

Fucking Maison. Of course, he would catch something before me.

"Damn, it's something big, too," he boasts, pulling the line and pretending to struggle with it for dramatic effect. He pauses and looks at me. His face grows serious and darkens. "Don't fucking hurt her, man... Deal with your shit."

My head whips up to nothing, just the same trees and the same searing and sparkling wintery sky. "What the fuck did you just say?" A deep chill runs through my bones, much colder than the Arctic air around me.

Maison's talking to me. His voice is clear and unyielding, the same tone he took when our relationship turned sour and he started hating me. "Don't fucking kill her, Micah. Don't fucking kill her like you killed Olivia, like you killed me. Got it? Don't fucking kill her, man. I'll never forgive you."

Jesus, fuck.

My eyes shoot to the sky and find the position of the sun hovering westward.

Shit.

I've been gone for hours, sitting silently in my fishing spot. I must have fallen asleep, and the last thing I remember is my eyes growing heavy since I refuse to sleep at night. I must have passed out or fallen into one of my trances.

The weather warmed to balmy after a two-week-long deep freeze, and I had to try to get us some food.

"Get the fuck out of my head, Maison," I say out loud to myself.

Earthly silence

I sense him beside me—through the twin bond we've had from birth. His presence is thick in the frosty air.

I recall every word we said to each other that day we went fishing. It was also the last time Maison and I had a normal conversation. It was the night before we met Olivia and everything changed between us. My parents mistakenly thought I was heartbroken, but I wasn't. And I wasn't fucking jealous, like Maison assumed. He couldn't have been more wrong, and his jealousy almost destroyed us. Now I understand how he felt because I am jealous of him when I should be mourning him. I'm jealous of a fucking ghost to the point of insanity. Because, no matter what, he's still the better twin.

"Maison?" I say again, swallowing all the emotions built up in my throat. For the first time since he died, a nagging desperation to see him sits in my core—to hear his voice one more time. When I close my eyes, he is right fucking here. I see him, every memory of him leaving me stiff, senseless, and numb. Now that I'm alone and away from London, it's Maison who consumes my thoughts.

Fuck. I won't do this. I refuse to lose my mind. I can't mourn him because that would mean his death was real. Mourning him will end him, and I'm not ready to lose him yet.

I shake my head to snap out of it, pulling my hood over my head. Maybe the isolation is finally getting to me, like London keeps saying. Either that, or the lack of sleep. I try not to sleep while she's sleeping since I almost lost her the last time I let myself relax. Since she risked her life to go and chase a ghost in the dark woods, there has been a noticeable shift in her I can't ignore. That was a couple of weeks ago, and things have been off between us ever since.

Every day, she slips further away from me. Her mind is shattering, causing me to doubt her ability to rely on her own judgment.

I lean down and pull on my fishing line, hoping I don't come up empty. London's hungry, and I can't seem to keep her content anymore. She longs for something more than what I can give her right now.

I can tell by her eyes, by how vacant they are when I fuck her—not that I've had much to give her, either. The darkness is swallowing us whole, and she's asked a few times about the others. If, maybe, we should go check on them. *Yeah, not fucking likely.*

Maybe not today, but eventually, she will realize how fucked up I am and leave. Perhaps she's already come to that conclusion—it would explain her behavior, distance, and constant pandering.

She doesn't speak to me about it, but I can see the spark of life fading in her eyes the longer she stays here. I'm killing her, or the island's killing her, but I'm losing her either way. And if I don't have her, I just don't see the point in living anymore.

I pack up, knowing we will go hungry tonight. The fish aren't biting, and I'm not in the right headspace to stay here. I've been gone too long, but at least it will be a good test to see what she does when left to her own devices.

I head back through the thicket toward the ice-covered cabin.

As I approach the cabin, I freeze when I notice a set of footprints heading away from it. Smaller, dainty footsteps, unlike mine, leading in a completely different direction.

"Goddammit, London," I mutter as I pick up my pace, realizing the footsteps only go in one direction.

She fucking left.

"London?" I call out aggressively.

Nothing.

"London," I call out again, my voice trembling. She better be taking a piss or something and call out to me so I at least know she's okay.

Icy silence.

My fingers flexing is the only external sign of anger, but inside, I'm bursting. At the first chance she gets, she leaves. And I only have one fucking rule: don't go outside without me. It's not that fucking hard.

Although the temperature has improved, it's far from warm. She won't last long out there without me. Ice crystals hover in the air. The air is still so cold that I cough whenever I take a deep breath. I follow the footsteps to find her, but they lead to a dead end. Almost like she disappeared mid-air.

She hid her tracks, and she did a fantastic fucking job of it, too. I scan the forest, trying to find even the slightest sign of her. I taught her this trick the last time we were out. It never occurred to me that she would use it to hide from me.

Smart girl.

"Fine. Suit yourself, sweetheart," I mutter, hoping she's within earshot and can hear me.

Two hours go by, and the sun's about to set. I've paced the cabin a thousand times and put a dent in the creaky floor. I debate if I've made the right decision by not going after her—not wanting to admit to myself that I had no clue where to search for her and that she bested me.

The pressure on my shoulders mounts and my vision blurs when I realize she isn't coming back.

"Fuck," I cry out. I'm not sure why I bother standing here, all fucking composed. I grab a can of food and whip it against the wall so hard that it smashes open, and her precious beans splatter all over the place. Immediately, a layer of tension releases from my body. I grab the bedding and start tearing at that, too, throwing all her things around the room.

It's then that I realize it's her things I'm chucking. She didn't take her backpack. Her journal, her clothes, her precious fucking book are all here.

Which means...

She's probably lost, and with how cold it is outside... And I've been sitting here having a tantrum, testing her.

I run my hands through my hair, preparing to go into the forest to find her, ripping my hair out.

Breathe.

If someone was in front of me right now, I'd fuck them up. It wouldn't matter who the fuck it was.

A meek voice comes from the door. "Micah?"

My head snaps to her, and a fierce, animalistic sensation washes over me. Just the person I'd like to rip up. My despair turns into anger, my face seething, then full-on relief. I'm not even trying to hide it. I flex my jaw and take her in, ice crystals hanging over her hair, hanging off her eyelashes. The fabric of her sweater is frozen. I wipe all the snow off her and grab her freezing, icy hand.

Fucking helpless.

I close the distance between us and grab her shoulders, not sure whether I want to pin her down or hug her. She gasps initially, but then she wraps her arms around me and submits as I lift her up and press her against the wall.

Pinning her it is.

"London. London. London," I whisper into her ear, closing my eyes.

She's small, fragile, and perfect, like I could snap her in two. Her heart is pounding erratically, and she shivers uncontrollably from the cold.

Don't fucking leave me, then, sweetheart. Then, you won't be so fucking cold.

She peers up at me, her dark eyes wide as I grip her waist, thrusting my hips, and shove my lips on hers, my tongue dominating her mouth. I have so much I want to say, but all I can do is kiss her because her mouth tastes so fucking sweet and the urgency to consume her takes over. I inspect her with my hands—every part of her deliciously frosty body—while keeping my tongue inside her mouth.

I grab her face, then her chin, before I run my hands down her arms, her stomach, and the hand I'm desperately trying to fix. I keep my lips on hers, and she bites my bottom lip, kissing me with more vigor than I've gotten from her in weeks.

"Micah, I can't breathe," she finally gasps. "Let me talk for a second."

She wants it... She wants me more than she has in days. It's as if the fury simmering inside me has sparked her fire again. Witnessing her helplessness and how dependent she really is on me has also sparked mine.

My nostrils flare. "Where the fuck were you?" I grit, ripping my lips from hers, and arch my brow as she tilts her head toward me.

She blows out a breath. "Micah, I went out. Just like you, I needed space and fresh air. I've been cooped up here for six weeks."

I grab her chin and force her to look at me. Only at me, surrounded by silence and the sound of my teeth as they grind together. "I had one rule, London. One fucking rule. You could have gotten lost, you could have..."

I don't finish the thought.

She sighs as if realizing the anguish she caused me by leaving. "You thought I died?" She grabs my hand, running it over her chest and the swell of her breasts. I keep my head low so she can't see how fucking distraught I am or how fucking turned on I am. "Feel this, Micah," she whispers.

I pause and let her have her brief moment of control... because I plan on taking it back soon enough. "What the fuck for?"

She leans in and moves her mouth to my cheek. "Because it's beating, and it's yours. I just went for a walk, that's it. I was only thirty feet away in the woods; I didn't go far. This place is suffocating me. I just needed some time outside these walls."

The sensation of her lips against my skin ignites a fiery rush through my veins, intensifying my frustration. I may pretend I'm in charge, but this girl owns me. I slam both hands beside her head, and she winces. "So I suffocate you?"

Her gorgeous eyes flash. "I didn't say that," she responds carefully.

My hands trace up her back as I notice the sweater she's wearing. It looks like I'm not the only one thinking about Maison today. "What the fuck are you wearing?"

"Micah, don't be like that."

I'm being childish, but I don't give a shit. "Take it off."

"Micah..."

"Take it off, now."

Her pupils flare as she pulls the sweater off, wincing when she tries to use her injured hand. This time, I don't help her dress like I usually do. Her hand is yet another example of something I can't fix or change.

Just like I can't change the fact that Maison is dead.

Her real boyfriend is dead.

My fucking brother is dead... My twin, my best friend, my lifeline is fucking gone.

The pain of that thought hits me so hard in this moment. It's like the last two months of feeling absolutely nothing culminated into this very moment where I feel *everything*.

I run my fingers down her cheek. "Were you thinking about him today while you were away from me?" I keep my voice soft, even though I'm screaming inside. "Is that why you left?"

Tears form in her eyes as she stares at me with pity, and all my emotions reflect in her eyes back to me. She doesn't answer me. My jaw clenches as I watch her. The flicker in her eyes tells me everything I need to know. I keep my hands positioned so she can't move. She can't *avoid* my questions.

If words can slice, I want mine to make her bleed. "When you dream at night, do you dream about me... or him?" My breath hits her cheek. I already know the answer since she cries out for him almost every night, the memory of his death replaying in her mind as it does in mine. I'm not the only guy in her world and never will be.

A beat of silence goes by. Her body is shaking, and not from the cold.

Not anymore.

"I love you so much, Micah," she says, trembling but holding my stare. "But he was my first love. I'm sorry if that hurts you, but that's how it is. I can't change it. He was there for me at the beginning of all this. All I had was him, but that does not change how I feel about you now."

He was all I had, too. My whole goddamn life.

I try to breathe, but the tightness in my chest takes over, completely paralyzing me. She shifts, and her sweater hits the floor. She's wearing her sexy, tight-ribbed tank top, the one that makes her tits look amazing. I run my hand down her stomach and slip that off, too, so her tits pop out. Her naked body helps me breathe again.

My jaw flexes. My whole body is more rigid than my bone weapon. She runs her hand down her torso to the band of her sweatpants, and my cock is now a painful bulge against my boxers. "This too, Micah?" she breathes. "Is this what you want me to do?"

I bite the inside of my cheek. "It's a good start," I growl.

She grabs my erection, tickling it with her fingers through the fabric. "Will fucking me non-stop help you get over losing your brother instead of actually talking about him?" She pulls down the band of her pants. She's still so thin that they fall to the floor as soon as she loosens the drawstring. I loosen my drawstring and pull out my cock, cradling her up so her back is pressed against the wall.

Her pussy is ready for me, as it always is.

"Yes, it's what I fucking want." I slide right into her and begin sucking on her neck, mumbling into her skin, "You are all I ever want."

I rock inside her, and she keeps her head hung low to try to hide the fact that she's crying. I bury myself deep inside her, and already, the sex is better than it has been in days. I wipe her tears away with my thumb.

Maison's warning from the grave echoes in my ears. He doesn't like what I'm doing to London. He knows I'm going to destroy her.

But I am so in love with her that it hurts.

So he can fuck right off.

"Is this what you need, Micah? For me to show how much I love you?" Her voice breaks as she says it, and she grinds onto my cock. Her sniffles turn to moans as she fills herself up with the length of my cock.

I pull out of her, and using both arms, I pick her up and move her to the bed, laying her down and looking at this gorgeous girl in my possession. All the little marks I've given her when she said or did something I didn't like. She thought it was a game and I was teasing when I said I wanted to train her. But her training hasn't even begun, and those marks were just the beginning. She needs to understand that she can't leave me. Clearly, I've been too gentle with her.

I have to remind her how much pleasure I can give her.

I pull off her, the dim light of the fire making her skin sparkle beneath me. I run my thumb over the two bruises I left on her hips and press down.

Her breath hitches, and she shakes her head, pursing her adorable lips. "Micah, I don't want to play this game right now. You're scaring me, and I'm tired."

She's always fucking tired. All she does is sleep. But little does she know that it's time for her awakening. She's ready... so I press harder.

"Stop it, Micah."

I press deeper, and she goes deathly still, but her breath deepens, her cheeks flush, and her eyes darken. Her body is responding how I hoped it would, arching into me.

"Be very careful when telling me to stop, sweetheart," I whisper. "Because you only get to say it once, and I will stop. But I don't think that's what you really want me to do."

Her little heart is beating super fast now. *That got her attention.*

"Do you still want me to stop, baby?"

Her naked body trembles slightly, but she bites her bottom lip and her eyes sparkle. More vitality than I've seen in weeks. "No. But I think we should talk about him, eventually. You can't hide from him forever, Micah. You're not doing well right now. What happened? Can we talk about it? We have to come to terms with what happened to him."

I pause, and she waits for my reaction, which she must be aware will not be positive. I lean my forehead against hers, dominating her space because doing so gives me a slice of control I wouldn't have otherwise. "I'm not hiding from him, London. I can't get him out of my mind, but I'm not ready to deal with him. Because I'm worried that when I do, I won't come back from the places it will bring me to."

She's quiet, her breath causing her chest to rise and fall underneath me. "Micah…"

I press my fingers over her lips, quieting her. "The only person I want to think about right now, in what short time we have left, is you, baby."

A hint of fear flashes in her eyes. "Have you thought about going to check on the others? I mean, we just left them in the night. They probably think we are dead." She mindlessly plays with my fingers before grabbing my hand. "We can't stay here forever, Micah."

I nuzzle my nose into her neck, ignoring the clench in my stomach. "Yes, we fucking can," I remind her. Her doubts about me have started. I knew this was coming. The bliss of having her to myself could never last. She's quiet and contemplative now, scanning my face, looking for any sign of sanity, which I'm not sure either of us fully possesses right now.

I've got news for you, sweetheart… I've always been fucking crazy.

My body is pressed over hers, and I finally take off my sweater so I can feel her skin against mine. My finger finds her lips. "You really fucking pissed me off today." All this talk about going back to the others. I can never go back there… That's where *it* is—Maison's grave—as if he doesn't haunt my thoughts enough.

I kiss her, drawing it out, soft and sweet, before I pull up and look at her, my fingers reaching for her backside. "Do you want me to fuck you now, sweetheart? Like, really fuck you the way I think you want me to?"

She blinks twice, and her lips part. Her mind is on overdrive before she gives me the little nod of consent I was waiting for. It's time to unleash the demons within me because I think that's exactly what she needs to get the spark back she's been missing.

She arches her hips beneath me, raising one leg so it wraps around me. "Are you going to hurt me?" she whispers.

I perch myself on my elbow and arch an eyebrow at her as a wicked grin crosses my face. "Who said anything about hurting you? I don't plan on hurting you at all." I reach over and grab an old crappy T-shirt, using all my strength to rip it in two as she shuffles to the edge of the bed, pulling her knees to her chest and watching me, her matted hair falling down to her breasts.

She's never looked so fucking beautiful.

I grab my fishing wire and run my hand along her cheek as she parts her rosy lips for me. "Close your eyes, baby, and open your mouth." She hesitates only for a second before her mouth falls open and her tongue slips out. I place a gag in her mouth, then rub my hand down her neck. "I want you to learn what suffocating really feels like…"

CHAPTER SEVEN

LONDON

Today was hard.

Maison consumed my thoughts, and I cried for three hours straight, thinking about him, allowing myself to miss him. I waited for as long as I could, out by the snowy creek, until my toes were tingling and had lost all sensation, because this was the only time I could truly grieve him without Micah stealing my thoughts and dominating my reality. Even if it was pointless because it's not like I'm any better, and I knew Micah would be angry with me for leaving, which is absurd considering he was gone for hours, too. I needed to heal, and while I knew Micah wouldn't like it, I needed to try.

At this point, I'm not sure who's sicker, me or Micah. I should say no to him, stop him from hurting me and shoving a gag in my mouth. Because I'm not sure this is something people our age are supposed to do, let alone admit that it excites me. Micah's been breaking down these past couple of weeks, and seeing emotions inside him, anger or otherwise, is still better than watching him sitting by himself, carving wood and barely sleeping.

I enjoy the way he looks at me and how my heart pulses when he's enraged, foaming at the mouth, staring down at me like I'm food. He isn't Prince Charming—far from it—but he's my version of it. My body serves as his connection to reality, preventing him from descending into the abyss of his tormented thoughts.

I relax my body, allowing myself to go slack while he manhandles me. Fighting Micah is futile as he holds my belly down with one hand. I lie in horror as he effortlessly grabs my wrists, wrapping a wire around them and tying a knot, like he's used to kidnapping women on the regular.

I take a second to process what he's doing, the fact that he's actually restraining me. Heat pools between my legs and a flush hits my cheeks at how turned on I am by this. Of course, I am, because it's Micah, and I've been attracted to him from the moment I laid eyes on him. The depth of my trust in him is evident in my desire to please him by letting him do whatever he wants to me.

He slowly and methodically positions me in a way that suits him. My legs spread open, my knees up, my arms bound behind me, and my body put on display and vulnerable, reminding me of the first time he ever fucked me while I was in his brother's arms. He bites his lip, taking in my pebbled nipples. He grabs me and gives my ass a little smack. "Stay here, London. Don't fucking move an inch. I want to admire you for a bit, baby." His breath is raspy as he says it.

I stay deathly still, lying on the soft, furry wolf blanket he made me, but keep my eyes locked on him. Whatever he has planned, he isn't in a hurry. He moves to the fireplace, throwing on a log and some fuel so the flames ignite and blow up. Heat rises to my face, and it's a welcomed sensation in contrast to the chilliness lingering in the air. His muscles ripple beneath his smooth, olive skin under the darkening sky and flickering firelight. He emulates everything that is this cabin, shrouded in obscurity.

My god, he's sexy.

He isn't in a good headspace. His eyes are shadowed, like liquid onyx, and he appears disconnected from the world around him, except for his singular focus on me. I haven't seen this side of him in a while, and I've only ever experienced it once. Something must have happened today beyond my need for a moment away from him.

He's hurting... so deeply. I am part of the reason why he's hurting, although there is nothing I can do to change that other than show him I am here for him in all the ways he needs me to be.

My hand starts to throb, so I shift a little, just enough to ease the pressure. He's tidying the cabin now and pauses at my shifting, tilting his head as he beholds me. "I told you not to fucking move, London."

I freeze, my heart pattering, and I swallow a lump in my throat. The way he says it, I don't recognize him right now. Or maybe I do... It was his darkness that originally drew me to him; I was attracted to *his* story when I agreed to come on this trip to begin with. I plead through my eyes as he pierces me with a dark stare, then continues cleaning, ignoring me.

Obsessively cleaning.

I shift again, my hand now on fire. He walks over to me, crawling onto the bed and finally giving me the attention I've been begging for since he started *admiring* me.

He draws his chin to the side. "Does your hand hurt, baby?" he asks darkly.

Now he cares? I dare not tell him to stop, even though I should, because Micah doesn't make idle threats. I don't tell him my hand is throbbing, shooting pain into my shoulder. I'm not sure how far he's going to take this.

Would he stop?

He ponders for a moment. "Do you want me to untie you, London?"

He must sense my hesitation because he arches his sexy brows as if daring me to say anything. We haven't discussed what we are about to do. We've teased it. He's given me those bruises, and I asked for them. But it hasn't gone further than that, and we haven't talked about boundaries.

Are those even relevant now?

I shake my head and glimpse a hint of a smile on his lips. Dark, raw emotion.

I choke on my breath. What if this is what he wants, and he keeps me like this forever? I peer at him, telling myself this is just him fulfilling a sexual fantasy, that he doesn't mean it and would never actually tie me up in real life.

My skin radiates heat and vibrates with primal lust, every inch of my body craving him. I need this more than anything. I want to absorb all his rage and anger. He isn't the only one with darkness; it's inside me, too, and I'm slowly slipping into the void. When I slip entirely into it, I want us to at least be together.

I moan as his fingers tease my stomach, my breasts. He curves his fingers and gently pulls my hair, tying it up so it's out of my face, then wipes a bead of sweat from my brow.

Every second, every slight tickle of his body against mine sends my senses into overdrive. He leans over me and kisses my forehead before placing a shirt around my eyes, as if the gag in my mouth and the wire around my wrists weren't enough.

My world becomes black.

"Bite down on your gag," he warns. Seconds later, a sizzling burn hits the skin of my inner thigh, and I squeak and flail. He keeps the heat on my skin for what feels like an eternity, pinning me in place with one firm hand so I don't shatter my wrists.

Ash... The fucker burned me.

I bite hard, chewing the inside of my cheek. A few seconds later, he rubs a piece of snow on the blister, and the pain subsides. I'm left with something unexpected—raw euphoria. Heat explodes in my belly, right between my legs. Another mark, another notch on his belt.

I want more. My pain has become so constant that I need it like a drug to merely exist.

More fire, more pain, more heightened emotions.

My body pleads for him. I let out a long breath through my nose, trying to contain the beating of my heart. I arch my back, wanting and expecting more, as if we are precisely the missing puzzle pieces in each other's existence. It's deliciously terrifying.

His hands find my hips, and I lean into him, hoping he'll at least put his mouth on me after what he just did. He shuffles his body down. The electric current of his lips is so close, the kiss of his breath tickling my skin. Then... he abruptly stops. He pulls a blanket over my legs, rises, and wordlessly leaves the cabin, shooting an icy breeze that teases my bare skin as the door creaks behind him.

Fucker.

The gag is so tight that I barely manage an audible moan. He is going to leave me tied up like this and do absolutely nothing to me. He takes his time outside, then finally comes back in, *humming* to himself like a psycho. I use the opportunity to rest, keeping my eyes closed, even though I can't see anything anyway. I drop my head down, positioning myself like a turtle on the bed, bound and extremely uncomfortable as he rustles around the cabin. It doesn't take long for me to doze in and out of sleep, listening to the familiar, calming sounds of Micah working.

I shift my body carefully. My injured wrist doesn't hurt if I don't move it, so I lie utterly still, waiting for him and anticipating his plans for me. He grows quiet, so I listen to the snow falling.

And yes, I've come to learn that you can actually hear snow falling, and I don't mean the wind, the rustle of the trees, or the crunch of footsteps on top of it. When it's falling and you really listen, you can hear the millions of flakes as the snow blankets the ground. It's crystalline and something I've never noticed while in the city. Only in Alaska can I truly appreciate the sound.

Finally, after about an hour of meticulously taking his time doing whatever he is doing, I sense his heavy presence crawl up beside me. His hand gently pulls the fabric from my mouth.

"Are you hungry, baby?" he asks, running his hand across my cheek.

My stomach has been grumbling for the past hour while waiting for him. I soften as his warm hands run up my arms. I suck in a breath, feeling a ripple of annoyance at how bored I've been. "Micah, what are you doing to me? I'm cold and tired. Please let me go." I just want to lie down. He hasn't touched me at all, and this is *not* how I thought my first experience of being tied up would go. Not that I ever thought any guy would tie me up or that I would want someone to, but here we are...

"Eat," he demands.

"How long are you going to keep me like this?"

He shoves his fingers into my mouth. "Eat, London. You need food." I lick his fingers, and a delicious earthy aroma hits my tastebuds. I almost die from the deliciousness of it. It's spaghetti with marinara sauce, and I slurp down the noodle, savoring every salty bit of it. He's been saving this spaghetti for a special occasion. I've wanted to eat it so badly for weeks now, but he wouldn't let me.

He hand-feeds some more, and I moan at how wonderful the sensation of taste is when all my other senses are dulled. It's the best meal I've had here. It even tastes better than those cold, canned beans I shoved into my mouth when he found me at the plane site after I ran away.

I chew and swallow, licking my lips for more. He slips another bite into my mouth, and I devour it like an animal. "Take your fill, sweetheart." He chuckles.

I eat as much as he's willing to give me, wondering what the catch is. He gives me a few more bites and says nothing. Then he grabs the water, pulls my head back softly, and pours some into my mouth.

My stomach is full, with no hunger pains left, and now all I want is him.

He shifts and shuffles, and finally, his warm skin presses against my cheek, his hard cock near my mouth teasing me. He slaps my cheek with it. "Are you still hungry?" he teases.

Still blindfolded, I reach for his cock with my tongue and find the salty tip, which I lick. I was craving it, actually, waiting for this.

"Yeah," I breathe, instantly turned on again.

I'm surprised he even gave me something to eat first.

"Good. Because you're going to be sucking for a while."

Hmph. We'll see about that...

Sucking him off proves more difficult with my wrists tied. I can't do the things he likes with my hands, so I'm entirely reliant on my mouth. I suck as hard as I can, taking him as deep as possible while still trying to breathe. I can't see his facial expressions—the ones he can't control when I'm doing it right—so I wait until his muscled thighs tighten since that's the only other body part I can feel right now. I dig in deep into my current motion of opening my throat.

He's right... It takes me nearly half an hour of pure determination to get him off. And he doesn't touch me, even though my pussy is throbbing the entire time, waiting for him.

He doesn't even touch my breasts or my ass when his hands are usually all over me, and my nipples are tight like painful pebbles. I start to realize, ever so slowly, that this is part of my punishment, too.

He doesn't make much noise, but I imagine the expression on his face. Eventually, he quivers and spills into my mouth, and I swallow it down.

"Fucking hell." He rubs his hand along my tied-up injured arm. "That was so fucking good, baby. That was by far the best blow job I've ever had." He takes a warm cloth and wipes my mouth while I fight the swell of pride rising within me. He runs his knuckles along my cheek. "So fucking pretty," he whispers. "Such a perfect mouth."

I moan from his praise; it makes every fiber of my being sing. My skin is on fire as he continues running his fingers down and pinches my nipples.

Finally touching me.

My breath is heavy as I shift from my position on my knees and lie back to rest my head despite the awkward position of my injured wrist. He takes that warm cloth and starts cleaning me. I'm not going to complain about it. This is much, much better than my state of despair earlier today when I was grieving. And I want to see what else he has in store for me now.

He runs his hand along my cheek, and I lean into his touch, wishing he would touch more of me. "You want more, sweetheart?"

This is why I think I'm sicker than he is. Because I do want more. I want everything Micah wants to give me. I want to surrender to him fully.

My body trembles as I whisper, "Please."

He pulls my head back, gripping my hair in his hands.

"Please. Please. Please," I beg harder, trying to swallow a lump in my throat.

"Good fucking girl," he growls, my body inviting his, and I can hear the desperation in his voice, too.

This is a side of him I haven't seen yet. In all our time together, it's never been quite this dark. I start to wonder if, even though he's asking, I really have a choice in the matter.

I hear him shuffling, his strong, warm hands grazing my face, and I realize he's putting the gag back in my mouth. I flinch a little before his lips tickle my ear. "Trust me, baby, you're going to need this. Is your hand okay?"

I nod, although it's not okay. It fucking hurts and it's throbbing, but not wanting to end this yet, I hide its true intensity.

Once my gag is securely back in place, I relax my head against the three logs of wood that make up the headboard. Slowly, he starts kissing my stomach, savoring every moment as he moves to my breasts and finally gives me the release I've been craving. Every part of my body dissolves in pleasure. Rising to his feet, he maintains a calm and composed tone.

"Here's the rule, sweetheart. I'm going to kiss you now and slide my fingers inside you. You're not allowed to come until I say you can, and if you do, I promise the punishment will hurt in a way that won't make you moan. Do you understand?"

Shit, there is no way I can control that with him, and he knows it. It barely takes anything for me to get off with Micah. He touches me in one spot, and it happens.

"Nod if you understand, London."

I force myself to swallow and respond with a nod. As he runs his fingers along my sides, my heart pounds with more intensity than I've ever experienced with him before. It's as if I suddenly don't recognize the person I've spent the last six weeks with. The voice is his, but his body is different. His energy has intensified, and my heart rate spikes.

I shake my head, not wanting to play anymore, moaning and shaking for him to free me. He slips my gag out.

"What is it?" he asks, and the sound of his voice instantly soothes me. It's Micah; he isn't some crazed lunatic.

"Micah, I don't want to do this anymore," I breathe out. "You're scaring me. What happened to you today?"

He pulls off my blindfold, and I see his perfect dark eyes, his pouty lips, and a soft, pained expression on his face rather than the hard one I was expecting. His hair falls in soft waves above his dark eyes. He wipes a bit of sweat off my brow and the tear running down my cheek with his thumb.

"Will you tell me what happened to you today? Did you see something?" *Did you see him?* is what I want to ask.

He kisses me now, strong and hard. "Remember what I told you," he says, then pulls back, blatantly ignoring my question. "Don't come, sweetheart, or you're mine."

I'm already his, so I'm confused about what exactly he is referring to. He slides his tongue inside my mouth. My body heats in response as he crawls in next to me, grabbing my injured wrist as if just remembering it might hurt.

"Micah, please, answer me," I say in a meek voice. "Then you can do whatever you want to me."

A pause, and then he says, "Nothing's happening to me, London. I just want to do things to you that I haven't wanted to do to anyone else, and since we are going to die soon, I don't want to wait any longer. Do you trust me?"

Implicitly.

My voice comes out hushed and slightly broken. "Yeah, I trust you, Micah, with my life. I'm just worried about you." I shouldn't trust him—he's losing his mind. I don't understand the sudden panic, why he thinks we are going to keel over and die. We still have plenty of food, and spring isn't that far away.

"Do you want to stay here with me?"

"Yes, of course I do."

Why is he asking me this?

"Then close your eyes, sweetheart. This will feel better if you can't see what I'm doing." He puts my blindfold back on but, luckily, doesn't gag my mouth again.

"Remember what I said. Don't come, no matter how badly you want to."

My body tingles, and I try to ignore the already aching pain in my core. Micah's fingers barely tickle my thighs, and I let out a giggle.

"Quit giggling. This isn't funny."

"It's a little bit funny," I breathe.

"I'll put your gag back on if you don't take this seriously."

I suppress my laughter, shifting it to a mischievous grin. "What am I supposed to do?" I ask, wiggling on the bed as he runs his hands up and down my inner thighs and rubs his finger over the tender spot he burned.

"Relax your body and quit kicking so much."

I hadn't realized I was kicking, but even his soft tickles are making my body scream.

He runs his tongue along the same line he made with his fingers on my thigh and finally presses one finger inside me.

"Be strong, baby," he encourages, angling his finger in the way I like before adding another.

I'm so hungry for him that I clench around his fingers. As he presses down on my belly with his other hand, he leans down to kiss me. The motion is just right, and a little tingle runs through me. *A tiny orgasm, hardly noticeable.*

He pulls his lips from my mouth. "You fucking suck, London."

I loosen a breath. "I... I didn't. I swear."

"I know what your 'O' face looks like, baby. You fucking came, don't lie to me."

I shift uncomfortably, waiting for him to say something else. The wind picks up outside, along with my breath, and the draft that hits the bed causes goosebumps on my skin and sends a shiver up my spine.

"What are you going to do to me now, Micah?"

He pulls me down and positions his head between my legs before peering up at me through the gap between my thighs. "I'm going to fucking torture you, baby. And when I'm done, I'm going to take your ass."

He's going to take my ass?

I don't even understand what that means. Is my ass even big enough for him to take? My knees squeeze Micah's shoulders as he holds them firmly with both hands while his tongue laps up my folds and his teeth lightly scrape my clit.

I can't think. I can't process anything other than his mouth on me as my body tightens and the heat of my blood explodes through my veins. The sensation hits every nerve and limb, each toe and finger. My breasts are painfully swollen, my nipples raw from where he's been biting me for the last hour. The crippling fear of what he is planning to do to me afterward is still there, though.

Anal sex? Is that something I can do?

"Micah," I beg, if that's what you want to call it. I stopped begging him after ten minutes when I realized what he was doing. Now the sounds that come out of me are more like *Mmm* and *Aaah* noises that sort of resemble his name. I can't seem to catch my breath. "Please... I can't..."

I orgasm easily, I realize, and the human body can only sustain so many in a short period. Because this is torturous, in a very delicious and fucked-up way. My body doesn't decline between each orgasm as you think it would, and Micah's relentless with his mouth and fingers, only giving me a short few seconds before he keeps going. I've yet to fully climax. Sometimes, he changes things up, giving my mouth what it wants and pressing his lips to mine while keeping his fingers inside me.

He hasn't spoken to me since he started, ignoring my silent pleas, keeping me bound. Any time I try to squirm, he's there, holding me down and forcing it. He's still extremely gentle with me through every touch and every lick, as if my body is his temple.

It's not long until he's back down on my clit, pressing his tongue on my sensitive spot. It's so intense that my body finally gives up. He eases off me, chuckling. "Have you had enough, sweetheart?" After I catch my breath, he brings his lips to mine. "Taste yourself. Experience how fucking delicious you are." He slips his tongue inside my mouth, and I bite his lip, tasting my own wetness, my lips lingering for as long as he lets me.

He runs his fingers through my now extremely knotted hair and pulls off my blindfold. His dark brows are arched, and he's smiling, looking very pleased with himself. His face is certainly one I will never forget. Even in death, I can't imagine not seeing him every time I close my eyes, touch myself, or clench any part of my body. If I were to die before him on this island, my ghost would forever haunt him just to be near him.

He owns me...

He nibbles on my ear as my body seems to mold into his like I'm made of liquid.

"Micah," I whisper once I've caught my breath.

"London."

"Is this real?" I could very well be dead, and this is some sort of purgatory, caught between heaven and hell—the best parts of both.

He snickers, and he finds his way to my lips. "Yeah, sweetheart, it's real." He climbs on top of me, and I wrap my legs around him.

He licks his lips, and I gasp as he grabs the knife on the side of the bed. He expertly snips my binds, finally freeing my hands, the red welts on each wrist pulsing. I forgot that pain...

The fire crackles and pops, sending a red ember across the room. I forgot about *that* pain, too. I crumble into his waiting arms, having no fucking clue what time it is.

"I'm going to fuck you now, London. I want you to watch me while you climax, baby. I want to feel your breath on my skin and your heart beating, every part of you that makes you alive, okay?" He finally pulls my knees up, one by one. His motions are so composed. However, he can't hide the desperation in his words. His muscled body presses into mine, and he finally starts fucking me the way my body has been begging him to.

His cock is smooth as he slides inside me, my pussy ready for him. It takes me no time to hit my climax. I hardly recognize the moans that come out of my mouth as my body explodes into a nearly painful release. I keep my eyes open and on his the whole time.

Our breaths mingle as he rolls off me, pulling the blanket over his back, covering both of us. He gives my forehead a quick kiss and turns me on my stomach as I lie panting beneath him. After a few minutes, he gives my ass a little slap, shifting his attention there.

My stomach clenches...

He isn't fucking done. He never came; he hasn't even come close to climaxing.

It's dark inside now, just a small flicker of light from the fire he made earlier, which is dying out. The snow is coming down heavily outside. The small view of the outside I have from our bed reminds me of how alone and secluded we are.

Stranded.

I keep my attention on the outside and try to ignore what he is about to do.

He gently spreads my ass open and slowly slides a finger inside, then another.

My entire body tenses. "Micah... I don't think I can do this."

His lips brush against my ear. "You don't have a choice, baby, so relax."

I bite my lip as his fingers make gentle circles. "So fucking tight," he says, and I wonder how many times he's thought about doing this to me. I never thought I would ever do something like this with anyone. Ever.

"I don't think I'm big enough," I say, hoping he will change his mind. He merely snickers, then reaches out and grabs something from his side of the bed.

A bottle of lube?

Did he bring lube to Alaska to use on someone who wasn't me? My entire body bristles in jealousy at the thought of who he was planning on using that on.

"I found it in someone's luggage," he says as if reading my thoughts. "I never told you because you're always so fucking wet and never need it."

This appeases me for a moment as I attempt to relax, trying to make sense of the feelings coursing through me. But my body is tense. I'm not sure this is something I am capable of.

"Breathe, London. I don't want to tie you up again. I want you to do this willingly."

I breathe deeply as I focus on the fur of the wolf blanket, how soft it is and how much I love the guy who made it for me.

His fingers dig deeper, spreading out my ass further. He grabs a fresh cloth from ripped-up clothing and cleans me, then spreads some more. "Good fucking girl. Open up for me, baby. You're so strong, London. We have all night to get this right."

I've dealt with pain, and I told him on countless occasions that I could handle him. This is my chance to prove it. "You promise that it won't hurt?" I whisper to him.

He chuckles. "No. It probably will."

My breath hitches as he starts slowly, pressing the tip of his cock inside me after covering it in lube. Ever so slightly, he pushes himself deeper inside, and I seem to wrap around him, my body inviting the length of him instead of fighting against it like I thought it would.

Because I belong to him. I was made for him.

But it still fucking hurts.

I let myself go to the pain. With each touch, he evokes all the hurt, anguish, sorrow, and grief I've ever experienced. It's as if I can finally acknowledge it—manage it—in a way I couldn't before. He claims me, taking me gently until he's so deep that his entire body over mine is rocking back and forth. He fucks me like this for a while, slow and sensual, doing his best not to hurt me, kissing my neck, and breathing whispers of reassurance. A slow swell of pleasure rocks through me, shooting to my very core. The orgasm is just as intense as the others. I can barely make audible noises at this point as I muffle my breaths into the blanket.

He finishes relatively quickly, and I get a huge rush of satisfaction when his body comes undone, his breath so heavy and labored. He swears as he climaxes and keeps his hands gentle on me, not once doing anything that would truly hurt me.

I've unraveled him.

Every part of my body is throbbing now, even parts I never expected would be stimulated quite like that. He pulls off me, grabs some water and starts washing me again, wiping away all the sweat and sticky heat that came out of me. When I turn around and face him, he seems much cleaner than I do. It probably looks like I just went through a meat grinder and got spit out on the other side.

He cups his hands over my face and leans his forehead against mine before helping me put a shirt on. He cuddles up next to me, pulling me as close to him as possible. I can't talk; I have no words left, barely any coherent thoughts.

I close my eyes and finally let sleep take me, and I can't help the swelling of emotions that overtake me.

Grief, love, pain.

All of it.

"London," Micah whispers as the final bits of embers die in the fire and the shadows take over.

"Yeah," I whisper back, my body so relaxed and calm.

"Are you ever going to leave like that again?"

I swallow hard and squeeze my eyes shut. "No, Micah. I won't do that again. I promise that I won't ever leave you."

His fingers dig into me ever so slightly. "Will you marry me, baby? When we get out of here, I want you to be mine forever."

My body and mind jolt awake, and I turn to face him. His dark stare is as serious as I've ever seen it. His eyebrows are furrowed together, full of a deep, intense emotion. He isn't on his knee, and he certainly doesn't have a ring. He's just staring at me, eyes smoldering, lips pouting, his beautiful, handsome face waiting for me to say something.

I revel in the way he's looking at me. Images of the past four months consume my thoughts. The first day of school, him bullying me on the plane, the crash, the dead bodies, falling in love with Maison, falling in love with

Micah, the severed limbs, the isolation, the love, the fear, the hatred, and the betrayal...

Micah... it's just Micah now. That's all I feel, and it's all I need. He plays with a lock of my hair that has fallen over my eyes and moves it behind my ear. "Because if you want to marry me if we survive this, and I trust you will still be there, that would keep me sane."

His sanity. He knows it's slipping.

I press my lips to his because, deep down, I've already lost a part of my sanity. Perhaps our broken pieces can make up a whole. "Yes, Micah. I will marry you."

I kiss him again, and I keep kissing him all night because he got what he wanted, and now it's my turn, and all I ever want are his lips on mine.

CHAPTER EIGHT

LONDON

*S*pring

We are still alive and have officially survived winter. I think it might be early spring—or, at least, there are hints of it in the air. Subtle changes at first, things I hardly noticed, but that Micah picked up on immediately, like the sunlight lasting longer and pushing the darkness away. Some days are agonizing, and ever since the day Micah tied me up, the days have blurred together. Just wind and winter. Micah was there through the darkest part of it, always making me feel better.

When I'm alone, and in the odd times when I'm awake and Micah is sleeping beside me, with my hand placed over his beating heart, I hear the voices. It's as if they are lingering on the surface of my psyche, waiting to torment me. The other day, they came while it was light outside. Micah had only left for a few minutes, but I saw someone hidden in the shadows. When he came back, I was curled up in a ball, shaking. I couldn't bring myself to tell him why. When it happens, I usually seduce him, then submit to him in the ways that hurt the most. It's easier to get lost in him than to deal with what these voices might mean.

The night when he tied me up was only a couple of weeks ago, and somehow, I fell even more in love with him since then. He continues to feed me, fuck me, worship me, and he helps me get over my fear of dying here. We are still in the dark about the state of the others, and Micah still doesn't seem to care. He doesn't believe they are still alive, and I'm pretty sure he hasn't given them a second thought. Micah is still fragile and still hasn't properly dealt with Maison's death, although his temperament has settled. He thrives out here, in the wild, in this wicked place—with me.

So I try to forget them, just as Micah has trained me to forget Maison. It's only the two of us now, and even if somehow the others are still alive, no one else matters.

"Get ready, London. Pay attention; they aren't far ahead," Micah calls over his shoulder. He's standing with his back to me but doesn't turn to face me, keeping his focus on the paw prints of his prey.

I drop the wood in my hands, grab my spear, and crouch, trailing a few feet behind him. My long dark hair falls over my face, and my heartbeat picks up as it always does before a kill. I can only imagine how untamed we look. We're hungry, and Micah's hunting. He's so sexy in his natural state—like an apex predator—that watching him move makes me want to jump him right here.

It's April now; at least, that's what we think. The snow has melted to nothing but slush as the temperatures rise, and what was once a white and barren land now has hints of a lush forest terrain. I can't wait to see how pretty it is at the height of summer. The trees here are plentiful and diverse, with fir trees surrounding us. Fresh buds and muted greenery tease the bushes and ground. I've fallen in love with it here, away from the rest of the world.

And I've fallen so deeply for him.

I watch him move with grace as he crouches and crawls with his back to me, stalking a deer. His body is tense as he grips his bone weapon. His hood covers his face, and he's wearing his usual gray sweats. I can't see his expression, but I know his eyebrows are pinched in deep focus. I enjoy the heat from the blazing sun on my skin and the view of his fit, strong frame a few feet ahead of me.

He gives me a hand signal to stay put and jumps out of view, leaping almost wolflike into the thick woods. He thinks a deer is nearby, similar to the large doe I let get away all those months ago. We only ever catch one type of animal other than fish. A hare of sorts, larger than the rabbits we used to catch in the fall. On special occasions, or on the days when I don't think I can handle game meat anymore, he lets me have some of the canned food.

Micah and I haven't talked about that night we had spaghetti. He smiles more, as if he's aware he owns my soul. He knows I could never leave him—I haven't left his side since. It's easier that way, not having the tension of our past ruining our present, giving him the control he needs as well as my full attention. At least, this way, we can focus only on our survival.

I've been dreaming a lot lately, both while asleep and awake, my mind drifting off to the dark spaces in the forest, which lead to darker spaces in my mind. It's as if the forest likes to play tricks on me and knows we don't truly belong here. Sometimes, I have to pinch myself to make sure I'm really awake and not follow it. And unfortunately, even after I pinch myself, the laughter continues. I hear it every fucking night, and I have since the night I walked into the woods when I shouldn't have. The sound of Micah's breathing brings me back—he keeps my sanity from completely shattering.

Over the past weeks, on the days when the sun was shining, he would bundle me up and take me outside to help me clear my head and give me fresh air. He teaches me everything, every intimate detail about every northern animal, like which droppings are which, what types of animals we can find during winter, which birds to expect in the spring, and what I have to do to survive without him—which I never plan on doing anyway.

Right now, he's been gone longer than I anticipated, and he never leaves me alone like this. I twitch, trying to keep still and quiet like he told me to. I resist the urge to call out to him since it's incredibly important to be quiet while hunting. If somehow the doe gets past Micah, I'll aim for the heart or an eyeball because my stomach is shredding and I'm not currently feeling humane. In the meantime, I sit and wait, trying to blend into the earth.

I turn my head as the wind whistles through the trees. I can sense Micah hidden from my view in the shadows of the dense forest, so I keep my head locked in front of me. I glance upward, and my heart stills a single beat at the soft whispers in the woods.

It's Maison.

Soft, caring... concerned. His presence is like a soft feather on my skin. He says my name, calling out to me, and I search for him. He's there in his usual gray hoodie, outside my field of vision, watching over me. I've never seen him this clear.

"Micah?" I call out, and only stillness answers me. Too quiet.

I close my eyes, and when I look again, Maison's gone, although his whispers linger. Every memory—his crooked smile and his comforting presence—lingers around. It's pleasant knowing he's still with me, and I wish he would come closer so I could feel him. My heart flutters, and my breath catches.

It was Maison—I know it in my heart—and this fleeting moment I had with him wasn't long enough. "Come back..." I sob. Tears sting my eyes as the emotions of my stilted grief flood through me. "Maison, come back to me," I call out again, my voice breaking.

"London." Micah's voice snaps me back to reality, and for a moment, I recoil. "What are you looking at?

The whispers disappear, Maison's presence vanishes, and I pull back. Micah approaches me, and I find his gaze, making sure he knows I'm still with him. His eyes are like dark clouds as he studies me.

I swallow hard, the vision of Maison still stuck in my mind. Did Micah hear that? Did he hear me call out for Maison? I keep my voice steady, but inside, the cracks are forming, ready to shatter. "Nothing. I was just checking the forest. I was waiting like you told me to." I point to the spot where the barren forest floor peeks through, in the opposite direction of where I saw Maison. "You can see the ground over there. It looks like grass is coming in. I haven't seen the ground in months."

It's the place where I saw that footprint a few weeks ago in the snow. The one I still have not told Micah about. The one I think belongs to Nigel.

His eyes narrow as if not believing me, and he parts his lips like he wants to say something but holds back. Luckily, he doesn't press the subject as he walks through the slush with an animal in his hand. He tosses it aside and walks up to me, pressing his lips to the back of my head. His body is a steady, warming presence behind me as I gaze into the glistening forest beyond.

"Did the deer get away?" I ask, leaning into him, enjoying his warmth as a chilly spring breeze cuts through the trees.

He shrugs and tightens his fingers around my arm. "I saw droppings, so it can't be far. We'll have to get it another day, but I caught us lunch." The rabbit he threw a few feet away from me is still bleeding from its neck, where Micah likely sliced it. He leans in so his mouth tickles my cheek. "I caught this for you, baby. For your birthday." I decided it was my birthday this morning since my birthday is in late March, and he promised to make me something good. Food hasn't been as plentiful as I'd hoped. Every day is a struggle not to dip into our reserves.

I lick my lips and gaze at him as heat pools inside me at his words. He knows his way to my heart.

"Who were you just talking to?" he asks, with an edge in his voice that wasn't there earlier.

I scan the forest where I just saw Maison and draw a long blink. "No one. Nobody is here. I was just... talking. Thinking out loud."

"Liar," he says, and I wince. "Come on, let's head back."

He lets go of me, turns, and heads back to the cabin. I follow him, keeping my gaze steady on him as we make our way back. I don't want to ruffle his feathers, and I certainly don't want to admit to him the thoughts circling in my head. That perhaps, Maison is really here with us, or that I was calling out for him again. Micah didn't react so well last time.

Once we arrive at the cabin, he immediately sets to work on the rabbit. Opting not to go inside right away, I settle on a blanket outside with my knees up and my chin in my hands. He cleared the snow in this spot for us. I observe him as he skillfully preps the rabbit for skinning. With each precise cut, the fur is peeled away in chunks, leaving behind a disfigured creature that bears no resemblance to the adorable, furry animal of my childhood memories. Easter will never be quite the same for me after this.

He looks at me with cold, silent eyes, as if he's furious with me. I think it's more than that; he's in his head about something. Since the warmer weather arrived, Micah has been more paranoid than usual, and I don't think it has anything to do with Maison. He constantly checks around for animal tracks or any sign of anything out of the ordinary. He won't admit it, but he thinks the others may be alive and looking for us. He does this pacing thing where he circles without really *doing* anything. He's nervous, as he should be. Because if I were the others and I were still alive, I would come looking for us, too. Although we love the warmer weather, spring brings certain realities back—like whether we are still alone here.

He shoves the spear into the hare and roasts it over the flames, cooking it, focusing precisely on his task. When he's done and the site is clean, he adds a log to the fire and finally comes and sits next to me on the blanket, peering out into the woods again. He feeds me most of the rabbit, and I lie against him as he places small pieces in my mouth.

"London, I need to talk to you about something..." The way he says it makes my blood freeze, and I stop chewing. He must be considering venturing out, and I want to go with him when he does.

It doesn't take long before he pulls me on top of him, and I press myself into him on instinct. Nothing is really stopping us from fucking right here; we did it the other day. I feel him grow hard as I position my hips on him. But something tells me that he doesn't merely want to have sex. He has a look in his eyes.

"We can talk later," I murmur, biting his bottom lip, and he momentarily returns my kiss. Micah is not exactly a *talker*, so I know this won't be good.

I sit straddled over him, with my legs on either side of his torso, and he runs his hand up my back. I pull my sweats down and grind on him, giving myself a very satisfying orgasm as he grips my waist. I lean into a kiss, wondering why he's not giving anything back to me.

Something's very wrong.

"What's going on, Micah?" I finally ask him, breaking the silence and pressing my lips on his face, loving how his facial hair tickles me.

He doesn't mince his words. "I have to go explore and see what's going on out there. You're not coming with me."

My body goes rigid against him. It's as if he sensed what my reaction would be and knew how much this would upset me. He keeps me tight in his hold.

I wiggle beneath him. "No. No. No. Fuck you, Micah!" I scream at him, knowing my struggle is futile. I squeeze my knees together as if that would make any sort of impact. He planned this. He waited until he fed and fucked me and made sure I peed. I walked right into it.

I should have known.

"Calm the fuck down, London," he grits, grabbing my hands and interlacing his fingers with mine. "I'm not going for long. I just want to see if anyone's out there. I'll be back later tonight."

I squeeze his hands harder, to the point where my nails dig into his flesh. "So take me with you, then. Don't leave me here alone."

He shakes his head, grabbing my hands and moving them behind his back so I'm wrapped around him. "No. It's not safe. I don't know what's out there or who is out there. It's time to go and check; I need to see who's still alive."

He chooses now to finally give a shit.

My head becomes dizzy. A deep ache hits my belly as his hard body presses against mine, worried this is the last time I will ever feel him. "You promised you wouldn't leave me," I whimper. "You said we would do this together. Remember, you said that to me when Maison died."

He frowns at me, cupping my cheek. "I need to go check on Thomas and Jade. You're safest here until, at the very least, I know where Nigel and Ezra are." My head falls to his chest, and tiny sobs come out of me. Because he's already decided, and I know no amount of begging on my part will change that. He plays with my hair to try to make me feel better and attempts to explain himself. "I don't want them finding this place, or you. It's the same reason I refuse to tell you where we are, London. You're mine. I don't want to lose you, baby, and I definitely don't want you getting hurt out there."

I consider telling him about the footprint—that there is a tiny chance they are already here, already know exactly where we are, and have been spying on us.

"I'll follow you," I threaten. "If you leave me, I will get up and follow you. You know I will." After all this time, he still thinks that given the chance, I will leave him, that I will choose to stay with them over him. That's what this is truly about.

My body shakes as I hear a nearby nip in the woods—a growl of some sort, one of the many predators that stalk these woods.

He tweaks a brow and runs his hand over the back of his neck with a pained expression while I still sit straddled on him, half-naked, in my pleading, broken state. His eyes mirror my own madness, and it scares me to my very core.

He wraps his arms around my waist and squeezes, pulling me up with him as he rises, cradling me in his arms like a child. "No, sweetheart," he says with a razor's edge, "unfortunately, you won't."

What he doesn't realize is that he is my only lifeline, and I don't just mean food, water, or shelter. He is the only thing keeping me from going utterly fucking insane. He doesn't know how close to the edge I am or about the laughter I keep hearing. I've kept that part of myself hidden from him. Without him, I am nothing. I don't stand a chance out here alone.

A surge of panic burns through my heart. "Don't fucking do it, Micah," I scream, flailing beneath him. "I swear to god, if you do what you're thinking of doing, I will never forgive you."

I wiggle in his arms, not submitting to him on this matter. This isn't a fantasy anymore or some sex game to help us relieve our twisted urges of pleasure by intertwining our grief with love. This is life and death. And what he is about to do is *fucked up*.

He holds his hand over my mouth so I can't scream. Not that it would matter if I did. It's not like anyone can hear me. *He* just doesn't want to hear it.

He enters the cabin and drops me on the bed. I kick at him, but he keeps my torso firm in his hold. The way I'm positioned barely gives me room to move, and he already has the wire ready nearby. It doesn't take much for him to bind my hand and tie me to the bedpost.

My injured hand, he's tying my bad fucking hand...

I start to hyperventilate as the reality of the situation settles in.

"Please, Micah. Don't do this... We've come so far. Don't leave me again, please... *Please*!"

He runs his thumb along my hairline, then leans down and kisses me.

I don't return the kiss.

"You'll be fine, London. I'll only be gone for a few hours. I'll be back before dusk. Just try to sleep, and when I get back, I will make you spaghetti. You love spaghetti, don't you, baby?"

I squeeze my eyes shut. "Please," I whisper-sob one more time as my stomach tightens and starts to swirl. The last time I felt this sick, I was hurtling through the air in a toxic airplane about to crash.

Tears burn my eyes as I think of Maison... He wouldn't do something so fucked up. Maison's been warning me. All these months, his ghostly presence warned me of what his brother was capable of. Micah can't leave me alone like this; I won't survive the silence. Only a fraction of my grief is enough to swallow me whole and leave me drowning in its depths.

I realize with a sickening pit in my stomach that I've been captive for months. Ever since the first time he tied me up when I left him, he was signaling this. It's apparent in how close he keeps me at all times, watching over me even as I relieve myself. I thought he was being protective, that it was what he liked. But he doesn't trust me enough to bring me with him. The level of control he needs is diabolical, as Nigel once so elegantly called it. Those words have never rung so true.

Micah's dominating presence hovers over me, and I glare at him with fire and ice in my eyes. "Why are you doing this?" I ask, resolved to my fate. Perhaps Nigel was right about Micah this entire time, and Nigel's hatred runs so deep because he recognizes glimpses of his own malevolence in Micah. Evil begets evil, drawn to each other like a moth to a flame.

He squats so he's at eye level with me, darkness flashing in his eyes again. "I can't let you see that part of me again, London. And I can't let you go yet." He frowns, studying me, his eyes running up and down my body as I'm curled up beneath him in his favorite position.

"Micah, I'm fine. I'll be fine. I'll stay right next to you, I promise. You don't have to do this."

His hand finds my cheek. "I don't think you're fine, London. You can pretend you are, but I notice everything about you. You muttering to yourself, staring off into space, being so fucking jittery all the time. You hear things, don't you, sweetheart? This isn't fine, London, and I'm fucking worried about you."

I swallow bile down my throat. He knows... He always knows, as if my secrets are carved on my face.

Another flash in his eyes darkens his pupils as he rises and drapes my wolf blanket around me. I can't tell what emotion just swallowed him whole, but I simply don't recognize this version of Micah.

"Maison was right about you," I say darkly, gazing toward the window. "When he said you were going to hurt me and that you're sick."

He pauses at the door, his black hood pulled over his face before he departs. "Don't make this fucking harder than it needs to be. You're the one who's not well, baby. I'll make it all better when I get back. I'm the one who's here, London, and I'll be the one to take care of you, not a fucking ghost."

"I'm *healing*!" I unleash a scream at him, my voice carrying an unexpected force. The level of desperation pouring out of me is palpable. "That's what normal people do when they grieve, Micah. They remember their loved ones who passed. I imagine Maison because I fucking miss him. And that is normal. I'm not the crazy one, Micah, *you* are. You're a sociopath, completely and utterly psychotic and devoid of emotion. I'll never forgive you for this. I fucking hate you!"

I regret the words as soon as I say them—because I don't mean them—but I won't let him try to validate his reasons for tying me up like a prisoner.

He doesn't give me a chance to retract my words.

He's gone.

No kiss, no hug, no words of reassurance. Just gone, leaving behind a hint of wind from the shuttering door as it opens and closes.

I'm completely alone for the first time in four months, and with no way to defend myself should I need to. My heart clenches at the thought that he won't come back. That something will happen to him, and he will leave me tied up like this forever. I lower my head, allowing it to hang limply, as I desperately try to find a way to make myself comfortable. Thoughts swirl in my mind, wondering whether we can overcome this, if it's possible for me to forgive him, and most importantly, contemplating who I will become while he's gone.

CHAPTER NINE

MICAH

This side of winter isn't pretty.

In fact, from my vantage point, it's worse than I had imagined.

I squat on the opposite side of the meadow, soaking wet from the snow. The sun beams down on me, with blue skies soaring above, as I watch two survivors I barely recognize sitting by a fire.

Wild, hungry, and wind-burned.

Soulless.

It's like winter sucked every ounce of life out of them and spat frozen zombies out the other side. It's creepy as fuck watching them transfixed by the fire without blinking, staring at nothing but smoke and embers since the wood is too wet to burn. Unmoving in a way that's not natural.

No hope exists here anymore—or anywhere. It will be a long, slow, agonizing descent for all of us now. This island is killing them, and soon, they will turn on each other. The sooner they realize that, the better.

The walk back here was treacherous, even for me. The spring melt made it worse than the trek on that cold winter night when I brought London away from here. My calf muscles are burning as I squat in place for nearly half an hour, watching them, not ready to make my presence known until I have eyes on everyone. I sit detached, suppressing the weight of my emotions pressing against me. I refuse to let them consume my mind.

It's every man for himself now, and I honestly don't give a damn about the people who helped my brother's killer.

I notice Thomas first, based on his sheer size. He seems like he is doing just fine—physically, at least—as he rises and stalks across the field to what looks like their cooking site, set up in the middle of the meadow. He's down about thirty pounds, his hair to his shoulders and his face covered by the hood of a New Ocean hockey sweater. I grimace when he turns and I get a good view of his missing hand, which was healing before I left him. I made sure of that.

Still, it pains me to see it. It reminds me of all the blood soaking into the ground around him and the agony he endured. The putrid stank of the puss that seeped out of his injury. London covered in it as I severed his wrist. It's a memory I'd rather forget, so it was easier not to be around him.

Jade rises from her spot by the fire and follows him to the creek. The water is high, nearly cresting the bank from the snowmelt. She looks skinny, too, as to be expected.

Then James emerges from what used to be my shelter, looking strong and sturdy, his face all serious and shit.

Jade, Thomas, James.

Ollie, Nathan, and Serena are still not accounted for.

I scan the rest of the camp, finding their food covered by a tarp, and I have to say, I'm impressed they didn't eat all of it. They have a bit left, but not nearly enough to last them more than a couple of weeks unless they can figure out how to sustain themselves solely on the land. The site itself seems well-organized and intact, though.

I make a mental note of how easy it would be to sneak in here and take everything. They must not realize that I am an enemy stalking them because I've been eying up that food for the last hour. London and I could survive out here for so much longer with only the crumbs they have left. They would be fine since the creek has plenty of fish, and I left them a small knife to make do with.

Plus, my shelter is well-insulated—they are alive because of it. They should be thanking me; I built it with the intent of surviving in it myself and used fabric from the airplane to shield it from the cold weather. And it was good enough for me, so it should be good enough for them.

You're fucking welcome.

Serena finally follows James out of the shelter, and the four of them sit together now, engaged in conversation. Muffled voices carry across the meadow. I don't want to make myself known until I have eyes on every person alive or, at the very least, their dead body. I can't take any chances without knowing their headspace.

Desperate people do weird shit.

I also take note that Ezra and Naomi aren't here, either, which doesn't surprise me. After what Ezra did to Thomas, I can't see them welcoming him with open arms. However, I am surprised Naomi is not here with Serena. Thinking of Naomi always triggers a subtle twinge of shame in me.

Fuck, I did that girl dirty.

I don't hate her, despite London's contempt for her. She's the only person I am curious about other than London, although I'd never admit that to London because I know she'd castrate me.

A snap of twigs has me on full alert as Ollie slips out from the forest, a mere ten feet from where I'm hiding. The hairs on the back of my neck stand on end because I didn't even fucking see him and he could have stumbled right on me.

I have to be more careful.

I sink deeper into the shadows and continue watching. A few minutes pass, and they still don't notice me. James and Serena are cuddled by the fire. I can't really tell what state they are in, but they look healthy enough. James was always a tough little shit, so it's unsurprising that he's taken care of her.

Suddenly, I realize I've only seen Ollie. No sign of Nathan yet, and he's never too far away from Ollie. Those two are stuck together like glue.

So, where the fuck is Nathan?

I watch them for about ten minutes until I am certain Nathan isn't with them, and I then step forward just as Thomas and Jade step back to the fire.

Thomas sees me first and tilts his head in an unpleasant greeting.

Yeah, I know. I look like shit. So do you, buddy.

He keeps his expression neutral and flexes his jaw. "Where the fuck have you been?"

I step closer, keeping my chin high. "Not even a hi or a how are you? Okay, I see how this is going to go."

The rest of them snap their heads up and stare at me. I run my hands through the facial hair on my chin and try not to smirk at the peach fuzz on the rest of them. James immediately stands in front of Serena, and the other three exchange looks.

I glare at him, trying not to roll my eyes since sarcasm won't help the situation. "Relax, Turbo. I'm not here to hurt anyone. I'm just here to talk."

James's stare is unwavering, and his body language is tense, which is less than ideal for me right now. Especially since I still don't have eyes on his other dipshit friend. Serena stares at me, all wide-eyed and curious, but says nothing. Jade's reaction is the one that surprises me the most. Out of all of them, she's changed the most, and it's got nothing to do with her appearance. She tilts her head and narrows her eyes at me with an expression I can't interpret as anything but contempt.

I'm starting to regret making my presence known so soon, but I need information from them, so it's a risk I'm willing to take.

"Where's London?" James asks, causing Serena to wince. James seems oblivious to her reaction. I get it; London has that effect on people. Serena has a right to be jealous, but London's mine. Like fuck I'll let her near James. I see the way he looks at her.

"She's safe," I mutter, keeping my eyes locked on Jade as she jerks her head toward Thomas.

James lifts his spear as if that will scare me and squints while Thomas sits next to him.

Interesting.

"I don't think I like the fact that she isn't with you right now," James says.

I lift my chin slightly. "I don't really care what you think."

"Is she alive?" Jade asks, causing me to shift my attention to her. The command in her voice is unmistakable in the way she says it. Jade, the blushing girl who could barely hold a conversation in my presence our whole lives, seems to be the one in charge.

What kind of question is that? And when the fuck did I become the enemy?

My lips curve into a smile. "Yeah, she's fucking alive."

They are quiet, all five of them staring at me, waiting for me to do something. I live for awkward silence, so I wait until they get uncomfortable enough to say something.

Surprisingly, it's Thomas who speaks first. "Why are you here, Micah?"

I relax my tense posture, changing my smirk into a grin, but keep my grip firm on my bone weapon. These aren't my friends. Not anymore... Not with the frostbite evident on the tips of their ears and noses.

"I came to see if any of you had a razor." No one laughs, even though I think I'm fucking hilarious.

Thomas jerks to his feet. "This shit isn't a joke. You both left us out here, man." He's eyeing me like he wants to tear me apart. "You're looking pretty good for someone trapped outside all winter."

Thomas could mutilate me if he wanted, so I don't relent on my rigid stance. Thomas would win physically, but I am much quicker and could get him down if needed. But I won't. He's pissed at me, sure, but he's loyal, and ultimately, he won't hurt me.

James, however, is an entirely different fucking problem as his jaw flexes and his hands shift into fists. "Tell us where she is, Micah. I want to see her. It's not enough for her to just be alive. She needs people in her life, man. And you're clearly out of your mind."

Out of my mind? What gave them that idea? I shake my head. "Not fucking happening. But you can go ahead and tell me where the others are."

"That's not how this is going to work, Micah," Jade says, tossing another log into the fire, looking almost bored. It's as if they anticipated this conversation, like they expected me to pay them a visit.

"Tell me, then, Jade, are we going to have a problem?"

They all stare at each other, having some silent conversation like a little fucking family. How cute.

James shakes his head and slides his arm around Serena. "You know what, Micah? You are the fucking problem. We get that you lost Maison, so I'll give you a pass, but we've lost people, too, so apologies if your shit isn't at the top of our priority list."

An icy jolt hits my core.

"Nathan didn't last through the winter, Micah," Jade says calmly.

Well, fuck.

I keep my face neutral as I stay outside their circle. "I'm sorry to hear that," I say, and I am genuinely sorry. I guess that explains his absence. I just... don't have the energy to care. Over the last few minutes, I've realized that taking London away was the right call, and so was tying her up in the cabin so they don't have access to her.

I've become the enemy; they blame me for something that was inevitable.

"Why should we tell you anything?" James asks while Thomas grimaces, clearly having turned his loyalty elsewhere. And honestly, that's fine by me. One less person I have to give a shit about. "And how much food do you have left, Micah?"

I catch Jade's eyes, the vacant stare she's giving me. Then she blinks at me twice, which perks my attention.

She's trying to tell me something.

I focus on the guys, trying not to expose her. It's time to leave. I won't get shit from them, not unless I give them something in return. "Well, this was fun. I guess I'll be seeing you." I turn my back to them and start walking away with the full intention of circling back to meet Jade, assuming that's what she was trying to tell me.

"I mean it, Micah," James yells at me, and I do my best to ignore him, even though I hate empty threats. "Go back to wherever the fuck you and London are hiding and stay away from here. Or better yet, bring London back here, and you fuck off."

I freeze, my adrenaline spiking. It's not the reaction they want from me right now. And here I thought I was being nice. Ever so slowly, and probably more theatrically than needed, I turn around and step toward them.

My voice increases an octave, and I suppress the lurch in my stomach. "Listen to me real fucking carefully. I don't give a fuck about Nigel, Ezra, or any of you. I plan to find them. You can count on that. But if you breathe London's name again or threaten to take her away from me one more time, I will fucking kill you." I direct my gaze to Thomas so he can properly comprehend as well. They all jump to their feet at my threats. "I will kill you, too, buddy. You won't win over her. None of you will." Thomas visibly tenses, and I jerk my head toward Serena and Jade. "I won't touch the girls, but if you're dead, I can't see them lasting too long out here, so why don't you back the fuck down."

Serena's breath hitches, and she covers her mouth. Jade glares at me, shaking her head and placing a comforting arm around Serena.

The flicker in James's eyes is the exact emotion I was trying to evoke. Even Thomas stands down, and I draw my eyes to his stumpy wrist, reminding him that I have no qualms about doing what I need to do when pressed. He knows me well enough to believe I'm not fucking around. He's scared, and right now, I need them to be scared of me. I don't want them to do anything stupid, like coming to find us.

"I'll be seeing you," I say as I walk away for real this time.

I should feel guilty for leaving them and for leaving London the way I did.

But I fucking don't.

If London had come with me, she would have ended up staying here. She denies it, but I've watched her unravel day by day, and she's better off with me, even if she doesn't believe it.

I plan on going back to her as soon as possible and making it up to her. She might be mad for a little while, but she won't be able to resist me once I get my hands on her again.

       ➤

"Was threatening us really necessary?" Jade asks dryly, without turning around, as I approach her by the river about five minutes away from the others. She must have heard me coming despite my stealth. Her senses are keener than I was expecting. She might look weak, but every single survivor is strong in their own way. Given they are still alive, I can't underestimate any of them.

She's peering down the creek and into the dark forest beyond, her gaze meeting the unknown, as if she thinks there is a darker enemy than me lurking somewhere out there. The air carries a chill, and my stomach squeezes as the earliest part of dusk hits the sky, knowing nightfall is only an hour away. Jade kept me fucking waiting.

Cautiously, I pause a few feet behind her, my weapons tucked away in my pack and my hands in my pockets. She still doesn't bother turning around.

"Yeah, I agree," I tell her. "That didn't go well."

She whips around to face me, her eyebrows pinched together, and I can't help but smirk.

Her face darkens, and she shoves her finger in my side. "Look at you, laughing. I haven't seen you even crack a smile the entire time I've known you, and you choose this moment to laugh? *Nothing* about people dying or this situation is funny."

I pull my hood off in a gesture of neutrality and take a step back, not wanting to admit that her little poke in my ribs hurt a bit. Plus, I did, after all, just threaten to kill all of them, so she's right to be wary of me. "Let's keep our hands to ourselves, Jade." My tone heeds a warning, even though I'm trying to be nice.

She tweaks her head, crossing her arms. "Why? Because you might cut them off?"

Oof. I deserved that.

As she shifts, I get a clear view of her under the layers of clothes she's wearing. She's just as thin as everyone else. She's got this grayish skin tone that has lost all its former brightness, and there is a hint of frostbite on her wind-burned cheeks. I suspect she's lost a solid twenty pounds since being here, but she's mentally strong based on the strength in her eyes, although the change in all of us is in our eyes.

"Where have you been, Micah? Can you at least tell me that?"

"No." I'm especially not telling Jade, as she seems to have a particular bone to pick with me.

She scoffs, and her eyes flash. It's as if a layer of wildness has seeped into us, blending our boundaries so that we can no longer distinguish where we end and where the wasteland begins. The only difference is that I've always been this way.

Finally glaring at me, she shakes her head. "After everything that's happened, how could you and London abandon us like that? How could you do that to Thomas?"

I cock an eyebrow and step back. It's actually quite endearing that she missed us so much.

"We had our reasons," is all I say back to her. "What do you want to tell me? Or were you just twitching your eyes at me so you could give me shit?"

Jade's nose crinkles when she's mad, a quirk I hadn't noticed before. I don't think I've ever seen her this lit up. I always just remember her being a blubbering mess, but I like this new and improved version of Jade.

Survival suits her.

Her face hardens, her eyes casting off to that distant enemy again. "We barely survived the winter. It was brutal and changed everyone here. You have no idea what we went through or how hard it was. Or how worried I was that he..."

I cock a brow. "He?" The one no one wants to talk about.

Her eyes glaze over. "How worried we were about you," she whispers, catching herself. I let it slide, although Nigel is more of a taboo topic for me than Maison.

I scoff. "I'm standing here, too, Jade. London and I survived exactly what you did."

She bites her lip as if reliving those specific memories, and because I do have a shred of humanity left in me, I feel a twinge of guilt for the intense emotions that overtake her.

"Sure, if that's what you want me to believe, Micah. You can't blame James and Thomas for being pissed at you. You took the fucking first aid kit and half the food."

"A third of the food," I correct her.

She rolls her eyes, and a hint of a forced smile hits her lips. Then she shakes her head as if just remembering how exacerbating I can be. She pauses for a moment, branches shifting in the wind and the babble of the creek hitting what's left of the ice, and finally, as if it pains her, she asks, "Is London okay?"

"She's okay."

She quirks her head. "Just okay? Was it your idea to take her away? Did she want to leave with you?"

I cock a brow at her. "Yes, she did. Sorry she didn't want to stay with people who helped her boyfriend's killer. You chose a side as soon as you gave them a *third* of our food."

She blows out a breath and shakes her head in my direction, giving me the look I hate the most. I despise being pitied. "That's not fair, Micah. And I don't think I ever told you how truly sorry I am for what happened to Maison. He didn't deserve that ending."

My insides stir at the mention of Maison, and I quickly suppress any fucking emotion that bubbles up.

I shrug. "Then or now, it doesn't fucking matter. Every one of us is going to die soon, Jade."

Her eyes flash, and she pauses for a brief second before speaking. "I have information you might find useful."

"Really? And what would that be?"

She arches a brow but stays silent. I draw in a long breath and try to contain my anger. If Jade had planned to tell me anything useful about the whereabouts of the others, without wanting something in return, she would have already. I have to pretend I don't give a shit, even though their whereabouts are exactly what I want to know.

"So, out with it, then. Where the fuck are they?"

She shakes her head. "I'm not telling you unless you make me a promise."

"I already told you; I'm not telling you where London is."

She scoffs, and the tone of her voice is like nothing I've ever heard from her before. "You two are so into yourselves; it's sickening. You think this entire island revolves around you."

I frown. "You mean, it doesn't?"

Her mouth gapes. "I don't want another mouth to feed. I said I wanted to know if she was okay, not that I wanted her back with us. She made her choice when she left. What I want is the medical kit, or at least part of it. There was a possibility we could have saved Nathan if we had had it."

An amused smile forms on my lips at how bossy Jade has become. She really has toughened up; she never would have spoken to me this way before surviving an Alaskan winter.

I cock a brow. "You think a band-aid would have saved Nathan? Because I've got news for you, it wouldn't have mattered. We are all going to die eventually. This island will pick us off one by one if we don't kill each other over food first. Does Thomas know you're talking to me?"

She pauses and crosses her arms. "No, he doesn't. I'm doing this because, despite how mad they are and how much of an asshole you're being, telling you is the right thing to do. And you are right about the food, Micah. It's all anyone can think about."

Maybe for them, but for me, I think about other things. I stop talking now; I wait for her to say something. She is the one who brought me here, and I'm sick of whatever game she's playing. "If you have something to say, Jade, just say it. Otherwise, I have things to do."

She's quiet, contemplating, the wheels turning in her head. A wave of emotion overtakes her. After a few moments, she says, "The six of us had to huddle together for days in those shelters. We barely had enough firewood to sustain two fires. The night we realized that was the night Nathan died. But it was too cold to move him, so we left him there, and we all moved into one shelter. We couldn't leave the shelter for more than five minutes at a time, so we barely ate. I still don't have proper feeling in my hands and feet. None of us could lie down, so we had to take turns sleeping to make sure we kept breathing. It was torture, Micah."

I remember that cold snap; it lasted two weeks and was by far the worst part of the winter. London and I screwed like rabbits for most of it. But what's her fucking point?

"You're alive, Jade." I tap on my chest. "Your heart is still beating—that's got to count for something." I scratch my facial hair awkwardly and soften my voice. "Most of you made it. The shelter I left you was warm enough; I made sure of it." Before I left, I even dug holes in the snow around the shelter to deepen the insulation on top of the layers of upholstery I took from the plane. It was good enough for me, so it should have been good enough for them. I refuse to be blamed for Nathan's death.

She tenses her shoulders. "Yeah, your shelter saved our lives. I'm not disputing that, Micah."

I chew the inside of my cheek, my patience wearing thin. "So, what are you getting at? And how do I know that what you are going to tell me is worth giving you part of the medical supplies?"

A tear slides down her icy cheek, and she wipes it away. "They are going to attack us if we don't give them what they want."

My stomach is on fire. "How do you know that? Did you see them?"

Her lip quivers before she darts her gaze away from me. "They left us a message."

"What kind of message?"

She steps toward the riverbank and kicks something a few inches from my feet. At first, I thought it was a rock, but now looking closer—

"We found this in the middle of our site last week. I'm assuming it came from Nigel. It seems like something he would do." Her voice breaks when she says his name. She has the same fear of him that London does. It's as if his motive was something deeper than just revenge—like it wasn't a motive at all but an instinct.

I look down, and my stomach heaves.

A bone, a femur from the looks of it. Human, most likely, probably one of our fallen classmates. I recover from a quick swell of emotions, remembering when I put those souls to rest. I gather myself enough to look at Jade, who is observing me.

"They have the upper hand," she says quietly, "because we don't know where they are, and they know exactly where we are. I gave in and dropped off food at the lake, and it seems to have appeased them, or him. I'm not really sure who from that group is still alive, but I'd bet you money Nigel is, and he's going to great lengths to hide himself."

"So they are not living at the lake?" I ask, and for some reason, that surprises me.

Jade shakes her head. "It appears they have moved. That's what I wanted to warn you about in case you decide to go there. Just be alert, Micah."

"I'm always alert." I jerk my head toward the camp. "Why couldn't they tell me this?"

Her eyes blaze. "Because they don't trust you, and can you really blame them? They're not worried about the bone threat. They think they can rely on their strength to fight anyone who comes near our camp, including you."

I flex my jaw. "Well, they're right. Stop giving them food, Jade. And Nigel's not that fucking smart."

She shakes her head. "Yes, he is. Don't underestimate him, Micah. He's patient and manipulative. Look what he did to your brother and what he got you to do."

My pulse flutters as a dangerous swirl develops in my belly.

"What are you talking about? He didn't make me do shit."

Her eyes find mine. "You left London alone. You were so desperate for information that you left her vulnerable to him. And he has a strong ally out there, considering what you did to Ezra."

Well, fuck.

An icy breeze sends a chill through my veins. "They won't find her," I say, curling my lip.

I pause as another tear slides down her cheek, and she wipes it away just as fast. Guilty energy is pouring out of her. "What did you do, Jade?" My voice is calm but deadly as I suppress my primal rage.

She wraps her arms around herself, looking like the timid little girl I'm used to. Tears swarm her face now. This is going to end up with me realizing just how fucked it was for me to leave London.

She lets out a sigh. "They might not be scared of Nigel, but I am. It was a really long winter, Micah. I'm terrified, and I just want to live through this. None of us are the same anymore. You have to understand that."

"What the fuck did you do, Jade?"

Her eyes cast downward. "He wrote something in the mud. A question. I saw it when I went to drop off a can of food, and I answered it." She swallows hard.

"What was the question?" I ask through gritted teeth, wishing she would just spill it out already.

"The message said, 'Where is he?'"

I tilt my head, and my voice comes out like steel—strong and cool. "And what did you tell him?"

She can't even look at me anymore. "*North.*"

It took all my willpower in that moment not to end her. The dark urge was overwhelming before I contained it and watched Jade's tears of betrayal with a mask of indifference and clenched fists, which is never a good sign for anyone near me in those circumstances. I regained what sliver of humanity I had left and walked away before I did something I *might* regret. Hopefully, I reminded her that a femur bone is not the worst of her problems and that Nigel isn't the worst enemy to have on this island.

I'm sure I made my point.

I shove my guilt inward as the sun hovers dangerously low in the sky, knowing I've already let London down by not being back by dusk like I had promised.

She'll have to wait a little longer, even though I'm sure she's beyond seething by now. As soon as I untie her and she gets her hands on her pointy spear, I'll be fucked.

I stalked to the lake site as fast as I could, needing to see for myself what was going on there, even though I was heading in the wrong direction.

It's dusk as I approach the muddy shores of the rocky beach and the familiar forests surrounding it. Long shadows loom over the lake's edge, the giant mountains glistening in the evening light.

I linger alone in the perimeter, my hood over my head and the winter wind still cutting through my skin. The temperatures are dropping quickly, and I suppress a yawn, knowing I will not be sleeping anytime soon. Nothing will stop me from getting back to London tonight—especially after what Jade told me.

However, I'm not worried about her.

The cabin is well-hidden, stuck in the middle of the thick woods. I barely found it myself, and I have much more experience than any of them regarding wilderness. Even if they got close, locating it would be like finding a needle in a haystack, and that is the only reason I didn't kill Jade when she admitted to betraying London and me.

A mist swirls over the lake and hovers in the air, creeping over the abandoned camp. At least, it looks abandoned. I'm not so sure.

"Where the fuck did they go?" I mutter, resting my elbows on my knees as I squat.

After a few minutes, I figure it's safe to walk over to the fire pit, the circle of rocks in the middle of the clearing where the main fire used to burn. The spot where my brother died is just a short distance away.

The snow has melted, exposing the dead, charred earth around the former fire pit. My heart aches for a moment as I absorb what I am seeing—Maison's dried blood has frozen, the haunting stain marking the spot.

I stare at the blood-stained ground, paralyzed, knowing I let the person who did this to him get away. I can't bring myself to look away. My eyes don't seem to blink as I recall that night and relive it at least a hundred times. What I could have done differently, why I consistently fail the few people in this world I actually care about...

Olivia included.

My pulse quickens, and I instinctively start to fortify the shield around my heart, redirecting my attention to the air I abruptly stopped breathing. Bit by bit, I replace the stone wall until, once again, I feel nothing, and the burning memory in my mind is extinguished.

I focus all my energy on moving away from this place, reveling in the fact that, at least, I made Ezra pay for putting a knife to my neck. There is no denying the intense satisfaction I felt when chopping Ezra's fingers off. He must have known he wouldn't be leaving that situation unscathed.

My knees bend as I lean down and touch the ash in the fire pit, rubbing it between my index finger and thumb. It's warm, and a heady smoke lingers in the air... There was a fire here recently, and the tracks are fresh. I rise and let the ash fall from my fingers.

I force myself to move on from the fire pit and check out the rocky beach until I'm satisfied that I'm completely alone. I wasn't sure how I was going to respond to being here. Even though I lived here for weeks, this place never felt right. It never felt like home, not the way the cabin does now with London there. Seeing this site completely abandoned only proves my point.

My bone weapon is in a tight grip in my hand as I shift my attention to the shelters. Even in the dim light, I can tell they are trashed. Only one is barely intact, but then again, one is all someone needs to survive.

I cautiously make my way to the shelter, my footsteps barely audible since I'm conscious that if someone else is present, they are probably aware of my presence, too.

A moment of panic overwhelms me as I get closer. This could be an ambush. Jade could be working with them, tricking me into coming here instead of heading directly to my girl like I should be doing. But my curiosity was always a problem for me, and I had to see for myself what became of this place.

Keeping my body rigid, I dip down and peer into the darkness of the shelter. My old shelter, of course, is the only one still standing. The others either burnt down or fell into a pile of moss and sticks.

I strain my eyes in the dark, and amidst a slight shift in the light, I catch a flicker of bright eyes just as a whimper escapes into the silence.

Someone's in here, trying to stay out of sight. I crawl in further and see platinum blonde hair sticking out of a hood. Naomi's shivering, with her arms wrapped around herself, staring at me with her big brown eyes.

My insides tighten at the sight of her. Withered, skinny, broken, and the last fucking person I wanted to see here. I whip my head around to see if this is an ambush because why the fuck would Ezra leave Naomi like this?

The wind greets me, and the silence of the forest is the only menacing presence. No one jumps out. Nigel and Ezra don't make some grand fucking entrance because no one else is here. I know this because I stalked the perimeter for an hour, making sure of it.

"Naomi," I say with caution, barely recognizing the girl I grew up with. The girl I fucked recklessly in the bathroom, stealing her innocence before she was even of age.

I was a predator even then.

Without blinking, she breathes my name, her tear-stained face streaked with mud and her unwavering gaze fixed on me. "Is that really you?"

I drop my bone weapon to my side, a feeling of protectiveness resurfacing along with the guilt for how I treated her over the years and how quickly I dropped her when London gave me a sliver of hope I had a chance.

And now I stare at this girl who has suddenly become a wrinkle in my plans, sitting by herself and barely holding on to her life, knowing I can't just walk away from her in her current state.

Fuck.

I have a decision to make.

Which girl am I going to save first? And why do I have a gut feeling I'm going to make the wrong decision?

CHAPTER TEN

LONDON

"I hate him. I hate him. I hate him," I whisper to myself, over and over again, as the sun drifts across the sky and the day turns into night. If I say the words enough times, maybe it will become true. Maybe I'll believe it.

I shift to my knees to give my wrist a break, but the weight of my body might as well be a ton of bricks with how sharp this wire is. My skin is raw as the edged restraint grazes the bones of my hand like a steak knife. The skin on the rest of my body is crawling, tingling, and burning, all the sensations blurring together.

I shiver as I have kicked off my blankets in foolish frustration, and despite how well-insulated the cabin is, it's not immune to the Arctic freeze, even if it is spring. I'm not sure how much longer I can endure this.

Where are you, Micah?

I stare longingly outside, waiting for Micah to come back. He said he was going to come back by dusk. And after managing to sleep for a few fitful, nightmare-induced hours this afternoon, it's now well past nightfall, the long shadows in the room causing my mind to play tricks on me. The buildup of worry inside me intensifies with each passing moment, like at any minute, my body might explode.

I have no choice but to put aside the throbbing pain and focus on what I can control, which is turning my mind off and numbing myself to the pain, like Micah taught me.

The problem is that I have to pee so badly that it stings, and I'm not sure what kind of robot I'd have to be to ignore that kind of discomfort. I clench my legs together in a desperate attempt to hold it until he comes back.

I refuse to piss myself or endure that kind of humiliation. He'd come back to his girlfriend lying in a puddle of her own piss. But worse? I'd be lying in it and smelling like it. I underestimated how kinky he was, but I doubt he's into that. He would never look at me the same again.

I let out an audible chuckle... or maybe it's more like a psychotic laugh. After everything he's done to me—the manipulation, the control, the possessiveness—all I care about is whether he will fuck me again.

That is how good Micah Matei is.

As I sit pining over him, I twist and contemplate a dark thought...

What if he doesn't come back?

The way the wire is positioned on my wrist, I could easily keep digging it into my skin and sever the vein until I bleed out. It would be a quick death and has to be better than this.

I blow out an icy breath.

He will come back; he promised he would.

A gust of wind sends a chill through the room, and the door shutters. Micah didn't leave me with any heat or bother to light a fire, like the fucking gentleman he is.

I shiver, sweat, and cry, realizing that he isn't coming back. Because he'd be here by now if he were—I can now only assume he's dead.

He wouldn't just *not* come back to me.

After a while, laughter chimes in my ears, and I welcome it after a long, long day of excruciating silence. I keep my eyes closed. Not that it matters since tonight is dark, with no hint of moonlight in the sky.

It is a memory, I've decided. The laughter. A different memory for each person. Everyone laughing at me on the airplane, then Ezra and Naomi laughing at me when they were going through my stuff after we crashed.

And Nigel...

Not that he laughed much, but it's the moment when he found me alone, right before he killed Maison—that dark, sinister laugh. When I hear it, it's the anger from that night I cling to that keeps me from completely breaking.

None of the laughter belongs to Micah because he never fucking laughs. No one is here, or near, watching me. I'm hallucinating all of it and have been for months.

The laughter lasts most of the night until a streak of light finally appears in the sky and I can make out the shadows of the room.

Nearly twenty-four hours have passed since Micah left me like this.

My stomach grumbles. I've grown accustomed to eating regularly due to how well Micah takes care of me.

I ignore it.

My hunger is the least of my concerns, and I can deal with going without food for days on end. It's the pit in my stomach that hurts from the grief and the fear he won't ever come back. It's my dry lips and cracked skin from the lack of water.

A loud bang startles me, as if someone threw something on the side of the cabin.

A rock.

Then another, a soft bang this time, from the other side of the house.

I squeeze my eyes shut as the walls start to close in on me. The laughter begins again, and I realize I am not hallucinating this time.

Someone's here.

More than one person, from the sounds of it, and they are fucking with me. They keep throwing them, one after another, before the rocks bang into the siding like a drum. Every time one hits, I flinch until my body clenches so hard I have no choice but to collapse.

I let out a whimper, knowing there is nothing I can do because Micah left me helpless to them. I sway slowly and bite the inside of my cheek, waiting for them to stop, and eventually, the banging stops. But it's the whispers of my name that make every hair on my skin stand on end. I wish they would come in here and do whatever it is they have planned for me instead of taunting me like this... I'd much prefer the physical pain to the mental anguish of knowing I can't fight back.

My bladder lets loose, providing me with instant, blissful relief. I'm able to shift my body so most of it drips onto the floor, though there isn't much that comes out.

Still, it's so humiliating.

"Micah," I moan out, calling for him, hoping that, somehow, he will appear.

"Micah's not here, baby," a soft, deep voice whispers in my ear.

I startle. My eyes open and scan the limited scope of my vision. My heart tightens, not in fear but in relief. The familiar voice has my body instantly softening.

"Maison," I manage a small whisper. The laughter outside disappears, and a stillness fills the air. "Is that you?"

He appears to me in the corner of my eye. I want to reach out and touch him so badly. He crouches beside me, just out of reach, but I can see him. He's wearing his gray hoodie, the one he died in. He looks so real, so tangible—nothing like a ghost.

"It's really me, baby." It even sounds like him.

I let out an uncontrollable sob and lay my head down, staring at his pretty dark eyes and soft face. "I miss you, Maison. I miss you so much. You have no idea how much I miss you."

I see his face, the one I have not let myself picture during these past few months with Micah. I never used to notice the subtle differences between them, but they are so clearly etched in his expression now. He lets out an adorable grin, one I hadn't realized I longed for since Micah still prefers to scowl. He peers down at me. "I've missed you, too, but I'm not gone, not really. I'm still here with you, baby."

"He won't let me think about you, Maison. I'm sorry I've blocked you out. I wish he had died instead of you."

He tilts his head. "You don't mean that, London. But Micah's like that, baby. I warned you before you fell in love with him."

I stare at him. He doesn't move or disappear, not like during the fleeting moments I've seen him before. He's still as a statue beside me.

Not leaving me.

He looks at peace.

His soul isn't tormented like Micah's and mine because Maison's soul was never tormented to begin with. I think tormented souls in death were tormented in life, too. Either you're tormented or not, and being dead or alive simply doesn't matter.

"Can you help me?" I ask in a whisper, still aware someone might be lurking outside, wondering now if that was a hallucination, too. As if, somehow, whispering will make them go away.

He shakes his head. "It doesn't work that way, London."

I blow out a breath, but not because he can't help me. Of course, he can't help me. He's not real. But because I desperately want to touch him.

He leans forward, even closer but still out of reach. He smells the same, that heady scent I fell in love with. Sometimes, you can hear music while dreaming, and you can smell using your memories... This is the most powerful memory I've had so far.

"I think someone's out there," I finally say after a few moments of peaceful stillness, taking my time just to watch him, to appreciate him, even if I can't have him.

He nods and looks at the door, his hair a tousled, sexy mess. "Sounds like it, doesn't it? They are coming for you. They are still alive and out there somewhere. Can you free yourself, London, and get away from here?"

I sniffle, aware of how cold I am, tied up and shivering alone. I laugh because this is hilarious to me right now. The level of crazy in these four walls is unmatched.

My lungs struggle to expand. "I can't go anywhere, Maison. And even if I could get free of this wire, I have nowhere to go."

He leans down and grazes his hands over my knotted hair, his fingers causing a light tickle to my senses. Or is it the draft that always hits me in this spot? Regardless, the thought of Maison's fingers is much better.

I close my eyes and appreciate his touch on my skin. "You need to get away from him, London," he whispers. "He isn't well. You know that, right? I've kept telling you this. I've warned you so many times."

Tears well up in my eyes. "I don't think I'm well either, Maison. I'm hallucinating right now, and the worst part is that I like it. I don't want you to leave. Will you stay with me?"

He tilts his head. "I told you I'd love you forever, London King, and I meant it. I'm not going anywhere, baby. I'll stay as long as you need me."

My breath grows heavy, my eyelids even heavier. Before I slip into unconsciousness and he vanishes, I steal one final glance at him. The tightness in my stomach cripples me. It's like losing him all over again. He's watching me like he used to when we spent countless hours gazing into each other's eyes. Micah and I don't gaze. Our chemistry is different; we fuse our bodies as if we are one. But I miss gazing, and Maison was so good at it.

"Maison," I whisper.

"Yeah, baby?"

"I love you."

He sits next to me, out of reach. "Rest now, London." His hand rests on my back, then slides up to my cheek. The pressure of him kisses my skin. How am I able to feel him?

"He isn't a terrible person," I say as my eyelids grow droopy. "And he's taking care of me. He's doing this to protect me because he's afraid to lose me. He'll be back soon."

The lies I tell myself to validate Micah's actions... Saying it out loud makes me sound even more pathetic, and I'm not sure if I believe it anymore.

I can hear Maison breathe. Somehow, I can hear the air pass through his lungs, the same sound I listened to for weeks when I was with him. It's calming, dulling my senses.

"He isn't coming back to you, London. You have to get out of here. Because if you don't, you will die. You need water to survive, baby, and he didn't leave you any."

He didn't leave me any water… Why didn't he leave me any water? He wasn't supposed to be gone this long. He wasn't planning on leaving me like this.

"Something happened to him, Maison. He loves me."

He shrugs. "Maybe, but look at how he left you, London. Would someone who isn't sick in the head leave someone like this? I would never leave you like this, not in a million years."

He's right. He was always right about his twin. After all, Maison would know him best. He's also right about the fact that he would never, ever leave me in this condition.

Bile seeps into my throat at the thought of what he's insinuating. "I'm so tired, Maison. I just want to sleep. Can I sleep?"

He sits at the end of the bed. His presence is so real that the bed shutters beneath him.

"Take a nap, baby. We can figure it out afterward. I'm not going anywhere."

"I want you to lie down with me."

He wipes his nose and crawls in beside me. So close, but he doesn't touch me. It's enough, though… He suffuses the air around me. I let out a huge breath, the kind when you settle for the night and shift from a state of alert to a sense of peace.

I doze. I'm not sure how long I sleep, but the laughter is gone, and it's the first time I've truly slept since Micah left.

It's just Maison now.

I let sleep take me, and it's glorious.

When I wake up, it's late afternoon, and the shimmering snow is reflecting outside as it usually does.

My wrists are raw, burning from the wire hitting my flesh. But I'm rested and ready to face the challenge awaiting me.

"It's time to get up, baby."

I lift my head to see him and smile. Maison's still here, just as he promised he would.

He cautiously raises a brow. "Are you ready?"

I swallow hard and nod. "Yeah, I think so, but I can't get out of this bind."

His firm hand sends a warm shudder down my spine. He gives me an adorable, faint smile. "You know exactly what you have to do, London. Your hand isn't fully healed, is it? Micah never really made it better. You still feel the broken bones, don't you?"

I wiggle my fingers. The tightness in my hand sends a shooting pain up my wrist.

Micah didn't tie the wire completely. A sliver of space exists between the wire and my wrist. I'm conscious of what I need to do, but there is no fucking way I can do it.

I sob, painfully aware I'm not strong enough. "I can't do that, Maison. I can't re-break my hand."

He pauses for only a moment. "You have to, London, or you will die. I don't want you to die yet because you're not meant to die here. You're meant to survive this."

I shake my head. "He'll be back. I trust him with my life and my whole heart."

Maison bites his lip as I shift to relieve my leg, which has gone numb from the awkward position I'm lying in. "You heard them outside earlier throwing stones at you," he says. "They will get to you before he gets back. They will kill you, and if they don't, you will die the way you're positioned right now. I can't see you die like that, baby. I refuse to watch Micah kill another one of my girlfriends."

I shake my head as if only realizing how fucked up I am right now. What am I even contemplating doing to myself? Perhaps Maison being here isn't as good for me as I thought it was. He's poisoning my mind against itself.

"Do it, London," he begs. "Please, do it for me."

"I can't, Maison," I breathe.

"You have to, baby."

I squeeze my eyes shut.

"Bite onto the mattress. Otherwise, you will hurt your jaw when you do it."

"Stay with me," I demand, knowing he could be out of my grasp within a second.

"I will, London. I promise, okay? When you get out of here, make your way back to the others and find Jade. That's the only way you will live through this."

South. I'm positive about that. At least, I'm fairly sure. It's a partial guess, and I really have no concept of how big this island actually is.

A feral noise fills the room, like a wounded animal getting killed. And only after a few agonizing seconds do I realize the noise is coming out of me as I pull on the wire binding my hand with every ounce of strength left in me.

Maison's voice keeps me going. "Come on, London. You're almost there. You're so fucking strong and beautiful. You can do this." His encouragement is all I need.

Sweat drips down the bridge of my nose despite how cold I am, but I continue because it's either a broken hand, dying of thirst, or being torn apart by whoever or whatever is out there watching me. Or being killed by those wolves that I fear so much.

I don't want to die. I've gone through too much.

Eventually, my hand slips through, each bone fragmented and each ligament torn apart, almost like they never healed at all.

An audible snap.

My limp, frozen bones and flesh slide right through the wire and my body is free. For a few agonizing seconds, I can't breathe, my body in utter shock before it all comes crashing in on me.

Reality.

Maison's gone. My hallucination's over. Just a faint wind left where he was sitting on the bed. Nothing but particles of dust because my living and breathing boyfriend is missing and needs me, and apparently, I cannot bear to think about both of them at the same time.

Micah might have tied me up, but he wouldn't have left me this long. Maison's wrong. I know in every part of my soul that Micah would never abandon me.

I'm angry... pissed off at him, but I love him.

And right now, he needs me.

I wipe the sweat off my brow and pull on Maison's hockey sweater, which is conveniently close by. I barely manage to change out of my pee-soaked pants, whipping them across the room.

Enough is enough. I need to grieve him, and in order to grieve him, I need to remember him. His sweater still smells like him, which is probably what I was smelling when I was hallucinating.

I spend a moment basking in the scent of his sweater before I fully comprehend the pain in my hand.

I'm bleeding... badly.

Blood wells from the flaps of skin where the wire cut my wrist as I refractured it to pull it through. Tiny droplets of blood soak the bed and create a trail across the floor as I crawl over it. I hate looking at it—the crimson. It's a reminder of how much blood has been spilled already and of the terror building up from the nightmares of losing my hand.

I find the little compartment where Micah hid the medical kit, opening a trapdoor in the ground. Micah dug to hide it, should anyone come looking for it, and it's a clever hiding place.

I do what I can to clean my wounds and wrap my hand in a bandage the best I can before hiding the kit again and setting my sights on the door. Hopefully, the bandage and tight wrap will stave off any infection. I'll come back for the medical kit. I don't dare take it out yet, remembering all the strife it caused on this island.

Micah left a bit of food on the table, which sets off my senses as if I were a feral dog. I push myself toward it, ripping it to shreds with my teeth and devouring it. It's enough. I find what little water we have, made of melted snow, and chug it. My energy comes soaring back, although it doesn't take much to satiate my hunger, which is still a constant tug in my belly.

Instead of leaving, I pull myself back to the bed and lie down, completely exhausted from what I just did to myself but relieved I am no longer tied and bound.

I stretch my legs and arms and twist my torso, relieving all the kinks in my back, neck, and shoulders. The door shutters in the wind and I watch it, hoping that, at any second, Micah will walk back through the door and see me sitting here, unbound. Being the obedient girl he likes so much, not leaving him like I had promised.

The sun's rays are shining through the window, and I stare at them for what seems like hours, in a trance, as they shift across the room. I should have stayed tied up because it's not like I'm moving anyway. I want to leave, but I am unable to muster the courage to do so.

"Go, baby. You can't stay here with him."

I seek out Maison, but he isn't here. Only his voice in my head. I sway back and forth and bring my hands to my knees, careful not to agitate my broken hand.

I whisper out to him. "He'll be so mad at me if I leave him, Maison. I'll lose him..."

"You've already lost him." His words echo in my ears and create a sharp ache in my belly.

He appears now in my peripheral vision, out of reach and out of sight, his ghostly presence disappearing as I come to my senses.

I sniffle and wipe the tears stinging my face. Then I will myself to grab my pack and move toward the door before I overthink my decision to leave.

I'll head south and hope for the best. I'll see if I can find him. If I follow the stream, it should eventually take me to the others' site.

The mid-afternoon light blinds me. My head shifts around, and I blink a few times, not truly understanding what I am seeing. Large pieces of ice layer the ground—hail. It looks like it hailed. The voices, the laughter... they were probably from the thunder. I scratch my head, but my hairs stand on end like I am being watched.

I could very well be the last living soul on this island.

My head is heavy as I slowly walk southward, trudging through the wet mud. My feet and legs are completely drenched after only a minute. But now that I've started, I can't stop until I find the others.

Or Micah... whoever comes first.

Ten minutes go by, maybe more. I've lost track of time on this island a long time ago. I stick near the creek so I won't get lost.

An unusual noise causes me to freeze. I glance around, half-expecting to see Maison. Instead, I spot a footprint, and my blood curdles.

He's smiling, as if he were there all along, watching me through the trees, throwing stones at me. He looks thin and haggard, and his blond hair is long and stringy. For a fleeting moment, I question his existence. Then he clicks his tongue, and a deep panic settles in. The irony of my broken hand throbbing is not lost on me as I stare at the guy who caused the injury, walking toward me with a hockey stick spear in his hand.

His approach is slow and deliberate, and the mere thought of his name sends a chill down my spine. Out of nowhere, strong, rough hands firmly grab me from behind.

Argyle.

CHAPTER ELEVEN

Micah

Two scenarios are playing out in my mind.

Either Jade is lying, and this is a trap. Some really fucked-up plan to access my food and get rid of me. Thomas's anger toward me and James's little crush on London are the motivating factors for their clear betrayal. And the trap was well executed because I walked right into it.

Or...

London is in real danger, Nigel is still alive, and Naomi is really alone at the lake camp, half-dead and abandoned like she seems to be. I'd almost prefer the first alternative. It would give me an excuse to slaughter everyone on this island, feed this beast within me, and finally acknowledge the rage simmering deep inside. Also, it would be easier for me to decide what to do right now. I'm already treading a fine line with London, but Naomi alone at the lake camp is way too enticing, and blondes push me into making terrible decisions.

Plus, she's half-dead, and leaving her here would seal her fate.

"Micah, is it really you, or am I dreaming?" She blinks a few times. Her pupils are dilated, like she can see me but can't focus on me.

I tilt my head down as I crouch in the dark entrance. The whites of her eyes are shining in the ray of moonlight seeping through the roof, but they are bloodshot, which concerns me.

"Yeah, it's really me."

"Are you going to hurt me?" she asks, keeping her distance in the far corner of the shelter. It's beyond weird seeing a girl who's thrown herself at me her entire life shrinking away from me. To see her as a shell of who she once was, her eyes filled with genuine fear.

I crawl into the shelter and kneel a few inches away from her. The heat of her fever is radiating off her.

"That depends," I admit. "Are you here alone?"

She nods carefully as I try to get a better view of her. She looks rough, covered in mud from head to toe, her hair in dreadlocks. She's in a much worse state than Jade and the others. Skinnier, if that's even possible. She's wrapped herself in a single blanket, and she's shivering despite the fact that she's clearly burning up.

I can't help it; I reach out and run my hands down her frail shoulders. As I expected, the skin on her neck is on fire. "Fucking hell, Naomi. What happened to you? Where's Ezra?"

She shouldn't be here, especially not alone, but she's in no condition for questioning, given that she's shaking. I pull out some water from my pack and place it to her lips. I only have a small amount, but I let her take her fill. I'll get more tomorrow.

She lies down, curling into herself. "I left him," she whimpers, but she's barely coherent. I will hold off further questioning until she's more lucid. Plus, I'm not sure if she would even tell me the truth.

She drinks the water and lays her head down, seemingly falling asleep immediately. It's almost like my presence makes her feel safe enough to finally sleep, like she's confident I will take care of her.

Which I will...

She looks so peaceful, her face in a serene state.

These girls give me their blind trust, and I take it greedily. Just like London thrives on praise, I yearn for their obsession with me, as if it validates my existence.

Constant reassurance.

I wait a few minutes to see if her condition improves. She coughs, and her face twists into a grimace, her peaceful sleep now induced with nightmares.

I watch her for a moment, not really grasping that Naomi is here, alone and nearly dead. I have to make a hard decision, knowing London is bound back at the cabin and likely a target.

Naomi's a twist in my plans I wasn't expecting. If I leave her tonight, she'll die. But I can't bring her in this condition in the dead of night. I'll have to wait until the morning.

I think for a moment.

When I left London, she was well-fed and healthy. She should be able to last at least one more night. Tomorrow, I will go back with Naomi, and we can figure things out from there.

My stomach clenches, and for the first time on this island, I'm second-guessing my decision. This girl is half-dead. Maybe I should let nature take its course and let her perish.

I'd be doing her a favor.

That's now the third time today I've seriously considered killing someone. In fact, I've had murderous thoughts about everyone I've come into contact with since leaving London.

It's not normal; it can't be. However, these thoughts seem to circle back in my mind, like perhaps they have been there all along and I've always been this way. Like Nigel and I are more alike than I care to admit.

As if on cue, Naomi lets out a moan. I'm not sure if this is some devious plan Naomi concocted with Ezra to lure me away. I don't hate Naomi, but I don't fucking trust her. She's a phenomenal actress when she needs to be. However, she isn't faking a fever.

Her body twists and turns in her sleep. The experiences she endured leading to her current condition were undeniably real. Despite my desire to believe I'm the focal point of everyone's existence, I'm sure she's been through the wringer, just as we've all changed since being here.

"What are you up to, Naomi?" I whisper, my nerves dancing dangerously in my stomach. "Where have you been, pretty girl?"

She shivers in her sleep, teeth chattering, as I reach into my pack, grab my blanket, and crawl in beside her.

Choosing Naomi over London is a bad fucking idea. But what the fuck am I supposed to do?

This is Naomi. And I'm not actually choosing her.

I can save both of them.

I give her space and am careful not to touch her as I pull my blanket over the two of us. Even in this weather, her fever will keep her warm, but the chill in the air will only get cooler as the night goes on. Eventually, she will need my body heat.

The sips of water I gave her should help ease her pain. Even one sip of water can mean the difference between life and death, and I've seen enough death and destruction on this island to be able to tell Naomi is at a tipping point.

As I drift off to sleep, I keep my brain focused on London waiting for me, lying in my favorite position.

One more night, baby. I'll come back to you.

One night... I tell myself over and over, as if it somehow makes it better or changes the fact that, no matter what I do, it won't be the same when I get there.

Naomi's condition worsened overnight to the point where I couldn't get her to regain consciousness. The pulse in her neck is barely detectable under my thumb as I pick her up. She's too incoherent to make the trek back to the cabin. After a long, rough night of taking care of her, I'm really fucking tired. It will take hours, but I hadn't planned to stay out here even one night; I don't have sufficient supplies. If I don't take her now, she will die.

I pick her up, but she doesn't wake as I walk in the direction of the morning sun. "Come on, Naomi," I mutter. "Time to go see London."

I carry her in my arms like a bag of bones, and she doesn't move, keeping her head flopped down and her blonde hair falling toward the ground. I'm not upset about leaving this place behind and going home.

After an hour of meandering through the woods, she finally groans in my arms. Her eyes flutter open, and she peers up at me. "Where are you taking me?" She coughs, and her breath is labored.

"Shh. Don't talk. You're going to need your energy."

Sweat pours down her face as her fever breaks, and she's at least more alert now, even though she gazes at me inquisitively, which is annoying.

It seems like her fever has broken, at least for now. "Where is London?" I push down my annoyance; Naomi's always more tolerable when she isn't speaking.

"Don't make me regret saving your life by talking, Naomi. You will not be the one asking questions."

That shuts her up. But the corner of her mouth tilts upward as she presses herself against me, wrapping her arms around my neck and resting her head on my chest.

Yeah, keep smiling, sweetheart.

Fucking hell.

She's asleep again within minutes, her body burning up once more.

It's a painfully slow walk, just as it was when I carried London all those months ago. I seriously dread seeing London's reaction to me bringing Naomi in like this, or her reaction to Naomi at all.

I haven't been in a relationship before, but I'm afraid of her reaction to me... period.

I'm hoping London can understand why I'm bringing Naomi back and, perhaps, can see the humanity left in me after what I did to her. That she can realize I'm doing this to prove I'm worthy of her. Because even though London hates Naomi, she's too pure to leave someone dying like that.

She isn't me...

A couple of grueling hours go by, and Naomi's barely conscious during any of it. Sweat drips off my forehead as we finally approach the stream near the cabin.

Naomi's like a heat locker, which I'd normally like, but the sun is getting stronger, and sweating too much is a risk out here. I place Naomi down and refill my water bottle with the crystal-clear winter runoff. I pour some over my head to cool off. It's always a risk to drink unfiltered water like this, but in these situations, it's always better to drink the water and risk the sickness than dying of dehydration.

Like muscle memory, my eyes immediately scan the area. Other than the constant sound of snow dripping off the trees, the forest is still. My nerves fire up when I notice footprints leading toward the woods, and my heart sinks. One set of footprints, not two. Whoever these belong to is alone.

They are fresh and tiny, and they come from the direction of the cabin.

"Fucking hell, London," I mutter as I follow the trail with my eyes and see that those tiny footprints lead into the forest beyond.

South.

Smart girl.

She sensed what direction to go, even though I was very careful not to tell her. She also figured out how to get out of my bind, which was fucking impossible. Something isn't right... She wouldn't have left. Even if she got out, she wouldn't have fucking left.

This is an ambush.

Naomi is awake now, peering up at me. I don't give her a chance to move before I grab her and shove my hand over her mouth. I could have my bone weapon on her neck in an instant.

She squirms beneath me. "Micah, what is it?

I press harder. "Shut the fuck up, Naomi." I need to listen. These tracks are fresh, and whoever it is could be close.

Her heart is beating out of her chest as she lies limp in my arms and I turn in every direction.

Listening. Probably looking paranoid as fuck.

After a few minutes, I determine that no one is here... And if they are, they are doing a really good job staying out of sight. I drop Naomi, and she crumbles to the ground.

"Micah, please," she whimpers, curling into a ball. "I need your help."

I crack my neck, unleashing the strain of carrying her all day. I keep my voice composed. "Where's your boyfriend, Naomi? Is Ezra here?"

She blinks at me from the ground. "He isn't my boyfriend. At least, I doubt he wants me anymore. And I don't know where *here* is, Micah. All I see are trees."

I squat so I'm at eye level with her and tilt my head. She doesn't even flinch as she meets my stare, and I try to make out if she's telling me the truth. Her eyes are still hazed, likely from extreme hunger.

"You're fucking lying."

She has to be. There is no way she'd leave her only lifeline willingly. Unless... I guess she managed to find another.

I conceal my deep regret as a new wave of panic settles in. Again, I've walked right into this and led them straight here. Or maybe they were already here, waiting, and took London. Either way, the past two days have been full of shitty decisions on my part.

Naomi closes her eyes as her head starts to sway. "I'm not lying. I think I'm going to be—"

She doesn't finish her sentence before she hurls vomit on my feet, then folds her body on the ground.

She sits in the mud, waiting for me to pick her up.

I don't. I'm actually rather disgusted.

Instead, I stare at the footprints and try to figure out what they mean as Naomi cries and moans at my feet.

I shift my gaze down to her. "When was the last time you ate, Naomi?"

"I can't remember," she says as she gags one more time before looking up at me with tears in her eyes and snot on her face. "It's been a few days, at least." That would explain the vomiting and her inability to keep any liquids in.

"You had food. A third of it, to be exact. Is it gone?"

She bites her lip and doesn't respond; she just lays her head down—not answering but answering all the same.

I grind my teeth and shake my head. "Get your ass up, Naomi. We need to move."

She whips her head up. "Micah, what the fuck? I can barely move."

I start in the direction of the cabin and call over my shoulder, "Then stay here, Naomi. It's up to you. If this is some sort of trap, it won't be good for you."

The best-case scenario is that she stays in a puddle of her own puke, then goes back to Ezra, who's waiting somewhere, too chicken shit to show himself, which will confirm she was lying. The worst-case scenario is playing out how I think it is.

She pulls herself off the ground and musters enough strength to follow me. I suppress a twinge of guilt, knowing how sick and weak she is. But if London is watching, I don't want her to see Naomi in my arms.

We carry forward, and I slow my pace so Naomi can stick close to me, although I track her movements. She can barely walk, and when I turn to check on her, she's dripping in sweat. Naomi needs to understand the seriousness of the situation, and if she had any part in it, she will pay. And until I'm certain she isn't lying to me, I'm not coddling her, although admittedly, I can't carry her any longer. My body is sore, and my knees are screaming at me now.

She huffs, and I hear her footsteps crunch on the ground behind me. I pull out my bone weapon sticking out of my pack. Keeping it firm in my hand, I signal for her to stop just before the cabin comes into sight. She knows this signal; she trapped animals with me for weeks when we first crash-landed.

"Micah, I... Please, I can't do this anymore."

"Shut up, Naomi," I snap at her, drawing my eyes to the trail London left. If Nigel is here, Naomi has already announced our presence with her incessant talking.

I peer around, and my heart sinks. One set of tracks... It's like I want there to be more... Somehow, if she had been taken, it would have been easier to swallow. There are no other tracks, no sign of Ezra or Nigel. I can only conclude they haven't been here.

Naomi lets out a gasp as she catches up to me. "Is this where you and London have been all winter?"

My eyes are laser-focused on the door, which was left partially open. "Yes."

She clearly doesn't realize that London isn't here. And I don't want to say anything until I'm absolutely sure.

"Do Jade and Thomas know where you two have been? Is *she* in there?"

Finally, she thinks to ask about London.

I face her, my anger starting to boil over the edge. "I don't owe anybody anything, Naomi, and I thought I told you not to ask questions." I edge the door open slightly and peer inside, keeping one hand on her and the other gripped firmly on my bone weapon. Blood rushes to my head when I see that the spot where I left London is empty, with dried blood splattered in a line across the floor and on the bed. The stench of urine and sweat is heavy in the air.

My heart stops beating.

She's gone.

The cabin is messy. It looks like she left in a hurry, and I can't deduce what actually happened or how she got out of her restraints. I resist the urge to check on the food—I don't want Naomi to know anything more than she already does.

I turn to face Naomi, trying to get a read on her, but her eyes are glazed and it looks like she might keel over. She's shaking beside me, and I arch a brow. From the terror in her eyes, her fear of me is authentic right now.

"Where the fuck is she, Naomi?"

She stands, shaking, wrapping her arms around herself. "Micah, I don't know where she is. You have to believe me. Please."

My nostrils flare as I grab Naomi by the waist and gently toss her on the bed. She whimpers as her body hits the foam mattress. I crawl on top of her, placing both arms by her head, and she stares back at me, her eyes as fired up as mine as I put my hands on her. "You need to listen to me real carefully, Naomi. I don't want to hurt you, but if you hurt London or know where she is, if I find out you are lying to me, it won't end well for you. She is my life now. Nothing and nobody else matters the way she does, not even you. So tell me where the fuck she is."

She bites her lip in clear defiance.

"Fucking tell me what's going on," I scream, slamming my fists right next to her head. "Why were you alone?"

She curls up beneath me, cringing at my sudden outburst of anger as if just realizing how serious this is for me. "I told you. I left him," she cries out. "I left when he was meeting Nigel. I didn't even tell him. I just fled."

I shift my body slightly so I'm not pressing down on her. "I highly fucking doubt that, Naomi. Why would you just leave him? It doesn't add up."

She closes her eyes before they glaze over. She's warm again, her fever cutting in and out. She needs to eat before she passes out for good.

I run my hand over her burning forehead and give her some water out of my pack. Then I pull a piece of hair from her eyes so I can really inspect her. If she's lying, I'll be able to tell. My anger quickly dissipates as I meet her soft brown eyes and see the girl I was friends with my whole life. For a few seconds, she is not the enemy as I viewed her over the past few months, the person who had a hand in my twin's death.

She's just Naomi, and I'm losing her, too.

"Why haven't you eaten, Naomi?" I soften my voice. My hot temper doesn't work in getting what I want from Naomi... It never has.

She swallows hard and looks at the door as if she wants to flee. "We split the food with Nigel. Ezra and I had to share, and Nigel took most of it. I don't know where Nigel is. We weren't staying together, and Ezra wouldn't let me near him."

I tilt my head. "And why is that?"

"Because Nigel is sick in the head, Micah. He killed Maison, and Ezra cannot simply ignore that."

I scoff and suppress a twinge in my stomach as I run my hand through my hair. "Ezra chose his side. Tell me where you were staying."

She blinks at me, then bursts into tears, her body radiating heat as she shakes her head. "No, you're going to hurt him. I won't let you hurt him again, Micah. But I promise you, they don't know about this place. They have no idea where you are."

I clench my jaw, not sure how to respond. She's quiet now, whimpering as she turns away from me. Streaks of mud line her face, the dirt from her body all over the bed.

"Fuck, Naomi," I mutter, checking myself, grasping onto whatever sliver of humanity I have left in me. "What am I going to do with you?"

I sigh, trying to compose myself, grappling with the complicated feelings I have for Naomi right now. I walk to the stove, turn it on, and boil some water. I need to at least clean her up and let her rest.

I watch her as I clean up the mess London left behind and bite back a swell of emotions as I pick up the sweats London was wearing when I left her.

I toss them into the corner and shift my attention back to Naomi, whose chest rises and falls in a slow rhythm. It reminds me of the way London sleeps.

The wrong girl is in my bed.

Fuck, London. Why did you leave, baby?

The outside world inevitably seeped into my distorted version of paradise. An outcome I can only blame on my regrettable choices. It's like a punch to the gut thinking that London may never lie with me in that spot again and how it could very well be Naomi with whom I spend my final days.

I already miss the hell out of London.

I walk over and delicately place one hand on Naomi's torso, the warmth of her skin teasing my fingertips. Slowly, I glide my hands down her stomach, carefully tugging at the waistband of her sweats, guiding them down her legs. She doesn't even flinch as I grab her shirt and pull it off, leaving her completely nude.

My dick betrays me as I stare at her tits and watch as her nipples harden. I refuse to feel guilty about seeing her naked and enjoying it. It's not like I haven't seen her before, because I have—many times. But this time, it's different because under no circumstances will I act on it. I'm sexually attracted to her—that was never the problem with Naomi, per se. I just don't overly like her personality. I do my best to ignore her and shift my attention to London's clothes, anywhere but Naomi's body, picking out a new outfit for Naomi as she lies on the bed, her eyes barely open and her body still burning up.

"What are you going to do with me now?" she breathes out, her eyes closed, looking completely defeated.

I lean to her earlobe, and her body tenses beneath me. "You smell like shit," I tell her. "I'm giving you a bath."

Even in her semi-comatose state, a small smirk forms on her lips, and I ignore it as I drop a T-shirt into the hot water and soak her skin with it, starting with her arms.

"Whatever you say, Micah," she mutters, but she's clearly enjoying this.

I work my way up to her neck, then down to her legs, ignoring the obvious parts. She can wash those herself once she's better.

Her eyes remain shut as she enjoys the warmth. I do my best to scrub every inch of dirt and grime off her legs and torso and help her clean her hair. I do everything not to touch her sexually.

Then I turn her around and clean her backside. I've gotten pretty efficient at this. It was my thing with London, and London ate it right up, too. The way Naomi leans into it makes me wonder how Ezra is with her. Judging by her current reaction to me, it wouldn't surprise me if he was shit in bed. I've never understood Naomi's attraction to him to begin with. He's inferior to me on every level.

Once done, I step back and lay a blanket over her. She lifts her knees, exposing herself to me, and my dick immediately betrays me. She knows it. Believe it or not, I've only fucked this girl a handful of times, but given how horny I always am, this is like torture.

Fuck. Why do I have to be so easily distracted by pussy?

I help her put on an oversized T-shirt, and before I help her get fully dressed, she lets out a deep breath and mumbles, "I hate you, Micah. I hate you for leaving me for her. I hate you for the years you've treated me like shit."

With a grimace, she launches a kick in my direction, narrowly missing as I dodge out of the way and catch her foot in my hands, restraining her.

"Fuck you, Micah," she spits, her voice full of venom and delirious with fever. She's bawling her eyes out, and it kills me. I really hate making girls cry.

I grab hold of the arch of her foot to calm her down and stop her from kicking me again. It works. She immediately melts into my touch as I dig my fingers into her foot. "I owe you an apology, Naomi. I should have at least given you an explanation. Just let me take care of you right now."

Let me make something right.

This seems to appease her. She closes her eyes and falls back asleep while I rub her feet to make sure she's relaxed. When I'm confident she's out, I reach over and grab the dirty bucket of water.

She opens her eyes briefly when I drop her feet.

"Stay here. I'll be back," I tell her.

"I'm not going anywhere; I can barely move. Where are you going, Micah?"

"Fishing." I let the door shutter behind me.

I need space to think right now. I can't just abandon Naomi again, and I certainly can't fuck her, even though she will eventually try.

I resist the urge to follow London's tracks right now to claim her and bring her back tonight.

Is she expecting me to follow? Her absence is a pretty clear answer. She knew how I'd respond, that her leaving was the one thing I truly feared. She's done with me, and I can't blame her, even if I'm not quite done with her. As soon as Naomi gets better, I'll drop her off with the others and take London back—whether she wants me to or not.

CHAPTER TWELVE

LONDON

I ce, I've decided, is very dangerous, especially when it gets cracked over your skull and used as a weapon. My hand is throbbing, the excruciating pain only dulled by the intense explosions in my head—my body can only comprehend so much pain at a time. I keep my eyes closed because I'm certain of whose arms I'm in right now. The stub of his hand, where his fingers should be, is wrapped around my waist, poking into my side.

Ezra.

Nigel must be the other set of feet crunching and slugging in the snow behind us. I've been awake for a while, but I don't move or say anything as my body hangs limply, my legs down Ezra's front and my head over his shoulder. He certainly doesn't hold me with the comfort or grace Micah does—the rhythm of his body is more abrupt. His smell is different, too. His sweat is more... putrid.

Apparently, Ezra and Nigel don't speak to each other since they haven't uttered a word since I woke up.

I try to squeeze my hand into a fist and find, with horror, that I can't move my fingers. A fresh wave of panic consumes me. My wound is bad, and I doubt these two will care enough to tend to it. I attempt to calm myself, recalling all the better ways Micah has taught me to react in a situation like this: surrender to the circumstances and take charge by influencing the environment and the people around me.

Breathe, London. Dull the pain. Focus, survive, then kill.

Kill.

I remain listless, keeping my eyes partly closed, and hone in on my surroundings. Based on the position of the sun, I'm reasonably confident the cabin is north. This means we are northeast of where Jade is, which is where I need to flee once I escape.

Ezra stalls, and he heaves me up as his hand—or should I say, lack thereof—slips. The silence of the snowy landscape is interrupted by his voice.

"She's fucking heavy," he mutters and pulls me up over his shoulder, my wounded hand hitting his side. "And she stinks." It takes every ounce of my willpower not to cry out.

I want to scoff because I am *not* heavy—he's just weak.

However, I can't argue with the fact that I probably do stink.

The last time Ezra touched me, he had pulled me out of my shelter feet first and let Naomi beat the shit out of me. I'll never forget that, or what any of them did to me for that matter. Especially how Ezra betrayed Micah and Maison. If I have the chance to kill them both, I won't hesitate. I will finish what Micah was incapable of doing when he had the chance—when I foolishly stopped him.

The greatest regret of my life.

They caused the loss of my best friend and changed my relationship with Micah before it had even started. I could have had both of them, but they took that from me.

"Quit whining and keep moving. He could be following us." The sound of Nigel's voice is worse than his breath, which I can smell as he steps closer to me. It's as if he has a lingering cavity that never got filled, now worse from being on this island with the lack of dental hygiene. Even back in New Ocean, his breath sickened me. That was in the beginning, when we used to be *friends* and I hadn't realized what a vile creature he was. His obsession with

Micah started long before I arrived and has since festered into something seemingly more sinister.

"How much longer?" Ezra continues, grunting and carrying me like a brute.

"The airplane is close. Please shut up, or you'll wake her." A fresh wave of nausea overwhelms me at Nigel's voice and the thought of where he's taking me.

However, the hint of panic in his voice makes me smile. It's nothing like the mocking laughter that echoed around my head all winter. He's human, just like me. He can die as easily as I can.

The airplane is an obvious place for Micah to search for me—if he comes for me at all. If he's still alive, he would have seen the evidence of my fleeing by now. He will meticulously inspect every inch of the cabin, diligently searching for any clue of other people's presence, but all he will find is my blood and sweat. He will believe I left him because he won't have any proof otherwise.

Suddenly, Ezra heaves me to the ground, and I find myself face-first in the snow. I can't help but moan as I land on my hand.

Fuck.

"I'm not taking one more step until you tell me where we're going, man," Ezra barks. "It's getting dark, and I don't want to be out here at night. And we need London alive. Otherwise, she is fucking useless to us."

I whip my eyes open and glare at him for treating me like a rag doll. No point in pretending I'm asleep anymore.

Nigel's already grinning at me like the serpent he is. "Good morning, sunshine. Did you have a good sleep?"

I quirk my lips upward, mimicking his smug smile. Nigel thinks Micah is the one he should worry about, but I'm actually the one he should fear. I'm stronger than he realizes. That's how I survived this far, how I got out of Micah's ties, and truly, how I survived Micah at all, as he has clearly begun his descent into insanity.

Just as I have.

"When he finds out you've taken me, Micah's going to kill you, Nigel. Then you can join your sister in hell."

To my surprise, Ezra laughs, and Nigel glares at him, only confirming my assumption that the two of them are far from chummy. I turn my eyes to Ezra. "He's going to kill you, too, Ezra."

Ezra merely snarls, and Nigel lets out that dark laugh of his. "Oh, London, I've missed you so, so much. How was your little honeymoon with Micah? I'm sure you constantly thought about Maison and really mourned him. I did you a favor by killing him, didn't I? He isn't in your way anymore. Now you can find true happiness."

The sound that comes out of me is feral. Hearing Maison's name from his mouth guts me.

He clicks his tongue. "And no, London. He's not going to kill me, because he's not going to find me or come looking for you at all. My guess is that he's... distracted."

Distracted? *Not dead.*

Ezra curls his lip but says nothing, and I get a punch to the gut when the realization of what he means hits me. Micah's distraction, I bet, is in the form of a five-foot-seven blonde bitch, who is suspiciously missing from this expedition. I can see from the look on Ezra's face that he's none too happy about it, either. But he says nothing, and the fact that he's allowing it means Nigel really is the one in charge.

I sit up on the snowbank and lean back on my good arm. I take a good look at them now. Haggard would be an understatement to describe their appearance. Stringy is more like it. Both have dirty, blond hair that looks more like straw.

Barely human.

Vile, hideous, and evil.

Winter obviously wasn't as good to them as it was to Micah and me. Each has black patches on their face from obvious frostbite, and it puts a smile on my face. Even if they were to torture me, break all my fingers, or cut off any part of my body and kill me slowly, I would still die happy after seeing the amount of damage on their faces caused by winter. How cold they must have been while I spent my winter making love and falling deeper than I thought was possible in a warm, inviting *home.*

However, right now, I doubt I'm much better. I pull my hand to my mouth and laugh. But Nigel's dead eyes make me pause, and the hairs prickle on my skin.

He looks at me, and his eyes reflect the shadows in his soul.

A tremor courses through me as I avert my gaze, unable to stomach him for one more moment.

Ezra speaks first, breaking the deathly silence. "What's so funny?"

I push myself to my feet and wipe the mud off my ass, keeping my gaze down until the last possible second. I finally peer up at him, avoiding Nigel's death glare, wondering if Ezra really knows the kind of monster he's aligned himself with. "You believing you're going to win over Micah is comical to me."

"Stop talking, or I'll gag you," Ezra spits.

A smile hits my lips at how seasoned I've become at being gagged and tortured. His threats don't scare me, and I shall embrace death if it comes to that.

Ezra reaches to pick me up, but I slap his hands away. "Save your energy since I'm so heavy for you to carry," I snap at him. "I can walk by myself." Ezra hesitates and twists toward Nigel as if needing permission. I merely roll my eyes and stomp ahead before he can stop me. It wasn't that long ago when Ezra was one of our esteemed leaders on this island, and his deference to Nigel now is unsettling. "I won't run away. I promise." The words float over my shoulder. As if I have enough strength to run away from them, as if my body isn't giving out. I can sense the heat in my hand spreading to my wrist. I have a headache, and the chills of a fever are starting to spread over every limb and muscle of my body.

Ezra forges ahead, and I raise my brows at him as we make eye contact, his face unreadable. Nigel strategically positions himself at my back, and Ezra visibly exhales, grateful to be free from the weight of carrying me. I follow Ezra through the wet snow and into the darkening night. We walk for at least an hour, away from the safety of the thick trees. We continue past the death holes with melted patches of snow, rock gleaming underneath it, and toward the one place on this island that truly makes me squirm.

The place where thirty-two of our fallen classmates were put to rest above ground and where their corpses are still frozen in time. The place that started it all.

Every one of those tortured souls still haunts these charred trees—it's in my bones, in the fibers of the air. Sometimes, I can still hear them scream, and it chills my soul.

Breathing in this place is difficult.

We arrive at the airplane site right as the darkest part of the night descends upon us. Hopefully, this is the first place Micah will look when he finds me missing. Unless he's dead already. Because that is the only reason I will accept for him not coming back when he said he would.

Distracted or otherwise.

As we approach the break in the trees where the plane's wings seem to have been swallowed by branches and debris, the eerie whispers of my classmates who didn't survive start to fill the site. The pungent smell of acid fills the air, a haunting reminder of the nearby corpses that have yet to be cleared away.

The whispers are so clear that I wonder if the others hear it, too. The sound binds my feet to the ground and has me searching the woods to keep the corpses in my line of sight as if to convince myself I'm not imagining it.

Nigel kicks me forward. "What on earth are you staring at? Keep moving. Micah's not going to save you right now, London. He isn't hiding in those woods, I assure you."

I groan as I stumble toward the plane, and Ezra turns around to see what the commotion is about.

Perhaps it's because my condition is worsening by the second, but I'm only moving right now out of pure desperation and with the hope that I can rest my head on a seat when we get there—if Nigel even allows me that level of comfort. I'm not so sure what their endgame is with me.

Ezra opens the back door first, and Nigel nudges me inside. I immediately crawl to my regular spot and curl up in the seat, leaning my head down, hoping they are just as tired as I am and will leave me alone.

That seems to be the case as Ezra takes a seat nearby, one that wasn't destroyed in the fire or torn apart by the crash but across from where I sit so he can watch me.

Nigel, however, hovers over me as some of his argyle shirt pokes out from under his hoodie. His eyes look tired and tight, and they flicker as he tilts his head. "How much food do you and Micah have left?"

My eyes narrow into slits. "I'm not telling you that." Food. Of course, that's what this is about; they probably don't have much left. They found me, another food source for them.

A new lifeline.

"Oh, you will tell us, London. Eventually, you will tell me everything I want to know. You might feel like, somehow, you're in control of this situation, but you're not. You're ours now, *sweetheart*. So if you want to eat, you need to tell us where you've been hiding and where your food is."

I fold my arms, refusing to engage. A simmering pit of fire is steadily forming in my stomach, spreading over my skin. I'm always hungry; I can't manage the hunger the way Micah can.

It makes me deranged.

Nigel's barely hanging on by a thread. I can tell by his eyes and the subtle dragging of his feet. He barely survived winter; I'm surprised he even survived himself.

To my extreme relief, he turns and finds a place to settle in for the night. "Don't think about running away while I'm asleep because I will follow you and kill you," he says flippantly.

I blow out a breath when he stumbles to the front of the plane to take a cushy seat. Even he's too tired to torment me right now, and Ezra's already snoring somewhere beside me.

It's only a matter of time before Nigel does decide to hurt me, though, and by then, I truly might be fucked.

Two sunsets have now passed since Micah left me, and I'm numb about it.

"You'll be fine, sweetheart. I'll only be gone for a few hours. I'll be back before dusk. Try to sleep."

Liar.

I close my eyes as Nigel and Ezra drift off into whatever bodily state they consider sleep, but unsurprisingly, it eludes me. I think of chestnut eyes as I attempt to get comfortable and lay my head on the window. I'm just not sure whose eyes they are anymore.

Maybe both of them.

Perhaps they are the same to me now.

I haven't slept a wink since Micah left me, other than when the ghost of Maison was with me.

And I am *not* fine.

The darkness outside creeps into my soul, blurring the edges of my heart. Pain and hunger consume my brain, leaving little room for anything else. The chill in the air makes my bones shiver, specifically my teeth as they slam into each other.

"Shut. Up," Ezra gripes from the middle of the plane, but it's not like I can do anything to stop it. I press my lips together and try to focus on my breath as it circles in the air in front of me. The last thing I want to do is agitate these two more than I already have.

My mere existence seems to accomplish that just fine.

He can't see it, but I flip Ezra the bird, and the gesture is immensely satisfying.

I shift and jerk, the side of the seat digging into my back, before I finally lie down as restfully as I can, focusing on the pleasant memories I had in this spot. Tonight, I will dream about Maison, and only Maison. It was his hands holding me when this plane crashed, his hands that have never hurt me. And it's *his* memory I will cherish from the horrors that occurred that night. When I first flirted with him and started falling for him... The day this all started.

Maison, Maison, Maison.

The memory instantly warms me while thinking of Micah endlessly hurts. What is he doing right now? Who is he with? Why is he not with me? I think of the mediocre fuck that is Naomi Wilson and what lengths she would go to get Micah back. The thought cripples me more than it should. Nigel knows how to get under my skin, planting that seed of doubt, even if it's not true. However, I can't deny the fact that Naomi's not here.

Nope. Not thinking about Micah.

After a few minutes of snores and grunts from across the damaged plane, the cabin grows quiet. I peer outside the window for the rest of the night, staring at the outline of half-burnt trees, which seem to glow from the reflection of the melting snow and moonlight. A hint of smoke teases the air, and my nostrils twitch.

Why is there smoke?

I spend the next hours counting every pounding heart-beat, every throb in my hand, every second that ticks by, finding gratitude in the stillness of the moment and the fact that I get to live one more night.

Finally, I drift into a restless sleep plagued by night-mares. It's always the same circular thoughts of severed hands, chopped fingers, blood, and guts. Images of Micah fucking blonde girls, then making me cut off my own hand.

My eyes shoot open, and my heart rate bolts.

Laughter.

A dark chill overcomes me as the shadows swallow me whole. Because the person laughing at me is sleeping a mere ten feet away in the front of the plane, which gives a good sense of my current mental state. Only it's not him laughing...

It's me, and the laughter is coming from the darkest parts of me.

My eyes are wide open, but my body is frozen as I listen to the soft snores of the others. And I sit here going crazy, just... *laughing* as if this were a carnival.

I snap out of it, my eyes focused on a bloodstain on the ground beside me as a hint of morning light trickles inside. The person who caused that pool of blood also laughed at me at school before his body bled out days later in the crash.

"What's so fucking funny, London?" Ezra grumbles from a few feet away. He is not happy, which makes me laugh even more. It's the morning now anyway, and I'm not sure what's so funny. Truly, I don't.

A heavy boot hits my shin, and a stalky shadow looms over me.

"Fuck, Nigel," I cry out as pain shoots up to my knee. I curl back from him and then glare. "What did I ever do to you?" Nothing, is the answer.

His deviant smirk indicates he's plenty rested now, ready to torture me.

He tilts his head. "Are you ready to tell me where you and Micah are staying, or am I going to have to bleed the answers out of you?"

I can't help but grimace and violently shake my head, his words causing my entire body to tremble. "I don't know, I really don't." It's true, I think. I'm not certain I would be able to find that place again, even if I wanted to. Micah had made sure of that.

He reaches down and pulls me up by my hair with one hand and grabs my bandaged fingers with the other. I yelp out, pain shooting up my arm. "Want to try again? Or should I pull your fingers off one at a time?"

I suppress the bile that builds in my throat, the pain blurring the lines of my vision, and choke on the acidic smell radiating from him.

It smells like he's decaying...

"North," I whimper, fighting the dusty tears in my eyes from the dirt layered on my face. I don't want to give him the satisfaction of hearing me scream. "It's close to where you found me. Maybe another twenty minutes... North. It's a cabin."

He looks at Ezra, then back at me, and I wince when his eyes draw to my hand again. He merely smiles, flashing his teeth. "You better not be lying."

I pull my hand away from him and whatever wretched thought he just had. "I'm not lying," I say through gritted teeth. "Say hi to Micah for me." I laugh again because, apparently, it's the only way I can express my emotions at the moment.

He kicks me again—hard this time—in my side. Those dead eyes of his peer down at me as my head slams into the wall from the force of the blow. "You're a funny girl, London. My sister was funny, too... It must be what he sees in you."

The wind knocks out of me, and I manage to swallow, not daring to laugh again, keeping my gaze on the window. "It's near a stream," I finally say. "Find the stream and head north."

I hope it's enough to appease him, and he'll leave. At least, if I give him the location, maybe I won't have to spend the day with him.

He pauses and runs his hand along his chin as if contemplating his course of action, then looks at Ezra, who's kept to the shadows with zero involvement. "Keep her here until I get back, and I will give you half of what I find. Watch her like a hawk and don't trust a goddamn word that comes out of her filthy mouth."

Jesus.

Food. This is all about food. I put the pieces together... They don't fucking have any.

My eyes whip to Ezra as Nigel slips out through the airplane door, and I fall back into my seat.

Tense.

Nigel makes me incredibly skittish, seeing how far he's gone now and what this island has done to *him*, specifically. What I think he's capable of... I don't understand how anyone could be near him, especially Ezra, who was Maison's best friend.

Ezra's beady eyes haven't left mine since Nigel kicked me, his angry gaze boring into me and his straw hair hanging in front of his eyes. All sorts of thoughts are swirling around his head, all centered on me.

Ezra, Ezra, Ezra.

He doesn't scare me like he should—not the same way Nigel does. I stare back at him, unblinking, and only when Nigel's a comfortable distance and the tension melts from my shoulders do I finally say, "You ate all your food?"

"We were hungry," Ezra retorts, keeping his heavy stare. No wonder Naomi left, if that is indeed what happened. That food should have lasted longer; they certainly had enough of it.

He breaks the stare first, sitting in the seat across from me, placing his elbows on his knees and running his hands through his hair. "You're not going to do anything stupid like run away, are you?"

I shake my head and blink. "No."

He's stressed, the tension on his face pouring out of him like he's trying to find his words. Almost as if I make him nervous, which is strange considering I've spent countless hours on this island with him and we've barely interacted. In fact, I think this is the first conversation we've ever had. He always speaks around me, over me, but never directly to me. Even back when we were all trying to survive together, we hardly interacted. It was like I was invisible to him, and he was supposedly Maison's best friend.

And Micah's enemy.

I cock a brow. "So, you're taking orders from Nigel now? He's fucked up, Ezra. You must see that."

He scoffs and waves his hand. "Anyone who's still alive on this island right now is fucked up." He lays his head back against the seat and closes his eyes. "Now, can you please shut up? I'm not in the mood to talk."

I press my lips together but ignore his request, acknowledging he looks... defeated. "Where's Naomi, Ezra? Why isn't she here?"

He lifts his head only momentarily, but I don't miss the flash in his eyes at the mention of his girlfriend. He doesn't answer me, just flexes his jaw, giving off the masculine alpha energy I've gotten used to receiving since being here.

I don't relent, even though sitting in silence sounds enticing, especially since my energy has depleted so much. Not to mention, my tongue is dry, and it's hard to swallow since they've given me no water since capturing me.

"So, are you going to kill me, then?"

Because I plan on killing you if you side with Nigel.

His eyebrows twitch, and he scowls. "Only if you keep talking," he gripes. Everyone from New Ocean is always so broody and miserable.

I sigh and lean back but keep my eyes on him. It bugs him—the way I look at him, my eyes piercing into him. I can tell by the way he shifts and tugs at his collar, by the sweat beading on his forehead.

My eyes draw down to his four missing fingers and his thumb. I stare at his nubs in complete fascination, remembering Micah was the one who had caused it.

I never inspected Thomas's wrist and how it ended up looking. For the few days I was at their camp after Maison died, Thomas kept it well-hidden and spent most of that time in bed. I haven't seen him since.

Ezra wipes the beads of sweat with his thumb as they drip down the bridge of his nose. He's frightened of me—or of Micah. Probably of Micah. Either that, or guilt is eating at him for the role he had in his best friend's death and seeing me now is bringing out those emotions.

"Quit staring at me," he says without lifting his head.

I pause for a moment before responding, "I'm thirsty."

He huffs, but to my surprise, he rises and heads to the front of the airplane. When he returns, he hands me a bottle of water, keeping his face void of emotion. "Here you go. Now, shut up."

I grab the bottle with my good hand and guzzle it all down as if I were a camel in the desert. The liquid rushes down my throat. He watches me for a moment as I toss the bottle to the side before he takes his place in a seat one row up so I can't stare at him anymore.

I shift uncomfortably, now dealing with a very full bladder. I sigh and try to get in a position where my bladder is not burning.

He must sense my discomfort. "What's your problem now?"

"I have to pee."

A pause, and then he says, "Jesus Christ, you're worse than Naomi."

I can't help but laugh at that. I stop to think for a second about what it's like for those two behind closed doors, what their pillow talk is like. I never cared to observe their relationship outside of Naomi treating him like shit.

I let out a sigh. I am not above begging. "Please, Ezra. Otherwise, I'll pee in here, and then you will have to smell it and listen to me whine."

He lets out a loud, dramatic sigh. "Fine, but I have to watch you. If you run off, I'm fucked."

Why would he be fucked?

I slide over two seats and face him, placing my legs on the floor of the plane. "Fine. Watch."

I rise to step outside and hear him following a few feet behind me. I ignore him and revel in the sun shining and how much warmer it is now that it's springtime. The sun is warming the land day by day, melting all the snow and revealing all that lies under it after months of frost. Today is particularly warm, and the sky is clear, the sun shining bright. I try to enjoy the small, pleasant moments I am afforded, so I bask in the warmth of it. I've long lost track of the days since Maison died and Micah took me away, but it seems like spring has finally arrived and cemented itself, and the change in the landscape proves it.

I take a few steps and relieve myself. When I peek over at Ezra, I'm happy to see he isn't looking. His back is to me, giving me the privacy I deserve.

Once I'm done, I pull up my sweats and take a deep breath. No part of me wants to go back on that plane right now. He senses my need to stay out here for a second and sits on the plane's stairs as I gaze out at the tundra and the wilderness beyond.

For a few minutes, both of us seem to lose ourselves in it, but eventually, he coughs. "Let's go back inside, London. Time's up."

I turn to face him, and for the first time, he isn't looking at me with complete disdain. In fact, he just looks fucking tired. And hungry...

He jerks his head toward the door, his patience limited.

I need to get inside Ezra's head. He's the one person on this island I've never really understood, and right now, he could be the key to getting out of this mess. There must be some substance under there; he can't be as stupid as he looks. Naomi must get a much softer side of him—the same way I get a softer side of Micah... sometimes.

Like I did with Micah, I have to pull it out of him.

I peer into the woods once more, then follow him into the airplane and back to my spot. Once I'm comfortable enough and he's settled back in his row, I finally dare to ask him the same question I dared to ask Micah once. "Ezra, why do you hate me? What did I ever do to you?"

He doesn't even pause to think about it. "Because Naomi hates you. It was just easier for me to hate you, too."

Solid reasoning, I suppose.

So where is Naomi, then?

I pause and swallow hard. "They're together right now." Not a question, so the real question is, why is Ezra okay with it?

"Probably," he answers. "I wouldn't put it past them." My stomach stirs at his clear admission. The way he says it, though... It's as if they can't stay away from each other, and he knows it.

He must not be in a good headspace about it.

"And you're okay with them being together?" I say over the seat since I can't look into his eyes right now.

"Stop trying to get fucking answers out of me, London."

Jesus.

Is his desire for revenge on Micah truly stronger than his love for Naomi? Is that what this is about? Or is it about food? Only hunger drives anyone anymore.

"Whatever you're planning to do, it's not going to work. Micah's too smart. He will see right through it."

Silence.

I don't care what he says; this is my moment, and I have to seize it. I just saw a crack in his facade, and now I need to wedge it open. It could mean life or death for me.

"You could let me go," I tell him. "Or we could go find them together and end this feud today, no questions asked. I want to be with Micah, and you want to be with Naomi.

You and I shouldn't be together right now." I sound desperate. "We can offer a truce... I'll vouch for you, Ezra."

I mean what I say, even though he certainly played a role in everything that happened. The question is, can I forgive him? And can Ezra forgive Micah for chopping off his fingers? Nigel plays off Ezra's emotions, which is no doubt what he's using to control him—to manipulate him.

I need to remind Ezra what his life could be like if he just let go of his hate. He doesn't respond, but I will take his silence as a sign that he is contemplating what I said.

"I saw that it wasn't you who killed Maison, Ezra. You did nothing wrong. I don't blame you for Maison's death. We were all there; we saw Nigel kill him in cold blood."

"Don't fucking talk about Maison," he blurts out. "You knew him for a month, and you think because you were fucking him that, somehow, his death hurts you more than it hurts me? He was my best friend for fifteen years, London. So shut the fuck up about Maison. You cheated on him the first chance you got, and with his brother, no less. You don't deserve to breathe the same air as me."

Tears sting my eyes at the cruelty of his words... at how little Ezra regards me and what I shared with Maison. It was real, and he was my first love. I shouldn't have to explain that, but I seem to have to continuously defend my feelings for Maison and how his death tore me to pieces.

I've had the same conversation with Micah, over and over, until it was just easier to suppress my feelings to the deepest parts of me. Well, I refuse to do it anymore.

Maison deserves better.

I let out an uncontrollable sob. I hate that I let a guy like Ezra get to me.

Wiping the tears from my face, I straighten, my words coming out sharp. "I understand it's hard for you to comprehend what I went through with the two of them, but I loved Maison with my whole heart. I'm not the one betraying him right now by siding with his killer." I pause for a moment, my voice catching. "But that is exactly what you and Naomi are doing."

More silence.

No aggressive retort or snarky comeback. And even if he did, I'm done talking... Ezra wins. We can sit in utter silence for all I care, but I hope the truth of my words rips into him and slices him from the inside out.

My stomach grumbles. The hunger pains have returned after weeks of not having them because Micah kept me fed. I don't bother asking Ezra for food because I know what his answer will be.

He doesn't fucking have any.

So I sit as quietly as I can, trying not to let the pain and hurt overwhelm me.

Fuck Ezra Schwartz.

CHAPTER THIRTEEN

LONDON

A loud bang startles me from my doze as Nigel barges into the airplane, his eyes wild. I raise my head as he storms the aisle and lunges right at me. I barely have enough time to lift my non-injured arm to protect myself before he grabs me by the collar and pulls me out of my seat, flinging me to the floor, where I land in a jumbled heap, lying in a cold sweat.

"You lied," he muses, his gaze predatory as he steps over me.

I chew on the inside of my cheek until a coppery metal tang hits my mouth. I landed on my broken hand, and agonizing pain shoots through my entire arm and into my neck, causing my vision to blur. I bite my cheek harder to fight off the agony.

I'll take it that he didn't find the cabin.

I glare up at him, my hair falling in my face. "I didn't lie to you. It's well hidden; I warned you about that."

Nigel kicks me in the ribs, quickly reminding me that I am his captive, that he is the one in control right now, and that I need to potentially watch my mouth.

"London. London. London... You're not making yourself very useful to me right now." The moment his boot connects with my wrist, a scream erupts from me, the sheer agony impossible to suppress.

"I will continue to torture you until you tell me where the fuck your hideout is."

"You can go to hell, Nigel. If you haven't found it by now, you won't."

He quirks his head and kneels so he's somewhat at eye level with me.

The madness inside him is apparent in his eyes.

He's gone. Any part of him that was good, pure, or innocent has disappeared.

"No, London," he says darkly, "but you can."

The light reflects off the blade he's holding, which flashes for a second before he presses the dull blade of the ice skate against my neck. I scramble for a second before my body goes limp beneath him and my eyes roll back in my head. He is on top of me, pressing his knee into my chest and crushing my lungs. Tears well up in my eyes from the sheer amount of pain I'm in.

Ezra stands behind him, and my vision is blurred, but I can tell he's doing nothing to stop Nigel. In a last desperate attempt, I seek Ezra's eyes, giving him a silent plea as all the blood rushes to my head.

Nigel positions himself between us. "This skate is sharp, London. It was Micah's first spear he made from his hockey gear. Poetic, isn't it?" He leans down, his spit hitting my cheek. "If I press down even an inch harder, I will sever the artery in your neck, and you will die. Is that what you want?"

I can't respond because I can't breathe.

"And if you don't know where the hell that cabin is, then I doubt your usefulness to me."

"Just fucking tell us, London." Ezra's voice is distant, like he's speaking through a tunnel. Distant but desperate. Surviving seems to have taken priority for him. "Don't make this harder on yourself."

Ezra and I were sitting in glorious silence for the past few hours, and he didn't put his hands on me once. He even tossed dried food at me, saying nothing, of course, but the gesture told me enough. He's not a monster; he's just hungry.

At least he's not a monster yet.

And that little piece of food sufficed to stop the gnawing feeling in my stomach.

My heart beats so fast now, and I close my eyes, waiting for Nigel to end it. His face is not the last thing I want to see.

"Stop it, man. You're killing her. She's the only leverage we have," Ezra finally says. "If you kill her, we'll never find him."

Nothing... I feel nothing as Nigel presses that skate into my neck, crushing me, mutilating me.

No fear, no pain.

I'm numb.

Because I think I'm already dead inside, immune to Nigel's blind rage.

And then... it ends. Nigel releases the pressure on me, removing the blade from my throat. My body convulses as I suck in a breath, choking on it. My vision returns, but I don't dare to move. I keep my eyes closed, my cheek lying in the pool of dried blood beneath me.

Ezra pulls me up, and I crawl back into my seat and face them. Nigel composes himself and stands with his arms crossed. His smile comes straight from hell.

"Good point," he says, wiping the blood off the blade on his shirt.

My blood.

I place my hand on my neck... A trickle of blood seeps onto my fingers. So meticulous not to have killed me. A small drop of that blood rolls down my neck and drips to the ground beneath me.

"Looks like you get to live today, London," he says, observing me as I watch the crimson stain the seat.

Do I want to live?

Even if he hasn't killed me, I will still have a scar from what he just did, leaving more permanent marks on me. I wrap my hand around my neck to stop the stinging pain. But I can breathe, and at least, I have a new source of pain to focus on so I can ignore the ones in my heart and hand.

Nigel steps back. "Time to go. Get up," he says abruptly.

My head whips up, and my eyes narrow.

Go? Go where? I just assumed this was where they were living.

I laugh again... I can't walk. I can barely breathe, so I just laugh silently to myself.

The wind howls around me.

"What if he comes after her today and follows us?" Ezra asks. "This is the most obvious place to look for her."

"He won't," Nigel quips. "Not if he found Naomi. Last I saw, she was waiting for him at the lake site. I doubt he will leave her to die. He will have to choose between Naomi and London, and then our dear London will finally see what kind of person he is and, hopefully, make the right decision."

Ezra curls his lips at the mention of Naomi. I can't put my finger on what happened between them exactly—if Naomi left by herself or if they had planned this to lure us out of pure desperation.

Nigel rolls his eyes at Ezra's emotional response to her. "Relax. I'm sure your dear girlfriend is doing just fine." This does nothing to calm Ezra down. He's vibrating, pulsating in anger like he would whenever Micah used Naomi to taunt him.

I pull myself to my knees as Nigel walks away, prepping for us to leave the airplane. His words hit me then as I wonder just what kind of state they left Naomi in. And if Micah would really choose Naomi over me.

The fact that he isn't here right now answers my question and also explains why it took him so long to come back to me when he had promised he would only be gone for a few hours.

Nigel pushes the airplane door open and heads outside while Ezra helps me to my feet. "Move," he orders.

Begrudgingly, I follow, keeping my face emotionless, not allowing myself to *feel.*

The sun settles in the sky. That hint of smoke still teases the air, and Nigel looks at me with a sly smirk as he passes me. "Let's go home, shall we? Ladies first."

A sick feeling pools in my stomach. Ezra ignores me and trails behind, knowing I don't have the energy to run away from him. I stare into the dead forest. One small step at a time, my feet connect with stone, and we head north. Something tells me that, no matter what, this is the beginning of the end, and the airplane was a sanctuary compared to where I'm going.

Every bone and muscle screams at me as I follow the two boys through the barren wilderness.

One evil, one stupid—both desperate.

We walk in silence through the charred skeleton trees, the barren land discomposed by the destruction that occurred here. The island this far north is dangerous. Much more so than the airplane or the lusher forest Micah and I briefly called home.

I drag myself forward, now wishing Ezra would carry me. My skin is on fire as I try to keep up, burning up with a fever from the scrapes and pulled flesh on my hand. My body has endured too much.

It's starting to break down.

Withering away.

Beat by beat, my heart is slowing.

A rhythmic buzz teases the air, and I can't quite put my finger on what it is...

Ezra pauses to take a sip of water, the very last of it, before filling up his bottle with melted snow pooling on the ground. It's skanky water we have no business drinking. Even now, Micah's deep voice is in the back of my mind, lecturing me.

If you have the choice between drinking or not drinking water, drink it. You will one hundred percent die if you don't, okay? London! Baby, it's important that you pay attention to this; it might save your life one day.

All the words of wisdom Micah shared with me all winter, relaying all his expertise about surviving out here. Preparing me for when he wouldn't be here to take care of me, as if he knew this would happen eventually. My mouth salivates at the thought of drinking, and my heart breaks at the thought of him.

Nigel snatches the bottle from Ezra's hand before he can give me any as a powerful gust of wind blows through, and clean air is replaced by the putrid smell of decaying flesh, now thick on my tongue.

The severed souls that haunt us.

The air is suddenly thicker, the stench revolting, and the buzzing hovers in the air like an apocalypse. Completely unnerving, given what's near us.

Flies. Maggots. Insects feasting.

Nigel is already puking before we register the mountain of bodies next to us.

All thirty-two of them are piled near each other or on top of one another, and in the early evening light, some of their eyes are still open as we walk by.

Their bodies are still decaying, frozen in time from that fateful night. The colder weather must have partially preserved the bodies, or at least, the remnants that were picked at by vultures and rodents before the snow fell and the temperatures dropped. A few of them have been pulled away and torn apart by animals, rotting where they rest... what's left of them anyway.

"Keep moving," Nigel gripes, still gagging from the sight and smell of those dead bodies melting into the earth. I hope he dies from that tainted water. Karma at its best. Once again, this shows me how sick he is because he led me right here. He must have forgotten they were so close.

Inside, I'm screaming, but I don't dare laugh. The utter disdain on his face tells me he will kill me if I do. Then I will be converted into a pile of bones.

I shudder as I stare at these poor dead souls, none of whom I really knew. Surviving instead of them fills me with a deep sense of guilt. Each was an athlete, a cheerleader, or a leader in the community and school. They will be deeply missed by their community, but I won't be. I was barely a blip in my father's life before this school year started.

They are faceless now... The only identifiers are what's left of their Armani suits and the fabric of their blue cheerleading outfits. I can't help but gape at them, and Nigel, who has recovered from his vomiting, smirks at my reaction. All the blood rushes from my face, and Ezra merely stands a few feet away, scowling.

"Oh, suck it up. It's not like you haven't seen this before," he says to Ezra.

"Dude, have some fucking respect," Ezra barks. "You might not have given a shit about them, but these were my fucking friends." I smile because it's nice to see the old Ezra again—the one who hated Nigel. I miss the days when they loathed each other and Ezra had a backbone. I was completely unnerved when they became inseparable, back before that fateful night when this island became truly divided.

Nigel scoffs and keeps walking past the cemetery as if it's the most normal thing in the world. He actually starts whistling to himself as he glides ahead, and Ezra shakes his head.

I finally make eye contact with Ezra, though he doesn't give me any hint of emotion other than the blank stare he's been giving me for the two days I've been with him. His face is entirely unreadable, and I wonder if he—among others on this island, including myself—is simply shutting off his emotions to cope with the stark realities that we live in. That would explain Ezra's sudden lack of interest in Naomi and how he became a shell of the alpha athlete I knew only months before.

I need to find a way to reawaken the essence of his true self, and Maison holds the key to that. I can sense that he genuinely cares, not necessarily about me, but about the people in his life. The mere mention of Maison brings him to life. Maison seems to have that effect on everyone, even in death—except for Micah, who seems to want to erase him from existence.

My eyes glance down to Ezra's hand as I walk, and I'm immediately reminded that it might not be so easy when I see his thumb twitching—sticking out from the four scarred nubs where his fingers used to be.

I watch him, even as he turns his head back to keep an eye on me, and I wonder how he survived that, how he's coping with the loss of his fingers, and how he and Nigel survived this deep freeze, if not on the airplane.

Most importantly, why does Ezra have this strange loyalty to Nigel?

I guess it's not like he'd be welcomed by the others, so perhaps he has no other choice. This island is truly divided, and I have no idea whose side I'm actually on.

My heart sinks thinking of Micah with Naomi and how quickly things have changed. She's now the one wearing my clothes, eating my food, and sleeping in my spot, all the while plotting to steal from Micah by wrapping her lips around him. Or, perhaps, he was her goal this entire time. If she's the reason why he hasn't come after me, I will never speak to him again.

That's unforgivable.

We finally pass the bodies and head north along the tundra. Slowly, we start to veer west. To my relief, we begin a descent into the lower terrains, where the land is lusher and the number of death pits reduced. The clear sky is now an inky black as dusk settles upon us, and I'm not sure how long they expect to keep going. We must be close to wherever they are taking me.

Nigel is ahead, and I wonder if I could push him into one of the open pits in the earth if I were fast enough. He would fall into oblivion, and no one would miss him.

I'd be doing this world a favor.

Nigel abruptly stops in front of one of these said death pits. "We're here," he says sweetly, turning around to look at me.

I narrow my eyes in confusion, straining to see any sign of movement or life.

Just darkness and ice.

He pushes me, and I fall into that darkness, landing with a maddening *thud*.

"Fuck," I cry out as I land hard and a sharp pain snakes up my hand, the wind stolen from my lungs. I have to bite the inside of my cheek to will away the pain. As I regain my senses, I turn my head around, standing on all fours—almost catlike—to get my bearings.

It's not a deep hole, but it's deep enough that I can't get out on my own, which was likely the point of throwing me in here. This was well-planned. It seems that everything they are plotting is connected to their belief that I am essential to their survival. A crumpled blanket lies frozen and wet inside the pit, with extra sweaters nearby.

Planned indeed.

"You can't just leave me here," I scream at them, mustering any energy I have left. "I'll die tonight." The cold alone will kill me if not an animal or the lack of water or food. As the temperature starts decreasing sharply, goosebumps rise on my skin. It's a stark contrast to the day's earlier teasing warmth from the sun.

It's even colder down here.

It's Nigel who answers me. "This is where you get to stay. It's your new home, London, so settle in. We'll be back."

I shuffle myself up and scramble to the side, trying to climb despite my lame arm. "How long do you plan to keep me like this?" I scream. We are so deep in the wilderness. Micah will never find me—if he's even looking.

Nigel's stalky silhouette looms above me, and he shrugs. "Maybe forever, or perhaps, until you decide you'd like to cooperate. You don't seem like you want to work with me, London, and that insults me. We used to be such a team."

Me. Not us. And here I thought he and Ezra were aligned.

I bite back a snarled response. He completely used me at the time, and I easily fell for his lies. However, perhaps I should thank him. After all, he's the reason I fell so deeply for the twins, and my bone-crushing love for them was worth it.

Nigel disappears, and Ezra slides into my field of vision.

He hesitates, just for a second.

But a second is all I need.

"I can help you," I say calmly, almost in a whisper, hoping Nigel doesn't overhear. "Instead of just leaving me here to die, I could help you hunt, help you find food. You know Micah taught me a lot about trapping animals." I pause, waiting for him to respond, but he remains quiet and still as a statue.

His eyes stay locked on mine, his face torn between conflicting emotions, which urges me to continue. "Otherwise, you'll die. Both of you will wither away and fucking rot. I'm the best chance you have, Ezra."

His only chance since, clearly, Naomi is not in the picture any longer.

"You don't know that," Ezra says, running his hands through his hair. "You don't know anything."

I slap the side of the pit with my good hand. "Bullshit. You ate all your food. You're beyond desperate right now—I can tell by how thin you are. Ezra, I can help you go back to the others. You don't need him."

He shakes his head. "No, fuck that. You need to experience what we all went through this winter, London. You have no idea." He seems to be battling with himself—a part of him wants to help me, I know it.

I shut my eyes. "Please, Ezra. Don't let him do this." Chills run through my body, and not because of the ice in the air. My injured hand is infected. It burns and oozes from where the wire scraped my bones. My nightmare is playing out, and I've seen firsthand what can happen.

I truly don't know if I will survive the night. The only other nights I slept outside in the elements like this were when Maison or Micah were with me, at least.

"Ezra," I plead again, and he pauses for a moment as if wanting to say something meaningful.

"I can't help you, London. I'm sorry," he says before disappearing, leaving me in this dark hole alone with my misery.

"Please don't do this," I shout once more out of pure desperation, grasping my hair and pulling it. "Please, please, please." My screams are reduced to shallow whispers, swallowed by the silence around me. I don't know what's worse: the vast emptiness of the Alaskan wilderness or the inky stone walls crushing every ounce of hope out of me.

The air embodies death.

The wind doesn't rustle the trees in this place; there are no trees. No waves crashing, no calming sound of the creek.

Just frightening silence as I lie in the unsettling quiet, grasping my throat, sliding my thumb over the tiny cut. The realization of how narrowly I escaped death hits me like a punch to the gut.

Even though I've thought about death more than I care to admit over the past couple of days, the human spirit has an innate will to live. That is why Nigel, the miserable creature that he is, is still alive. Given the choice, the instinct for self-preservation compels most individuals to choose life, even in the most dire of circumstances, only considering the latter when life doesn't seem like the best choice anymore.

I'm getting close to that point...

Once in a while, through the sounds of my chattering teeth, I hear the earth crack, as if these stone walls might come tumbling down. Eventually, I wrap my hands around my knees and shiver, holding on to one sliver of hope: Ezra apologized to me... He's never once apologized for anything, and that is what is keeping me from drowning in panic.

Too tired to keep my head up, I plant my face against the ground and shudder as the cold pool of slush nearby trickles into my mouth and nose. My bones are chilled to their very core. If I'm lucky, I will suffocate in this slushy snow.

I keep mouthing the word *please* as if that will make any difference. Micah needs to come for me; I'll die otherwise. However, I know he won't. He won't find me here because, even with his tracking skills, this cave is too well-hidden.

I start to numb my senses, disregarding my wet hair and soaked clothes. My vision blends into the darkness, but my mind is solely focused on the thought that Micah might be with her. It's a painfully vivid image, one I've unfortunately witnessed before.

I let out one more sob before my eyes close from utter exhaustion, resting my head against the cold stone wall. "Micah, where are you? Please find me." Even after all I've been through, saying his name comforts me, and begging is natural at this point.

At least an hour goes by, then another. I refuse to sleep, worried I might never wake up if I do. Eventually, the laughter returns, low at first but there all the same. I begin to pull my hair, willing it to stop, knowing this is a sign of my growing insanity. I pull it hard, then start to scratch my arm, digging my fingers into my flesh to keep myself awake. I only manage to stay alert by observing how my breath seems to slither and shine as if frozen in the moonlight peeking through the clouds. I shift my gaze upward, and my heart stops when a flash of green blooms from the dark inky sky above me and dances through the night.

The laughter eases, and my mouth momentarily gapes. Tears sting my eyes as I remember that fateful first night I spent with Maison, and I'm able to stall my descent into delirium and calm my painful breathing by focusing on that memory.

Hope. A sign. My lifeline.

The whispers ebb and flow, and time seems to stand still. I'm not asleep, though I'm certainly not awake. My stomach is like liquid clay, and the pain is excruciating.

I close my eyes and sway back and forth. I wish Maison would come to me as he did the last time I was held captive like this.

When Micah held me captive.

Maison doesn't appear... but the laughter returns.

Nigel's laugh... and it takes me a few seconds to realize I am not actually hallucinating.

"What the fuck do you want, Nigel?" I ask him, feeling his evil presence lingering above. He's alone. "Where's Ezra?"

He clicks his tongue. "Ezra doesn't trust you, London."

I scoff, the sound echoing over the rocks, my feeble attempt at hiding the cracks in my spirit. He's breaking me. "Just kill me, Nigel. I know you want to."

Anything is better than staying here like this.

"Oh, I plan to. I'm going to starve you, London. But before I'm done with you, you will feel true hunger, and you'll know what it was like for the rest of us this winter while you hid in your glamorous life."

I shudder at the thought. He would do that, too. His hatred for me, as unwarranted as it is, runs deep. Our emotions are so heightened that his true self shines through, as it does for all of us.

Who am I when stripped to the bare minimum?

I haven't stopped to think about that. My existential crisis is short-lived when Nigel kicks rocks down on my head. I bite the inside of my cheek and place my arms above my head to stop them from cracking my skull.

"You had the same amount of food as we did," I remind him, happy I still have some sense of wit. "So, what's the real reason why you're doing this?"

He snickers and kicks one more large rock, barely missing my head. "Because I can, London. Do I need any more reasons than that?"

He finally stops and chuckles to himself, and I let him humiliate me, not even trying to move.

A few agonizing seconds go by before I finally say, "Where have you been hiding, Nigel? Aren't you tired of your miserable existence yet?" I'm egging him on, but I have nothing left, and me egging him on makes him weak. He's emotional, just like me, and he usually gives me information when I push him. The astute journalist is just as stupid as I am. I've outwitted him several times on this island. I just need to stay strong.

"You're fucking looking at it." He takes a heavy breath. "Have you ever seen someone die of dehydration?" he muses as if he is looking at the dancing lights above us, too.

He pauses as if I am actually going to answer him.

"Your blood will thicken. Your organs will shut down one by one. You'll shit yourself and hallucinate. I've heard dying of thirst is a terrible way to die. Even your brain cells will start to shrink. Your stomach will eat itself, and your veins will dry up."

I wonder if that is why he is the way he is. His brain cells have morphed so much that he has become a shell of who he once was. That's why he has become a predator, a murderer—utterly psychotic.

"Nighty night, London."

Psycho. He's lost his damn mind.

I sit stiff as a board, my back pressed against the rock, hoping that he somehow falls into one of these pits on his way back to whatever dreadful hole he calls home. I let out an uncontrollable sob when he finally shuffles away.

It's a calm night, the moon now completely hidden within the shadows of the clouds. I can hear the snowfall as it hits the earth, though, as still as the night itself. With each flake hitting my face, I feel a chill as a short storm blows through this already miserable night. As if it could get any worse.

I'm not sure how much time goes by. Every time I drift off, my head hangs to the side, waking me up only so I can whip it back up. Alerting myself once again.

I guess I want to live, after all.

I listen to the sounds around me to bring myself some comfort. Just like I did with Micah. I used to listen to the snow, and he would tease me about it and say it was impossible for the human ear to hear a snowflake fall to the ground. I argued that it wasn't a single snowflake but a million snowflakes falling at once. How could you not hear it?

He would smile at me like I was an idiot, but then he would explain all the sounds of the forest. Describe every bird's call. Make me listen while he annoyingly told me what insects each bird eats. He would go on about it for an hour while I secretly listened to the snow and pretended to care. But really, I would stare at him, so happy he was showing me a part of himself that I knew he never showed anyone else.

Another whisper hits the air.

Another voice.

"London." I whip my eyes open but can't see anything, just shadow, darkness, and spring snow. A ghost, probably of one of the fallen. I'm no doubt hallucinating the tall figure standing before me—the Grim Reaper finally coming to claim me. Either that, or it's Nigel again, and I'm not sure which one is worse.

"Get away from me." I scramble back and kick at him, my foot connecting with flesh.

"Fuck you! That hurt."

Ezra!

I take a moment to decipher if it's really him, not trusting myself anymore. I blink a few times, and he puts his hand on my arm to settle me. "What are you doing?" I ask him.

"I came to get you."

I sniffle and wipe the wetness dripping off my nose. "Why?"

"Because you're useless to me if you die of hypothermia. You're coming with me."

I cock my head at him. "Does Nigel know you're doing this?"

"No, and he won't... Not yet, anyway. Get up. He'll be gone until morning."

I have so many questions, but I don't linger. He helps me up, and as my knees weaken and my hand throbs, I fall into his arms.

I stare up at the dark outline of the steep rock wall in front of me. He jumped right in here and landed straight on his feet. That's something I could imagine Micah doing. It must be an athlete thing. I forgot how good of an athlete Ezra was, too.

He crouches on all fours. "Stand on my back and pull yourself up."

My eyes widen, but I don't argue. I stand on his back, and as unsteady as I am, he is a firm anchor beneath me. I can barely reach the top, but it's enough to grip the rock with my good hand. I need to use both hands, but I don't think I can. The pain is immeasurable.

"Shit," I cry out as I fall behind him, landing right on my tailbone. "My hand... I can't."

He grinds his teeth together and shakes his head in frustration. "Fuck, fine. Come here."

He wraps his hands around my knees and hoists me up. I'm higher this time, and he positions himself underneath me. I'm able to get a steady footing on his shoulders and a better grip to, hopefully, pull myself up.

Ezra moves faster. He isn't nice about it as he crouches and hurls me up over the rock, where I slam into the slimy ground.

"Fuck," I yell at him. "Do you have to be so rough?"

I'm still on the ground as he pulls himself up effortlessly, even with his lame hand. A commonality we apparently have.

He grabs my elbow and leads me through the dark. "Come on, my shelter's this way."

His shelter? So they do live here, in the most hellish part of the island.

This should be interesting.

We walk for a bit through the gnarled trees. I follow him, clinging to his arm so the branches of those trees don't reach down and eat me.

Smoke... a thick, dense smoke fills the air.

More than a campfire—this looks like a forest fire. I can taste the ash.

"There's a fire nearby." It's not a question. Something surely isn't right, and this landscape seems ripe for fires.

"Yeah, the smoke came in an hour ago. The moon is red."

I glance up and see the blood-red moon, full and bright above us. It looks like it bears the mark of the devil. I shudder, thinking about what that could mean given how clear it was earlier.

Ezra leads me into the night, and I lean into him as he helps me take every step. He sighs and, eventually, pulls me into his arms as he navigates in the dark.

I instantly warm up, and I hate that I like it. I so desperately wish it was Micah warming me, but Ezra Schwartz is better than nothing.

We finally come upon another small death hole, and my stomach drops when I see a faint glow. He pauses in front of it, and I peer down, still in his arms. Red embers radiate from inside. A few feet away, a tiny hole is dug into the earth, with the only tarp we have on this island expertly placed inside it. Apparently, his shelter is in a death hole. The same as my prison, but this one is much nicer. I peer down again. It's not as deep as the hole I was in, and he has blankets—lots of them—piled up. No roof per se, but a natural dip in the earth creates a small cave deep within, and the tarp would do the trick to shelter from the elements.

I'm actually impressed. This is a fantastic place to hide and would have provided exceptional insulation during the deep freeze. I'm sure Nigel has his lair somewhere nearby, too. All the pieces start to fit together in my mind, especially how they are still breathing.

"Is this where you live now?" I ask him.

"Yeah, it's better than that fucking lake site and the shithole shelter Micah made us. I'm covered from the elements, and I can have a fire without the fucking thing burning down."

I chuckle because the way he says it tells me he knows from experience.

I look around for Nigel, for any spark of human life other than the two of us.

"Where is he?" I ask cautiously. Saying his name out loud causes my body to have a visceral reaction.

"He's close."

I don't push my luck to ask where or how far, grateful I get to sleep on something much more comfortable than the bedrock I was forced to lie on for the past few hours. The thick pile of clothes and blankets he used to construct a bed will do just fine.

He twitches his head, his beady eyes taking me in. "Get in."

He's sharing his bed with me, and I don't know what to make of it. I hop down and sit cross-legged on the bed as he joins me. He fusses beside me, blowing on the embers so they heat but don't flame. It's enough to provide a comforting warmth in the tiny cave, and it casts a pleasant glow of calming, flickering light. As I watch him, he reminds me of Micah, not settling until the very last minute. Focused, brooding, and stronger than I gave him credit for.

He survived some serious shit, and as much as I hate him or am supposed to hate him, right now, I am grateful for him. Dare I say, I'm seeing, just a teensy bit, of what Naomi sees in him.

A kernel.

He sits beside me, sprawling his long legs out in front of him and finally relaxing, as if my presence here makes him super uncomfortable. I am stiff, too, like I don't really know whether I should lie down or not. He did, after all, kidnap me and keep me in captivity for two days, and he was the one who knocked me out.

"I'm not making a fire tonight, so settle in," he finally grunts. He looks stressed, his elbows on his knees, his head in his hands. I hesitate, secretly worried that he will choke me in my sleep, that this is some sort of ruse to get me to trust him.

This *sad* version of Ezra is... interesting.

He senses my nervous energy. "I'm not going to hurt you, London. At least, not right now, so go to sleep." I might have been feisty earlier, but being with these guys has certainly broken my spirit and humbled me. My looks have little effect on Ezra and Nigel, unlike Micah and Maison, who started swooning the moment they laid eyes on me.

"Why are you suddenly being so nice to me?" I ask him, feeling brave. Shifting to get more comfortable, I enjoy the heat from the embers on my skin. I lie down, using my arm as a pillow, my injured one cradled against me.

His sad eyes shutter. "I don't think you would have lived through the night, despite what Nigel thinks. And... I don't want to be fucking alone, and I don't want to spend time with him. Since you're here right now, you're kind of my only option."

I can't help but look at him—how tired he looks, how ravaged he is, and how hard it must have been to admit that to me.

"But don't fucking test me," he snaps as if sensing how nice he's being. He finally lays his head back. He hands me a bottle of water, and I accept it, although I inspect it before drinking. "It's fine. It's from melted snow. It's clean; I've been drinking it and haven't gotten sick."

I take a swig and drink down the entire thing. Instantly, I feel better.

Water. Always drink the water.

Until it melts to nothing.

"You have no clean source of water here," I point out. "You know you can't last much longer in this place. Once the snow melts, you have to go back. You can't hide from Micah forever."

He answers with a grumbling stomach.

Awkwardly, he lies down beside me, close enough to provide a blanket of warmth, but far enough to be appropriate given the circumstances.

"Get some sleep. We're hunting tomorrow."

I huff. "I can barely move, Ezra. My hand is..."

He reaches for it, and I wince. He slowly unwraps the bandage and inspects it, shaking his head. "He did this to you, didn't he?"

I don't respond. I don't want him to know what Micah did to me. I've been trying to downplay it since it happened. I hoped he wouldn't care enough to look.

He grabs what's left of the clean water and washes the scrapes and the bits of hanging skin. I haven't wanted to see how bad it is, but the discoloration says enough.

The swelling, the bruising, the cuts... It's bad.

He wraps it back up without asking any more questions.

He knows... He senses how toxic Micah and I are.

I wipe the sweat dripping from my forehead. "I need to eat, Ezra. Please, can I have something?"

A pause, and his entire body goes rigid. "There is no more food, London. It's gone... all of it.

My breath hitches. I knew they were low, but out? Completely?

I blow out a breath. "Is that why Naomi left?" She was clearly here; her mark is all over this place. The two of them spent the winter in this very spot. Surviving, relying on each other, easing their pain, loss, and suffering, just like Micah and I did. Yet, both decided to leave us...

His mouth curls. "She said she was going to see what she could find and come right back. We both knew the others wouldn't welcome me back, so we couldn't go together. We knew I'd ruin any chance we'd have of living. So she left, and she never came back... so fuck her."

Traitorous bitch.

"I'm sorry, Ezra. You didn't deserve to be abandoned like that."

He scoffs. "So, if you want to eat, you have to help me hunt. There is no fucking choice. Either that, or you die."

He must have something... *anything.*

"If you want me to have any fucking strength to hunt, I need something now..."

I can imagine his eyes rolling. "Fucking chicks, man," he mutters but hands me a piece of dried meat he had hidden.

I knew it.

He pulls a blanket over him and rolls over in the other direction. "This is the last of it. There is no more fucking food, London."

I take a small bite and savor the taste, swallowing it slowly.

He's wrong... It's not the last of it. I know exactly where more food is—a whole pile of it. Am I capable of betraying Micah by telling Ezra where the cabin is? Micah seems to have no problem betraying me.

"Ezra, I..."

"Go the fuck to sleep before I throw you back in that hole. And if you fucking snore or do any more of that weird laughing shit, I'm going to gag you."

With a dismissive scoff, I roll in the opposite direction, avoiding any further conversation. With a sense of contentment, I drift off to sleep and am grateful for the companionship that banishes the echoes of laughter that have plagued me for countless nights.

CHAPTER FOURTEEN

MICAH

I take my time walking back to the cabin with two small Northern pikes in my hand. I've spent most of my time at the river for the past two days, and Naomi has only been awake for a fraction of that time. She's been fighting a fever and moaning in her sleep. Twice, I thought she was dead, and twice, I thought about killing her myself and putting her out of her misery. Once last night and once this morning.

I was so close... if she only knew.

London is back with Jade. I'm not entirely sure, but I have a strong feeling that's where she would have gone, and just thinking about it makes me fucking furious. I stared at her footprints for an hour, playing out what could have happened—how she got free and how she knew where to go after repeatedly warning her not to leave. All signs now confirm that she's gone. She practically screamed that she didn't want to be here anymore, and I ignored her.

But deep down, I knew—*I fucking knew.* That's why I tied her up.

I've been tempted to go and see for myself, but with Naomi's condition worsening, I couldn't bring myself to leave for longer than a couple of hours. She'll die if I do. I also can't leave her alone with my food and supplies because I don't fucking trust her, which leaves me in quite the predicament.

I stride to the firepit, grab my knife, drop to my knees, and stab the fish in the eye, gutting it. As I cook, I sit back and wait, playing with the tip of my bone weapon, letting it pierce my flesh and watching as the blood trickles down my skin.

The unsettling part isn't the choices I'm contemplating; it's the fact that I'm unbothered by them. Once the thought of killing Naomi entered my mind, it became impossible to erase. It proves that the darkness within me has always existed, and right now, my only connection to humanity revolves around one person.

London.

She is always the one keeping me sane, even if she doesn't realize it. And Naomi is merely in the way. A problem easily solved.

Eventually, I head inside. I push open the door to the cabin and step inside, staring at Naomi. My emotions are hollow—a dark void somewhere deep within—and I can't be bothered to find them. Naomi hasn't moved since I left her, sleeping soundly like a lamb to the slaughter. Her blonde hair is splayed out on the bed, combed and clean because I made it that way.

Fucking helpless.

Goddammit.

My dick gets excited thinking about the times I've fucked London right in this spot, as helpless as this girl in front of me who's moaning in her sleep, and how much I enjoyed London being just as needy.

My groin tightens, and I slide in next to Naomi, checking her fever. I keep my distance and control these intense urges I have as I watch her chest rise and fall in my bed, fantasizing about what it would feel like to take the air from her lungs while simultaneously thinking about fucking her. I'm fully aware of how messed up that is.

I remind myself I'm only turned on because I'm used to getting my dick sucked daily, and right now, the wrong fucking girl is in my bed, even if she's slowly becoming my backup plan.

Fuck, London. Where are you, baby?

I fall asleep quickly, even though it's the afternoon. I usually don't like to waste the daylight hours by sleeping, but I'm fucking tired and clearly not thinking straight.

My eyes shoot open a little while later. My mind is fuzzy, my body alert. I was asleep—a deep fucking sleep—which rarely happens. I can tell Naomi is awake, even without looking, because her energy has shifted. Her head is propped on her hand, and her big brown eyes are scrutinizing me. Her pupils are dilated, but she's more aware than she's been since I found her. I turn to face her, seeing she's been awake for a while.

Her fever broke, and beads of sweat pool over her forehead. I arch my brows, not letting her know she has rattled me. It was so careless to fall asleep without realizing she was awake and alert like this. She could have done anything she wanted to me, and I would have been powerless to stop her.

She parts her lips. "What are you going to do with me now, Micah?" she asks in a tone that's equally sexual and hostile. She's wary, as she should be. I don't recognize myself anymore, either.

I keep my voice even, trying not to scare her yet. "I'm not going to do anything with you right now, Naomi." Her lips tilt upward, and her eyes flash. Clearly, she's enjoying this and has no idea that London is the only reason she's still breathing.

"Why did you bring me here, then?"

I roll over her, pressing my hands on either side of her, and keep my body a healthy distance away. "You're not going to be the one asking questions, Naomi. Where are Nigel and Ezra? How long had you been away from them when I found you?"

She pauses for a moment before answering, probably thinking long and hard about whether she wants to lie to me right now. "One day, as soon as the weather broke, I left him."

At the same time I left London. What are the fucking odds?

"Stop fucking lying, Naomi. Is London with them? Why did you leave them?"

A massive knot forms in my stomach. What if I'm wrong, and I missed something? What if London isn't with Jade... and she's been with Ezra and Nigel these last few days? I could never forgive myself for choosing to help Naomi. What if London covered her tracks well enough, then something happened in the forest?

I should have left Naomi at the lake site. The others would have found her eventually.

A flush hits her cheeks, making me feel like she's lying, and I suppress the urge to resort to physical violence to get her to talk. If London is with Ezra and Nigel, Naomi is the only living person who can help me find her quickly. And she can't help me if I suck the air out of her lungs.

I lean down so my mouth is close to hers. "Fucking. Tell. Me."

She stiffens beneath me and bites her lower lip. "I don't know. How the fuck would I know where London is?"

My eyes narrow. "So, why did you leave them?"

She blinks, keeping her gaze steady, her body warm beneath mine. "We ran out of food," she admits. "I was trying to find the creek camp, but I didn't make it. I'm not lying to you, Micah. I would never lie to you. You know how I feel about you."

Feel... as in present tense.

I lock my gaze with hers, searching her eyes for any sign of lies, and remain silent. My jaw flexes, annoyed that her story is actually adding up. I can tell she isn't totally lying, but she definitely knows more than she's letting on, which gives me extreme pause.

She shifts her body and raises her knee between my legs. Fuck.

I ease the tension and roll off her. She knows me well enough to know I'm turned on right now and is playing it to her advantage. I rise out of bed and pull on a sweater. Grabbing a piece of wood, I start carving. Anything to keep my hands busy and ignore this half-naked girl in my bed.

She pretends to ignore me as she pulls the blanket off her and leans over the bed to grab a new T-shirt that's not sweat-stained from her fever. I can't help but watch her change, and when she pulls up, she smirks at me.

It looks like the confident Naomi is back.

She lies down, resting her head on one of the bedposts, and picks at her nails. I side-glance her way as I blow wood dust off my carving, and she looks anything but impressed. Bored almost, even if she still looks pale as a fucking ghost.

"Do you want to fuck me right now?" she eventually asks, not looking up.

I cock my head, steadying my knife. "Nope. I want to know where my girlfriend is."

"Liar."

I scoff at her brazenness. "What about Ezra?"

"What about him?"

"Aren't you with him, Naomi?"

She raises an eyebrow. "Does it look like I'm with him?"

Good point.

Fuck. Naomi will be the death of me.

I flip the knife in my hand, focusing on it instead of her. "I have a girlfriend, Naomi, so get any ideas you have out of your head. Despite her absence right now, I'm still loyal to her."

She shakes her head. Sitting cross-legged, she begins to comb her hair with her hands. "So, suddenly, you're loyal to only one girl? Is she the one, Micah? The one who finally tamed you? Because I call bullshit. I will never understand the two of you together. You don't belong with her. She was Maison's... and so was Olivia. Why do you go after Maison's girls?"

This has my stomach turning in on itself. "Who the fuck do you think I belong with, Naomi? You?"

She presses her lips together, and her eyes glaze over. "Look around. You might not have a choice in that matter anymore. You can fight it as long as you want, Micah, but we always get pulled back to each other. No one put a gun to your head to bring me with you when you found me, but here we are. She isn't here, and you seem rather surprised by that, like maybe she left voluntarily. So maybe you care about me a bit more than you think you do."

My fingers clench. "You know nothing about my relationship with London, so quit pretending like you do."

The hurt in her eyes is evident. All that emotion is bundled up and manifests into the look she's giving me right now.

I never properly ended things with Naomi. I quit talking to her when I realized who I was in love with. I did the same to her when I broke things off with Olivia and tried to use Naomi to make Olivia jealous. I told Naomi I'd date her after I stole her virginity by the urinal to make her feel better.

Finally, after a few seconds, she says, "What do they have that I don't?"

I blink at her, not really understanding her question or who she is referring to. I cross my arms and say nothing.

After Olivia died and I came back to New Ocean, my anger got the better of me, and I hated seeing how happy everyone was. I started fucking Naomi again to see if that would make me feel alive and to get revenge on Ezra for stealing my glory goal and basically a whole hockey season from me. But it didn't work; I was still tortured inside. It wasn't fair to her, and I guess it was a harsh punishment for Ezra.

"Olivia and London," she responds carefully, knowing I probably look confused. "You chose them over me. Did you not like having sex with me? Am I not pretty enough for you?"

I shake my head and sit on the side of the bed. As much as I don't want to have this conversation, it seems like it's happening, and the last thing I want is to upset her. "You're a gorgeous girl, Naomi. You know that, though."

She folds her arms as if suddenly feeling self-conscious that she's throwing herself at me again and that I'm denying her. "So what is it, then?"

"Naomi. Don't do this."

She purses her lips. "I want to understand... I thought, after the Gala, before all that Olivia shit, you said... You lied to me, Micah. And I didn't deserve that."

I lean up and place the blanket over her tits to hide her naked body and to help distract the physical response to her I shouldn't be having.

She rolls to her side and lets me tuck her in. "Were you having sex with her at the same time as me?"

I lower my eyes and draw my hand back. "Yeah."

Her eyes widen at my sudden admission. "Do you even know which *her* I'm referring to right now?"

"No," I admit.

Shit... I really don't. I was screwing Naomi when I first became attracted to London. When London watched me with Naomi in the woods, I knew right then that I wanted her and it was the wrong girl pleasuring me. I could tell how much London wanted me then, even if she didn't know it yet.

Naomi kicks at me. "Fuck you, Micah. Just fuck you."

She looks tired and pale, and right now, I don't have the energy for this shit, and I certainly do not want to have this conversation.

I crawl in next to her as she lays her head on the bed, defeated, refusing to look at me. "You need some water and rest." I grab the bottle I left near the bed and lift her head. She takes a tiny sip and sinks back down on the bed, her eyes locked on the outside. Her eyes are still sunk deep into her face and blood-shot. She's far from the healthy and vibrant girl I had considered a friend. I help her get more comfortable, covering her with an oversized sweater.

"Are you hungry?" I ask.

She nods hesitantly but still refuses to look at me.

I'm not sure when she ate for the last time, so I hand her a piece of leftover fish and give her some space to eat it, sitting on the edge of the bed with my elbows on my knees.

"Eat up, Naomi. Because as soon as you're feeling better, we're leaving," I say, turning to face her.

Her eyes widen. "Where are we going?"

"You are going to show me exactly where your boyfriend is hiding."

She blinks at me a few times before taking a bite of fish like it's poison. The opposite of London, who would have ripped that fish out of my hands to get her teeth on it. "Are you going to hurt him again?"

"That depends."

"Depends on what?"

"It depends on whether you're lying to me right now."

After two days, Naomi's health shows signs of improvement. I feed her what I can, which isn't much since the fish aren't biting and having her is throwing me off my game. I've been tense, more than usual, missing the fuck out of my girlfriend and wishing she was in front of me so I could apologize, worship her, and make everything right.

A warm breeze brushes my skin as I crouch and watch the furry squirrel eying the bait I set inside the wire trap a few minutes earlier.

That's right, eat the bait, you little fucker.

I followed the critter for an hour, waiting for the perfect moment to place my trap to catch it. The hunger pains are constant, but it's my desire to hunt and kill something with my bare hands that drives me. Maybe then, this void in my heart will be filled, and this relentless craving that has taken over me will finally be satisfied.

I've been avoiding spending too much time with Naomi because the intensity of this feeling is growing. Every time I hold my knife, slicing little pieces off the wood, I'm drawn to the graceful curve of her neck as she swallows and watches me from her deathbed, drilling me with a death glare of her own. If she only recognized the insidiousness of my thoughts.

The snow is melting more every day. I hold on to the hope that London will walk up through the shadows of the trees and come back to me. Now that spring has arrived, more animals are out. The birds are migrating, so the forest is much more cheery and alive. I bet London would love it right now after being cooped up inside for so long. I wish I could show her all the species of birds that live in these woods. I want to prove to her that life with me isn't terrible and that she didn't have to leave. Anything to go back and do things differently so she was still here with me.

As time goes on since I've been away from her, I've gotten more withdrawn, enjoying the quiet of the wilderness a little too much. I'm slowly starting to become one with it, losing myself in it—not caring about anything past the hum of the forest or planning my next kill. I lurk around these woods, studying every branch and every paw print in the mud of an animal that will eventually become my prey.

I've lost sight of the squirrel, but it will be back—the smell of fish is too enticing. I'm not bothered; I can easily sit for hours in silence, merely existing in my domain.

Watching... Waiting... Hunting. It's what I live for.

Sometimes, I hardly notice if I'm breathing. Anytime I hear Maison, I expel him from my mind.

The squirrel squeaks as it scurries across the ground right in front of me while I lie on my stomach in wait. It notices me and seems unbothered, and I stay utterly still. It stops, waits... twitches its face.

As soon as it gets tangled up in my little web of wire and takes my bait, it's mine. My stomach grumbles thinking about it, and I push that sensation out of my mind, too. I have to be stronger than the forces that work against me. I have to be stronger than everything else and not let something as trivial as hunger weaken me, and to do that, I must transcend.

I still have enough canned food to last me at least six more months if I don't eat it. Theoretically, I could last another winter. The problem is everyone else still breathing who will want it, and I'm not giving it up—over my dead body.

Finally, the squirrel bites, and I almost miss it. I regain my focus on its speckled tail long enough for me to pounce. I catch it and jab my bone weapon right into it. The kill wasn't satisfying enough, though.

I need something bigger next time.

I grab my meal and head back to Naomi. A coiling rage burns inside me for reasons I can't fathom right now. Of course, she's sleeping, but I note the fresh firewood piled up nearby. She was always better at gathering firewood than London. London, however, is better at other things...

She sits up, and her gaze cuts to me when I walk in. "Where were you, Micah? You were gone for four hours. I thought you weren't coming back."

I almost didn't. I spent two of those hours contemplating whether I should just cure this desire by jumping into the river. The problem, I'm realizing, is that there are few desirable ways to kill yourself on a deserted island—none that would be efficient enough for me.

I let the wooden door slam behind me as I walk in.

She jolts back. "What's wrong with you?"

I'm getting really fucking sick of people asking me that.

I cock my head. "Sorry, sweetheart. I don't answer to you. I apologize if life with me is not what you were expecting."

Apparently, it wasn't for London, either.

I pull off my sweater, and her eyes draw down to my abs. I've lost a touch of weight, although I am still strong and as lean as I used to be. I ignore her lingering eyes and crawl in next to her. When we sleep at the same time, which is rare, it's in the same bed, but I make sure not to touch her, even though she's pressed right up against me every morning. I usually wake up earlier than her and slip out of bed before she can try anything. Luckily, she's been too tired and weak to do much other than sleep a lot.

I don't berate her about where Nigel and Ezra are hiding, but she continues to endlessly whine and complain about literally everything. Those are the moments when I think the most about putting an end to her misery.

She asks why I won't tell her where I'm hiding the food or why I won't feed her any of it.

She complains that she's cold and tired. And that the shack smells funny, that London's things are everywhere, and how that's weird for her.

And, and, and...

Fucking hell. If I end up spending the end of my days with Naomi, I'll have to teach her to shut up. I'm not sure why Ezra is so obsessed with her.

I turn to face her, and my heart sinks when I see her cheeks are tear-stained. Fuck, I hate seeing girls cry. Seeing them emotional is my Achilles heel and the only reason that keeps me from believing I'm a *total* asshole.

I arch a brow at her, giving her my brooding gaze that makes her swoon. "I'm sorry, Naomi. I really am. I'm just really fucked up."

She doesn't smile; she radiates nothing but ice-cold contempt toward me. However, the color is back in her face, her edges are filled in, and her hair has regained a layer of gloss. She's still so mad at me for rejecting her, and I honestly don't blame her, but she can't deny that she's healthy. It seems I have a knack for leaving emotional scars on girls, but physically, they are in bliss when they are with me.

London was no different.

Seeing her in London's tight-fitting tank top makes my jaw clench. My stomach twists, thinking about all the times I've admired London in it over these past few months. However, the tank top is not the same on Naomi because her tits aren't nearly as fucking nice as London's. Which serves as yet another reminder of how badly I've fucked up.

London wore it on the plane, and it took every ounce of control not to reach out and touch her—to see if this girl was real. She thought I was tense because I was angry, which I was, but my physical reaction to her started then. She looked so fucking good standing there, scowling at me, and she didn't even realize it. That's what I love the most about London; she doesn't have to try hard to look good because she's gorgeous all the time.

I can't help but stare at Naomi's tits anyway.

Naomi notices and her energy shifts, which is the exact response I need from her. "So, what do we do now?" she asks cautiously.

I shift my eyes up to meet hers. "I need you to show me where Ezra's hiding."

She shakes her head. "No. I can't do that, Micah. Not after what you did to his hand. I may not want to be with him anymore, but I don't want you to kill or hurt him again."

I wish I could guess exactly where London went so I could go directly to her and not waste any more time than I already have with Naomi and her bullshit. The other side of the island is calling me. Something is itching at me, telling me it's where I need to go first. For that, I need Naomi to cooperate. And since she responds much better to honey than poison...

I sweep the hair falling into her face and brush it behind her ears. "You have to show me, Naomi. You don't have a choice."

She lowers her gaze to my lips, then back to my eyes. Her expression is pained and confused, with a flicker of hesitation. "What is it about her, Micah? It could be us, the future you're imagining right now. I've never left you. I've never wavered in my feelings for you. You were always my first choice. Can you say the same thing about her?"

I regret messing around with Naomi in the early days of being stranded here. My motive was one of pure jealousy, ignited by witnessing Maison's connection with London. London's wandering eyes in the forest filled that hollowness inside me. She wanted me, and I wanted her to want me. I was manipulating Naomi then, and I'm manipulating her now.

She grabs my wrist, then laces my fingers in her hand before twisting them above my head and straddling me.

Fuck. She was always good at playing games, too.

"Naomi," I warn.

"Micah," she whispers, lips tickling my cheek and pressing her chest against me. "London's gone... She left you."

I move my hands to her hips to push her off me, but she doubles down on her grip on my thighs. And fuck me, considering she was nearly dead three days ago, she's strong.

I shake my head, even though I can't dispute what she's saying. "You don't know that."

She runs her hand over my cheek. "Micah, I'm here now. *This* is your reality."

This reminds me so much of Olivia. How Olivia acted when she was manipulating me, and I couldn't see past her pussy. I'd like to think I've grown since then.

Olivia ruined me.

She slides down like a worm, pulling my sweats down with her. My fucking cock is hard, betraying me from her grinding on it, and she moves to take it in her mouth. I close my eyes as it throbs, and Naomi expertly cups it in her hands. I drop my hands, not knowing where to place them.

"You have to stop this, Naomi." I push her just out of reach because if her lips make contact, it's a line I can't uncross.

She knows what I like. Part of me wants to let her do this. My cock twinges just thinking about it and how easy it would be to just let Naomi suck it, as she has so many times before. My body craves it even now.

Just not from her.

Fuck.

London's not here. London fucking left me, but every ounce of me is screaming no, that I need to go find her. This is Naomi's desperate attempt to stay here with me. There is no way this is what I want right now.

She narrows her eyes and fidgets beneath my grip. "Don't feel guilty," she says, peering up at me through her lashes. "I'll do that thing you like with my tongue." Fire blazes in her eyes. "She was never yours, Micah. She was Maison's girlfriend, just like Olivia was. Now she's gone, and you're stuck with me."

I whip her around and slam her on the bed, my hard-on immediately subsiding. This is the girl who beat the shit out of London for no good reason. I won't betray London like this, whether she's dead or alive. No fucking way. I've already let it go too far.

"She is mine, Naomi," I hiss. "She is mine like no other girl has ever been. Not you, not Olivia, not anyone, and I will fucking move mountains to get her back."

She startles and stiffens, her eyes like saucers. "It sure seems like it," she scoffs.

I grip her brittle shoulders with my hands and narrow my eyes. "What the fuck is wrong with you, Naomi? I've treated you like trash for three years. Don't you have any fucking dignity?"

The pain in her eyes surprises me. Like she actually thinks she has a chance.

She laughs darkly. "There you are, Micah. I thought you went all soft on me."

I shake her. "Is this a fucking joke to you? You're not telling me the full story of what happened between you and Ezra, so start fucking talking."

She loves it when I get like this. She constantly tries to pull this reaction out of me; she seeks it out. It's not reciprocated. No more teasing, no more games. I don't want Naomi Wilson, nor do I want to spend the rest of my life with her. I have to find London.

"I have nothing left but my sense of humor, Micah. Because, apparently, you stole my dignity along with my virginity. Which, if I recall, you enjoyed doing."

I ease my grip and tense my jaw. I'm playing right into her games because when I get mad, I get horny, and she is fully aware of that.

"Don't test me, or I'll abandon you in the woods somewhere. If you don't start talking, you'll end up dead because I won't take care of you anymore. I'll drop you in the most remote place I can find, and I'll get the fuck away from you."

"I told you. We ran out of food," she snarls. "I had no choice but to leave him. He wouldn't exactly have been welcome anywhere else. I wasn't in the mood to die, so I left him to find the others. I told him I'd be back... and I just never went back."

She pauses for a moment, a break in her thoughts. "Their plan has always been to find you and take her from you to get you to give up the location of your food. They got your location from Jade."

I listen, pause, and consider, even though this information isn't new to me. What I didn't realize was that Naomi was in on it, which changes everything.

"And your plan, Naomi?"

She slides her eyes to mine, meeting my gaze with fury. "Does it seem like I have a fucking plan?" Her eyes flash with pain. "You won't hurt me, Micah. You can pretend all you want, but we both know you won't."

Heat rolls through my stomach. She has no fucking clue how many times I've thought about killing her these past few days and how I might even enjoy it. Or how many times I've thought about killing myself. I'm turning into a monster. Slowly, day by day, I'm drowning in my darkness as I always knew I would.

I lean forward and cup her cheek, grazing my thumb along her neck. She swallows, and her face goes white.

"Yeah, Naomi, I would hurt you," I whisper, "and that's what you are not quite comprehending."

I rise and pull her up. She fights me but gets on her feet, and I start to yank her forward. "Come on. Get fucking dressed. We're leaving now."

"What do I get out of it?" she snaps, scrambling to put some clothes on and slapping my hand. "If I tell you where they are, what are you going to do with me?"

There she is... This was never about me or her fake feelings for me. She can't be fucking pathetic enough to still want me this badly after the way I treated her. This was planned... meticulously fucking planned. I walked right into it, and now London is probably with some seriously deranged, starving lunatics—one of which killed my brother in cold blood.

I throw on some warm clothes and stuff an extra sweater in my pack, then grab my knife and my bone weapon. I forcefully push Naomi out the door before she even has a chance to blink. "I swear to god, Naomi, if this is some sort of game or trap to lure me away from here, or if they hurt London... I will kill you."

CHAPTER FIFTEEN

LONDON

Day unknown

Sometime in April
Something's happening. Our time on this island is end-ing. I've been held captive and betrayed by the person I trust-ed above all others. And the worst part is that I'm unsure if he is still alive. Ezra, Nigel, and I might be the only people left. If anyone reads this, things are not okay. Real evil exists in this world and comes in many hidden forms. It lingers in all of us. The signs were always there. Nigel needs to be punished for what he is and what he has done. For the world's sake, I hope this pretty little island kills him. If I can manage to stay alive long enough, I won't let him survive this. I will find a way to end him because he doesn't deserve to live through this.

I shut my leather-bound journal and rest my head against the rock. I unwrap the bandage around my wounded hand and attempt to move my fingers. The skin on my hand is scabbing and starting to heal to the point where I'm not worried about infection anymore. Howev-er, it's the lack of pain that scares me the most. By the time I'm done, I'm nearly sweating. I am unable to move a single finger, not even my pinky. Focusing on something other than my hunger or the fact that I have no idea where Ezra has gone helps pass the time, at least. He left an hour ago and said he would be back.

I'm much better today, my body no longer weighed down by extreme fatigue. My fever broke, and Ezra did what he could to keep my hand clean and my fever down. I think he saved my life last night by keeping me hydrated, letting me sip on water from the pools of what's left of the melting snow. It's not ideal, and he knows it. It's only a matter of time—days, if not hours—before we have to find somewhere else to go. That pooled water will start to rot; it's already turning black with mold. Yesterday, I slept the day away, trying not to cry or draw too much attention to the fact that I was there, in his space, sleeping in Naomi's spot.

He left on a few occasions without uttering a word, effortlessly vaulting over the edge of the cave wall and vanishing in a manner reminiscent of Micah. I kept the fire going while he was gone, staring at those embers, which mesmerized me so much that time had no rhythm. When he came back, he handed me my leather-bound journal, which I stared at in awe, and went about his business, engrossed in whatever he does to keep himself occupied.

I took it as a peace offering since I had lost the book when he slammed ice over my head. I assumed I had dropped it and didn't give it much thought. Ezra seems content with my presence now and hasn't killed me, even though he had every opportunity to. There would have been no resistance from me; I would have willingly surrendered to that darkness.

I press the leather against my cheek, happy to have it back, even though the words written inside terrify me. My eyes grow heavy, so I rest them, and I'm not sure how much time goes by before Ezra jumps into the cave.

"It's time to go, London. We have to meet Nigel."

Tired. I'm so fucking tired of this island and the people on it.

Especially Nigel.

My eyes wearily open, and Ezra is scowling. I thought that at least Ezra didn't want me dead, but forcing me to meet Nigel is basically a death sentence.

"I'd rather not," I say flippantly.

He bends down and grabs me effortlessly, like I'm made of feathers. "We have to meet him. He'll know you're gone by now, and I don't want to make him angry."

"Why is that such a concern for you?" I ask, needles prickling my skin. Ezra lifts me up, placing me on the ground above the cave. My knees are weak, my body thin and broken, and under my baggy clothes, the grime on my body is melting into me.

He jerks his head for me to follow. "Because I don't want him to find this place. I've managed to keep my location a secret from him, and I'd rather keep it that way. He left me a message, though. He wants me to bring you to him."

I hitch a breath and follow him, keeping my eyes wide open. "Ezra, please let me stay with you," I beg.

He doesn't answer, or at least, he pretends he didn't hear me, and I follow him through a few thickets of brush and over the barren rocks, plumes of mist hovering over the wet parts of the ground. The safety and warmth of his cave are replaced by an icy chill cutting through my clothes. I stay near him, almost touching him but not quite. After a few minutes, he reaches back and grabs my good hand, which I hadn't realized was trembling.

"Let me handle this. Don't fucking say anything," Ezra says quietly as we approach wherever their hidden meeting spot is. He holds a hockey skate spear in one hand and hangs onto me with the other. I step back behind him, half expecting Nigel to jump out of the woods and slice me open.

"Why are we even doing this?" I ask him. The last couple of days have been peaceful. Just existing for once, with no intense energy from Micah, no Nigel. Just a peaceful co-existence with Ezra, who seems just as sad and empty as I am.

His sandy blond dreads fall in his face as he turns to face me. What's left of him—which is very little—is reflected in his eyes. "We meet every three days. I think he has more food, and he gives me some if I cooperate with him."

My blood freezes. So his plan is to trade me to Nigel for food?

"Ezra, you're not thinking straight," I whisper. "There is another way."

What I've learned from Ezra is that he gives information in small spurts, but if I push him too much, he will shut down. So, instead, I don't push him and stand by his side. "We can find more food... Nigel isn't the answer."

We approach a small clearing. The ground is dead and muddy, as is everything else in this godforsaken spot. Ezra pauses in front of me. "Quiet, we're here."

I'm not sure where *here* is, exactly. I notice small remnants of a cooking site, with empty cans strewn around and a circle of ash sitting between two fallen logs. My skin crawls as Nigel joins us, emerging from the trees as if he's been watching us for some time. His hair hangs in his face, and his stalky body is withered beneath his clothes.

"I see you've let the bitch out of her pen," he mutters, otherwise dismissing me. A flash of anger flickers in his eyes. In fact, he's seething. He must have gone to check on me—to torment me—only to find me missing. I wish I could have seen his reaction.

Ezra bristles, and because I haven't let go of him, the fingers of my good hand move from his wrist to his muscled back. My body is silently shaking as Nigel carves his deadly eyes over me, his gaze lingering for a moment before his eyebrow twitches.

His wicked presence is so thick in the air that I could choke on it.

"She would have died otherwise," Ezra barks back at him, "and that wasn't part of the plan."

This plan of theirs.

The plan I will derail once I dig my claws further into Ezra. He's already mine, and Nigel senses my hold over him. That's why Nigel's proceeding with caution as Ezra flexes his body in a protective stance. Nigel circles me with his usual snake-like smile like he just captured a mouse.

"You don't get to keep her," he says with finality.

Clearly, Ezra and Nigel can't stand each other. I can't comprehend how Ezra can stand to be around him after what he did to Maison. However, it's not like Ezra has other options. Unless... I'm slowly becoming one.

"Just kill him," I whisper. "You don't need him, Ezra. We'll find his food; it has to be around here."

My heart nearly stops when Nigel steps toward me, keeping his eyes on me the entire time. He pulls something from behind his back and waves it in front of us.

A can of Heinz beans.

My mouth salivates.

Such a simple thing, yet it wields so much power over us all. I understand why Ezra is bound to him. Ezra and Naomi have two mouths to feed, while Nigel has only one. It makes sense that Nigel would still have some food, but they don't.

Nigel merely raises a brow and smiles as Ezra eyes that food like a rabid dog.

Asshole. Vile, despicable asshole.

So humiliating.

"You mean, this food?" Nigel merely shrugs and grins. "Hand her over, and it's yours. And I can forgive you for taking her to begin with," he says, his tone so casual—as if he owns me. As if I'm merely a possession to barter. This is likely why, I'm realizing, Ezra saved me to begin with.

Would Ezra actually hand me over to Nigel, knowing what he's capable of?

Ezra runs his hands through his hair, contemplating. And I can't blame him. I'm nobody to him. He peers at me, then back at Nigel. The pain in his eyes is evident as he grapples with the weight of this seemingly simple choice. I guess that hunger will do that to you.

I refrain from making any sort of facial expression, especially when I can sense Ezra coiling up with tension beside me.

Finally, he says with a shrug, "No, man. I think I'm going to keep her. London is officially off-limits to you."

I suppress a smile, and Nigel's stare hardens as he takes me in, hiding behind Ezra's tall frame.

Nigel takes a careful step back and studies me. "You truly possess a remarkable vagina with extraordinary powers, don't you, London King? Maybe you will let me have a go."

Ezra doesn't respond or react to that insinuation or disgusting threat, and I do my best to stay hidden behind him. I hate Nigel, but he scares the fuck out of me. He killed Maison with zero hesitation in front of everyone. Who knows what he will try to do to me? Ezra is protecting me right now, even though he has no good reason to. This means he has some sort of ulterior motive with me as well.

Nigel scoffs and flicks his wrist. "Do you really want to eat rodents for the rest of your miserable life?"

Speaking of said rodents, one crosses the clearing as if on cue. A muskrat. My instinct is to catch it... Kill it. Eat it.

My stomach twists at the primal urge, and I lunge forward on instinct.

Wild.

It crawls toward Nigel, slow and steady, and we all stare as it squeaks. Ezra takes his spear and throws it. It severs the rat in the heart, a mere foot from Nigel's feet, causing Nigel to stumble back. Ezra steps over to the rat and stares down at it, then pulls the spear from its fat, furry body and rises.

"Yeah," he says, looking at Nigel, and flexes his jaw. "I do."

I could kiss him—I won't because it's Ezra and that's just *gross*, but I could.

Nigel holds his spear, gripping it tightly as if realizing now that he should be scared of Ezra. He steps back, keeping his distance as he walks backward, and finally says, with an acidic lace in his voice, "I'll be seeing you very soon, London. It will be only you and I left on this island. Ezra can only protect you for so long."

That threat will forever haunt my dreams.

Ezra grabs our meal, then my good hand, and pulls me away from the clearing.

I turn to face Nigel, sensing his cold stare piercing my back.

When we are out of earshot, Ezra turns to me. "Quit staring at him, or you'll piss him off more. If it were up to him, he would kill you right here, right now."

My heart stills at that thought and at Ezra's confirmation of what I have long suspected.

Nigel is a stone-cold killer.

When I turn back, Nigel has disappeared into the shadows and mist, and I can breathe again. If only for the moment.

We don't talk on the way back, but I watch him. For whatever reason, Ezra just chose me over food, and I'm not sure why. We make eye contact, and he doesn't smile. He shows nothing, barely blinking.

He's supposed to loathe me, and it's clearly paining him not to. I'm not sure if he likes me, but I don't think he harbors any animosity toward me, either. He's certainly not acting like he hates me. Eventually, I pull my hand away from his and stop walking. I need answers, and he needs to start talking to me. "Why don't you just let him kill me, Ezra? What's your endgame with me?"

He grimaces and shrugs. "I'm bored, and you're better than nothing. And you're definitely better than him."

I cross my arms and cock a brow. "I'm not going anywhere with you until you tell me what headspace you're in. What's going on in that mind of yours? What's your plan for me, Ezra?"

Stalking forward, he ignores my question. His hood is up, and his sandy hair sticks out at the bottom, reminding me of a scarecrow. It makes me smile, although none of this is funny.

"Fine, stay here with Nigel, then. Suit your fucking self," he says, calling over his shoulder.

The mere thought of that sends a shiver down my spine.

"Wait," I call out and run after him, eager to leave the cold, malevolent energy behind me.

After a few minutes, I can barely keep up with him, and I start crying, the tears pouring out of me. He turns his head at me and grunts, but I offer to hold the muskrat. So he sweeps me into his arms, and I let out a sigh from not having to put pressure on my legs anymore. He carries me the rest of the way, probably because he doesn't want to hear me whine.

Relaxing to the rhythmic sway of his arms, I stare down at the lifeless eyes of the rodent I once would have gagged at.

Sweet victory.

What we need to survive is protein, but primarily fat. It could put life back into us for a few days until we consider our next move. Micah showed me how to render it, cook the fat, and consume it with liquids. Even a flat rock can be used to pool it. That's what's truly kept us going all these months. I wonder if Ezra knows how to do that, though somehow I doubt he does.

When we finally arrive at his camp, he carefully helps me into the shelter, lifting me by my hips and gently setting me down. He lights a fire with a bit of fuel he has in a water bottle—he stole it from our collective supplies. Fuel is yet another resource that is becoming quite limited. The flames flare up, casting a warm glow around us. I stare up at Ezra, who still hasn't spoken since we left Nigel.

"I'll be back," he says.

My skin turns clammy as a wall of terror slams into me. I stare over the cave lip, half expecting to see argyle hovering over it. I look at Ezra with pleading eyes. "Please don't leave me. He's going to come for me, isn't he?"

Ezra pulls his spear into his hand, prepping to leave me. "Yeah, I wouldn't put it past him. I'm going to check the area and make sure he didn't follow us."

"You're scared of him, aren't you?"

His beady eyes flash. "I'm not scared of anything anymore. But I can understand why you are. Naomi didn't like being around him, either. She said he was suspicious. But he helped me hunt; he saved my life when your fucking boyfriend decided to mutilate me. If it wasn't for him, I'd be dead." He presses his stubby hand to my chest. "And you serve as a reminder of what Micah did to me, so I'm sorry if I'm a bit conflicted on what to do with you."

"He killed Maison in cold blood," I remind him. "Or are you blocking it out because it's inconvenient for you?"

His eyes shoot daggers at me, his lips turning down. "There isn't a fucking day that goes by when I don't think about it, London." He jumps out of the cave with ease.

Shit. I pressed him too hard.

Still, Maison is the only topic that fires him back to life. Maison is the key to winning him over; I know it.

I curl up in a ball, enjoying the flames on my face, and start to daydream about Micah. My tall athlete in his dark hoodie, with his dark eyes and equally dark soul, each of which sets alight my fire.

Five days of nothing but my own haunting thoughts after spending months with him, through which he was my entire existence.

Five days...

Micah hasn't come for me.

Five days...

I haven't even heard a whisper from him. It's as if he never existed at all.

Eventually, and I have no idea how long I waited, Ezra returns, and the muskrat we caught is skinned and cooked. He watches me with disgust as I curl into a ball. He's obviously still pouting from when I called him out. However, he still hands me a hunk of it and some fresh water. I carefully scan the liquid for mold but end up drinking anyway.

"Nigel's not around. I checked everywhere," he tells me. "But stay close to me, no matter what. He doesn't like you, London."

I scoff. "Evidently." I have a feeling in my gut that this is not the last I'll see of Nigel.

Ezra sits with his lanky legs out in front of him, chewing on his meat. "Do you want to know the real reason why I want to keep you around?" he asks me with his mouth full.

My heart stops at the way he says it, as if he has no plans to let me go.

He plans to keep me... like I'm a possession.

I tilt my head and run my hand over my matted hair, which I was able to pull into a braid earlier. I don't respond, keeping my eyes focused on my dinner instead.

"You're the last reminder I have of him," he says.

My eyes shoot up.

He leans his head back against the stone. "He looked happy with you—more than he had in a long time—before Micah fucked it up for him. He'd want me to look after you and protect you in the way he would." A swell of emotions run through me at the thought of Maison still protecting me from the other side. But this is Ezra, and he's been an ass since the moment I met him, even when Maison and I were together and happy. "But mainly, it's because when Micah finds out I have you, he will fucking *hate* it."

That's it, then. Revenge on Micah.

However, I suppose it could be both.

"Why do you and Micah hate each other so much? And please don't say it's because of Naomi unless you want me to vomit."

He tilts his head up and scoffs, but a smile hints at his lips. He's loosening up...

"Maison and I were always close—he was my best friend growing up. Micah was always there, but..." He casts his gaze downward, a fleeting moment of hatred before it's gone.

I rest my hand on his leg. He twitches but doesn't move it. It's not sexual but comforting. I want him to know I'm open to his friendship, should he want it.

"But what, Ezra? Help me understand your dynamic with Micah." My eyes draw down to his hand. It always seems to provoke his anger when my gaze lingers there. I move my hand to his and run my fingers over his scars. He lets me inspect his impaired hand before slowly pulling it away and tucking it into the cuff of his sweater.

"Micah's an ass," he mutters. "He's always had it out for me. There is something seriously wrong with that guy. He was jealous of me. He can't stand when he's not the center of everyone's attention. His jealousy of my friendship with Maison is the real reason why he cut off my fingers. He saw an opportunity to hurt me and jumped on it."

I can't say I disagree with him right now.

The more I think about it, the more I realize that Micah could have let Ezra go. Perhaps I disagree with his decision to cut off Ezra's fingers, even if it was in the heat of the moment. Sure, Ezra had a knife to Micah's throat, but it's not like Ezra was the one who stabbed Maison.

"I'm sorry, Ezra," I say to him, "if I had any part in it."

My eyes draw to my shattered hand, and I internally laugh at the irony that Micah indirectly caused this injury, too.

However, Micah has also been my savior in more ways than I can count.

Ezra continues, and I watch him. It's as if he's replaying something in his mind. "It's like Micah doesn't have a soul. Like maybe he wasn't supposed to be born... Like it was always supposed to be Maison, and Micah was a fucking accident. A freak of fucking nature that never should have existed."

I never really stopped to think which of the two was older. I just assumed Micah was... not that it really matters.

"What else did he do to you?" I ask him, genuinely curious. What did Micah do to Ezra that makes him look so tortured whenever he's around him?

His jaw tenses. "He fucked me up when we were kids. And I mean, he was obsessed with making my life hell. My mom said I had to put up with him because of my parents' business dealings, not to mention that the whole town fucking caters to anyone with the last name Matei. But she didn't know what he was really like. Maison did, though. He saw it, too, and he turned a blind eye to it. That is, until Micah raped his girlfriend, then killed her."

Jesus.

I blow out a breath. "Ezra, you know Maison was the one who killed Olivia."

"Yeah, well, Micah still fucking raped her."

Christ... I can't dispute that, either.

I scoff. "So, who cares? That's his business with Maison. Everyone gets bullied once in a while, Ezra. But you grow up and grow out of it, or you stand up for yourself."

His pupils flare. "You don't fucking understand. You think this island is the first time he has crushed my neck? He did that to me behind closed doors for years. I swear, he has almost killed me at least three times when we were younger and I was smaller than him. He was obsessed with torturing me—it's like he got off on it or something. Something is not fucking right about him." He pauses for a moment. "And he'd get this glazed look in his eye... like he was there but not really there. His pupils went all black and shit."

My heart pounds as he describes Micah's eyes because I've witnessed what he's talking about, although I've only seen it once. The night he called me Olivia when he went all unhinged and hurt me, and not sexually.

The bruises he left on Olivia.

The bruises he leaves on me...

The particular style of how he likes to pleasure.

I bite my lip and listen, hanging my head down and letting him continue, my lower belly filling with heat. Because I know what he is saying is true. I hope he can't see it... can't see that I like that side of Micah.

It's why I was so drawn to him.

"You know what I mean, don't you?" he finally asks me. "You've seen it."

I sniff and look up at him. "I've seen that side of him, yes. But he has a good side, too, Ezra. You have to have seen it. He takes care of people he genuinely loves. He's not soulless; he's just damaged."

No one's ever made me feel as alive as Micah has. How could someone who's supposedly soulless do that to me?

"Tell me one good memory about him. One redemption moment, Ezra. He's got to have one. It couldn't have been all bad growing up."

"Why the fuck should I?" he snipes.

I soften my gaze. "Because holding onto toxic memories will hurt you more than it will hurt him. You have to live your life differently now, and when the pain of what he did to you overwhelms you, hold on to something pleasant in your mind about him. That way, it will hurt less."

Ezra grabs a bone from the muskrat he's been drying on the fire and starts to pick his teeth with it, his face scrunched in a scowl as if it pains him to even come up with one happy thought about Micah.

"Just one, Ezra," I encourage him. "One pleasant memory. It won't kill you."

He stokes the fire with a nearby stick. "He taught me how to shoot a puck properly."

My eyes whip up, pulling my gaze away from the mesmerizing embers. "Keep going," I urge him, giving him all my attention. "Tell me all about it."

"I always struggled with the execution of shooting, and it was holding my game back. He spent a summer with me at the rink and taught me how to do it. Now I have the best shot on the entire team. He said if I was going to play on the same team as him, then I had to step it up because he doesn't play with losers."

I snicker. Such a Micah thing to say, and the image of them working together on something brings a smile to my face. I need to focus on my happy memories of him, too, because right now, my anger might destroy me. "See, he's not all terrible."

He merely scoffs. "You may be right, but he gets bored easily. And that's why you're here with me right now. Naomi gets bored, too, which is why *she's* not here with me."

My stomach turns. I hate thinking about Micah this way or about the possibility he's with Naomi.

"So, are you going to try to move on from her, or are you just going to sulk?" I try to change the subject.

He sneers and jerks his head toward my wrist. "Are you going to tell me what happened to your hand, or should I just assume? You look like hell, London."

I have no flippant response to that. Closing my eyes, I imagine the sensation of my hand gliding through those restraints. In a single instant, every bone that Micah had painstakingly mended for me shattered into fragments. It's as if being broken is my destined state.

When I open my eyes, he's studying me, then crosses his arms. "Like you, maybe I'm not over her yet, so sulking seems like the right thing to do."

"You're too good for her," I tell him. "When we get out of here, I bet you'll find a new girlfriend within a week. You'll be the star hockey player in college and meet new girls. I bet they will throw themselves at you."

He stares down at his missing fingers and shakes his head. "No, I won't. Because Micah fucked that up for me, too. Plus, it's always been Naomi. I can't imagine being with anyone else."

I roll my eyes. "You're what, like nineteen now? You really think she is the one you are meant to be with? Just cut your damn hair, and you will have girls flocking to you, I promise. Hockey or no hockey. You're a catch, Ezra. You just need to see your worth." And get rid of this blind loyalty to Naomi, who doesn't deserve it.

He scowls at me. "What do you mean, cut my hair? What's wrong with my fucking hair?"

I arch a brow. "Well... I don't know. It doesn't really suit you. It makes your eyes look small and beady."

"Fuck you. Naomi likes my long hair."

I place my hand on his leg again. "Naomi's not here, as you pointed out."

His body bristles, but he's not the only one who can remind me the one we really want isn't here.

We sit in silence while he broods, my thoughts now consumed with Micah and how much I miss him. I watch Ezra, and I desperately want to know what's going on in that brain of his, but I don't dare ask. He's calm right now and almost pleasant. I don't want to ruin the moment by speaking.

Every time I push him, he responds aggressively and we digress, and I'm finally getting through to him. Eventually, he reaches over to his pile of things and grabs a black bag, then pulls something small and sharp out of it.

Scissors. A whole shaving kit, actually. He leans over and hands me the pair of tiny silver scissors.

"What are you doing?" I ask him.

"I want you to fucking cut it."

I blink at him a couple of times and shake my head. "I thought Naomi liked your hair?"

"She does," he snaps at me. "That's the point."

I scoff at the tiny scissors hanging off my pinky and stare at his thick, dread-like hair. "I can't cut your hair with these. It will take forever. It's too long and thick. What you are asking me will literally take me hours. Plus, your hair is dirty, and it stinks. I don't particularly want to touch it."

He sits in front of me, stretching his legs out. "Good thing we have tons of time. Now, get to cutting."

Fucking hell.

I suck in a breath as he pulls his hood down, revealing just how much hair he has. It nearly hangs down to his shoulders.

"Fine," I mutter. "Sit closer so I don't have to lean in. And remember, I only have one working hand." I sink back into the rough texture of the rock face, appreciating its solid support against my back. I rest my hurt arm on his shoulder and start to take tiny snips, working my way from the bottom. He fidgets, clearly uncomfortable to be sitting so close to me.

"Quit moving. If you want me to do this right, sit still. Otherwise, I will just shave it bald."

He merely grunts. "Do a good job. Make it look good."

"I will."

A half an hour goes by as I focus on my task, the sun moving across the blistering blue sky. Cutting his hair is almost mesmerizing.

No voices, no worries, no fear—just cutting... I see why Micah spends all his time carving.

I'm about halfway through his haircut when he turns his head toward me. "What went on with that teacher and you, anyway?"

I pause momentarily before continuing my snipping. "I fucked him once in a hotel room. His wife found out about it because he was sloppy and left receipts. She was obviously suspicious of him. My entire school blacklisted me once it got out."

He chuckles. "That's actually pretty savage."

I slide the scissors down his neck, and he stiffens. "I don't want to talk about it. He doesn't matter. In fact, he's irrelevant to me now. It was wrong, and I feel like I've been punished enough for it."

"Sorry, I was just curious. I thought we were bonding," he says cautiously as I work the scissors near the longer hairs by his ear.

"Don't apologize. It is what it is, and it's over now. I just don't see a point in discussing my mistakes."

He shifts forward. "Well, what do you want to talk about, then?"

I ponder for a moment and smile at the fact that Ezra Schwartz wants to talk to me at all. "Tell me about Maison. I want to hear everything, and I want to hear something about him I don't know."

I've spent the last three months with someone who would rather forget Maison, so it's nice to be with someone who brings him alive in my head again.

"When he was in his junior year, he had a goal to fuck every girl in our graduating class."

I poke him in the ribs. "Not funny." *But it's likely true.* "Tell me something else."

"He was a poet."

This catches my attention.

"He was good at it, too. He always had a way of seeing the bright side of everything."

I smile at the thought, and it doesn't surprise me, not with how well-read Maison was. He did, after all, switch personas with Micah in English class. He loved it when I read *The Great Gatsby* to him; he appreciated it in a way Micah doesn't. "Tell me something else..."

I listen to him speak and reminisce about his years of friendship with Maison. I can't help but question Ezra's role as the villain despite all the terrible things he's done. His parents got royally fucked by the Matei family, and his reactions were always centered on that.

I love hearing his stories about Maison—the imagery it creates in my mind. I could listen to Ezra talk about Maison for hours. It's the perfect distraction for my duplicity and rebellious thoughts against Micah.

What I'm contemplating doing.

I cut Ezra's hair to the point where I think it looks decent. I make careful snips, trying to make it perfectly even for him, then blow on his head. "There, you're done. Turn around so I can see your face."

He turns, and as he does, I barely recognize him. He still has beady eyes, but I'm taken aback. I forgot how cute he actually is. When he's not being Ezra, he's a pretty attractive guy. I thought so the first time I saw him, too. Until he scowled, and I was able to tell how mean he was.

He narrows his eyes at me. "What? Why are you looking at me like that? Do I look horrible?"

I shake my head and smile. "Not at all. We will get you a new girlfriend in no time." The best part is how much Naomi loves Ezra's long hair and how good it felt to cut it all off knowing that.

He hoods his eyes for a second, and I realize how dry my mouth is—how little water and snow melt we have. "We can't stay here much longer," I tell him.

"I can't go back to the other group, London. We could go to the lake site, but I can't guarantee you'll be safe there. Nigel will go there eventually because he has no other choice, either."

I tilt my head. "You know, you could just apologize to Thomas and the others. All you have to do is be genuine and swallow your pride. You never know; people might surprise you. I think Micah chopping off your fingers was enough punishment, and they might feel the same way, too."

I have to think there is a shred of goodness left on this island.

Forgiveness. Love. Hope.

Anything else than hatred.

His mouth twitches. "No fucking point. Plus, I doubt anyone left alive will want to share since we've already divided the food equally."

My heart sinks. He has a point.

I bury any last traces of guilt for what I'm about to suggest. I stare down at my bruised and lifeless hand, then slowly raise my head to meet his gaze. "Ezra, I know where

Micah is hiding the rest of the food. I can get us to the cabin."

CHAPTER SIXTEEN

MICAH

The evening looms as we step outside the warmth of the cabin. At this time of night, when both the sun and moon share the sky, the shadows are the longest. It's not an ideal time to go looking for London, but I can't stay here without her for another second. Especially now that I am certain that Naomi is playing games.

Naomi stumbles forward, and my fingers tighten around my bone weapon.

Fresh footprints mark the melted mud and snow. Two sets of them lead right up to the window, then back into the forest, where they seem to disappear again. Whoever it was wasn't even trying to hide themselves. Someone was here recently. These muddy prints were not here when I was out here twenty minutes ago.

My stomach tightens when a flicker flashes in the corner of my eye. I lift my hand as Naomi opens her mouth to speak, only to close it again as I grab her and pull her into my chest, covering her mouth. "Someone's out there, watching us," I whisper.

"What? What did you see?"

I press my hand harder. "Shh, Naomi. Don't fucking talk." She freezes in my arms as I scan the darkness. "London?" I call out and listen.

My ears are keen. Only the familiar sound of silence answers me.

"London, answer me. I know you're there," I yell out as Naomi wiggles and squirms in my arms, which only causes me to tighten my grip on her mouth, suffocating her so she will shut the fuck up. The wind rustles through the thick trees while Naomi shakes, then goes limp. Just the raw, rugged sounds of nature.

I wait.

Listen.

I barely let Naomi breathe.

The shadows close in on me, and my heart rate spikes. London saw me with Naomi; she must have. She saw what Naomi was trying to do to me, what I let her do to me, when all along it was London I needed—the one I obsessively craved.

"London, come out. We can talk this through."

Silence. No London, no ghost, no figure peering from the woods, and for a moment, I wonder if my mind is playing tricks on me. My paranoia is finally catching up with me. It wouldn't be the first time I've seen things I shouldn't have in these woods.

I hang my head low and listen. Really listen... This island is so quiet that if they so much as move, I will hear them.

A few moments pass, but I'm patient, keeping my focus.

Then a muffled wind echoes from the trees, bringing along a faint cry that has my ears perking up. The shadows are messing with my sense of direction. In my mind, I can hear her as clear as day—her sweet voice calling my name, so low that I wonder if it's real. It could be my mind recalling the entire winter when I had her pinned down, teasing her with my tongue. I recall the soft skin of her thigh as it brushed under my fingers while I made her squirm and squirt, bruising her with my lips as she lay fully under my control.

Her final cry when I abandoned her.

My heart falters from the pain in that cry and her last words to me before I left, foolishly dismissing them as an outburst.

"Don't fucking hurt her," I say in no direction in particular, but I can imagine Ezra is with her and Nigel is somewhere close, watching me. *Enjoying this.*

Naomi bites down on my hand, marking my flesh with her teeth, and I drop her.

"Fuck. Micah," she coughs out, grabbing her neck and touching the red marks I left on her. "No one is here. You've lost your damn mind." Tears flow out of her eyes as she chokes on her breath and keels over. I had no clue how hard I was holding her. I flex my jaw and blink, coming back to reality, then smile.

My dick isn't so enticing now, is it, sweetheart?

I ignore her scowling and continue to scan the forest as we edge toward where I think I heard London. Or someone...

Naomi waits and crosses her arms while every hair on my arm stands on end. "She's here, and I don't think she's alone."

"No one is here, Micah," Naomi scoffs.

I stare at the thickest part of the woods, where her cry echoed from. I heard them flee after Naomi bit me. My instinct is to chase London, but I won't. I'll hunt her instead... I'm better at that.

I nudge Naomi forward. "Move."

She frowns but nods and takes a tentative step into the darkness.

"Good fucking girl," I mutter under my breath, watching her, making sure she listens. Her blonde ponytail swings as she faces me. Her eyes flash slightly and a brief twinge appears on her lips before she turns away and struts forward—every ounce of pep back in her step.

Fuck me, this girl loves the abuse.

They all seem to with me.

I take one final glance at the cabin, wondering if I will ever make it back here or if I'm turning my back on it forever. My eyes are drawn to the footprints, and I falter.

The snow has melted, so perhaps there were no footprints, or perhaps they were ours all along. I recall my last steps just an hour earlier. I came back from the woods and walked around the cabin to the cooking site. Naomi was here the whole time. She could have left those footprints.

So why are my senses screaming at me?

She is here.

Five fucking days, and I promised London I'd only be gone a few hours.

"Micah, I can't walk that fast," Naomi whines as I set an intense pace toward the airplane and she struggles to keep up. "Can you please just take me to the others? I'll tell you where Ezra is if you let me go. Please, Micah. Please. I don't want to go with you back there."

I whip around to face her, my knife flashing in the moonlight. "Nope. Keep up, Naomi. And stop fucking whining. I'm trying to think."

Naomi's strength is back—she proved that to me when she pushed me down and straddled me. If she has the energy to take my cock down her throat, then she can keep up to help me find my girlfriend. In fact, I think she has been better for a while now and was just pretending to not feel well because I've been doting on her.

The fear in her eyes is real now... finally. She sees me for what I am as her hands keep drawing up to the bruises on her neck. I'm not proud of it, but it's time she knew what I am. Now she can stay the fuck away from me and, hopefully, keep her life intact.

We walk through the dense woods, deeper into the night, until the landscape finally starts to change. I know I'm close and fully aware this could be a trap to lure me away from the cabin again, but I don't care. The food is well-hidden, and getting London back means everything to me. The woods are too quiet, everything in the air is off, and I hate the feeling of not being in control. With my bone weapon sticking out of my backpack and my sharp knife in my hand, I hack at the dense bushes standing in my way of finding her.

I scan the woods immediately in front of me and finally spot what I'm looking for—fresh broken sticks, proving that someone was here. Almost as if there was a struggle here mere moments before.

"They aren't far ahead," I say to Naomi as she struggles to keep up. "We have to get to the airplane. That's where they are headed."

London, I'm coming for you, baby.

Naomi finally admitted where Nigel and Ezra are staying, in a cave system close to the airplane. I know these caves; I found them in the fall when I stalked this island from end to end. The problem is that there are hundreds of these holes scattered everywhere, so it would be like finding a needle in a haystack.

I slow my pace, the ground slippery as we head toward the airplane, and I let Naomi join me as we enter a dangerous area full of cracks in the earth. As much as she drives me crazy, I'm not ready yet for her to fall to her death inside one of these things. I grab her hand and make sure she sticks close to me. She leans into me as we walk, enjoying my hand in hers way too much.

"What are you going to do when you find them?" Naomi asks as I grab her waist and lift her over a dark hole. I pause and release her back to her feet.

"I'm going to return you to Ezra."

It's not what she wants, but she doesn't have a choice. I'm banking on the fact Ezra won't be able to resist Naomi when he lays eyes on her. Especially with how shiny and pretty I've made her.

He'll want her back.

She lets out a sob. "You're so fucking predictable, Micah. This is so typical of you. I'm not telling you what cave it is. You can't make me go back to that place."

Pathetic.

No wonder they are so desperate. There is no fresh running water anywhere. Only rodents, bottom feeders, and dead bodies. I look around at the barren land in disgust, grateful for the cabin I found for London.

"Why did he move you here?" Inquiring minds want to know. What drew them to live like this? At least the lake site offered fresh water, a place to bathe and fish.

Her eyes whip up at me. "To hide from you, Micah. For a few weeks, Ezra was petrified that you were going to come back and kill him."

"He should be petrified," I say, hacking some brush. I probably would have killed him, and I definitely will now if he has London.

Naomi stops walking, crosses her arms, and scoffs. "You're not as smart as you think you are, Micah. Maybe give Ezra some credit; he remembered all these holes in the ground. We took a chance, checked them out, and found one to live in. Some of them have tiny caves buried in the earth. They provided good shelter, better than what we had at the lake. It doesn't seem like much, but it kept us alive... not that you care at all about us living."

Interesting. And I hate to admit it, but smart.

She casts her brown eyes up to meet mine, her words causing a chill to run up my spine. "He's obsessed with his hatred for you. He's not himself, and he hasn't been since that night. I couldn't look at it anymore. I couldn't deal with him any longer."

"Look at what anymore?"

"His *fingers,* Micah. The ones you chopped off, remember?"

How could I fucking forget?

The wind shifts, and I can tell we are close based on the putrid stench of decaying flesh nearby.

My sight is drawn to the broken silver tip of the airplane as I pull Naomi into me. She loves it, her body responding with a slight arch of her hips against mine.

I lean down and whisper, "There is a lot you don't know about me, Naomi. I'm much smarter than you think I am. And just so you know, I'm never going to fuck you, so quit trying. I'm only keeping you alive to try to prove to my girlfriend that I'm not the monster she thinks I am. Now, shut up. We're here."

Her eyes widen when she finally notices how hard I'm gripping the sharp knife in my hand and that I'm holding it two inches from her face. How tense and rigid my body is. How fast my heart is beating.

She bites her bottom lip, her frosty breath teasing the air. She turns her head in every direction as if only realizing what I've known for a while.

We are being watched...

She sucks in a breath as a wolf howls in the night. "Micah... I'm really scared."

I scoff. "Well, he's your boyfriend, sweetheart, and you caused this." Oddly enough, the one she should be most frightened of is me, yet that fact hasn't cemented in her brain yet.

I keep my eyes laser-focused on the plane and the burnt brush that envelops it. The growth, dust, and mud caked on it allow it to blend into the natural surroundings.

I scan for any sign of the others as we huddle down on the cold earth. Naomi can sense that I'm not playing around, and eventually, she sits cross-legged in the dirt and leans back on her arms, peering up at me. I watch the trees and the plane as I listen to the wind. Any sign that will trigger me.

She stays quiet.

They are here; I know it. They weren't that far ahead of us. Whoever it is, I have to admire their level of patience, which leads me to believe it's Nigel... since Ezra has the patience of a pit bull, especially when it comes to waiting someone out. His dumbass would have made himself known by now.

After about twenty minutes of obsessively watching nothing moving, I take a few steps and jerk my head toward Naomi. "Come on, get up. Let's go check it out."

It's not that I'm scared because I know I could take anyone out. However, I'm not sure I can take on the two of them if it comes down to that. I refuse to put London in a position where she's ever on this island without me. Even if I'm unsure where London's head's at or what side she's on after what I did to her.

We walk up to the airplane, and I push down the bile in my throat, ignoring the goosebumps rising on my arms. The memory of this place suffocates me as I remember when we were crash-landed and I thought I was about to lose my brother. That's all I gave a shit about in that moment. The joke's on me... I fucking lost him anyway. I never would have thought the girl he was comforting that day would become my fucking obsession, though. My only reason for living.

As we approach, I easily pull the door open.

Red flag number one.

The last time I was here, I closed it. I distinctly remember securing the doors after I pulled the upholstery apart to create the shelter. Someone was here, and it wasn't fucking me.

I clench my jaw as I peer inside, then keep Naomi behind me as I step in, trying not to show how much this place creeps the fuck out of me. I couldn't sleep for five days after hauling all the dead bodies to that open grave. I didn't lie down; I paced for hours in the same spot, hidden in the trees away from the others, trying to settle myself down. It's not an image I'll soon forget. It nearly broke me that night, and I almost didn't come back from it.

"What do you see?" Naomi whispers behind me. I press my arm against her chest, looking in both directions. The broken windows, the carnage, the blood... I give her a warning look, and she bites her lips shut and wraps her little fingers around my arm, digging her nails in.

The last time I was here by myself, I swear that I saw someone who was supposed to be dead. In fact, I distinctly remember carrying this kid's body to the pile of corpses the night the plane crashed.

But there he was, standing ghostly still in an Armani suit by the bathroom at the back of the plane, staring at me like a creepy ass motherfucker. It was a junior named Troy, a friend of James, Ollie, and Nathan. And he looked pissed, like he's the one who should have been alive instead of me. He watched me the entire time I was in here. He scared the ever-loving shit out of me, and I couldn't get out of there fast enough. I told myself that was the last time I'd ever come here.

As my eyes adjust, my heart stops. Right in the same spot as where the ghost was standing is London. A sense of dread settles in my stomach. I don't recognize the girl in front of me. She's battered and bruised, her hair is falling in her face, and hatred is spewing from her eyes.

I blink twice to convince myself she's real. Her head shakes, and my gaze falls upon a shadow standing menacingly behind her, his thumb firmly holding a knife to her throat.

Ezra Fingerless Schwartz.

CHAPTER SEVENTEEN

LONDON

I stand alongside Ezra as we step through the dark tree line and the wooden cabin comes into view. We stand utterly still, side by side, our hands a mere inch from each other—mine mangled, his with missing fingers. It's a decrepit, creepy cabin now that I really get a good look at it. And why it's even here, in the middle of nowhere, is the creepiest part of it all. Watching it from afar, it's almost like I'm somebody else and this wasn't where I spent the last four months. A different girl arrived in this cabin a few months ago. It's not the same girl standing here now.

"Micah keeps the food under the floorboards," I whisper as we approach. My insides are screaming at me for betraying him like this, but I'm desperately hungry. I've never coped well with the hunger.

"There is a trapdoor in one of them, with a secret compartment inside." I often wonder why whoever built this place put that hidden compartment there.

Who or what they were hiding from...

Ezra's eyes narrow as he takes in the cabin—the secret Micah fought so hard to keep.

"Seems cozy," he mutters, keeping his eyes on it as he shifts beside me.

I don't respond to that.

We have no plan. We left as soon as I told Ezra I knew how to find the cabin, but I made him promise he would stick with me and give none of it to Nigel. And if Micah is there, I made him promise to let me handle him.

He agreed. I trusted him, and we departed in the early evening, trying to hide among the shadows of the night. We walked through the dreadful forest, past the fallen trees, dead souls, and tragedies. He carried me a bit of the way when I lost my footing, but we barely spoke. We stopped at the creek where I filled my bottle, and now we are here.

The cabin is dark, lonely, and haunted, and I wonder how I ever thought of such a wicked place as a safe haven. A circle of fir trees stands watch over it, blending the shack into the surrounding landscape—protecting it—as if this cabin is part of nature itself. If you didn't know it was there, you would never even notice it. But I paid attention to the markings around it and studied the woods so I could find it again if I needed to. I also left a marker, a small hair tie I was relieved to see was still hanging from the branch where I left it. Either Micah isn't paying attention, or he is losing touch with reality.

My stomach sinks at the view of the flickering light inside and the realization of what I am seeing. He's in there without me. And that means he hasn't come to find me. Because if he had, he would have succeeded. He would have found a way.

Ezra watches me in my torment as I stare at the cabin and the woods beyond. "I told you he isn't a good guy," he says. "He doesn't care about you, London. The only person Micah cares about is himself."

What Ezra doesn't understand is how little I feel in this moment or the fact he's not much better than Micah. After all, he is keeping me captive, too. I guess when there are no other alternatives, people become valuable possessions—possibly as valuable as food. And I think, somehow, I've become a possession to merely barter for something better and more useful.

With a lump in my throat, I cautiously tread through the slushy mixture of mud and snow behind Ezra. My legs grow heavier with each step, but my mind clears up. We peer inside the small, dirty window—the only window, the one I spent months gazing out of into the wintery night.

That feels like a lifetime ago.

It's hard to see through the pane as it's layered with grime and fifty years' worth of dirt. My eyes are weary, and the light is the trickiest at this moment of the night, but shadows dance inside. There is clear movement in the single room near the bed. Two shadows intermingled together.

Micah isn't alone.

We only watch for a moment, but a moment is all I need before I stumble a couple of steps back. Because I am numb and utterly detached from myself watching him with her, just as Nigel and Ezra had predicted.

Even without looking at him, I can feel the terrifying energy Ezra emits behind me. Something shifts in him, an audible snap, and his body chemistry changes. I turn to face him and the heat is radiating off him. The nice guy I've caught glimpses of over these past few days is gone, and the one staring back at me is feral—the boy he has become after enduring the horrors of this island. My heart stills at the look in his eyes as they glaze over and darken like the evening sky above us.

And they are directed right at me.

I fidget under his hardened glare. The wheels are turning in his head as he stares at me, then to the window, and then back to me, his lip curling. I know that look—the raw, unhinged emotion radiating from him. Seeing Naomi with Micah was the final straw, and his sanity is shattering.

"Ezra, you don't need her," I whisper.

A wicked grin spreads over his face, one I've not seen on him before. "You're right," he says darkly, looking at me like I'm meat. "I fucking don't."

I hate the way he's looking at me. It's not him... This isn't Ezra. My body is frozen, and a cry is building in my throat as he closes the few inches between us. I twist away from him toward the cabin, the door a mere ten feet away. So close... Micah's so close to me, but I don't know if I can call out to him.

I stand frozen, the anger swelling inside me so potent, but I need him.

I need Micah.

I open my mouth to scream...

"Don't fucking do it, London," Ezra warns, fully aware of what I'm thinking. I bite my lip, too scared to move. "Don't scream, London. Don't make a fucking peep. I have nothing to lose anymore, and I don't care if I live or die. If you cry out, I will slit your throat before he has the chance to save you."

Ezra lies when he says he doesn't care... Because if he didn't care whether he lived or died, he wouldn't be threatening me to begin with. Why wouldn't he just make his presence known and let Micah kill him? Because he wants to live, and saying otherwise is bullshit.

He grabs me before I can react and clamps his hand so hard on my mouth that I can't gasp for air. He has his hockey skate spear digging into my neck. I can't bear the image of Naomi on top of Micah, so I close my eyes.

"Open your goddamn eyes and watch them," he orders, his fingers digging into me.

Micah and Naomi. They are impossible *not* to see. Even with my eyes closed, it's an image I'll never forget.

"This is what I was warning you about." His voice cracks—raw.

I swallow hard, watching them. Tears sting my eyes as I take in what I know is killing him inside, too. I'm gutted and absolutely torn apart watching them as they embrace. My body shakes as I see her lean up, and even from this distance, it's impossible to mistake what they are doing. I close my eyes so I can't watch.

"Tell me who you see in there." I don't recognize Ezra, the raw pain in his voice.

"Micah and Naomi," I whisper, and it pains me to say it, too.

"That's right. Micah and fucking Naomi. Now someone else gets to experience the pain of witnessing them together. This is what I've experienced for years. This. Is. What. They. Do."

Taking advantage of his moment of pain, I twist out of his grip. He reaches out for me, but I'm quicker, finding whatever inner strength is left inside me. Instead of screaming, I turn and run as fast as I can into the woods. He catches me quickly and pushes me to the ground.

He chuckles as he presses my shoulders down. His eyes blaze like starlight, his brute strength pinning me beneath him. "You think I'm going to let you get rescued? You're a liar, just like she is. You were never going to give me the food, were you?"

He's wrong, so utterly wrong. I would have; I was going to. I didn't think things through. Part of me hoped Micah wouldn't be here, that maybe, just maybe, he was dead, and this food is rightfully mine.

I can't breathe. I can't find the words to beg Ezra to stop because he's crushing my lungs. All I can manage is to stare up at him with pleading eyes as they begin to sting with dirty tears. He presses on me harder. "Quit struggling. I'm all you have, London. And trust me, you're not my fucking first choice, either."

Somewhere in the distance, I hear Micah call for me.

"London, answer me. I know you're there."

One scream. All I have to manage is one scream. But I'm too petrified to utter a word, not with how unhinged Ezra is and all that rage burning inside him. I understand it all too well, given the intense emotions this island brings out of us. One single overwhelming thought has the power to cripple you. At this moment, my mind mirrors Ezra's, shrouded in darkness.

I've underestimated him.

Ezra is just as capable as Micah to do fucked-up shit, and right now, he is wounded and vulnerable. He cut Thomas's hand, pressed a knife to Micah's throat, and pulled me out of my shelter and let Naomi and Nigel hurt me. *He* took me and held me captive these past few days.

I finally realize what I should have known all along. I'm alone here. Truly alone. We all are. Everyone still alive is fucking deranged.

My anger consumes me, a dark cloud blotting any amount of light within me.

I hate this island. I hate everyone on it.

Especially Micah Matei.

Ezra drags me deeper into the woods with his hand still clamped over my mouth, which is entirely unnecessary. I'm resolved to not scream. I'll never scream again.

As my oxygen dwindles, darkness engulfs my world.

I should have known... I'm not special to Micah. He needs release, and he will get it from whoever will give it to him. The only person who really thought I was special is dead.

Micah taught me all winter to crave him like a pet—to only want him, obey him, and prioritize his desires. Only after was he completely satisfied would he finally give me what I wanted, and by then, I yearned for it so intensely that my skin felt like it might liquefy.

He made me fucking *needy*.

The weight of my grief for Maison cripples me, the force surpassing my hate and anger combined. Bundled up in Ezra's arms, I watch as Micah and Naomi pass us in the woods. Darkness ripples, my body descending into it.

"Don't fall asleep...The fun's only beginning." Those are the final words I hear Ezra whisper before I go limp and fall into an oxygen-less bliss.

It's the stench of decaying flesh that awakens me. A hint of acidic smoke teases my nostrils to the point where I almost choke on it.

I slowly regain my senses. Strong arms are wrapped around me, and cold steel is pressed to my neck. My body is numb and limp, and every muscle screams at me as I stand, barely mobile. If it weren't for Ezra holding me up, I doubt I would be standing. I'm completely reliant on him... I have nothing left.

I'm inside the airplane, I realize, and the residual acidic smell of the crash still lingers in the air, even after six months. I will recognize this smell for the rest of my brief life. Even in my death, it will still haunt me.

I have no memory of how I got here. The last thing I remember was Micah walking by as Ezra suffocated me.

The anger that erupted within me.

I felt all of Ezra's rage and sadness as if they were my own—the last moments before his breaking point. Seeing Naomi with Micah was his undoing, as it was mine. I keep my eyes closed, seeing no point in opening them.

But Ezra is shaking.

Why is he shaking?

I hear Micah before I see him. Ezra tightens his hold on me in warning as two figures emerge at the front of the plane. We stay hidden among the shadows in the back as Micah steps in and looks from side to side. His eyes are narrowed and his jaw flexes as he takes in his surroundings.

Ezra must have beaten him here.

The moonlight shines bright on Naomi's platinum hair, and I can tell, even from here, how shiny she is. How much better she looks than me. My hair, full of mud and sticks, hangs over my face. I can smell myself, and it's not pretty. The stench from not bathing for days combined with blood, sweat, and whatever odor is coming out of the wrap on my hand.

I finally make eye contact with Micah and shake my head, knowing Ezra might do it if pressed. He might kill me. His hatred for Micah runs that deep. I didn't think it would be Ezra ending my life. And oddly enough, Nigel is entirely missing.

Nigel would love this, and I wouldn't be surprised if he was lurking somewhere nearby, watching the rest of us deteriorate.

Micah stands tense in front of Naomi, as if protecting her from *me* as I spew my anger toward them. His hair is tousled in his face, and I can't make his expression in the dark, but I can imagine it.

He came for me... He finally came for me. And for a tiny moment, that's all that matters. Something sharpens in my chest.

"*Ezra!*" Naomi screams from behind Micah, and she steps toward him. What Micah does next surprises me.

In a swift motion, Micah pulls Naomi in front of him and places his knife to her throat. Her eyes bulge at the force of it and at the blade grazing the tender spot on her neck.

The sight of it ignites something inside me. It lights a fire, if only a flicker of it. Micah's eyes don't leave mine, and he has a pained look on his face I recognize so much.

Ezra bristles and tenses as if taken off guard by this after what we just saw them doing. For a few tense seconds, it's as if no one breathes. The four of us are staring silently at each other in the dark. In the place that started it all.

Mist from the forest and melting snow circles the air outside—a deep, thick fog rolling in for the occasion.

"Micah..." Naomi whimpers, peering up at him. "Why are you doing this?"

Micah cocks his head and pulls her into the crook of his arm. That muscled arm I miss so much. As much as I miss the softness of his sweatshirt, his dark, sexy demeanor, and the way he always smells so manly. Why does Micah have to look like a fucking god? Even when I hate him, my body pulses at the sight of him. He's never looked so good to me—with his intense energy as he sticks a knife against Naomi's throat and his hood over his face.

"Don't fucking talk, Naomi. Keep your fucking mouth shut right now." His voice is deep and cutting, and my cheeks heat at the sound of it. His brows are furrowed and his jaw clenches as if he's stressed—like he wishes he could keep us both but is ultimately choosing me.

She bites her lip and goes wholly still, her eyes watering. Finally ripping his eyes from me, Micah shifts his focus to Ezra. He talks slowly, with intent. "Give me London, and I'll give you Naomi. A simple trade. This doesn't need to get ugly, Ezra."

I bite the inside of my cheek, waiting and wishing Ezra would make the trade.

It's a good one.

I can guess his response and imagine the snarled look he always gives. Naomi keeps her eyes on Ezra the whole time, and to my surprise, Ezra laughs.

"You would think I'd want Naomi back," he says with a nonchalant shrug, his tone betraying his mask of indifference. "Keep her. Do what you fucking want with her. She's dead to me."

"Ezra, don't say that," Naomi cries. "I was coming back to you. Micah took me before I could get back. I almost died."

Liar. She's so good at it, and Ezra falls for it every time. He softens at her voice—she's already piercing his walls.

"Don't fall for it," I whisper, though I truly don't know why. My hatred for this girl is strong right now. I don't want her with Ezra because she deserves to rot alone.

Micah narrows his eyes. "Really?" he says carefully, drawing it out. Both boys assess each other, nearly mirroring each other's movements in an intense, overdue stand-off.

Ezra tilts his head. "Yeah, really," he says in a sarcastic tone. "Do you hear that, Naomi? You're. Fucking. Dead. To. Me."

Micah scoffs, contemplating for a moment. He's so skilled at hiding his emotions. He grows quiet, still, and focused—the tells that make him distinctly Micah. "That's bullshit," he finally says and yanks her in front of him, her shirt riding up and baring the skin of her tight stomach. He twists her into an unsightly position.

Ezra doesn't move. He doesn't flinch as Naomi whimpers and moans, her skin glistening, soft and clean.

"Micah, don't do this," she begs before looking at Ezra, the one she abandoned. "Ezra, please make the trade."

Ezra merely shakes his head.

"What do you want, then, Ezra?" Micah says.

Ezra snickers as if signaling to Micah that he has won this battle. "All of your food. Every single can of whatever you have left. I want all of it. And if you don't give it to me, I'll hurt London. I don't want to, but I will if I have to."

Ezra pulls me in and grabs my hand. I scream out in pain and almost drop to my knees, but Ezra keeps me up and firm within his control.

Micah lurches for me, but Ezra digs in the skate of his spear, making Micah falter.

"Don't come any closer, man. Don't make me hurt this girl more than I already have," Ezra shrieks. "Just give me the fucking food, and you can have her. You can have both of them."

Micah's gaze descends to Naomi, who is now trembling. His eyes shift down to her taut, exposed stomach. He slowly lifts her shirt, revealing the bra she is wearing underneath. His fingertips glide over her smooth skin, causing my toes to curl. He glances up at us, raising an eyebrow, and a wicked grin spreads across his face. "You sure about that? Look at her, buddy. I even cleaned her up for you."

This elicits a reaction. Ezra loosens his hold on me, and I swear, I feel his cock harden along my back because I am pressed so deep against him.

I can hardly blame him. Her skin is smooth and ivory, and her body is much fuller than mine at the moment. Her breasts peek out, showing off their perkiness. The image of her on top of Micah makes the pit in my stomach explode.

He's mine.

"Take the trade, Ezra," I tell him, still hanging from his arms. "I'll make sure Micah gives you the food. But you can't ever trust her again."

Micah's fingers are still on Naomi, and I'm not even sure he's aware of it. Those fingers that have explored every inch of my body are now touching her. He's so comfortable caressing her skin, and it almost looks like she's enjoying it.

Do I even want to go back to him?

A bang interrupts that thought, and all four of us direct our attention outside. There's a hint of movement in the corner of my eye, and the back door swings open.

Fuck. It better not be Nigel. He is the last person who needs to attend this party.

"I think you better put her down, man," a voice says from outside.

Not Nigel...

A deeper, sweeter voice. Caring. Friendly.

I blow out a breath as James steps through the door near us at the back of the broken plane.

He shakes his head. "You're all seriously fucked up. Hand her over, man. Whatever is going on here is over."

"What the fuck are you going to do about it?" Ezra fights back, his voice coming out desperate.

Another voice cuts in, and another shadow enters from the dark mist. Jade follows James inside the airplane, gripping a pointy wooden spear. I can hardly believe my eyes...

Why are they here?

James steps into a protective stance in front of Jade. "It's what we're both going to do about it," she says calmly. "You're outnumbered, Ezra, and we can take you." Her eyes flash to me, her face sunken in, but she otherwise looks healthy, and for that, I'm eternally grateful.

She continues, "So fucking drop her, Ezra. Or Thomas might have something to say about it, too." Another physical response from Ezra. This time, his body shudders. The look in Jade's eyes is nothing short of terrifying. She runs her eyes over me, and even in the dark, I can tell she has changed. No hint of kindness lingers in those hard eyes.

I glance over at Micah, and he's already gone, vanished. And he took Naomi with him.

He's so fast. Always so fucking smooth when he disappears like he's so good at doing, leaving scars in his wake.

Ezra hardens his grip on me. "Get back and give me space. I'll let her go, but get the fuck away from me."

James lifts his arms. "Alright. Okay, man. Just let her go."

"I'm sorry, London," he whispers, then drops me like a lead balloon. I fall with a *thud,* and before I can take a proper breath, Ezra flees into the night.

CHAPTER EIGHTEEN

LONDON

It's not long before I'm in James's arms. He pulls me up and places me on a plane seat, his hand firmly gripping my chin as he studies my eyes before his gaze moves down, inspecting the wounds that mar my body.

He frowns and looks at Jade. "Should we go after him?"

Her eyes are blank as she peers down at me, then flicks her gaze outside. "No point. He's gone. We'll look for him tomorrow." Her head tilts in my direction. "Why were you here? With Ezra?" A simple, pointed question. No greetings or niceties, although I suppose I don't deserve either. "And where's Micah?" I can't help but try to examine the girl looking back at me and how hardened she looks.

It gives me pause.

I swallow hard, barely grabbing onto words, unable to form a proper sentence. My mind is finally catching up with the fact I'm with someone safe. At least, I think she's safe. I'm not sure about anything anymore. There is a subtle wildness in Jade, a husk deep in her eyes.

I can't imagine what the last few months were like for her... What it would have been like living in a shelter made of snow and sticks. While Micah and I were safe and warm, I deliberately avoided thinking about it—it was easier that way.

Jade crosses her arms and awaits my answer.

"Micah left. He... left me alone to go find you," I finally say, keeping my gaze down. I can't bear to look at them, should they see how truly broken I am. "After a few days, when he didn't return, I escaped and followed him. That's when I ran into Nigel and Ezra while trying to find my way back to you. Micah was just here, and he's with Naomi." I can't hide the bitterness in my voice. He must have slipped out so quickly if they didn't even see him.

"What do you mean, escaped?" James asks.

Shit. Did I really say that?

He kneels in front of me. "Did Micah hurt you, London?"

My breath hitches. How do I even respond? "He... he was trying to protect me." Even after everything that happened, my natural instinct is to protect him.

I peer up at James. He looks different, too, much older than he is. His sandy hair is longer, but he's still clean-cut, unlike Micah with his sexy ruggedness or Ezra and Nigel with their feral-like appearances. James seems... steady, normal even.

"You're safe now, London," James says calmly, pulling a strand of hair out of my eyes—hair that was stuck to my forehead and caked with dirt and blood. "I'm not going to let you go near either of them again."

Is that what I want? Protection from Micah? Is that what I need?

James isn't the fondest of Micah. He respects him, yes, but there may be more to it. Something that has to do with me. He notices my bandage and grabs my hand, and I wince as he holds it gently.

His brows knit together. "Did Micah do this to you?" He's piecing it all together—the string of darkness that is my bond to Micah. I respond by shedding a single tear. All my intense emotions manifest into one tiny tear. No others come to join it.

"Fuck," he mutters. "I'm going to kill Micah for doing this to you. He should have protected you. If you had been with me, I wouldn't have let you out of my sight."

I don't respond. Instead, my stomach twists, the hunger taking over. I can't think of anything else, let alone defending my boyfriend, who doesn't deserve to be defended. "Do you have any food? Anything? Please, I just need a little."

I'm not above begging, as I've learned, and I haven't been accustomed to going hungry.

James nods and pulls out a piece of cooked meat. I grab it from him and shove it into my mouth, eating it like a vicious animal, baring my teeth and ripping through it before he can take it back.

James and Jade watch me as I finish, then lay my head back and close my eyes. James pulls me up. "Come on, let's get you out of here. We will deal with Ezra later. Can you walk?"

I pause, uncertain of how this will be received, my heart pounding in my chest. How should I address the fact that Ezra, despite his shortcomings, is also in need of rescue? That he's a lost soul but has the potential for redemption.

I stand, then swiftly descend into James's muscular arms as my legs barely have any feeling left in them and my muscles are completely wasted.

"Ezra's scared... and he's alone. He saved me from Nigel. He didn't want to do this to me; I know he didn't. He acted out when he saw Naomi and Micah." I had him under control until he saw her with him. At least, it's evidence that he's still with me and that his sanity isn't completely gone.

"We can't leave yet," Jade interrupts. "We haven't gotten what we came here for. Believe it or not, there are other people on this island besides Micah and Ezra. And we didn't exactly come here to save you."

With confusion etched on my face, I look at Jade, who is scowling. If they weren't here for me, then why are they here?

"Ollie's missing," Jade says curtly. "He went missing last night. He didn't come back to the camp, so we came looking for him."

I narrow my eyes, leaning on James for support to stand. "And Nathan?" Only now am I realizing that James not being with either of his best friends is strange.

"Nathan didn't make it, London," James says. "He died months ago."

I gasp, pulling my hand to my mouth. "I'm sorry... I didn't know."

Jade stares out the window, a flash of something in her eyes, her brows drawn. Jade is tormented, just like I am.

Anger, fear, rage, hunger.

A mix of emotions.

"Where was Nigel during all this? You said you were with him," she asks.

"Unfortunately, yes, I was," I mutter. "But I don't know where he's staying. It's in a cave north of here. That's all I know. Ezra protected me from him. Nigel's... *unhinged.*"

She runs her hand through her hair, surely thinking about Nigel. They were best friends for years, and I wonder if she knew what he was the whole time.

Jade signals to James. "Fine, we'll go back tonight and let London get some rest away from here. We can continue looking for Ollie tomorrow."

We start to walk into the mist of the night, James keeping close to both of us. He's very strong—very much the hockey captain he once was. "Let's go back and drop her off. We can come back out tomorrow."

As we walk, I steal glances at Jade, hoping to catch a glimpse of the girl I once knew. From what I can tell, she's gone. She steps ahead, confident and withdrawn. I stay close to James, my muscles aching like my body might cease working at any moment.

"We saw Micah," Jade finally says, cutting the tense silence other than the sound of our footsteps against the rock. "When he left you, he came to see us. We don't know what happened to him after that. Ollie went missing a few days later. We've been searching for Ollie on and off for two days."

"How are the others?" I ask, leaning into James to take the pressure off my feet. "Serena? Thomas?"

"Alive," she says with her back still turned to me.

James stays behind with me, supporting me as I walk slowly. Jade keeps her distance and continues to move forward. I appreciate that she's not pressuring me for anything at the moment, but I'm mentally preparing myself for the conversation we will need to have. I will have to explain my grief and pain and why Micah and I had to leave the group. Of course, only if she wants to talk about it. I can't help but feel like I lost her, too.

James grabs my arm to keep me steady and squeezes me. "She'll come around," he whispers.

Am I actually welcome back there? Do I even deserve for her to come around?

I'm too tired to care. I can barely keep my eyes open as we walk, just grateful to get away from the dead and the stench behind us and back to a place I once considered home.

My eyes tear up, and I last about five more minutes before I collapse and James has to carry me the rest of the way. I doze in his arms, happy to have someone warm and comforting. I've always felt safe with James.

"We're here," he whispers, and my eyelids flutter open. A fire is blazing in the meadow, and two people rise when we approach the clearing.

The only two people left here other than us.

James leads me straight to the shelter—Micah's shelter, the one he constructed for us to live in. Thomas and Serena fix their gaze on me, their silence palpable. As we pass by Thomas, I can't help but glance at the stump on his wrist, illuminated by the flickering firelight and cleverly concealed beneath his sleeve. Catching me staring, he swiftly withdraws it from my line of sight. I don't say a word to any of them and crawl into what I used to consider my home. It still smells like Micah. It still feels like he's here and should be here.

I miss him... so fucking much.

Jade crawls in with me, and James stays outside. "Get some rest," she says. "When you wake up, we can talk."

I nod, appreciative of the warm and comfortable bed made of pine boughs and a crap load of soft blankets from the airplane. "This is where James and Serena sleep now," she informs me. "So we will have to figure something out tomorrow."

I'm sure Serena is thrilled to have me back. I'm not here to cause trouble, but this will *never* be Serena's home. It will always belong to Micah and me; it's where we first connected.

James pops his head in, his face soft. "I'm heading back out first thing tomorrow. You will be okay, London. The group might be pissed at you right now, but no one is going to let you get hurt. Get some rest and sleep, alright? Thomas and Serena are staying up. They are taking the night shift."

I should have chosen James. Day one... I had connected with him before the twins completely consumed me. He would have been easier. But that's not where my heart pulled me.

"Where are you going?" I ask as I lay my head down to get more comfortable, wishing he wouldn't leave so soon.

"I'm going to get some sleep, and then I'm going to find Ollie. But I'm going alone. Thomas will stay here and watch over you girls."

I whip my head up. "James," I whisper, hoping the others can't hear me, even though they are close. He turns back to look at me, ever so stoic as he always is. I hope Serena treats him well.

"If you see Ezra, don't hurt him. I think..."

"What is it, London?"

"I think Ezra has paid enough for what he did... There are pieces of himself still inside him. He opened up to me a bit. He protected me from Nigel in the best way he could. He's hurting and in a lot of pain, and I think he's terrified. Please don't kill him... He needs forgiveness."

He nods, his baby blue eyes still full of light. "What do you want me to do if I see him?"

I pause for only a moment. "I want you to bring him back here."

He lets out a sigh. What I am asking him to do is hard, knowing Ezra won't be well received here. "Okay, I'll do that for you. I'll bring him back. And if I run into Nigel?"

I flick my eyes up at him. I want Nigel dead, but he's proving to have nine lives. And considering he's the cause of all my torment, I don't want him hurting one more person I care about. "If you see Nigel, promise me you will run. Don't interact with him, don't engage, just fucking run." From what I've witnessed and experienced the past couple of days, Nigel is the most dangerous person I've ever encountered. He's turned into something none of us understand, and every single person left alive has good reason to be terrified.

CHAPTER NINETEEN

MICAH

I brought Naomi back to the cabin for one more night. She wouldn't speak to me through the long, cold walk home. Even as I helped her over the dark patches in the rock, her iciness ran deep. It appears I have finally succeeded in breaking Naomi Wilson—traumatizing her is more like it. I've never heard her be so quiet.

As soon as James and Jade had arrived, I quickly had led Naomi out through the plane's back door, ensuring she wouldn't have a chance to scream or be noticed by them. Trying to explain why I had a knife to Naomi's throat would have been extremely difficult in that moment.

Her face is as pale as the moon as she steps inside the cabin and curls up on the bed. "Don't touch me, Micah," she snaps, her voice breaking. "Don't come near me."

I run my hand through my hair, taking a moment to remember the bond we formed as childhood friends. She's not an enemy nor a threat. She's just Naomi shaking like a leaf because she fears me. If Ezra had done anything to London, she'd be dead.

I sit down next to her. "I'm going to take you to Jade, Serena, and the others tomorrow. This is over with me, and you'll never have to talk to me again."

She doesn't respond because there is nothing more to say. Our friendship is broken; it always was. I'm not that guy for her, and I never have been. And I'm doing a terrible job being the guy I want to be for the one girl who has ever truly meant anything to me.

I don't crawl in next to Naomi, even though my body is dead tired. I won't sleep tonight anyway. Not that I ever really do, and especially not with Ezra lurking around. I don't know what transpired on the airplane after I left, but I plan to find out as soon as the sun rises.

I head outside, letting the wooden door creak behind me. There's a tease of pink and green light in the sky as the Northern Lights break through the stars sparkling across the sky. I make a small fire and sit next to it, placing my head in my hands. I try not to avert my gaze, knowing it's a sign. Maison loved these lights. He used to go and chase them—a benefit of living in a northern climate. He's with me right now, and I bet if I looked hard enough, I'd see him watching me.

I finally stare at the sky and at the stars behind those celestial lights and think of every way I've failed the few people I love in this world. Maison's presence is all over me, hovering around me and suffocating the air I breathe. His judgment is pouring in from the other side.

"Yeah, I know, brother," I whisper. "I fucking know... Now, get out of my mind."

He has no business being so self-righteous. He killed someone after all. He took a life. He fucking *died* and left me. The devastation of that is unforgivable. He can rot in hell.

I'm not a killer. I'm not a monster.

I whisper those two phrases to myself over and over as the fire dwindle to flickering embers and ashes. She was right there... I fucking had her within my grasp, and I let her slip. London's eyes were glazed over, and she looked at me like I was a stranger.

I sit in silence for hours without moving in the cold, frozen and still as the wind cuts through my hood and bites my face. My mind is in a prison, the guilt eating me alive for my heart being the one that's beating right now. My throat tightens... and for nearly an hour, I can't breathe.

It's a hint of light in the sky that shakes me and pulls me back to reality. The morning breaks through the clouds, and I rise, head inside, and nudge Naomi awake. She is sleeping soundly, sprawled out like she's on vacation—like I didn't nearly slit her throat eight hours earlier. "Get ready. It's time to go."

Without uttering a single word, she rises from the bed and begins cramming her stuff into her bag. Her demeanor has noticeably shifted since last night as she appears more collected and composed.

She finally makes eye contact with me. "They aren't going to want you there when they find out what you did to me last night. I'll tell them what you are, Micah."

A smile hints at my lips, and I open the trapdoor in the floorboards. "Yeah? We'll see about that." Her eyes widen as I pull out the medical kit and some canned food and stuff it into my backpack. "This is my peace offering, and they'd be stupid not to accept it. They have no food either, Naomi. It's my peace offering to you too. Take what you want."

I'm not worried about Naomi seeing my supply stash. It doesn't matter anymore. I won't need it because I won't be here next winter to eat it.

"How do you have so much left?" she asks as she leans down, cautiously grabs a few cans, and places them in her bag. She doesn't take it all, and she doesn't question why I purposely leave some behind.

"Because I know how to live off the land," I answer. "Nature has everything you need to survive."

She waits with her arms crossed and her lips pursed as I finish packing and head outside. She follows me as I scan both directions of the dark forest, half expecting Ezra or Nigel to pop out. A fresh breeze hits my skin.

I head south along the creek. She says nothing to me, still frightened or scared but quiet, which is what I always prefer when I'm with Naomi. That's why I used to just shove my dick in her mouth. However, that tactic wasn't an option this time around.

After about an hour of walking at a steady pace, she stops in her tracks. I ignore her and keep walking until I realize she isn't planning on moving until I acknowledge her.

"What is it, Naomi?" I ask with an edge of irritation in my voice.

She bites her bottom lip. "What if they don't want me here? I haven't seen them in months."

I tilt my head. It's not like Naomi to be so insecure. "Serena's there. You'll be fine."

She sucks in a breath, completely unsure of herself. "I... I don't know, Micah. Am I safe with them?"

I let out a laugh. "You're safer with them than you are with me." I pause for a moment, contemplating those words. "Naomi, for what it's worth, I'm sorry for doing that to you. I love her... I really fucking love her."

She looks away as a flash of emotion flows through her eyes. Pain, jealousy, or perhaps longing for what she has with someone else that she royally fucked up. "I know. You've made yourself abundantly clear. Let's get this over with," she mutters as we approach the meadow.

I try to breathe out the pent-up tension I'm holding inside, knowing London is here, too.

As we walk up, I notice Thomas, Jade, and Serena before they notice me. They are in the middle of the meadow, where they have set up another more central fire spot. They are huddled around... but there are only three of them. James is missing.

I hang back and watch for a second.

"Serena!" Naomi runs through the thicket and the meadow, all ponytail and pep, capturing their attention.

For fuck's sake.

This is why I prefer to fly solo. She has absolutely zero clue these people have changed, and her initial instinct to be weary was the right one.

Serena's eyes flicker up, then she bolts with excitement. "Naomi?"

The next few seconds are full of shrieks and hugs, and it's like we are in the halls of New Ocean Prep and the two of them just came from a pep rally—the bane of my existence—oblivious to the fact that Jade and Thomas rise, and neither look happy to see her. Jade's eyes tighten as she peers into the forest, right in my direction. Her knuckles are so tightly clenched that even from here, I can tell they are white.

She has good reasons to hate Naomi since she was the one who pinned her down when Ezra cut Thomas's hand. And Naomi is, of course, oblivious to the hatred spewing out of Jade. Thomas looks up toward where I'm standing. I step behind a group of fir trees, immersing myself in the comforting scent of pine needles.

"Where's Micah, Naomi?" Jade asks without pulling her gaze from the trees.

Naomi looks in my direction and frowns. I should leave right now and not have this conversation. I'm tempted...

She shakes her head. "I don't know. He was right there."

"Come on out, Micah," Thomas says, his massive frame intimidating the fuck out of me even from here. And I don't say that lightly.

I grip my bone weapon, readying it. No point in hiding my weapon. He's not my friend anymore, and he's twice my size even after surviving the hell of winter. Plus, James is not in my line of sight, which makes me really fucking nervous.

I've come to terms with having no one by my side. I have effectively isolated myself, but eventually, we will all succumb to turning against each other—an inevitable outcome as our resources diminish.

I keep my hood over my head as I step out from the shadows. "Thomas..." I say casually and with as little emotion as possible. I don't need this to be a recap of how shitty of a friend I am or how tortured they were all winter.

Thomas gets all bristly and puffs his chest but doesn't come near me. Instead, he steps in the opposite direction. Jade and Thomas both turn toward the shelter and then toward me.

It catches my attention.

"What are you doing here?" he asks, and Jade stays wholly still beside him, observing me. I doubt he knows Jade and I had our little rendezvous after our last meeting. I'll keep her secret... for now.

"Calm yourself down, dude. I'm not staying. I came to drop Naomi off and give you this." I drop the contents of my bag—containing all the canned food I could carry and the medical supplies—to the ground. The cans roll around, and the food scatters.

Jade and Thomas exchange a glance, as do Serena and Naomi. None of them know how to handle me... Thomas takes yet another step in the opposite direction, keeping his eyes on the threat.

Me... I'm the threat.

He can't help it; he's a defenseman. He's never been a fighter, but his guttural instinct is to protect. So why does he think London needs protecting?

I cut my gaze to Jade—since clearly, she's the one in charge—and jerk my chin toward the shelter. "Is she in there?"

Naomi and Serena grow quiet, although still hanging off each other. The air electrifies between us as Jade grabs her spear. "Micah, let's go talk."

I shake my head. "Nah. Why don't you just tell me why Thomas is all jittery? What do you think I did?"

Jade bites the inside of her cheek, steps toward me, and points in the direction where I just came from. "Forest... Now, Micah."

Fuck.

I decide to appease her and not cause a scene. I step back toward the tree line, and Jade follows me. As soon as we are away from the others, I whip around. Jade jolts, but her spear is up in an instant, the tip pointed right at me.

"London's here, Micah. She's not well, but I think you know that. We are jittery because Ollie is missing, and we don't know who to trust right now."

I don't know if I should be relieved or royally pissed off. Like fuck I am going to let Jade or Thomas stop me. I direct my attention to the shelter where London is resting.

"Micah, wait..."

I take a step forward as she doubles down on the grip on her spear. "No. I don't think I will."

Jade grabs my arm, and I bristle. "She's not well, Micah. Leave her alone right now. Trust me."

I pause dangerously and turn to face her. "If she's here, she needs me. No one else can help her the way I can. Can you understand that and get your spear out of my fucking face?"

She closes her eyes for a moment, composing herself, then opens them. "What I understand, Micah, is that she was with you, and then she wasn't. And she was hurt badly by Nigel and then Ezra. I also suspect she was hurt very fucking badly by you. So you can storm in there and proclaim your presence, but all you are going to do is upset her, and she needs to rest."

My eye twitches, her spear poking into my chest. "You can't stop me with a fucking stick."

She drops the spear an inch. "You're probably right, but then you will have to get through Thomas in order to get to her." She shrugs. "Good luck with that."

I let out a heavy sigh, knowing damn well Thomas will be an impenetrable wall for me, so I guess I have to play nice. "Well, what the fuck do you expect me to do, then? I can't just sit here."

She waves her hands. "I don't know. Go fishing or hunting. Find us some more food and contribute, considering we now have three more mouths to feed, soon four. That might go a long way with us. When she wakes up, I will let her know you're here."

As I scan my surroundings, my anxiety intensifies. James is still nowhere to be found, and it makes me really fucking nervous having so many rogue people roaming this island.

"Where is James?"

"He went to find Ollie who went missing a few days ago."

I place my hands in my sweats' pockets, trying to calm my raging heart. "What do you mean, he went missing?"

She sits on a nearby log and places her hands over her neck. "He went to the creek to get water and firewood and didn't come back. We searched for him for hours. It's not sitting right with me. Nigel's still unaccounted for. What if he has Ollie?"

I pause at how ridiculous that is. Ollie is twice the size of that short motherfucker. "Why would you think that?"

She sniffles and runs her hand over the bridge of her nose. "That's what I've been trying to tell you. There was another message..."

Another human bone.

I pause for a moment and compose myself. "That's why I'm not leaving. If London's here, then you're stuck with me too. I haven't seen Nigel, but Ezra is a liability as well. He's the one who hurt her, Jade, not me. If she just fucking stayed put like I told her to..."

"No one said you had to leave."

I need to explain myself; judgment is pouring out of her eyes. "I didn't mean to hurt her, Jade. I was supposed to go right back to her, but I got distracted by a nearly-dead Naomi."

"No one said that you did."

I run my hands through my hair, wanting to rip it all out. "I fucking love her. If something happens to her. If I lose her..."

Her eyes finally soften a bit. "I know, Micah. But pull yourself together before you talk to her, for her sake and yours. Go clear your head and come back. She's not going anywhere, and she's safe right now and resting. I'm watching over her. Just please trust me and calm down."

The tension radiates off me, the hurt inside hitting a breaking point, and poor Jade is about to take the brunt of it.

My fingers curl into a fist as the rage inside me boils over, melting the all-consuming love I have for the girl lying a few feet away from me. Someone needs to die for what happened to my twin and for forcing me to watch the girl I love deal with the pain of his death. How could she ever love me with that dark cloud hanging over our heads? We were doomed from the start.

"You want me to calm down? Like it's that fucking easy, Jade. You are the one who moved on when Maison died, like you didn't give a shit about him. He was slaughtered before your eyes, and you let his killer just walk away. You even gave him food. And you're telling me to calm down?"

It takes all of two seconds before Thomas is suddenly behind Jade. I watch him carefully as my world starts to turn gray—that dark place I get where I don't know what the fuck I am capable of.

"Step back, Micah. We're not your enemy," Thomas says, then places himself in front of Jade as I begin to shake and pace.

Weak.... I'm fucking weak for breaking down like this. For allowing them to witness my raw vulnerability. I need to get the fuck out of here.

Jade blows out a breath and shakes her head. "Micah, please understand. We had to focus on our own survival. I'm sorry about Maison, I really am, but we've been grieving Nathan, too, and everyone else that's lost their lives here."

My teeth grind together, a fiery heat rolling through me. "It's not the same. Nathan wasn't murdered."

Thomas tilts his head, stepping between Jade and me. "No, but the outcome was still the same, man. He's still gone."

I look her up and down. Then I look over to Thomas, to Serena and Naomi, who are eavesdropping only a couple of feet away, and finally to the shelter.

No sign of life. Nothing. London must be in a pretty shitty state if she hasn't come out yet. If I lose London, I might as well kill myself right now. She is all I have left; she is all I want and will ever want.

I look directly at Jade. "For your sake and everyone else's here, make sure she doesn't fucking die." I pull my pack over my shoulder, then pick up the knife and grip it to make sure everyone can see it. "Don't eat the food all at once. I'll be back soon."

I arrive back at the site just before dusk, as promised. I caught a fish and a rabbit, which I'm hoping will be well received by the others. I single-handedly doubled their food supply. I did as Jade suggested and took a breath and focused on what I do best: hunting, stalking, getting control of my surroundings.

Killing things.

I spent the better part of the day circling the perimeter of the camp to make sure there weren't any more *messages* sent by Nigel. I saw no sign of him anywhere. In fact, I'm confident he's nowhere near us, at least for now. My anxiety can ease, although I still don't think I will sleep knowing he and Ezra are out there.

Jade was right to send me away. A day in the woods helped clear my head and gave London a chance to sleep. My rage, however, is still simmering within me, ready to be unleashed at any moment. London can help with that once she's better and I can finally get her alone.

As I enter the meadow, Naomi and Serena are cuddled together by the fire. Thomas is working on skinning something while Jade, I notice, shoots daggers at Naomi. Naomi, in return, shoots them at me. Obviously, Naomi updated them on the reunion we had on the airplane last night. Their faces say it all as they behold me.

I approach silently, and Thomas shoots me a warning glance as he looks at the shelter. I hold up my kills in a gesture of neutrality and walk up next to him. He moves over, grunts, and tends to his skinning as I take out the knife and begin to prepare my kills.

Jade lifts her head as I approach, giving me a tight look. "She's asleep, but don't worry, she's still breathing." I can sense her maintaining a healthy distance from me ever since my emotional outburst earlier. I give a small nod, signifying my agreement, and then redirect my attention to my kills.

I want to go check on her, at least lay my eyes on her, but I'll give London space if that's what they think she truly needs. Or worse, if that's what she asked for.

Everyone is anxious around me, staring at my knife and the casual way I wield it. I'm not sure when I became the enemy on this island or when everyone became complete strangers to me, but here we are. The only person who seems unbothered by my presence is Thomas.

Together, we skin my kills, and I try not to stare at his wrist because I know it will set him off. But I marvel at how skilled he is with one hand, and I'm secretly proud of him for how he's been adapting to it since the last time I saw him. It has healed well from what I can tell, and that's because of the clean cut I gave him when I severed it with the same knife I'm holding now.

Like fuck I'm telling him that, though, because he's acting like a fucking baby.

We finish cooking our meat, and I find myself a stick to carve out a new spear. It's second nature to me now because I've known for a long time that my hands can't be idle.

I don't make eye contact with anyone, but I keep a careful eye on the shelter. After about an hour of sitting in silence, I blow the dust off the new spear just as a figure emerges from the darkness.

The moment James lays eyes on me, his body goes rigid, and a mix of fear and anxiety churns inside me when I notice he's not alone. Ezra steps out from the shadows and stares at me with a fucking cocky grin. I jump to my feet, and I'm not the only one. Thomas is right beside me, looking just as pissed.

James lifts his eyebrows and centers his attention on Thomas. "What's Micah doing here?" He also takes in the additional presence of Naomi, and his fingers curl into a fist.

Well, this just got fucking interesting...

Jade slowly rises, and Naomi's mouth gapes open. I guess Ezra's presence is a surprise to all of us.

It's Naomi who speaks first. "Ezra, what the hell happened to your hair?"

He chuckles, running his hand over his head. "My new girlfriend cut it for me." His words are cold and brutal, and he looks at me as he says it.

This has me jumping out of my skin, and I get to him before anyone can stop me. All the rage coiled in my stomach erupts out of me.

My fist connects with his face, knocking his ass to the ground, thinking of how close London must have gotten to him to cut his hair so nicely. How much care and attention she gave him...

What the actual fuck?

He rises to his elbows and grins up at me from the ground as blood stains his teeth. My bone weapon is against Ezra's neck before James or anyone can blink. He doesn't put up a fight as I pull him up and get him into a chokehold in a way that cuts off the oxygen to his brain. The same way he was holding London yesterday. It's not the first time I've done this to him, and it feels just as fucking good as it did the last time.

He always knows how to get under my skin; he baits me to act this way. Only this time, if anyone comes near me, I will kill him.

I grind my teeth together. "What the fuck did you just say?" He can't respond. His body goes limp underneath me as I restrict his ability to breathe. He doesn't try to fight back, but his chest rises and falls with laughter.

He's fucking *laughing* at me.

I yank him a few feet away from the others, positioning myself so no one can get behind me. "Tell me why I shouldn't kill you right fucking now?" I say with my mouth against his ear.

"I think he should," Thomas says, and it makes me smile. Just like old times.

"Thomas, stop. We talked about this," Jade says, holding him back by simply pressing her hand to his chest. "This isn't your fight."

I dig the bone tip into Ezra's neck. "One little slice, and we'd all have one less mouth to feed. I'd be doing everyone a favor."

"Micah, stop this shit," James says, taking a step forward. "You're scaring the girls."

Naomi and Serena are shaking like leaves. Jade, however, is watching, her face unreadable.

"What the fuck is he even doing with you?" I snap at James. "He had a knife to London's throat."

James curls his lip, his fingers now curled in a hard fist. Thomas steps back, not interfering, which was the exact response I was hoping for. "You had a knife to Naomi's throat too, man, yet you're here. And he's here because London begged me to bring him here, so talk to your girl."

Not the fucking same.

"He killed my brother," I retort.

"He didn't," Jade says, stepping forward. "That was Nigel, and you know it."

"Well, he was a fucking part of it."

As I squeeze, the pulse in Ezra's neck throbs in my hand from how fast his heart is beating. I want to experience it...What it's like to suck the soul right out of someone.

My anger is overwhelming. I squeeze harder. I'm not even sure the others realize he can't breathe at all anymore. One more second, and I could end him.

"Micah, stop! If you kill him, I'll never talk to you again."

The sound of her voice nearly cripples me. I whip my head up and see her.

Wild, beautiful, and broken.

London's watching me as if I'm a monster—the monster I kept telling myself I wasn't. I drop Ezra, and he immediately gasps for air, clinging to his throat. I'm so tense that no one dares come near me, but Naomi rushes over to him as London takes a step back.

I immediately chase after her. "London, baby, come here."

London stands there, and everyone stares at her, then back at me. Ezra moans from the ground but finds his voice. "See, I told you she was mine now," he says in a mocking tone.

London shakes her head, turns around, and disappears into the darkness.

"Fuck," I mutter.

Jade turns to James. "Get Ezra out of here," she growls, and James grabs Ezra, pulling him to safety. "Micah, calm the fuck down. And Thomas, you're not helping. This won't solve anything. Micah, if you can't compose yourself, then leave right now and don't come back."

James walks Ezra across the meadow, and Ezra stares right at Thomas, then at his missing hand. "He fucking cut my fingers off, too, man," he mutters as blood stains the snow beneath him. James shakes his head at him. "An eye for an eye."

James pats him on the back. "Ezra, you're not making any friends, man."

I ignore them. I jump over the cooking site and am out of view before Jade can stop me. I step toward the shelter, only to find it empty. Luckily, it's a clear night, and the moon and stars create just enough light to sort of see where I'm going.

"London," I call out for her, but she doesn't answer. I pause and listen—for her breaths, her rustling, her heart-beat—for any sign of her. She can't have run far, so she's hiding.

"London, I'm never going to stop looking for you, so you might as well come out and talk to me."

I hear a faint sob and a crunch of snow. I take a few steps and see her kneeling down, her head hanging in front of her. Her hair is muddy and messy, but she looks so fucking sexy. My stomach knots with a mix of emotions, aware of where she is standing and who is currently consuming her thoughts.

And it's not fucking me.

"London," I say in a low voice. She's so close, yet so far away right now.

"Stay back, Micah. Don't touch me right now. This isn't a game."

I tilt my head, but she continues to keep her eyes down-cast. "Talk to me, baby. Let me explain."

However, I don't really have anything to say about it. I did all the things she is mad about.

I tied her up and left her alone.

I abandoned her.

I didn't chase her when I should have.

She looks up at me, and her face is expressionless and cold. She opens her mouth slightly to say something, but no words come out. She won't give me a fucking word.

I reach out to her, needing to touch her. I grab her hand, and she flinches when I squeeze it. Something's wrong. Her hand is limp and distorted.

"Your hand is broken again." My stomach turns, thinking about what she must have done to get out of the binds I had her left in. What must have been going through her head as she shattered her own hand to escape me.

She probably thought I wasn't coming back, that she had no choice...

No wonder she can't look at me.

I kneel in front of her, pull her chin, and force her to look at me. Even though she's caked with dirt, all I can see are her gorgeous, full lips in the moonlight.

"I didn't mean to do this to you," I tell her.

"Ezra was right about you," she whispers, pulling her hand away. "I didn't want to believe she was the reason why you didn't come back for me or try to find me. But she was, wasn't she?"

I wipe some of the dirt on her face with my thumb, and damn, she's the most beautiful girl in the world. I don't know if I can be this close to her without her being mine. "Ezra hates me, London. He's poisoning your brain."

She stands, and I stay on my knees, placing my hands on either side of her slender waist.

She's so small, so breakable.

"Ezra didn't tie me up and leave me for two days," she mutters and turns her head away. But her little body is pressed right against me, sending a throb right to my cock.

She tries to wiggle away, but I don't relent on my hold. I breathe her in, so fucking happy to have her in my arms again, and I don't let go. Her fingers find mine, and she unwraps them one by one. She looks down at me, her expression chilling me to the core.

I squeeze my brows together. "Please, baby. I'm so sorry for doing that to you. I'm on my knees for you, London. I'm begging for you to hear me right now. Can you not see that was the worst mistake I've ever made?"

She grazes her fingers over my cheek, not touching me, but the heat of her fingers lingers. "You left me," she breathes. "I waited for you even after I got out. I so desperately wanted you to come back, but you didn't. You left me so vulnerable, Micah."

My eyes flash as that rage rolls through me again, thinking of Ezra. "Did Ezra hurt you?"

She pinches her lips together. "No more than you did. And he's not the one I was referring to."

I recall the level of comfort I just witnessed between them. His claim on her... Something happened between them. She had a chance to kill him and didn't. She fucking pampered him instead, gave him care and attention she should only reserve for me. I can tell by his cocky grin alone that he liked it.

I press my forehead against her stomach and shut my eyes, as if not seeing her will make this better. "Did you fuck him?"

She pulls away, and her eyes flash. Then she slaps me hard, right across the face with her non-mangled hand. My body is like stone, but the weight behind that slap hurts—the emotional punch she packs that turns me on so much about her. I take in every second of it; the pain is blissful because it means she still cares.

"Did you fuck Naomi?" she asks.

"No."

"Did she try?"

I should lie because that would make my life so much easier right now, but I'm a fucking terrible liar and I'm pretty sure she saw Naomi and me. "Yeah, she tried. But I didn't do anything with her, London. I swear. You're the only one I want, baby. I pushed her away before it got to that."

She bites her lip, and the swell of emotions in her eyes keeps me going. She's standing close, so I keep my forehead against her stomach and my hands to myself. Finally, she softens.

"I fucking missed you, London." My voice comes out as a whisper. I'm so hungry for her, and having her so close and not being able to touch her is torture. I just want to devour her so fucking hard. Especially as the image of her and Ezra together infiltrates my brain and I think of London cutting his hair. How long that would have taken her, and the fact she had scissors to his neck and didn't shove them into him.

I grab her hips again and pull her closer, so happy to experience the heat of her body again. I have memorized every curve and line on this girl, and I can't get enough of it. How does she not see that she is all I want?

I gaze up at her. "I can't be around you if you're not with me, London. You're mine, baby, remember? That doesn't change in a matter of days... It never fucking changes."

A twig snaps near me, and I pause for only a moment, then shrug it off. I doubt that with the performance I just put on, anyone would have the guts to interrupt me right now. I dig my thumbs into her in a way I know she likes as agony pours through me.

"Everything has changed," she hisses. "The moment you left me and didn't come back. That's when it changed. You shouldn't have chosen Naomi," she says coldly, and the sting from her slap still burns.

I run my hand along her stomach, down to the drawstring of her pants to remind her how little has changed, but she stops me, gripping my hand with hers. Annoyance tugs at me. She has never not given in to me, which tells me I must have really fucked up.

"Please, baby. I need you right now."

Her voice comes out ragged and raw. "Micah, you scare me... You really scare me. You don't seem right in the head, and I don't think I'm right in the head, either. I can't do this with you right now. I need to... process."

Process? She needs to process? *What the fuck does she need to process?*

"What the hell are you talking about, baby?"

"Please, Micah, don't make this harder than it needs to be."

Please. How many times has she said that to me?

Please.

Please.

Please.

Fucking needy, which is exactly how I want her. I'll remind her how good it makes her feel.

Suddenly, an annoying voice rips through the forest. "I think the girl told you to back off her, man."

My body stills, and every hair on my skin bristles. For fuck's sake. Of course, it would be James interrupting me. "Mind your fucking business," I yell out to him. This kid is really starting to get on my nerves.

"Nah, I don't think I will," he calls back.

London's eyes widen. He stands a few feet away with his head turned at least. Not that I care about James watching me as I claim my girl—or about anyone watching, for that matter. Let him watch.

"Get the fuck out of here," I gripe back at him with no intention of stopping.

The moment, however, is ruined. London pushes away from me and shakes her head, begging me not to make another scene.

"Look, man," I call out again, "I'm just having a moment with my girlfriend." At least, I think she's my girlfriend. She's looking at me like I'm a stranger right now, and I don't like it.

"London, are you good?" James asks.

"Of course, she's fucking good," I snipe.

"I wasn't talking to you."

"I'm fine," she responds weakly. "Micah and I are just talking. We will rejoin the group in a few minutes."

James pauses for a moment as if he doesn't believe her.

"Did you fucking hear her?" I ask, wondering why he's still fucking here.

She nudges me. "Micah, stop it."

"Yeah, I heard her, man. Jade called a meeting. We all need to chat about a few things. It would be appreciated if you both came and you didn't kill anyone or chop off anyone's fingers in the process."

"Can't promise anything," I yell back.

I tilt my head and peer down at London, whose big brown eyes are staring right into me.

She jerks her head in the direction of where James's voice came from. "Let's go, Micah."

I finally relent, and she shuffles away from me as fast as she can. "I can't fucking wait," I mutter, trying to ignore the painful fucking bulge against my pants.

CHAPTER TWENTY

LONDON

I wasn't sure how I would react to seeing Micah again. My love for him is undeniable, yet there's a lingering sense of unfamiliarity that troubles me. Perhaps I've never known him or understood the chilling whispers of his senseless brutality. He's always had demons inside him, and I love him regardless of them. Because I have that anger, too... but right now, it's directed at him.

I'm so fucking mad at him.

We rejoin the group, and I'm fully aware of how utterly disgusting I am as we approach the others huddled around the fire, Ezra included.

I'm tired, so exhausted, but I'm more hungry than anything. I'm always hungry. My stomach never settles, even when I'm able to eat scraps of whatever anyone cares to give me. I've never gotten used to the hunger, unlike Micah, who seems superhuman and can seemingly go days on end without eating or sleeping.

Always prowling.

As soon as we approach and I see Naomi sitting next to Serena, my body goes wholly still. My anger... it's directed at her, too. We make eye contact, and for a moment, we are the only two people here. She's no longer the cocky, confident girl who thought she owned the school and everyone here. Her golden hair is pulled back, and her eyes are...

broken. I recognize the emotions swimming inside her. If I looked in the mirror, I'd see the same.

Because Micah broke her, and he broke me, too.

And she broke Ezra.

A vicious, toxic cycle I am now the center of, yet I have no time or energy to sympathize with her. She's the reason why Micah didn't come back to me and I had to break my own hand to get out of those binds. I have no idea how much longer I could have endured that. The dehydration alone almost killed me—though, what I was planning on doing to myself scares me the most.

I can't be by myself. I realize that now.

As I cautiously step inside the circle, I can't help but notice the palpable intensity of Micah's energy right behind me. Ezra hangs to the side alone, not quite a part of the group but not an outsider anymore. We make eye contact, and he frowns, then tips his head to the side as if saying—

I'm sorry.

Naomi notices our interaction and frowns, wrapping her arms around herself. Everyone watches me as I sit cross-legged on a blanket Micah grabbed from his pack.

Micah keeps his distance and stands away from the group, gripping his bone weapon needlessly since no one is attacking him right now.

Although my earlier rejection pains him, I can't be what he needs me to be at this moment. His eyes somehow grow darker, and he pulls his hood up and sits at the edge of the circle. I don't owe Micah an explanation to make him feel better.

Whenever Ezra steals glances at me, he smiles—a calculated display meant to taunt Micah, who is watching closely. The four of us are seemingly engaged in a treacherous game of heartbreak and betrayal.

"Now that we're all together, we need to talk," James says, looking over at Jade.

Together... is that what we are?

Jade casts her gaze between Micah and Ezra, sensing the tension among us. "And we mean talk, not fight it out like dogs."

"Quit fucking looking at her," Micah grits to Ezra.

"Ollie is missing," Jade snaps. "Can we please focus on him rather than London, who is safe right now?"

That shuts everyone up, and I lower my eyes, focusing on the fire, hating that the attention is once again focused on me. Micah sits behind me, laying a blanket over me and pulling me between his legs. I fall into him, too tired to fight it, and he wraps his arms around me tight.

This behavior... It's very Maison-like.

The public displays of affection, the claiming... He's never done this before; he was always so distant and cold. Then again, we haven't really been together in front of everyone. I don't know how to act, and deep down... really deep down, this still seems like a betrayal to Maison. This group saw me on his lap in this same position for weeks.

"I didn't see Nigel when I went out, and unfortunately, I found no signs of Ollie," James says, looking directly at Ezra. "I found Ezra near the airplane heading north. I offered to bring him back if he could tell me where to find Nigel, but he claims to only know approximately where Nigel is hiding and swears he doesn't know the exact spot."

"Bullshit," Micah mutters.

"It's not bullshit, it's the truth," Naomi says, still leaning against Serena. "Ezra and I didn't know where Nigel was. It was part of our arrangement, and I was relieved and slept better at night because of it."

"He got worse as winter went on," Ezra says darkly, his gaze fixated on the fire. "He started saying some weird fucking shit, and I didn't like the way he looked at Naomi, so I kept Naomi away from him."

The mention of Nigel sends a chill up my spine, and goosebumps rise on my arms. As if noticing my tension, Micah's hands run over my shoulders, instantly warming and relaxing me. But he squeezes them in warning, harder than usual, which reminds me he's not Maison. And in this dark moment, he brings me comfort. His hand twists around my waist and settles on my stomach.

Everyone's still watching.

Ezra stays quiet and distant.

Naomi continues, her face solemn, "I think he has a cave similar to ours somewhere, and Ezra would meet him every few days to cook, hunt, and share food. But it's not like we left our cave much." She looks over at him. "Ezra and I were trapped in our cave for months during that big deep freeze."

I remember the deep freeze well. I spent it mainly cuddled up and warm.

Micah scoffs. "It seems like Ezra took real good care of you."

Ezra stiffens. "Well, we are fucking alive, aren't we? And that wasn't thanks to you... that was all me."

"You're barely alive," Micah says, running his hand over me, probably because my entire body tenses. "Naomi was hanging on by a thread when I found her. Do you even have a freshwater source?"

Naomi folds her arms. "No, we don't, which is part of why I left."

Ezra merely scoffs at that. "We all know she left for other reasons..."

"Why don't we just let him rot?" Thomas says. "He'll die there eventually. The snowpack's melting and drying. He won't have any access to water."

"I'd sleep better at night if we knew where he was," Jade says, her eyes set firmly on the flames. "If we find him, we'll find Ollie."

Ollie has been missing for several days now, and everyone seems reluctant to acknowledge the harsh reality that maybe Ollie has become one of the countless souls who now reside in the afterlife on this island.

"I'm going back tomorrow to look for him," James says. He exchanges glances with Serena, who frowns at him. "If he's still alive, I'll find him eventually."

Or his body.

I hope for Ollie's sake that he ended up somewhere the animals can't get to him. The bottom of the lake, perhaps, would be a good place where his soul could rest in peace. At least now, everyone understands the true threat that haunts us here. It's not the icy winds, rocks, animals, hidden shelters, or lack of food.

It's Nigel.

Jade believes it, even if the others don't. Out of everyone here, she possesses the deepest understanding of him. She knows he didn't kill Maison out of revenge for his sister but because he is nothing more than a brutal killer who probably would have killed eventually, regardless of his reasons why.

The little scar on my throat begins to throb like it always does whenever I think of him. No one talks or utters a word as we all relive the horrors of what happened when we were all last together.

He's out there. A murderer hiding in these woods, who is now also desperate and hungry.

Serena finally lifts her gaze from the fire. "We should all be safe enough together, right? I doubt he will come anywhere near here."

My head rests on Micah's chest, and I can distinctly hear the rhythm of his heart, but I swear it skips a beat, his body heat rising. Something about his energy shifts, and his body tightens. The silence is deafening; no one knowing how to answer.

Micah finally says, "I bet he is already here somewhere."

I swallow the acid in my throat at that very real possibility.

"What do we do now?" Naomi asks over the crackling fire. Hearing her voice makes my skin crawl. Visions of her beating me, holding me down while Nigel stabbed me in my side all those months ago... She doesn't deserve a place among us.

"We take turns staying awake," Jade says. "Some of us sleep during the day, and some of us man this fire. No one is ever allowed to be alone. We have three shelters, so we can split up, but keep your wits about you. All he needs is a fleeting moment." Thomas and James rise. "Two people need to stay up tonight."

"We'll take the fire," Micah volunteers before I even have a chance to protest. I look up at him, my eyes wide. It's still cold outside. My breath still teases the air, and I absolutely hate sleeping in the elements. But the fire out here is big, and they have a sufficient stockpile of wood. Besides, I spent the entire day sleeping, so I'm not tired anyway.

"It'll be fine, London," Micah whispers in my ear.

He doesn't understand. I'm not scared of the cold; I'm petrified of being alone with him. I hate how comfortable I already am in his arms. I need to remind myself I'm still pissed at him. We never finished our conversation.

Jade nods. "Fine, then tomorrow night, we can switch."

"We're not staying," Micah interrupts before she can finish her thought. "I'll take London back with me tomorrow. You can keep the food."

Jade tilts her head as if seeing right through us. She can sense my hesitation; everyone can. I've never been great at hiding my emotions from these people.

"Suit yourself," she mutters.

I bite my lip as everyone starts to shuffle away, getting ready to sleep for the night. A sense of dread eats me up inside—at the thought of staying here, at the thought of leaving... and at the thought of living.

How long can we truly live like this?

"Where the fuck am I supposed to go?" Ezra asks.

"We have a half-built shelter about a hundred feet down the river where Ollie stayed sometimes. It's not much, but it's better than nothing," James responds, rising and grabbing Serena's hand, but not before his gaze lingers on Micah, then on me, his eyebrows raised. "There is some wood stockpiled next to it, so you should be fine to start a fire."

Thomas, who hasn't said a word to anyone, walks out into the darkness, and Jade follows him, leaving Naomi, Ezra, Micah, and me.

The outsiders.

I can imagine how weird it is for the four of them to suddenly have four extra people to contend with. Ezra grimaces at Naomi, staring at her for a long second, anger seething out of him before he finally says, "Are you fucking coming or what, Naomi?"

She exhales sharply, scoops up a couple extra blankets, and joins Ezra in the darkness without even acknowledging our presence, leaving Micah and me alone once more.

Micah rises and throws a few logs into the fire, getting it nice and hot as I lay out a few extra blankets Jade has left us and lie down. I watch him, so confident and so strong. The ground, scorched by the flames, is dry to the touch, but a bone-chilling wind makes me shiver instantly. I can't relax; my joints are frozen, and my nerves are jumpy. My heart beats rapidly, reminiscent of the first time I was alone with Micah.

After all these months and everything we've been through together, Micah still has me on edge. It's as if my adrenaline spiked when I pulled myself out of those binds, and it never came down. I'm so lost in my thoughts that I jerk when he crawls in behind me on our bed.

My breath falters because I have no idea which version of Micah I'm about to get.

"Come here," he whispers, pulling me close.

The cuddly one apparently.

He runs his hand down to mine and pulls off the dirty bandage wrapped around it. I turn to face him, and the gold specs in his eyes flash as he pulls it off and checks the wound underneath it. I don't like to look at it or think about what it represents.

"I'll fix it," he whispers, pressing his lips to my brow. "I'll make it better."

No acknowledgment that he was the one who caused this, but a burning sorrow radiates from him. I can't shield him from that pain; he should endure it, and I hope it lingers until his last breath.

He bends my wrist, and I gasp as he tries to bend one finger. Every finger is swollen and bruised, the veins of my hand popping out. He frowns as he reaches over to the medical kit nearby and re-wraps my hand tighter than before, and it instantly feels better.

"We have to get some ice on it," he says, laying his head down and pulling my head down with him.

I enjoy his hot breath on my ear and neck. His erection is pressing against me, which causes heat to build in my core, adding to the already blazing fuel coursing through me that is my anger. My anger builds and intensifies with each passing second. He really thinks soft strokes and gentle kisses will make this all better?

He's relentless as his hands begin to roam my stomach, teasing their way up to my breasts where he cups one of them before moving back down to my belly.

Down.

Down.

Down.

"Micah, I can't do this right now," I protest, even though his soft hands are the medicine my body needs.

He runs his hand over my thighs. "I know, London. I'm warming you up; you're freezing."

The same way he left me—cold and alone. Now, suddenly, he cares?

"I'll rub you all night if I need to, baby," he whispers, nibbling on my ear. It sounds like an apology, although there is an edge to his voice.

I know Micah Matei well enough to tell when he's livid with me—his fingers hit all the right chords. And right now... he's raging.

This is usually the version of him where I get my best orgasms, which says more about me than it does about him.

My body reacts by leaning into him as if I can't control it. I crave him, even though I hate him right now. I hate how badly I want this.

His strong hands, which cover much of my withered body, rub every part of me, and my skin starts to thaw. The big fire he made us also helps as the flames heat my face.

He plays with the drawstring of my pants, and I clamp my fingers around his before he can get any further. "Fucking me isn't going to make me forgive you," I whisper.

He arches a brow and hits me with a pouty smile. "But you will fuck me? Because I've gone five days without sex, baby. I don't think I can hold back right now."

I don't respond, but I definitely don't say *no* as his fingers edge closer to the apex of my thigh. I close my eyes and revel in the heat, doing my best not to arch my back and give him any reason to believe I like it.

I don't stop him.

I'll let him make me feel good. I'll let him beg and grovel for once—it's the least he can do.

I'm not sure whether it's the heat from his body or from the fire, or the burning sensation in between my legs, but I begin to melt. The softness overtakes me. So much that I can ignore the rocks scraping into my side, the freezing earth beneath me, and the anger that just moments before consumed me.

After a few minutes, Micah's stroking stops. "You like these warm hands, don't you, baby?"

I don't like the way he says it, so I don't answer.

"Yeah, I know you do, sweetheart."

Goosebumps form on my skin despite how hot my body is.

He kisses my neck and teases his tongue on my earlobe, nipping it. "Because you will die out here without these hands, and you know it. So tomorrow, when I say we are leaving, you are going to come with me without saying a fucking word. Do you understand what I'm telling you, baby?"

My whole body freezes. Why can't Micah understand that we need to be with the others? That both our mental states are too fragile to be away from them. That they are really our lifeline, not each other.

"Micah, quit acting like this," I choke out a whisper as his hands move up to my neck. He doesn't squeeze, but the mere motion of it scares the shit out of me. The whisper is more like a sob because he is making me so helpless that it causes my heart rate to spike.

Every time I'm with Micah, I'm weak. It's the control he has over me. We've changed... I sense it—he must sense it, too. I know it pains him, and I don't know if we can ever go back to the way it was between us. When I was blind to the rest of the world, and only he mattered.

He made it that way. He made himself my only lifeline, my entire existence. It's the textbook definition of abuse. An abuse I apparently crave because I deplore that his lips are so close to mine and he's not kissing me. In fact, he moves his hands away from me, positioning himself a couple of inches away from my body.

My eyes open, and I turn to face him.

He moves his hand, and after a few seconds, he parts my lips and slips a piece of meat between them.

I salivate at the savory flavor and the rich, meaty texture.

It makes me weak, but I can't resist biting into that meat, licking the flavor off his fingers. I chew.... I think strongly about biting his thumb off as he presses it into my mouth as I swallow.

He chuckles darkly, running his fingers over my lips. "Don't bite the hand that feeds you, sweetheart."

I snap my mouth shut, and he grips my hips and squeezes, nudging his body against mine. He wraps his powerful arm tightly around me, the muscles in his biceps nearly suffocating me.

I turn to face him and run my fingers down the curve of his nose and under his eye. His broody, pouty lips tease me.

We stare at each other for a moment, neither making a move.

"Your choice, London King," he whispers, his voice rough and raw. "I'll never force you, and if you say no, I'll stop."

I devour his lips, slipping my tongue into his mouth, infusing him with my newfound energy. It's as if the breath I was missing suddenly floods back with a single kiss. He moans softly and effortlessly pulls me onto him.

I can't think about tomorrow or the day after. With my current mental capacity, I'm incapable of processing anything beyond my immediate physical urges and desires. Right now, I want him. Fuck, I want him more than anything. I'll worry about tomorrow and the hard decisions I have to make when it comes. The intensity of my desire for him surpasses all else, and at least for tonight, my anger relinquishes.

He is what *I* need in this moment.

I take control, biting his lower lip, then moving my lips to his neck. Longing for every inch of him, my kisses turn desperate. His hands slide to my lower back, and he slowly pulls off my sweats. He moans, and it nearly breaks me. He pulls my body closer to his, resting his hands on my hips.

"Pull those wet panties down, London. I want to see how badly you missed me." He kisses my ear and cups my neck. "Because I missed you, too, baby."

I snap my head up, my muddy hair lingering in my face. "This doesn't mean I forgive you," I breathe, but pulling my underwear down nonetheless.

He kisses me hard and deep, pulling me down to him. "Yeah, I know," he says after ripping his lips off mine. He turns me over so I'm lying on my back, the firelight making his eyes blaze as his muscled body looms over me. "But you still want me, don't you?"

His fingers find my center, stroking my clit. There is no hiding how much I want him. "Always so fucking needy," he murmurs. My traitorous body is dripping for him. I can't help my response to him because every part of him—the dark, dirty, soft, loving, every hard edge that makes up the fabric of Micah—is home to me now.

His lips find the skin on my neck, and his tongue begins to mark it. "Say those words to me, London." He smells so good... even his saliva smells delicious.

My stomach clenches at the toxicity of this. How broken we actually are... "Please, Micah."

His eyebrows arch. "Please what? I need you to say it, London." His face is pained like this is eating him up, too—or the guilt is, at the very least. The realization of how much control he has over me is slowly sinking in for him. Either that, or he missed me and felt our souls severing when we were apart.

I pause, aware of our surroundings: the blackened trees, the lingering threat, and how close the others are, probably listening to us.

I don't fucking care.

It's been five days of pure torture, hunger, thirst, and captivity—almost losing my sanity. I deserve comfort without the guilt that constantly affects me.

I move my knee between his legs, ignoring the rocks and hard sticks digging into my back underneath the blanket. He needs to know this is consensual. "Please, Micah. I want you inside me. I need you so badly."

"Fuck." He unleashes himself from his pants and enters me easily, my pussy clenching around him and a jolt of pleasure nipping at my core. Our hearts beat together as if they are one.

He's soft as he fucks me, and I whimper because my body is on the verge of collapse. He pushes in deeper, his hands roaming to my breasts, pinching my nipples and causing me to moan.

He cups my mouth as he pushes in and out of me. "Shh, baby. Keep it down. I don't want your little boyfriend to interrupt us again."

My boyfriend? He can't possibly be talking about James because that's ridiculous.

But it also makes sense. Micah is so possessive and can be extremely insecure. It brings liquid heat to my core, thinking of how much I own him, too. However, it pales in comparison to what he made me endure when I saw him with Naomi.

A dark smile plays on my lips. "You're so fucking jealous," I say, which causes his thrusts to deepen. I brush the hair from his face so I can see the soft shadow in his eyes and tilt my head toward him. "But James isn't the one you need to worry about."

This catches his attention.

"London," he warns. "Don't fucking do that to me."

I scratch his back as he continues to fuck me in typical Micah fashion. He's not soft, and multiple orgasms roll through me as he keeps his hand on my mouth and my legs wrap around him. I moan profusely as he moves his lips to my neck, grazing his teeth across my skin.

"I'll give these marks to you every night if I have to, sweetheart. Then, every time they look at you, they will know who you belong to."

I'm breathless, overwhelmed by the intense emotions he stirs within me as he vigorously pleasures me with pain. Biting me. Punishing me.

When I've finally had enough, he pulls his lips off. A satisfied expression covers his face as he admires the black marks etched on my body.

"Fucking. Mine," he growls. He then arches his soft, dark eyebrows, keeping his heavy gaze on me. "Say it, baby."

"I'm yours, Micah," I whisper as his heart beats against mine, savoring the steady rhythm in his chest. A moment of anger edges its way back into my heart, and I dig my fingernails into his back, which only cranks him up.

I kiss his mouth, and he nibbles on my lip, making me forget any sensation other than his softness and his muscled arms as he pins me to the ground.

No anger, pain, or sadness—or how fucking scared I am. For a few minutes, it's just him, and I forget everything else, including the pain in my hand, my ripped heart, and my fucked-up hallucinogenic mind. I quit caring what the others will think about the deep marks on my neck or if they can hear the moans coming from me.

We climax together, and when he finishes, he rolls off me and pulls me against him.

I'm not sure when I started crying, but he wipes my tears with his thumb and kisses the bridge of my nose. Then, I swear, he is asleep within thirty seconds.

I stare at the sky, unable to breathe or process what just happened. After a few long minutes, he finally says, "I thought I fucking lost you." He says it so softly that I wonder if he even said it at all. I'm not sure he's even conscious as his eyes remain closed.

He almost did lose me... and still might have. I get lost staring at him, and the tears pour out of me because I thought I lost him, too.

It takes ten minutes for my heart rate to settle, and luckily, sleep eludes me. I turn to face him and take him in. He is so familiar now, just like Maison once was—every line of his body, the way he breathes, how soft he is when he's sleeping. Even in this situation, near death, he still looks sexy.

I don't know what the future will bring, how much food we actually have left, or what we are going to do next, especially with Nigel still out there somewhere.

I'm not sure if I can truly forgive Micah.

Right now, I can't determine what scares me the most: Nigel lurking in the shadows, potentially watching me at this very moment, the perils of this pretty island, or the guy sleeping beside me, who I love so fully and who I think is out of his damn mind.

CHAPTER TWENTY-ONE

LONDON

I slip out of bed before Micah wakes up, and somehow, without him noticing. His arm was splayed out on top of me, and he didn't move it the entire night. His fingers gripped and teased me even in his sleep, pinning me in place. Anytime I moved, he would flinch and pull me in even closer.

Micah passed out in a way I've never seen him do—sleeping so soundly. He must've been exhausted but didn't want to admit it. Otherwise, he wouldn't have fallen asleep, so I didn't want to wake him. At one point in the night, I slipped into a semi-conscious state. But whenever I closed my eyes, I was plagued with nightmares, so I tried not to close them and focused on the flames instead. I stared at those flames twirling in the night, trying to ignore the images that haunt me.

Blood, crooked smiles, bone weapons and spears, dark chestnut eyes under a dark hood, and fishing wire. *Severed hands and argyle.*

I dared not close my eyes again. Keeping them open was better, even though the shadows played tricks on my mind and I kept thinking I saw a figure staring back at me. When I looked back, it was gone.

The temperature dropped, and we had no shelter, but Micah kept me warm. I got up a few times to put new logs into the fire to keep it burning, but I slipped back in beside him and he placed his hand over me again each time.

As I walk down the creek to the spot where Maison is buried, I look in every direction to make sure I'm alone. I'm on high alert, not wanting to become like Ollie—completely unaccounted for. As the sun starts to rise, I can tell the weather is going to be as dreary as my mood. The clouds are thick, and a heavy mist hangs in the air. The trees look as if they belong in a painting with their delicate strokes of evergreen, icy white, and muted gray.

I find the spot with two crossed sticks on the ground—a feeble attempt at marking Maison's grave but appreciated all the same. I sit with him for a few minutes as tears form in my eyes, but not because I'm grieving his loss. I am slowly coming to terms with that. I'm crying *for* Micah since he refuses to acknowledge Maison's death.

He cried out last night when he was asleep, yelling Maison's name. He was so alert when he did it that I thought for sure he was awake as pure anguish twisted his face. My heart broke for him.

Then he went quiet and fell back asleep as if it didn't happen at all. He merely reached out for me. I let go of my anger and took in his pain. A hint of a smile pulled my lips, knowing how annoyed he'd be if he knew how deeply I understood his grief. If he only knew he allowed me to see the most vulnerable sides of him...

Running my hands over the muddy spot where he is buried, I can't help but hope that Maison will appear just like he has done before and that the gentle whisper of wind in the trees is a sign he's here. However, he can't be because his lifeless body rests beneath me while his soul is hopefully somewhere peaceful.

I'm better now, away from the cabin and not as isolated. My body is much colder, but my mind is clearer. I was hallucinating and risking extreme dehydration when Maison appeared to me. I hope I never experience that state again and that if I do, I will meet a swift end.

The snap of a twig alerts me. My head whips up toward the sound.

Wind. Silence. Isolating pain.

"Fuck," I mutter as my heart rate spikes. I look around, seeing nothing out of place, suddenly feeling idiotic for coming out here alone. At least I can scream, and I doubt Nigel would get very far if he tried anything. Then again, I can't very well scream if I'm dead.

I'm so scared that I can't move. My body is frozen in this spot, and I lie down in the mud right over the cross. After a few minutes of heavy sobbing, I pull myself together and rise from the grave. The sun is peeking through the clouds over me, and I savor that sunlight, stripping my clothes and walking to the icy waters of the creek.

When I arrived yesterday morning, before I passed out from exhaustion, I changed into fresh clothes, but my skin is still caked with a thick layer of dirt and sweat. Micah must really love me because I'm not sure how he can stand the stench of me, let alone fuck me like this.

When I'm satisfied Nigel isn't going to jump out from behind a tree, I approach the icy bank and start by leaning over and splashing water on my face. I keep going until I've scrubbed myself as clean as I can, then quickly dip into the creek and let the flow of water wash my hair. When I come up for air, Micah's voice startles me.

"I don't like you coming out here alone." My eyes whip to him, standing with his head tilted. He has changed into black sweats and a white T-shirt and is holding a sweater. I avoid his heavy stare. I've been crying, and he probably can see it on my face, which makes me feel vulnerable with him.

I keep my eyes to the ground as I rise and walk toward him, and he pulls the warm sweater over my dripping body. I fall into him as he pats me dry. "I'm sorry. I just needed a minute," I tell him.

Last night was intense. I mean, sex with Micah is always intense, but last night was different. I can't read him right now, although I'm sure he can read me easily.

He helps me get dressed, then reaches over and hands me a spear. "At least, if you're going to wander off, take this with you. I made it for you this morning."

I narrow my eyes, casting my gaze to the sky, realizing I have no concept of where the sun is through the heavy, thick clouds. "You made it this morning? When?"

Micah's eyebrows rise. "London, you've been gone for three hours."

Jesus.

How long was I at Maison's grave for? Because I certainly wasn't bathing for three hours in those icy waters. Maybe my mind is not as clear as I thought.

He clasps his hands around my lower back. "I figured you needed some space, so I gave it to you. But my patience is thin, London, and I don't want to be away from you."

A wave of guilt washes over me. I can't bring myself to make eye contact with him because he's not going to like what I have to say.

He kisses the top of my head. "You know I love you, right?"

I flit my eyes up, his chestnut eyes flashing. He never says those words to me. In fact, I've only ever heard him say it twice before.

I'm quiet, letting him speak because I want to hear him say it.

I love you. I love you. I love you.

Not that it will change anything because I can't be with him.

He runs his hands down my arms and squeezes his brows together. "Every decision I've ever made on this island, everything I've hunted and killed, every life I've saved, I've done it for you. I'm keeping you alive, London, and now it's time to go home."

I lean up and kiss him, and a weird feeling washes over me. Like, somehow, we are saying goodbye instead of hello. It's entirely unsettling, and I dismiss the thought.

I have so many things I want to say to him. Like how he needs to deal with his brother's death, how isolating ourselves will only bring us more pain, and that we can't avoid our grief by immersing ourselves in each other. Because my grief is eating me up from the inside out, and I think it's doing the same to him.

I blow out a breath. "We should head back to the others and help."

He shakes his head and doesn't let go of me. "Not fucking good enough. Give me something else. Tell me what's going on in that head of yours."

I slap my hand away from him, my blind rage returning. "I don't owe you anything," I say through gritted teeth. "I know you want things to be okay again, for me to swoon because you finally decided to say what you're thinking, but I won't, not this time and not just to appease your precious ego. I'm not going back there with you, Micah. I meant the things I said when you left me."

I fucking hate you. I will never forgive you for this.

Arguing with him on this point is fruitless, but I do it anyway. He called me stubborn once, and now he is about to find out just how stubborn I am.

I cross my arms. "Take Naomi with you. I'm staying here until we are rescued."

It's silly being jealous right now in these circumstances—as if petty matters of the heart are what's important right now. But the jealousy is crippling, along with my anger for him leaving me like I'm a possession, and not a prized one at that.

Maison warned me. He warned me plenty, and I refused to listen.

Micah's eyes flash, and the vein in his neck pulses. "We're not getting fucking rescued, London. Look around, baby, this is it until you die. These idiots think that by lighting a tiny signal fire again, an airplane is somehow going to magically appear out of thin air. I have news for them and for you, sweetheart: it fucking won't. They can't make a fire big enough."

I shake my head. "I refuse to believe that, Micah. As a group, I think we have a better shot at getting rescued than if we split and give up." I've long thought Micah doesn't want to be rescued, and this proves it.

"It's not about getting rescued, London; it's about surviving. Why don't you see that? You will die here. Everyone here is going to die. We can live in that cabin, where we have a proper shelter—a home. We can't survive out here in the elements. Look at you... A week away from me, and you look like shit."

I press my lips together and glare at him. He knows... He knows this is a breakup. He slumps his shoulders.

Defeated.

It breaks me, but I can't be responsible for healing his heart anymore. I'm not his medicine... I'm his poison. And I'm not making him any better. It's sucking everything I have out of me to make him whole again.

My voice is broken. "You did this to me, Micah. You did this to us. You caused this fracture between us by not trusting me enough."

My eyes jerk to the forest floor, and my heart falters. Something is protruding off the ground, leaning against a nearby fallen log. Something that wasn't there before because I would have noticed it. My hand hits my mouth, tears fill my eyes, and my stomach turns as bile rises from the pit of my stomach, burning every inch of my throat, mouth, and nostrils.

Micah narrows his eyes. "London?"

The words get caught in my throat as I try to articulate the scene unfolding before me. He follows my gaze to Ollie's severed head on the ground, a few feet away from us. His eyes are staring at us like the pits of hell. His hair is still intact, and his eyes open. A fresh kill—

"Fucking Christ," Micah yells as he pulls my head to his chest, realizing what caused my reaction. "Don't look, baby. Keep your eyes closed." He covers my eyes immediately, but the damage is already done. I saw it...

I found Ollie.

"Why? Why, Micah?" My body convulses and shakes, knowing who did this to him.

"Come on, London. Let's get the fuck out of here."

I can't move. I stand, utterly frozen. "Nigel's here," I whisper. "He's probably watching us." He was probably watching me the whole time.

Grieving, crying, shedding my clothes.

That snap in the forest.

"He's here, Micah. He's here right now. That wasn't here before."

Micah grows deadly still, calm almost, before calling out to the forest. "I'm going to find you, Nigel," he threatens. "And when I do, I'm going to tear off every limb of your body."

Nigel.

I would barely call human what he has become and disintegrated into. He's nothing but a character in my mind now—a dark villain, a hunter, a killer among us. It's as if he's always been this way.

Micah and I walk back in silence through the heavy mist, with his protective hand on my back the entire time. I can't speak. The island, once again, seems to be deprived of oxygen.

The haunting image of Ollie's severed head will forever be etched in my mind—a constant reminder that his death was not caused by the plane crash, an animal, or the island itself. But by a sentient being making a cold, calculated decision and driven by anger, desperation, and pure instinct.

I'm still shaking as we come upon the meadow. The others are huddled there, preparing for what looks like will be an enormous fire. Micah grabs my hand and squeezes it before we get there, his lips brushing my ear. "I don't care what you say, London. I am not letting you go now."

I cling to his arm, regretting the entire conversation I just had with him despite speaking my truth in the moment.

If Nigel has his way, I will end up like Ollie. It's a miracle I'm still breathing.

James, Serena, Ezra, and Naomi are busy moving wood. No one spares us a glance; everyone is broken in their own way. We've all lost someone, and now, after everything we've had to endure, the real battle is just beginning.

"Where the fuck are Jade and Thomas?" Micah says as we walk up to them. Ezra merely glares from his spot on the ground, but he keeps his steady eyes on my neck, then grins and shakes his head.

I forgot about the bruises—the marking, the claiming. Micah spent a good twenty minutes licking and sucking me, as if those marks will somehow protect me.

Will Nigel care when he comes for me?

James rises at the urgency he picks up in Micah's voice and narrows his eyes, also noticing the new bruises on my neck. I can barely keep my head up, let alone try to hide them.

"They went to collect wood for the signal fire," James says as he carefully studies me while all the food in my belly slowly rises up my throat. "What did you do to her, Micah?" James can't hide his dislike for Micah any more than Micah can hide his jealousy of him.

Micah snaps his jaw tight as I seem to lose the ability to use my legs. "Don't concern yourself with London right now," he says, setting me on the log near the fire and rubbing his fingers over my lips in the way he does when we are alone—looking at me as if I'm the only person in this world. "Are Thomas and Jade together?" I keep my gaze to the ground and sway back and forth, keeping my hand firmly gripped on my boyfriend's arm.

My boyfriend.

I'm his, and he's mine.

The words exchanged last night were far from meaningless. The way Micah's holding me right now proves it. He's my home, and I fully appreciate that now, even if it took a severed head for me to realize it.

All their voices are distant, as if they are speaking into a tunnel.

"Yeah. They're together; that was our rule," I hear James say. "But seriously, man, what's wrong with London? She looks like she's seen a ghost."

Micah kneels next to me, rubbing the back of my neck. His fingers feel like paradise on my otherwise clammy skin. "She'll be alright. Go get them... Now."

Ignoring Micah's demands, James walks over and crouches in front of me. I raise my head to meet his soft, concerned expression, and I give him a nod. "Go, James. Please get them."

His eyes flash. "Alright, they're not far. I'll be right back." He starts toward the creek.

"James!" Micah barks out, and James goes wholly still, keeping his back to us. "Bring your weapon with you." Micah jerks his head to Ezra, who's busy staring at Naomi's ass as she bends down, picking up wood with Serena a few feet away. "Ezra, go with him."

Ezra merely scoffs, keeping his eyes laser-focused on Naomi as she bends over in a rather compromising position. "I don't fucking answer to you, man." He licks his lips in a way that makes it seem like they had plenty of time to make up.

James freezes, his body tense as he turns slightly toward us. "Are you going to tell us what's going on?"

Micah leans down and grabs the big knife he never keeps too far away from him. "London and I found Ollie. He's dead, dude. We saw his head. Nigel's here somewhere. He fucking slaughtered him."

I flinch.

Jesus, Micah.

James slumps his shoulders, a visible reaction, but he doesn't look back and picks up his pace, disappearing out of view. Micah crouches. "Stay. Right. Here. London. Don't fucking move from this spot." He yells over to James, "Hold on, man. I'll come with you."

The scream bursts out of me. "No. No. No!" Micah stops at my visceral reaction to not having his protective hands on me right now.

We have everyone's attention. Naomi and Serena come jogging back. "What's going on?" Serena asks.

Ezra, too, looks like he's seen a ghost. His cocky grin only moments before is replaced with pure disgust and terror.

"London." I can't let him go alone. Micah looks at Ezra, his eyes raging. "Did you have anything to do with this?"

Ezra's eyes widen, and he jumps to his feet. "What? Fuck no. I swear to god, dude. I didn't have anything to do with this. I just want my girl back. I only wanted food, man. I only took London because I was hungry. I swear. I fucking swear."

"What's happening?" Naomi asks, darting her gaze between the two of them, then to me.

I'm shaking, chilled to the core. My teeth are chattering, even though the air is still and the wind has died down.

Micah tosses the knife to Ezra, gripping his bone weapon.

His preferred weapon.

"Protect the girls. If he comes near here, end him. Don't fuck up again, Ezra."

I shake my head at Micah. "Don't leave me again," I whisper. "*Please.*"

He presses a kiss to my head. "I've got to go help James. Ezra will watch over you. I'll be back in five minutes, baby. I promise..."

"*I promise...*" *So many broken promises.*

I blow out a breath, watching as the love of my life walks away. Again.

The others' eyes burn into me while my body still processes what I saw—how close I was to being in Nigel's clutches.

"What do you think he wants?" Serena asks, sobbing.

"I don't know," Naomi says. "Ezra, did we do this to him? Did we cause this?"

"Fuck that," Ezra barks. "He's batshit fucking crazy. I'm not taking the blame for this."

Ezra and Naomi bicker for a few minutes, but I barely listen.

"I told you to quit helping him," she accuses him. "I told you about the way he looked at me." Eventually, Naomi huffs, and Ezra rises and starts to chop wood, enjoying the knife a little too much considering it was the cause of his amputation. "Don't worry, Naomi. If he comes near you, I'll kill him. London, are you okay?" Ezra asks, his voice sounding like it's in an echo chamber.

The bile lingering in my throat finally rises, and I keel over and vomit the remnants of whatever rodent Micah shoved into my mouth last night, unable to answer him. I cough for a solid five minutes.

A soft hand finally jolts me. Micah rubs my back, then pulls my braid away from my face as I finish the last of my heaving. I didn't hear him come back...

"Where's Jade?" Thomas growls, shaking me to my very core. "Where the fuck is she, Ezra?"

Ezra stops chopping, a defensive look in his eyes, gripping his knife and looking just as confused as I am. "I don't know where the fuck she is. I thought she was with you."

Thomas takes a menacing step toward him, utterly unbothered by the knife. "What did you do with her?"

Ezra steps up. "Nothing, man. She's not fucking here, and I haven't fucking seen her."

"Jade?" Thomas calls out frantically. "Jade, where are you?"

James stands and cups his hands around his mouth, yelling her name even louder.

My head spins, and I keel over again. Micah hands me a bottle of water. "Jade's missing, London. You've got to pull yourself together."

I pull my head up, my world completely uneven as his words register, and my stomach tightens all over again as I take tiny sips from the bottle. Micah's dark eyes are drawn in as he helps me up.

I was alone too... for hours. The message was sent to *me*. So why didn't Nigel take me when he had the chance? Unless...

Jade was always the target.

"She was just with me," Thomas says, visibly shaking. "She was only a minute away from me. I was gathering the last of the wood, and she said she was heading right back here. What was I fucking thinking, letting her go by herself?" I've never seen this level of emotion radiate from this big guy, including when he woke up and realized he no longer had a hand.

He begins pacing, unsettling the earth around him.

"She can't be far. I'll find her," Micah says. "I'll find Nigel, too, and end this."

"I'm coming with you," Thomas tells him, stopping in his tracks.

"Me too," James says next, his jaw tight.

Unsurprisingly, Ezra says nothing.

I watch James, who has displayed no emotion from losing Ollie. Deep down, it's as if he already knew the outcome and had come to terms with it. All those days he spent searching for him only to end up finding me.

Micah walks over and slaps a hand on Thomas's back. Only yesterday, Thomas might have tried to pull that hand out of its socket, but now it's like nothing happened. "Stay here, man. You're not in any condition to find her, and I need someone to watch over the girls."

"We can finish the signal fire," Serena offers.

"Signal fire?" I ask, finally putting the pieces together. All the wood, the flippant comment Micah made earlier about not getting rescued...

"Why are we suddenly building a signal fire?" I ask. The sky is cloudy—heavy and dense. We've been stranded for months without using a signal fire as a means of getting located. We even have a flare gun we didn't bother using because we haven't seen signs of humanity beyond this group.

James looks at me, his eyes sullen. "Thomas saw an airplane a couple of days ago. It was flying low, like it was looking for something. We want to be prepared in case it comes back."

Looking for something? The fire?

Or a group of missing teens, perhaps? A plane wreckage deep in the forest? Perhaps the world hasn't forgotten about us after all.

My mouth gapes open. Micah knew this and didn't think to tell me? Dread settles in my stomach. I want to have hope, but based on Micah's reaction, he doesn't think it matters.

"And you didn't think to say anything?" I say to no one in particular, but my question is directed at Micah.

"You seemed a bit distracted, London," James says, glancing between Micah and me.

So he did hear us.

James thinks I'm weak with Micah. He heard me firmly reject him last night, only to hear the passionate sounds of our fucking an hour later.

Thomas continues his pacing around the fire. "Can we talk about this later? We need to find Jade. She's probably dead already."

Micah rises and grabs his weaponry, throwing it in a pile, then grabs some canned food and opens it. "We all need to eat. Trust me, we'll need the upper hand on him."

Finally, he's not underestimating him. Nigel is smart, just as Jade had warned us and like I knew the whole time.

Even though I emptied the contents of my stomach mere moments earlier, the sight of that food awakens my hunger. We all help prepare the food and eat it in an unspoken agreement that our time here is ending.

We are clinging to that hope, shoving the food into us as fast as we can. When we finish, Micah flits his eyes to Ezra, who's busy wiping his mouth.

"Ezra, get ready. You're coming with James and me. You need to show us where that fucking shithole cave you lived in is."

Ezra nods, keeping his face neutral. A flash of sorrow hits his eyes—finally, the Ezra I saw back in his cave. His humanity is returning now that he's among his peers. "Yeah, I'll show you. Anything I can do to help."

Unsurprisingly, we all still defer to Micah. Even Ezra doesn't put up an argument. It makes me so proud to know that despite the darkness inside, his first instinct is to protect people. Even if he doesn't believe he's a good person, his actions from the beginning ultimately prove it.

Thomas sits, placing his head in his only hand, looking utterly defeated. All 220 pounds of pure muscle, and Jade has him soft as a puddle. His eyes find his former friend. "She's probably already dead."

Micah pulls his pack containing freshwater bottles over his back. "She's still alive," he says with confidence of steel.

"How do you know that?" Thomas asks, his eyes red and sullen.

Micah pulls his hood up, shadows haunting his face and every motion tight. "If you were Nigel right now, wouldn't you want to keep her?"

A shiver courses up my spine, shuddering at the thought of Nigel *keeping* her.

Micah's eyes find mine. "London, you good, baby?"

I stand, the canned food helping me regain my strength, and at least for the moment, my mind is clear. "Yeah, I'm good. I'm coming with you. I'm not leaving Jade again." To my extreme relief, he doesn't put up an argument. I grab my spear and stand next to him, trying to ignore the wobble in my knees. There is no fucking way I'm separating from him again.

Not ever.

I'd follow him to the ends of the earth if it meant I'd get to stay near him forever. I'll spend an eternity wherever he wants me to, healing him, doing anything he needs to take his pain away.

Needy, indeed. Because I fucking *need* Micah Matei.

CHAPTER TWENTY-TWO

MICAH

The first place we check is the abandoned lake site.

It's still abandoned, as I suspected it would be. Nigel wouldn't make it that easy for us. A glowing mist hangs in the air and wraps around the trees, blending the sky and the lake together and concealing the mountains beyond. Remnants of our old home are still evident everywhere. The circle of ash and stones around the fire pit, the half-built shelters fallen to dust, and the litter no one bothered to pick up because it's not like we have anywhere to dispose of it.

I can't read London's mood as she stares off at the lake, her body limp and her hand gripping my arm, which she hasn't let go of since we left the creek.

She and I are alone now, watching and waiting while James and Ezra walk back to the site to check things out. She's barely said a word since she saw Ollie. A blind panic is still evident in her eyes, and she's clinging to me like glue. I don't know if she meant what she said before, but the truth of her words landed like a punch to my gut.

She broke up with me, and I've never been broken up with. The ache in my heart still hurts from when she ripped into it. The truth of everything she said cut me raw, like an open wound. Then she saw a dead body... and now she's certainly not acting like we're broken up.

I'm not sure what to make of that.

What I do know is that I can't lose her, not when I just got her back, even if she's barely with me right now. This time, nothing will tear me away from her.

A twig snaps, and James and Ezra emerge from the haze.

"No one's here, Micah," James says, his face tight as he checks out London, who's peering into the lake like she sees something. "We didn't see any sign of Jade or Nigel."

I turn my head to see if I can make out anything beyond the trees and get a sense of what London's looking at. "Are you positive?" I ask him.

He runs his hands through his hair. "Yeah. We double-checked everything. We're the only ones here right now."

James is annoying, but I trust him. I still don't like him looking at London the way he does, but I can move past that, even if he thinks I don't notice.

It's fucked up, but I kind of trust Ezra, too. The way he interacts with London is different. He's still so blindly in love with Naomi Wilson; it's kind of pathetic. But who am I to judge? London trusts him, which means I need to trust him, too. And eventually, even if it might kill me, I need to apologize.

I jerk my head to the others, making eye contact with James, who can clearly tell something isn't right about London. "Let's get the fuck out of here. This place makes me shudder."

London doesn't move. She barely registers my voice as her eyes find the fire pit, then the dark spot where Maison died. Her gaze lingers, her mind drifting as she chews on her bottom lip and her tiny fingers gently squeeze my hand.

"Yeah, agreed. Let's go." Ezra's already a few steps ahead of us, yelling over his shoulder, "This place gives me the creeps."

I grab her arm and try to pull her with me. She hesitates, keeping her eyes grounded on that spot and her feet planted.

"Come on, London. We have to keep moving, baby. Stay with me," I press her.

She snaps her head up and finally acknowledges me, her awareness returning from whatever dark place she was in. "Did you hear that, Micah?" she asks me, looking genuinely confused, which breaks my heart.

"Hear what, baby?"

She blinks twice. "The laughter."

"What the hell is wrong with her?" Ezra asks.

With a single glance, I make him falter, and he stumbles back. He puts his hands up, his missing fingers in my face reminding me of what I did to him. "Sorry, I meant to say... It's just... no one's laughing." He stands back awkwardly next to James.

He didn't see Ollie. I got rid of the head so no one else had to endure seeing that.

"London's in shock," I whisper, running my hand over her face. She parts her lips at my touch, her gorgeous eyes finding mine, and her body trembles as she turns her focus to nothing.

"No one's here but us, London. Just stay close to me. I'm not going to let him near you." I want to know where her mind is at and what I have to do to bring her back to me. I want to promise her she's not in mortal danger, but I don't like making promises I can't keep.

This seems to appease her, and she relaxes, interlacing her fingers with mine and letting me lead her away. I wish I was taking her somewhere better, somewhere less insidious.

I wish I was taking her home.

It takes the better part of the day to get to the airplane, which should have only taken us an hour. London is slowing us down; her body is breaking down, possibly worse than her mind.

There is nothing I can say to her, so I choose to stay silent because what choice do I have? I scoop her in my arms and carry her most of the way. If I had left her again, I would have lost her. Nigel would have taken her from me. He would have found a way.

The three of us keep our eyes wide as we walk through the hazy forest toward the airplane. London, I think, is asleep in my arms.

Ezra hangs back with me as James storms at the front. Ezra's demeanor has changed with me since Ollie's death. It's a glimpse of what it used to be like between us when I actually gave a shit about the guy—before he got jealous of me and challenged me every chance he got.

"I don't want to state the obvious, man, but the longer we take, the higher chance that Jade might be dead," he says.

London shifts in my arms. "I know," I mutter. "I don't know what else to do. Just keep your eyes open." Helpless—I'm fucking helpless, as per usual. And finding Jade in this mist is worse than finding a needle in a haystack.

It's clear this fucker carefully orchestrated this. Nigel always worked best in the shadows, trying to slay me from afar because if I were to ever catch him face to face, it would end there. I need to figure out a way to outsmart him and do it without putting the girl I love in danger.

We reach the airplane, and we all cover our mouths at the stench of what's nearby. We don't stop at the plane; we keep moving past the pile of bones.

London stirs, and I press my hands over her mouth and eyes, trying to shield her from it. "Keep your eyes closed," I whisper. "You don't need to see this." I turn to Ezra. "How much farther?"

"Another twenty minutes," he says.

We walk in silence the rest of the way before Ezra pauses in front of a dark hole in the ground.

"You fucking lived here, man?" I ask him, inspecting the evidence of his home—animal bones in a corner he was using for God knows what, a few shredded ashen blankets, and empty cans of food.

He grimaces and shakes his head. "Fuck you, bro. I'm alive, aren't I?"

London gives me a warning squeeze, so I leave it alone. I'm sick of fighting with him, honestly. He hardly seems worth it anymore. I don't want to admit how good of an idea it was for him to move and take proper shelter here. The cave provides good insulation, and a greenhouse effect would have kept him warm enough. And there's dry kindling everywhere since this area of the island is a fucking wasteland.

The dry, cracked earth is almost like a desert, but it might have saved his life.

"Do you know where Nigel's cave is from here?" James asks. "You must know something. Come on, man, think..."

Ezra shakes his head. "I can show you where our meet-up spot is. From there, I have no fucking clue."

Even though I can't see the sun, I can tell the sky is darkening. London looks like the walking dead, and we aren't going to get anywhere hopping over the deep holes in the ground.

"I'm calling it," I announce. "We're going back to the plane. We can regroup in the morning."

Or I can come back alone and finish this.

No one argues. It's been a long day, and it looks like we get to spend the night in the airplane after all.

***

Fuck, she's beautiful.

I kiss the top of her brow, gently removing her head from my lap. She grimaces but doesn't wake up, and I slip from beneath her, draping the blanket over her to replace my warmth. The sun hasn't crested yet and stars fill the sky, but the faint glow of morning has begun. I stared at her all night, cradling her in my arms while she slept, wishing I would change my mind about the decision I'd already made. I couldn't take my eyes off her while she whimpered and laid her hand on my chest, and any time I'd move, she'd curl her fingers as if she knew exactly what I planned to do.

Because I'm about to fucking leave her again.

I take one last drawn-out look at her, then at James and Ezra, who are both sleeping nearby. James stayed awake most of the night with me—I could tell by the way his body shifted in his seat—though we didn't speak. Ezra was sawing logs within ten minutes, sleeping like a baby. London tried to stay awake, but my hands caressed her hairline and her eyelids grew heavy—she was out within five minutes.

Before I change my mind, I slip out of the airplane, making as little noise as possible, my bone weapon in my hand.

I'll be back for you, sweetheart.

I need to end this, and I can only do this alone. Nigel needs his reckoning, and I'm about to serve it to him on a platter.

London's already scared of me, and she doesn't need to see this side of me or the level of violence I'm about to unleash. She may soften my heart merely by existing, but this guttural rage deep within me will only be satiated by one thing right now.

Killing Nigel.

He's been watching me for years, studying me and my twin and gaining the upper hand in a war I didn't even know I was in. And so far, he's won every fucking battle.

A knot forms in my stomach as I venture into the night, mirroring the tight grip around my heart. The plan we discussed was to leave at first light to scour the caves, find where Nigel is hiding, and save Jade.

All well-intended, desperate, and fucking stupid.

Because I know exactly where Jade is and where Nigel is hiding her, and it's not in a cave. That's what Nigel wants us to believe. Knowing Nigel, he is much closer, in a more obvious place. For once, just once, I need to outsmart this kid.

I head south, the same path we took to get here. I head straight to the lake site and make it to the water just as the first beams of sun glimmer in the sky. The clouds have parted, and the sun rises over the lake in a shimmer of pink, reflecting perfectly over the water. My lips tug into a smile, knowing Maison's with me right now, helping me from his grave.

It was cloudy for days before this, so the sun shining... it has to be him.

And it's silent... blissful silence.

I watch and listen for a few minutes, ready for anything. I won't get caught like I did last time... the night Maison died. The early morning mist from the lake snakes its way toward the campsite. I slowly walk toward the shelters and see a slight hiss from the burning embers that blends in with that mist.

I almost miss it.

I bend over and place my hand on the ash. It's warm between my fingers... and wet.

Someone's been here and went to great lengths to hide it. I stare at the ash on my hand and then at the shelter in front of me, and unsurprisingly, it's empty. So I walk toward the other shelter that's half-fallen and toppled over.

A wave of shock washes over me when I come across Jade's lifeless form, her eyes shut, her hands bound tightly, and her face resting on the icy snow.

Similar to how I left London.

Her eyes shoot open—blood red, beaten, and black.

"Fuck, Jade." I crawl in to get to her and unbind her mouth, not even bothering to look around me.

She can barely whisper, and her eyes are swollen shut. "He has her, Micah," she mumbles.

My blood freezes as I pull up her shirt to check out the rest of her body. There are bruises and cuts all over her.

"Motherfucker," I grit out, and my stomach tenses at seeing those marks on her. Again, not all that dissimilar to the little bruises I gave London.

The parallels are uncanny.

Jade's bruises are black and purple against her ivory skin, which is cut up with tiny incisions all over her body.

Hundreds of them, like tiny paper cuts.

Not enough to make her bleed out, but enough to mark and torture her. This was meticulous. Nigel took his time doing this to her; he fucking enjoyed it. The sight of it even makes me squirm.

"What a sick motherfucker," I breathe out, then that little swirl of hypocrisy settles in my gut. This kind of sickness stems from something much deeper than just mere hunger or revenge. I know because I can identify it.

Identify with it.

I run my hands over her eyebrows, checking for a fever. Her body is scorching. Jade moans from the ground, trying to tell me something.

Fuck, she's bad. Like really fucking bad. He did a number on her.

I immediately cut off the wire around her wrists. She's so out of it that she doesn't move and her face stays stuck in the mud. "Jade, you're going to be fine. I'll get you out of here." That's the most important thing right now. Destroying the guy who did this to her will have to wait. I need to get her back to Thomas.

I turn my head toward the entrance of the broken shelter, searching for Nigel, who is nowhere to be seen.

She whimpers and lies limp in my arms. Adrenaline courses through my veins. This is my chance to grab her and go.

"Micah," she mumbles and shifts, "he has her."

I narrow my brows and pull her up into my arms. "London's safe, Jade. She's with James and Ezra. I didn't leave her alone this time."

"She's not..." She shakes her head. "You fucked up, Micah."

What in the actual fuck is she talking about?

My heart sinks as the realization settles in. That potentially Jade wasn't the target... She was the bait.

Jade's eyes are clear as I help pull her up and kneel in front of her. "Come on. We need to get you to safety."

Tears sting her eyes, and I can sense the desperation in her voice as she struggles to express herself. "He has her now. You shouldn't have left her."

Left her...

I fucking left her.

I close my eyes. The burning sensation on my skin feels as if my body is shedding while the monster inside me claws its way through the fragile edges of my mind.

Heat hits my face, and all I see is red.

Smoke tickles my nose, twigs crackling in my ear. My skin is burning as flames engulf the roof of the shelter.

I barely make it out with Jade before the entire thing lights up around me. I cough and keel over, my weapon slipping from my hand as I pull Jade away from the flames and the shelter starts to disintegrate.

I turn just as Nigel comes into view, and he's grinning as I'm brought to my knees from the lack of oxygen in my lungs. The knife in his hand shines in the brilliant sun, and he's dressed for the occasion in full Nigel attire—bow tie, argyle, and all.

My bone weapon is back in my hand within seconds, and I jump to a crouch. I'm facing him, protecting Jade. Nigel steps back and frowns, like he's surprised I can move so fast.

If he comes any closer, I will kill him.

The shelter is crackling and popping beside me. Smoke hangs in the air, and the fire starts to fizzle out on the wet ground.

"There is no way out of this, Nigel," I tell him, rising and ignoring my burning skin. He's not getting out of this alive. He must know that. "I'm taking Jade back. You're not going to hurt her anymore."

He runs his hand over his greasy, long hair. He looks like he hasn't showered in a year; the stench radiates from him like a pigpen.

He snickers and tilts his head, looking at me, then waves a dismissive hand I plan on breaking or cutting off entirely. "Take her," he spits. "I'm done with her anyway. She's no longer of use to me. She served her purpose."

I don't know what he means by that, and I don't like the tone he's taking with me. I'm quiet, seething, and not in the mood for his riddles. I know people well enough to know that they will eventually say what they mean, and I don't believe for one second that this fucker is just going to let me leave with Jade.

"How does it feel?" he asks me.

I curl my lip. He's finally playing. This kid can't help but get the last word. "How does what fucking feel?"

He snickers and takes a step back—likely because he knows he is going to lose a limb if he gets too close. "Being the reason you lose everyone you love. Everyone you get close to dies, Micah, or haven't you noticed that yet?"

I roll my eyes, suppressing the nagging feeling that what he is saying is true. "Are we still talking about Olivia?" I keep my voice even and emotionless, even though the thought of her dying still suffocates me. "She's not relevant to the conversation because I've got news for you, nerd, I wasn't close to her. Actually, I didn't give a fuck about her."

His hateful eyes flash, and my lips twitch with a smile. He doesn't want to talk about his sister, apparently. A slice of guilt hits me talking about Olivia that way—she was a piece of work, but she didn't deserve that ending.

He tugs at his collar as the flames beside us simmer out and the last of the shelter burns to a heap on the wet ground.

We both pause, and I make a mental note he must still have fuel hidden somewhere.

He looks at me and mirrors my smile, his teeth all rotten and black. I shudder at the sight of it, happy I at least had the dignity to keep up with my personal hygiene while on this island. Clearly, he lost his toothbrush along the way.

He speaks slowly. "No, Micah, I'm not talking about my sister... I'm talking about your little budding journalist."

I grind my teeth. "You're fucking bluffing." There is no way he has London. I came straight here. She was sleeping when I left her, and James and Ezra were with her. He had to have been watching us all night. I would have fucking seen or sensed him.

My hairs stand on end as my fingers curl around my weapon. "If you have her, then where the fuck is she?" The possibility that he has her cripples me, and it's the *only* reason he's still breathing.

He clicks his tongue. "So fucking impatient. You'll learn quickly I am not as emotional as Ezra, and also, unlike Ezra, I do not have a soft spot for London. You'd be wise not to poke at me right now. You are not, in any way, shape, or form, in control of anything right now."

"You can't fucking do anything to me, asshole," I mock him. "You'll wither away and die before me, and you fucking know it. And if you kill her, there is nothing stopping me from killing you."

"Micah... he will kill her. Don't test him," Jade moans from the ground. She's rolled onto her side, keeping her head down and avoiding looking at Nigel at all.

"Well said, Jade," he says, picking his nails. "And who's to say I haven't already?" He waves his hand at me. "Please. Continue your lecture, Micah. You are so good at protecting everyone else, but you can't seem to protect her, can you?"

A wave of nausea hits me. London has already been through so much because of my actions.

He clicks his tongue. "You're so predictable, Micah. I've been watching you and studying you for months, even before we came on this trip. In class, at the gym, on the hockey rink, and in the cafeteria. *Everywhere.* I know what you will do before you even do it. I'm not sure when you'll figure out I am smarter than you."

I look at Jade for validation of what he is saying. "He has her, Micah," she whispers as tears drip from her eyes.

Fuck.

"Where is she?" My voice is slightly more hesitant as I curl my fingers around my weapon. So close. One second, and I could end him.

So fucking tempting.

He jumps into the brush faster than I can blink, and I don't hesitate. I chase after him, leaving Jade alone, huddled on the ground and barely breathing, with her sliced-up body curled in a ball.

When I run into the brush, he's standing there, and London is hanging in his arms like a vision of death. His arms are around her neck in a chokehold, and he has a stupid grin on his face.

He knew I'd come alone, and he knew she'd follow. I fucking failed her, like I failed Maison and Olivia... Like I fail everyone.

I draw in one long breath. London's eyes are closed—I'm not even sure she's conscious. I stare down at him, and I desperately want to break his jaw.

"Why are you doing this?" My voice is broken and shaky.

A dangerous flash swirls in his eyes. "Because I can," he spits. "I don't need more of a reason than that."

"Is that why you killed Ollie?" I ask him. "Because you could?"

A feline smile tugs at his lips, and he shrugs as if killing his classmate is merely amusing. "I was bored, and he was just wandering around like a lost lamb looking for wood. Similar to London when she came out of the plane looking for you. It was easy... She's really lost her mind, hasn't she?"

London opens her eyes briefly before closing them again, her head hung low. She won't even look at me, and in the fleeting moment she makes eye contact with me, her eyes are like venom.

I fucking love her for it. She's still with me, and I'll take whatever venomous stare she gives me as long as she's still breathing.

Just hold on a few seconds, baby. Let me figure a way out of this.

"If you kill her, there is nothing stopping me from tearing you apart, limb by limb," I warn.

With a casual shrug, he maintains a vice-like grip around her neck, squeezing so tightly that her lips are turning blue. "Yeah, but she'll be dead. And as you've so elegantly pointed out, I'm a dead man anyway."

A few tense moments pass between us. Just the sound of lapping waves, the hiss of the embers when Nigel tried to burn me alive, and the wind as it scatters through the trees.

A snap of twigs has both of us whipping our heads around just as James comes into view. A red ember floats in the air and lands on my wrist. I stare down at it, thinking about how much it stings and how much pain Jade must be in from the hundreds of cuts he gave her.

I jerk my head toward the shelter. "Jade's over there," I tell him.

James makes a motion toward her.

"Don't fucking move," Nigel screams, and the intensity of his scream has all of us stunned. "Take one step, and I will slice her neck open."

James stands frozen, his forehead sweaty. "Look, man, I don't know how he got her. When I woke up and saw she was gone, I figured you two were together," James says, looking really fucking nervous.

I hood my eyes. "James, go get Jade. I'll handle this."

Another snap, another looming shadow in the woods. Ezra steps forward, darting his gaze from me to Nigel, the knife I gave him flashing in his hand.

"James, go now. Jade needs you," I say.

James pauses for only a moment before disappearing from view, hopefully taking Jade to Thomas, leaving me alone with Nigel and Ezra.

I look at Nigel, who is shaking with his eyes wide open and holding his knife right to London's throat, his focus solely on Ezra. "I'll give you food, Ezra. All of it—as much as you need. You'll have a better chance of surviving than if you wait for whatever crumbs they leave you with."

I scoff at the desperation in Nigel's voice, but Ezra has a vacant look in his eyes that I don't like. He doesn't move; he doesn't do fucking anything.

"Kill him, Ezra. I kept you safe all winter, and he mutilated you," Nigel orders, like he's been giving orders to Ezra the entire time we've been here. Brainwashing him. "Remember who saved you and kept you alive all winter."

Ezra flashes his eyes void of emotion at me, looking down at his lonely thumb and missing fingers. Ezra takes a menacing step toward me, causing Nigel to grin.

London's been defending Ezra for days—at every glare, every snide comment I make. I don't know what transpired between them while they were together, but I hope, for her sake, that she got through to him.

I soften my hard gaze. "I'm sorry, man. I'm sorry for what I did to your hand and what I did growing up. Don't do this for me, man. Do this for Maison, and for London. You obviously care about her now, and I know she fucking cares about you."

Ezra's face drops, and he gives me a nod. He turns to Nigel, who throws London like a sack of rocks at him, realizing she is in his way of making an escape. He takes a trembling step back, shaking now with his eyes wide open, waving his knife in front of him like it's actually going to stop me.

With a wide grin spreading across my face, I tilt my head to the side and crack my neck. That lethal pent-up energy is about to explode out of me. "You better fucking run."

CHAPTER TWENTY-THREE

MICAH

Nigel launches himself into the thick trees right as the threat leaves my lips. The motherfucker is as quick as he is slimy, but he got away from me last time. I won't let him get away from me twice. Secretly, I'm happy he ran because now I get to hunt, and that is much more fun.

London is a mess on the ground, and I have to make a split decision on either chasing Nigel down or tending to London. I sweep my gaze over to Ezra in a blind panic. "Protect her, please. And don't follow me. I need to end this."

London and I make eye contact as I say the last part, and her face contorts. "Do you understand, London? Stay the fuck here. He will kill you if he has the chance, baby. I have to finish this." I vanish before she can reply, leaving her with maybe the worst bodyguard ever, but he's the only person I've got at the moment. Although I hate leaving London again, this is my chance to finally deal with Nigel.

My nails dig into my palms as I step into the woods where he disappeared a mere ten seconds before, keeping my eyes open and my pace steady. A feeling I can only describe as lightning courses through my blood. The air is so still, and I focus on the sounds of the forest—the soft hum, the creaking branches. My nose twitches at the lingering smoke in the air. I become one with the forest; my senses are keen as if bolstered by my rage.

Nigel's very adept at being quiet, I'll give him that. But he is sorely underestimating my tracking skills. He's not that far ahead of me. If he even so much as snaps a twig or crunches his foot on a leaf, I'll hear him.

I stand frozen, not wanting to make the first move should he lead me astray. I don't want to resort to searching those caves for him. If he escapes there, he may be able to hide from me. Then he'll come for London again and again, and he won't stop until he kills her.

It's quiet. The branches and trees are still, as if the forest is on my side, refusing to provide him cover through its natural wards...

He's close.

"Come on out, bow tie," I taunt, my eyes finding broken sticks and twigs. I see an imprint on the ground, then another.

I smile as a sense of warmth engulfs me. "Got you, you little asshole," I mutter, walking over to a thick brush as a whirl of argyle snaps into focus. I'm amused by his pathetic attempt at holding his knife in front of him.

He swipes the knife, slicing the air, his skin a ghostly white and a sneer on his face. "Get back, Micah."

I confidently grip my bone weapon and approach him, completely unfazed by his sharper weapon or his ability to wield it.

He swipes at me again, and this time, I catch it between the bones of the antler and effortlessly toss it out of his hands, not wanting to touch the blade that recently beheaded one of my peers.

A twinge hits my gut as he falls to his knees before me, knowing all the power is mine. I grab him by the hair and yank him up. I want to understand the texture of death—not just watch someone die but experience it with them. The sensation when life is sucked out of them.

He twists his face, glaring at me and giving me no sign he's scared. I grin at him, and a rush of adrenaline courses through me. "You know, we're not so different you and I, Nigel," I tell him.

He scoffs, still acting tough. "Is that so?" he snarls, his face still radiating with supreme arrogance, even as he nears death.

My lips twitch into a smile as I forcefully slam his head to the ground. "It is so," I growl, leaning down to whisper in his ear. "You're not the only one on this island who has a desire to inflict pain on others. I've witnessed countless people die, though I haven't caused any of those deaths. I imagine it must be quite an emotional experience. Since I've suppressed my emotions for most of my life, this might ignite something within me I've been missing."

No response, partly because I am blocking his airway and his mouth is pressed in a pile of snow. But he can hear me. I know he can. And oddly enough, this is really the first time I've ever spoken to him. Even when we weren't on this island, I never deemed him important enough to talk to. For the few short weeks I lived near him at this very lake, he was insignificant to me. Even then, my instincts were spot-on.

I start my monologue with well-prepared words already in mind. I have spent weeks envisioning this moment. "Human beings are truly fascinating," I continue. "The depths of our capabilities, the twisted aspects that lie beneath the surface. What interests me the most is how fucking emotional we are. You see, what I have come to realize is that in the moment before death, individuals can only experience one emotion. It is a primal response to their circumstances. Yet, from what I've observed, that emotion is different for everyone."

I pull out my bone weapon and stick the tip right against his neck.

"Olivia... you remember her?" I snicker. "Yeah, of course you do. She was too fucked up when she died to have any real emotion. Her head just hit the side of the window, and she choked on her own vomit." He flinches at my words. "And Maison, my brother, my fucking twin, was happy and calm when he died because that's who he was at his core." I press his face further into the snow, watching his body convulse from lack of oxygen. "And right before Ezra thought I was going to kill him, he pissed himself." I chuckle at that one. "Tell me, what did Ollie say or do? Was he alive when you cut his fucking head off?"

I turn Nigel around so I can see his face. He coughs and spits out snow, some of it hanging from his nose. He doesn't blink; he just stares at me with idle eyes. "I want to see what emotion you have, Nigel." I shake him so hard that his head bobbles.

He gives me nothing, just as I suspected.

"You're a little fucking sociopath, just like London says you are."

His lip curls, and he starts to laugh.

I tilt my head to the side. "Fuck me, humor?" I snicker. Apparently, the laughter is contagious. "That's not what I was expecting from you, Nigel. I have to say that I'm surprised."

With a satisfied grin, I smile back at him, relishing in the victory and the satisfaction of finally getting something out of him. I almost don't want to ask him because I know he's up to something, but I can't help it. I need to know what's so fucking funny.

"What is it?" I say through gritted teeth. "What do you want to say to me, Nigel? What are your last fucking words?"

He licks his lips, swallowing something hard in his throat. Blood maybe?

"London's a whore... I hope you know I enjoyed every second of having my way with her. I ruined her for you, Micah. She will always be tainted by me now. My final present to you."

My stomach tenses. Rage boils through me as I tighten my grip on him.

He laughs again. "Don't worry. I knocked her out before I started, so she probably doesn't remember most of it. She was so tight, though, tighter than I thought she'd be given how worn in she is."

My fist hits his face with such force that blood spurts out of his nose. He doesn't get to talk again because the second punch breaks his jaw. Unleashing brute force is intensely satisfying. I do it *again* and *again* and *again*, ignoring the shooting pain in my wrist as I connect bone to bone. Fist to face, blood oozing from his eyes from where I'm indenting his skull.

I ease off for only a moment as he wiggles beneath me. I'm not going to make this a quick death. I won't just slit his throat or stab him. I will not make this humane...

He will die by blunt force.

I unleash on him. All of it, every dark piece of myself, and I punch him until my hands go raw.

All my hurt, anger, pain... all of it shoots through me and into him.

I rip his arm out of its socket.

"Fuck!" I scream as I break apart his bones.

I let go entirely. Somehow, his heart is still pounding in his chest as I lay my hand on it, finally ready to pierce it with my bone weapon.

"Micah, stop!"

London.

I jump to my feet and raise my head with a feral look on my face and blood on my hands. She's standing with Ezra in front of me. With her hand tightly clutching her spear, she takes a decisive step forward, her eyes vacant, wild, and broken.

I run my hands through my hair. I didn't want her to see me like this... so utterly fucking destroyed.

I narrow my eyes at them, my skin burning. My mind is consumed by a single, deadly purpose. "Why the fuck should I stop?" My voice is like chalk; I barely recognize it. "Especially after what he did to you, London?"

The pain on her face burrows into my soul. He might as well have killed her because what he did to her was worse.

All that pain—every bit of it—was caused by me because I couldn't protect her. Nigel was merely a vessel—empty and devoid of purpose. My destructive touch shatters everything in its wake. And I really, really didn't want to break her.

Now he might as well kill me.

By some miracle, Nigel is still breathing, and he manages a dark laugh. I pin him down, keeping him away from London. In his final breaths, he will still find a way to hurt her.

He twists his head and smiles at her with his bloody teeth, taking her in as she peers down at him, her hair falling in her face.

Without saying a word, she steps forward, and before I can stop her, she shoves the spear into his neck. His body convulses before it goes limp and life seeps from his eyes, though that wicked smile on his face remains intact.

I catch my breath and watch her for a heartbeat before I stumble back. The world feels rocky under my feet. She's shaking, clutching her spear, which she throws a few feet away as if it's made of fire.

"Holy fuck," Ezra mumbles, staring at Nigel's dead body. "That was messed up."

I stumble back, suddenly desperate for as much distance as possible between us.

Scared of the creature I've become.

My body trembles and is uncontrollably rigid as I realize what she just had to do. Once again, I failed miserably, and because of that, she now has to carry this burden. A deep part of me wants to be angry at her for taking this away from me. A bigger part of me is furious with myself for not finishing him before she did. I should have known she would do it, that she was strong enough.

For one last moment, I take in the sight of her. My vision returns, and I assess the damage I caused. Blood is splattered everywhere—all over me and all over her. Nigel's limp body is torn apart. His arm is broken from where I twisted it around his body and pulled it out of his socket in an unsightly way.

For the first time, I can't find words. My body shakes even harder as I run my hands through my hair, my stomach tightening and every vein in my body pulsing.

The world is so heavy, so fucking heavy. That weight is finally too much for me to bear.

I hear voices, but I can't register what they are saying.

"Micah, it's over. Try to breathe." London is the one speaking, but she keeps her distance. I'm still in a predatory stance, I realize, as she takes a tentative step toward me. Ezra holds her back, recognizing I'm not here anymore.

"London, give him a minute," he tells her.

It was smart because if she were to have touched my back like that right now, I might have pulled her arm from its socket, too.

They both look at me, and all I can seem to do is shake my head and stare down at Nigel's dead body—a physical manifestation of everything that pains me.

London parts her cherry lips. Those lips I spent the better part of the year kissing. Those beautiful lips I'll probably never touch again. So innocent... until she met me. I can't look her in the eyes, so I focus on those sexy fucking lips.

"Micah," she whispers. "Talk to me. Look at me."

I glance at what's left of Nigel, then at the gnarled branches of the forest beyond.

"Micah, no," she cries. "Stay with me. We need your help with the signal fire. Just stay with me. Please, I need you. It doesn't matter what he did." It kills me that she's begging again, knowing that I'm leaving her *again*.

She is aware of my thoughts, which are evident from my repeated glances to the north. She approaches me, and I instinctively take a step back. I feel my chest tighten, unwilling to let her make physical contact. If she were to touch me, everything would unravel because I would refuse to let her go.

I don't deserve to be saved; it's better if I fade into the shadows. London deserves better than me. I need to let her go. It's not our fucking time...

Ezra, who is standing awkwardly watching me, keeps London back. I shake my head, my eyes pleading. "Don't fucking hurt her again. Watch over her for me, man."

London screams, and I can't fathom how she has the strength. "Micah, don't fucking do this. Don't run away again. I didn't mean what I said yesterday... I didn't mean it!"

There is no strength left in me as I face her. "I love you, London King. Don't *ever* doubt that." I disappear into the woods before I have a chance to change my mind.

Her screams echo through the air, slowly transforming into desperate cries, but I continue to press forward. The wind cuts through my hoodie as I pick up my pace and head toward my home. My heart breaks for doing this to her again, but I can't give her what she needs or what she deserves.

It's time to finally admit to myself that she was right to break up with me, even if she regrets it or didn't mean it. She was right about my mental state, too. It's time I come to terms with the fact that I need to focus on my own healing and finally grieve the loss of my brother.

The only problem is... I have no fucking idea how to do that.

CHAPTER TWENTY-FOUR

LONDON

Day unknown

This will be my last entry. I no longer want to remember or document anything on this island. However, I think it's necessary to tell whoever may read this that Ollie was Nigel's latest victim. He was murdered in cold blood in the most heinous way. We've completely disintegrated. Only eight of us remain out of the twelve original survivors. Nigel is dead... I killed him.

Hunger, dehydration, and dread consume us. We thought we saw another plane yesterday morning. A brief shimmer in the sky before it disappeared within the cloud of distant smoke that lingers in the air from some fire on a different island. So our sole purpose is to keep our signal fire lit. It's our last sliver of hope as our food is running out. I've seen no sign of Micah since he left me two days ago. I saw the look in his eyes when he left. In those last seconds, it wasn't Micah staring back at me. I didn't recognize him; it was as if he wanted to kill me, too. The Micah I know and love is gone, and I don't think I can bring him back. I'd rather remember him the way he was—not wild, feral, and brutal, but as the boy I'm in love with. The soul-crushing love, the kind that hurts your bones. I won't go back to the cabin with him the way he is right now. He's broken, and I'm broken, and two broken people shouldn't be together. This pretty little island finally killed me.

I step outside the shelter after spending the last hour trying to nap since I refuse to sleep at night. I was numb when Ezra carried me back to the site a couple of days ago. And I'm marginally better, although I still struggle between the grip of dreams and reality.

The fire is blazing in the middle of the meadow, the flames nearly touching the sky as I approach the others who are huddled, their faces grim and tight. They are sitting around the fire, a sense of calm surrounding them since there is no more threat. Yet the actual threat is the worst it's been. Hunger is settling in as we've depleted our entire food supply.

I can't talk, eat, sleep, or breathe.

I sit next to Ezra, and Naomi grimaces, her jealousy coming off as no more than trite. Despite Naomi's glaring, he moves over and makes space for me. Everyone—except for Ezra—thinks Micah killed Nigel, and it's easier to keep it that way. The reality of what I did to Nigel settles in my stomach like a stone. What I am capable of... What we are all capable of, and how easy it was for me to do it. I'd do it again to anyone here if they push me.

The others don't know the true extent of what he did to me, and I don't know how to tell them... or if I should tell them at all. However, I think Ezra suspects it because he checks on me constantly, taking his oath to Micah to heart.

His promise to take care of me.

I observe Jade as she pulls her hood over her head, choosing to stay secluded while a dark plume of smoke envelops us. She avoids speaking to anyone, even to Thomas, who is sitting right beside her. Her gaze remains fixed on the flames, seemingly imprisoned within her own thoughts. The countless cuts scattered across her body are now nothing but cruel reminders—scars she will carry for the rest of her life. I want to help her heal, to reach out and talk to her, but I can't bring myself to ask her if he did the same thing to her he did to me.

He had her longer...

Naomi and Serena dote on her and, of course, gloss over me. While my wounds might not be as visible as Jade's, they run just as deep.

My mind is a blur as I nearly choke on the thickness in the air. I look around. The light is different; something isn't right. The sun, high in the sky, is blood red. Heavy smoke has settled around us, layered in the air. Pieces of ash bear down on us, lightly dusting the ground like snow. There is no way our tiny fire made all this smoke.

Two days went by, and nothing—no airplane, no rescue. We burned the fire for as long as we could until we just couldn't keep up with it any longer. And now we settle with a fire burning enough to keep us alive. The wood is still wet from the spring melt, the earth is damp, and the water in the creek is rising from the glacial melt. The days are warm, but the nights are still freezing, so we all sleep huddled together in the three shelters.

To Naomi's extreme displeasure, Ezra spent one of those nights with me, leaving her cold and alone.

I barely speak, still not truly trusting everyone. Especially not Naomi, who does nothing but stare at me and keeps her distance from me. The feud between us still lingers.

"Where is the smoke coming from?" I finally ask, ignoring Naomi's icy glare as Ezra drapes a friendly arm around me.

Or a guilty arm... He really is sorry for everything he put me through.

Thomas moves his arm from stroking Jade's back, and Jade doesn't acknowledge my question. "We don't know. It rolled in about an hour ago," Thomas says. "It came in fast and heavy, so wherever the fire is, it's close."

The island is burning.

My stomach flips, realizing what caused it. There is only one person skilled enough to make a fire this big, especially at this time of year.

"I think it's Micah," I whisper.

This garners a response from Jade, who shoots me a look but still refuses to speak, the spark of life within her extinguished.

"What are you talking about?" Thomas asks, keeping his attention focused on her as she blankly stares back into the fire.

I shrug indifferently. "The fire. Micah said a few times that we couldn't build a fire big enough to see from the sky. So I think that's exactly what he did."

My stomach tingles at the thought of Micah doing this. The butterflies he still gives me, knowing he did this to potentially save us gives me the hope I've been searching for.

A not-so-subtle sign. A message to me in the way only Micah would communicate.

Perhaps he's still with us, after all, and he's not gone completely wild.

Thomas blows out a breath. His muscles still flex, even though he's dropped at least thirty pounds since being here. "Yeah, Micah would do that, wouldn't he? This has Micah written all over it."

"How did he get it to burn?" Naomi asks. "We've been trying to burn this wood for days. It's too wet."

I blink at her lazily. Her hair is pulled up tight, her cheeks are sunken, and she is hardly recognizable. I keep my face neutral but don't respond to her. Instead, I focus on Thomas. I can't speak to Naomi; I still hate her. Ezra might have forgiven her, but she's yet to apologize to me for anything.

The most sinister thought consumes me. "Maybe he didn't burn wood. Maybe he burned something else." *Like a pile of dead bodies.*

No one responds to that.

"We need the flare gun," Thomas says, rising and throwing wood into the fire before directing his attention to me. "He has it, doesn't he?"

I merely nod. Micah has the flare gun—he's had it since the beginning. He didn't want to waste the only two flares in the beginning because no one would have seen it. I hope when the time comes, he will actually use it. And since he never gave it to us, he clearly wants it for himself.

I leave the others and walk to the creek, grabbing my pack to bathe. Before I do, I call over my shoulder, "Make sure you keep an eye on the sky. This fire might gain the attention we were looking for. Something's attracting those airplanes." This fire, in particular, is fresh, so whoever is out there will probably come looking.

At least, I hope so... Otherwise, we'll burn alive.

Once alone, I scrub myself to the point of obsession until my skin is raw and tears burn the back of my eyes. No matter what I do, I can't shake the feeling being caked with blood—Nigel's blood when it splattered over me like paint. It's like, somehow, it seeped into my pores and he's now a part of me. Afterward, I attempt to wrap my hand, doing my best to brace it like Micah would, and get dressed. Not that it matters anymore since I no longer have any feeling in my fingers. And that numbness is spreading through every nerve in my hand. Sometimes, I wonder if it's spreading to my heart.

Before I head back to the others, I peer at the sky. The smoke, dark and foreboding, is reminiscent of an apocalypse.

A perfect ending to this story.

It's quiet—eerily so—as if the spring birds, critters, and insects are hiding from the smoke, knowing their time on this island is ending, too.

It takes a few minutes for me to realize I hear something strange. It's more than the usual hum of wilderness, the distant crackling where the fire is burning, or the soul-sucking voices in my head.

It's a whooshing sound, low and close.

Like a machine.

Or a helicopter... flying low, heading in the complete opposite direction.

I drop my bag and run to the others, who see it too, each of them standing and staring up through the dense brush in the middle of the clearing. As if on cue, every single one of us, including Jade, jumps up and down in the meadow, screaming and waving our arms.

We scream until our lungs bleed. Then we scream some more.

The helicopter disappears into the heavy smoke, and we're all quiet again, out of breath and heartbroken. The silence is suffocating.

Naomi leans against Serena and starts to cry. I fall to my knees as my heart beats through my chest. The sense of doom I've been feeling takes over completely. My mind numbs, and my chest caves in on itself. We stare at each other as if silently saying, "What's next?"

But there is no next, and we all know it.

Perhaps my plans of offing myself will happen much sooner than I anticipated.

A few minutes go by, then a few more...

"What was that?" Ezra asks, breaking the silence among us.

"What the fuck did you see?" Thomas asks, furrowing his brow, still clearly harboring anger toward Ezra, just as I do for Naomi, but casting it aside for the moment for the sake of the others.

"It was a light in the sky," he says.

I whip my head up. "Are you sure?"

Ezra nods. "Yeah, it was a flash, but I saw it above those trees." He points northward.

The flare.

Micah.

He's alive and trying to save us. My heart swirls. I love him so fucking much for it.

We all pause, waiting for something.

At last, the helicopter reappears. We all go wild, waving our hands and screaming our lungs out. We let out a collective cry of relief as it flashes, its lights signaling that it sees us, and starts its descent into the meadow.

The whooshing sound overwhelms my senses, and it's such a serene feeling to see something human. Once it lands, a man in a blue uniform exits and the engine stops, the silence reverberating into the forest. My body releases all the tension, every muscle and fiber of my being giving out.

The man scans all of us, shaking his head incredulously. "I can't believe my eyes," he says. "The entire world has been looking for you folks for a very long time."

Two other men jump out, and within seconds, I am gathered inside strong arms and pulled in what I can only assume is an army helicopter.

Except it's not... They're wearing blue uniforms with the word *Police* etched on their chest.

"Who are you?" I ask him.

"My name is Sergeant Reynolds. I'm with the Royal Canadian Mounted Police, otherwise known as the RCMP."

"Canadian?" Ezra gripes, shaking his head as the men escort us onto the chopper. "You mean we're in fucking Canada?"

Sergeant Reynolds nods. "You are... Your plane went way off course. You're in the northern territory called the Yukon."

"Well, I'll be fucked," Ezra says. "No wonder you couldn't find us and it's so cold."

I can't help but laugh. All this time... We're not even in Alaska.

"Alright, come on," he says and mumbles something into a walkie-talkie, giving a hand signal to the pilot, who fires up the chopper. "We need to go now. Whatever caused this fire, it's spreading fast, so grab whatever you want to bring with you and get on. Are there any more of you?"

"Wait." I wiggle out of the officer's arms and run to the shelter, grabbing Maison's hockey sweater and nothing else. All my other possessions, including my journal, can burn. "There's one more person. We have to find Micah."

Sergeant Reynolds narrows his eyes. "Is that it? One more?"

Thomas steps forward. "No one else survived, sir." That is the understatement of the century.

Sergeant Reynolds narrows his eyes. "And where is Mr. Matei?"

I bite my lip. "We're not exactly sure where he is. But there's a hunting cabin north of here. He's probably staying there."

He shakes his head. "No, we cleared that site an hour ago. No one is there."

My stomach sinks as one officer carries me into the chopper.

"Was he the one with the flare?" Sergeant Reynolds asks, strapping me in.

We all nod. "We'll send a team to come back for him once the smoke clears out. Right now, my orders are to get the survivors to safety."

"Micah is a survivor!" I cry out, trying to get out of these straps.

My breath falters. The straps are too fucking tight. I rip myself out of them without anyone seeing.

My body convulses, and I let out a sob, but I don't bother arguing. If the chopper went to the cabin, Micah would have seen it. He went into hiding. He wants to die out here...

One of the other officers moves over to Jade, and his eyes must catch her scars because he lifts her arms and asks her permission to inspect her.

Sergeant Reynolds stops and really takes us all in. His eyes search every single one of us, knowing these injuries were caused by humans.

He can tell there's a story but doesn't ask.

The chopper takes off once we are all on board. The silent sobs and blind panic consume me as we rise into the air, matched only by the overwhelming grief of never seeing Micah again.

Once the chopper lifts, I peer outside. The view is hidden by the smoke, and I lurch off my seat. "No. No. No! You can't leave him."

Beg. Begging always works.

The officer has me in his grasp while the others just stare at my outburst. "Please, we have to find Micah. He's alive. I know he is."

"We'll come back for him, Ms. King. You need to take a seat."

Ms. King...

He knows my name. He knew Micah's name...

The entire world knows my name.

When we step out of this chopper, they will watch and see who steps out—who survived...

Forty-two people left New Ocean that day, but only seven will return. He has no fucking idea what we endured to get here, no one does. But they will... The world will want to know what happened out there.

They will force us to tell them as if we owe them something.

I sit with my head in my hands, rocking back and forth, looking at my peers who are all silent and thinking the same thing as me. Each of them is truly a stranger to me, just like when I stepped on that doomed plane all those months ago.

I never want to see any of them again.

Only now that I'm soaring through the air and the rush of the wind against my face is bringing back memories do I remember a promise I made to myself never to fly again. I spend the remainder of the flight trying to keep my food in my stomach. It's a lovely distraction from the pain in my heart, which is in literal pieces in my chest.

I wait in extreme anticipation until the chopper lands at an outpost, and we all get carted onto a large airplane, even bigger than the one we crashed in.

"I shouldn't have left him," I whisper to myself, knowing it's too late.

I repeat those words without a care about how crazy I look. I close my eyes and sway as panic grips me.

On the plane ride back, everyone has their eyes closed, dealing with their own internal torment. I'm in utter shock the entire plane ride to New Ocean.

I can't get Micah out of my head. His dark eyes, his olive skin, his warm, muscled body... How he looked at me and had been watching me from day one.

The day at the beach when he scrutinized me as I lay in my bathing suit, angry with the world. How alive he makes me feel.

I just left him... abandoned him to that inferno. I will never see him again, and that thought utterly destroys me.

The airplane lands abruptly, the screeching sound of the brakes piercing the air, and I take a deep breath as blind panic consumes me. I keep my eyes open because it's easier than closing them and reliving the horror of watching people die. And no one is here to comfort me this time.

Breathe.

I'm still breathing...

I'm at the back of the plane. In fact, if I ever fly again, I will only ever sit in the back since it did, indeed, save my life. I finally blow out a breath once the plane comes to a halt and the lights come on.

Air is coursing through my lungs at an alarming rate, going from not breathing to breathing heavily in a matter of seconds. I stare outside at the town I left, at the sea of people waiting for us. My stomach crawls its way to my throat.

I exit the airplane last and walk down the steps onto the tarmac of the small airport in New Ocean. They took us directly home. Word must have spread of our arrival and they let the media in because the place is swarming with reporters, people, and flashing lights.

The world is waiting to see what's left of us.

It's unnerving to see this many people after not being around anyone except one person for months. It's even more unsettling for me because I don't recognize a single familiar face.

I wasn't here long enough to matter to them.

Their disappointment is evident in their audible cries when they see my face instead of their star athlete. I'm the last to exit; there is no one behind me.

My heart races as I scan the crowd, the weight of the entire world's eyes on me. I'm glad I made the decision to leave my journal on the island. No one needs to know my truth. I'll keep my mouth shut forever to avoid reliving any of it.

As if on instinct, I reach for Micah, knowing he would protect me from the world that will want to consume me. I reach my other hand for Maison, also met with the icy emptiness that will now linger beside me forever.

The pain of losing them is crippling and shakes me to my core.

The crowd is filled with faces reflecting heartache and despair and families clinging to each other, their cries echoing through the air as they realize their son or daughter is never coming home. An entire generation was lost.

My parents push forward through the crowd, and my heart swells seeing my mom and dad together.

It's been seven years since I've seen them together, and here they are, side by side, waiting for me. My heart bursts at the sight of them. I hadn't realized how much I missed them. I let out a sob and run to them, ignoring everything else as I throw myself into their arms.

Cameras capture the moment.

My mom hugs me so hard and so frantically, as if she really can't believe I am here. She runs her hands along my hair and face and down my arms. Her hair looks dull, her body is frail and thin, and she looks like she has aged at least ten years. "London. Oh my god, honey. You're here. You're really here." I barely get in a sob because she's hugging me so tight.

She pulls off and studies me—every bruise and cut. She feels the ribs poking out of my sweater. "What happened to you out there?" she whispers. My dad stands a few feet behind her, awkward as always. I hug him, too, remembering our last moment when he dropped me off at the airport the day I was heading to the hockey tournament to spy.

I was a spy and a fraud, and now I'm a murderer. And a victim. In so many ways, I'm a victim.

I stumble over my words. Where do I start? I'll need therapy for the rest of my life to even begin to describe it.

Mom breaks down in sobs, and she and my father pull me in close as the media pushes through the barriers, shoving a microphone in my face. I have a moment of guilt, realizing that I was the sole focus of my mom and dad's thoughts during my absence. Meanwhile, Micah and Maison consumed my mind the entire time.

I hug them harder because I did miss them. So incredibly much.

I can't look at the others as the town fawns over them. We've all scattered into the crowd, and I'd be just as happy never to see their faces again. I'd give anything to forget it all—to forget everything and everyone I met while on this trip.

Even Micah. Because thinking of him hurts the most.

Eventually, the authorities pull us away, and they take me into a tent where an emergency doctor is waiting. They poke and prod me for a few minutes and, eventually, pull me onto a stretcher to run full tests on me at the hospital. There is red tape around the place, so at least the cameras stop flashing.

The paramedics take me through the back, and a woman catches my attention. I can't take my eyes off her striking high cheekbones, olive skin, and fabulously rich-looking outfit. She catches me watching her, her eyes in a lethal focus on mine. Neither of us can look away, so I keep staring in complete fascination.

I remember her from the pictures when I was investigating her sons, but also because of her striking resemblance to Micah and Maison. Clearly, they got their looks from their mother.

The pain in her eyes mirrors mine, and I want to cry out to her to let her know Micah is alive but that he's not ready to come home yet. I don't because I'm not sure if he will ever be ready to come home and I can't bring myself to speak.

For a moment, it's as if she has the ability to delve into my mind, her piercing stare effortlessly seeing beyond my walls and into my dark, cloudy soul. It's as if she can sense I'm desperately in love with them, and she watches me with a nurturing intuition while simultaneously assessing me to see if I'm worthy.

She leans into her husband's shoulders and starts sobbing. I understand her pain, and tears sting my eyes as my mother grabs my hand, only now realizing that it's shattered.

"London, honey," she says as she wipes the hair from my eyes in a loving gesture. "Will you please say something?"

I haven't uttered a single word since I arrived. I try to speak, but the words get caught in my throat. There is an overwhelming silence in my heart, and all I want is to escape New Ocean forever.

CHAPTER TWENTY-FIVE

MICAH

Before the Rescue

I stare down at the barrel of the flare gun I have pointed at my face. One flare left, and one chance to make that chopper come back. It would also be an easy way to end it, other than letting myself starve.

It's been two days since I left the others... since I left London. I've spent the whole time in a daze, dreaming of what it will be like if I pull the trigger and make it all go away. I'm sure the pressure of the gun would blow my brains out before my body could even comprehend the pain.

"Don't be a fucking cunt," Maison's voice echoes from the depths of the woods, and he appears to me like wind and mist. I glare at him, hoping he disappears into oblivion.

"Did you hear what I said? Don't be a fucking cunt. That's such a bitch move, man. Even for you."

My lip quivers and my body shudders at hearing his voice. It's not real; it's a memory. This fight happened when we were freshmen, and I threw popcorn at his face while we were watching a movie. I was just fucking around, and the guy lurched off his seat and punched me in the nose. Our fists flew after that, and Mom grounded us for breaking a crystal vase.

We spent two hours doing chores and refused to speak to each other until Maison decided he wasn't mad any longer. We made eye contact, and he flashed me his stupid smile. Then we cracked up, and everything was good between us again. Twin talk, we called it. We could always communicate without speaking, even when we hated each other. Because that's what we did. We fought, and we made up. We hated each other until someone messed with him, and then I saw red and wanted to fuck them up.

Except this isn't a fight. I'm furious with him right now, and his baby face isn't going to make me forgive him for leaving me.

"You're not even fucking real. Why don't you just disintegrate, Maison?" I spit out.

He doesn't. He just stands there, staring at me like a ghost from hell. The pain and suffering of his loss is unbearable. It matches the love I have for London.

Too much emotion. It's eating me alive.

He takes a step toward me, then another. "I'm as real as it gets, brother. And you know I'm right. If you use that gun on yourself right now, you'll kill her."

I don't look at him. I refuse to respond to a ghost.

"She's already dead," I tell him as my finger plays with the metal trigger. It's cold to the touch. "No one is looking for us. It doesn't fucking matter if they saw an airplane. This landscape is huge, and there are probably hundreds of islands. We're lost out here."

Now I'm confident I'm certifiably fucking insane.

A cool breeze brushes against my skin. Instead of looking at him, I watch the pile of dead bodies a few feet away from me. That's how fucked up I am; out of all the places on the island, this is where I chose to go.

He sits beside me like we used to when we would sit in silence and gaze at the water. "You don't know that," he says. "And you could always make a fire. If anyone can make this island burn, it's you."

"She's better off dying soon. And she's sure as hell better off without me."

"That's not fucking true either, man."

I look at him now, sitting beside me. I fully realize he's not real and that I'm talking to myself. But I'm happy I'm not alone.

"I left her, man. I hurt her so many times, and I let him have her. How could she ever look at me again? I'm possibly the worst thing that's ever happened to her."

Looking back, there are countless things I wish I had done differently—like not being born, not existing. I can't live without her, but I can't live with her knowing how sick I am.

So I don't want to fucking live.

"Yeah, you probably are the worst thing that's happened to her. You're fucking difficult and moody, you have a dominating personality, and you're crappy at expressing your emotions."

I scratch my scalp with the gun. "Alright, Maison. I get the fucking point."

"But she loves you, and she needs you, man. You've got to figure this out. Don't give up on her."

"I need to get better," I spit out. "I need to deal with you and all my shit before I can ever see her again. I'll only make her life worse if I'm in it."

"Then do it. Heal your mind, Micah."

"I don't fucking know how." My mind's been dark for so long, like I live in eternal night, which is probably why I prefer the midnight hours.

I rise and stare at the lifeless corpses in front of me. I stand back a few feet and clutch the fuel canister, nearly the last of my provisions until I can locate the rest of Nigel's supplies. With bated breath, I approach the bodies and toss the fuel on a few of them. The frigid Arctic winter has sucked all the moisture out of their bones, leaving them dry and brittle.

Like kindling.

If they want a fire, then I'll give them a fucking fire. I'll burn this island down if it means saving her.

Before I light the flame, I look for any sign of my brother. He's gone, at least for now, leaving me alone with these bodies lying in wait.

I flick the flame using my fire starter, and it takes no time to spread to the other bodies. One after another, they start to burn, melt, and begin their process of rebirth. I step back as far as I can as the fire catches on the nearby trees.

May their souls rest in peace.

Mine is the one that needs saving because right now... I'm about to burn in hell.

CHAPTER TWENTY-SIX

London

Four Months Later

"London, honey. Are you almost ready to go?"

I pull on a pair of loose-fitting jeans and stare at myself in the mirror, running my hands down my hips. Finally, I'm coming alive after months of looking like a zombie. Day by day, I'm slowly getting better—at least on the outside. The shine of my hair has returned, the natural blush to my skin is back on my cheeks, and my lips are a natural cherry red. I've gained thirty pounds, and my breasts are almost the size they once were. My womanly curves have returned.

However, it still takes every ounce of energy to breathe. I close my eyes and try not to think about Micah—which is nearly impossible.

He consumes my dreams, my thoughts, and every corner of my mind. And when I'm not thinking about him, Nigel haunts me. I'm honestly not sure which one is worse.

I fuss with my hair, trying to style it so it doesn't look completely disheveled. I should try harder, but I hardly feel like there's a point anymore. I might not look like a zombie, but I sure feel like one. So, instead, I pull on a baseball cap and rush out to meet my mom so we can walk to the beach, hoping no one will recognize me today.

We moved to California a month ago, and I'm still getting used to it here. I was going to move here alone, but my mom insisted on coming with me. So she sold most of our things, and we are starting over in a gorgeous two-bedroom condo by the beach. It's small and simple, but I can't imagine having anything bigger. I haven't stepped foot in New Ocean since we left four months ago.

Strangely, my favorite part about this place is the people. No one knows me here. I blend in much easier than in Portland and definitely more than I did in New Ocean, although sometimes I get hushes and stares as people recognize me from the news.

"It's that girl from the plane crash. She's one of the New Ocean survivors. The one that won't speak."

A spectacle who won't give the world their story.

The cool ocean breeze hits my lungs as we walk the three minutes to the public beach and stroll down the boardwalk. Eventually, we find a nice spot on the beach, and I sit back and stare at the ocean before bringing out my book. Since getting rescued, I don't know what scares me more: wide open spaces or tight confinement. Both chill me to my core, making every living moment a struggle.

I'm constantly looking for ways to escape.

I barely left my room for three months, crying and shaking in my sleep, refusing to speak about what happened out there. My mom finally shut herself in my room and refused to leave until I talked.

It all poured out of me, and I opened up to her.

The plane crash, our bullshit society, who really killed Olivia, my relationships with Maison and Micah, the death, the pain, the anguish, my hallucinations...

I couldn't, however, bring myself to tell her about Nigel—what he did to me, or in turn, what I did to him. I also didn't tell her the real reason I no longer have feeling in my hand.

My instinct is still to protect Micah.

She sat and listened and tried not to have a horrified look on her face. When I was done, she made a phone call to the police and forced me to tell them everything I told her. I was admitted to the hospital for the psychiatric care I desperately needed and also received two reconstructive surgeries to save my hand. I still have no feeling in it, but I can move it and use it reasonably well.

Out of the group, two of us were charged with criminal offenses. One simply cannot mutilate a hand and get away with it. Ezra and Naomi were charged with bodily harm resulting in loss of limb, and they are currently awaiting trial. Thomas's parents demanded justice when they found out what happened to him.

I refuse to testify against Ezra—he knows my secrets and keeps them to himself. I told him I'll stand by him through the trial, but I think he understands he will have to face the consequences of his decisions, regardless of whether I testify for or against him. It would mean standing in a courtroom and rehashing everything, and I simply don't think I can do it.

Some secrets are better left unsaid.

Naomi denies her involvement, saying Ezra and Nigel made her do everything. She can rot in jail for all I care. Me not testifying has nothing to do with her, even if she ends up benefiting from it. Due to the circumstances and heated emotions from all the families, it will likely be a long, drawn-out trial. I told the others all along we weren't above the law, and since Naomi was eighteen, they have to charge her as an adult.

Ezra's parents insist on pressing charges against Micah for the same offense he committed against Ezra. You can't, however, charge someone who is legally declared dead. They searched for him for months and found no sign of him out there.

I don't believe he's dead. There's something in my bones that tells me he's discovered the place that brings him joy, and I can't blame him for wanting to remain there. All I ever wanted was for him to find happiness.

My mom sits beside me on the beach and throws her head back, enjoying the heat of the summer sun, a bored expression on her face. I draw my gaze from my book to the hordes of people trying to cool themselves from the summer heat. Everyone looks innocent enough as they walk by with their upscale clothes, shiny purses, and fake smiles. Sometimes, I make eye contact with someone, and I see through the facade. The glimmer in their eyes is something different— something sinister.

A guy in his late twenties walks by us and smiles at me as we make eye contact. It makes me shudder.

"He's cute," my mom offers, and I shoot her a glare.

"Mom... No." I shake my head and glance down at my book.

After witnessing first-hand the depths of human depravity, I grapple with the idea of ever fully trusting anyone again. Beneath their seemingly innocent smiles lie their true psychotic selves. People terrify me now that I have witnessed their frightening transformation when they are pushed to their limits.

She bites her lips together and mouths an apology she thinks I can't hear. She grabs my hand, and I flinch. She pulls away as if I'm a delicate flower. "I understand it's hard right now," she says softly, "but eventually, you will heal, honey. You will find someone else if you open your heart."

"I don't want anyone else," I say with more emotion than I've expressed in months. "No one will ever *replace* Micah. He's not someone you can just get over."

I will settle... That is all I can do.

I let out a sigh, watching all the Californian muscled surfer guys, trying to imagine myself with any of them. One guy, with a similar build and frame to the twins, cruises by me on a longboard and trips, nearly falling as he rolls by us, checking me out.

I roll my eyes. If that were Micah, he never would have tripped. Mom's forehead crinkles before she says, "Honey, he's gone. And you're so young and have your whole life ahead of you." Those words eat at my soul.

Sometimes, I wonder what it would have been like if I had stayed with Micah. With the others gone, we could have been at peace. It was the life Micah dreamed for us. If I had managed to find a way to confront the demons in my mind, would I have experienced more happiness if I had stayed the day I broke free from his chains?

I'm not sure I'm capable of the emotion, at least not in the way that indicates happiness is a destination. However, perhaps I have experienced true happiness, even if I didn't recognize it at the time...

Twice.

After about an hour of sweltering in the sun on the beach, my mom shifts. I was just getting to the *first kiss* in my small-town romance book, and my stomach had started to swoon. Because, even after all I've been through, I still believe in true love.

"Come on, honey. I'm hungry. Let's go get some lunch."

We trail along the boardwalk and choose a cute coffee shop to stop and sit. The television is playing some soccer match in the background.

I order a half sandwich and a salad and sit near an open-air window. The television flashes on the wall beside me with no sound on. The server comes out and plops my food in front of me.

Hungry... So fucking hungry.

I rip my teeth into that sandwich as my stomach starts to eat itself. The sound of my mom's breath hitching is the only reason I pause and notice a few people staring at me.

"I'm sorry," I whisper, hanging my head as heat blooms on my face. This happens every time I eat. For a fleeting moment, food is scarce, and I eat as if it's my last chance. Usually, I can control it better, reminding myself to take careful, slow bites.

My mom frowns, her dark hair curled to her shoulders. "Don't ever apologize for what you went through. I just wish there was something I could do to take your pain away." There is only one thing that works to take my pain away. And unfortunately, Micah's lips are in the Arctic, and bruising myself doesn't seem to cut it.

A news alert goes off, and unsurprisingly, my face shows up. I let out a sigh...

I have become accustomed to seeing my face like that. It was one of those sensational stories that people will continue to follow for years. It's always the same picture of me, disembarking from the rescue plane. I appear emaciated and haggard, and it always pains me to see it. The photo has gone viral, forever marking my existence. I've learned to cope with it by pretending it's someone else.

Today, however, my face is short-lived on the screen, and it's the person they cut to that has me nearly falling off my chair. A live reporter is on-air in the small airport of New Ocean, and a breaking national news banner is at the bottom of the screen.

Something is happening.

I jump up and call to the server. "Can you turn the volume up on the television, please?"

The entire restaurant is glued to the screen as breaking news on the New Ocean survivors is about to be released.

A stunning blonde reporter speaks to the camera, the entire world likely watching. I recognize her; she's covered this story since it broke four months ago. She's the poster child for the New Ocean survivors.

Her voice cuts into me like glass. "This is live. After months of search and speculation, they've found the last suspected survivor of the New Ocean tragedy. Micah Matei was officially pronounced dead after numerous attempts at search and rescue in the area. I'm not sure how he evaded them for so long, but we have just received word that he has finally been found."

Or he allowed himself to be found.

"He's about to walk through these doors," she continues. "It's like he's risen from the dead."

My stomach nearly hollows out as he steps off the airplane, refusing to look at the swarm of cameras flashing around him.

His hair is long and wild, which puts a smile on my face. He's amazingly sexy and strong, as I knew he would be. His facial hair makes him look closer to thirty than twenty.

My heart fills as I stare at him, longing for him. I'm holding so much tension that I don't even realize tears are streaming down my face until a teardrop falls into my mouth.

With determination, the reporter moves closer and forcefully places a microphone an inch from his face. His eyes are cold and unyielding, staring directly into the camera as if piercing through the screen and into my soul. As if saying, "I see you, London."

The butterflies in my belly flap their silent wings, making my body sing. The physical reaction I have to this man, even after my vow to never let anyone touch me again, is unsurprising.

My mom wraps her arm around my back as we stare at the screen. I flinch at her touch like I always do. "Jesus, is that him, honey?"

My breath hitches, and I dare not to take my eyes off him for even a moment, should this be another one of my dreams.

"How did he manage to survive out there for so long by himself?" she asks incredulously. She's heard so much about Micah and Maison that she feels like she knows them.

I laugh to myself, thinking of Micah out there all alone, thriving. "Because it's Micah, Mom. Everything he does is a miracle."

The camera zooms on him again as he pushes through the crowd, and the weight of the world drops off my shoulders. It's as if seeing him again was the trigger I needed to heal. The warmth he brings me is my cure, despite the chills in my bones from when he wrecked me.

The icy absence of feeling in my fingers.

"Well, I'll give it to you, honey. He's incredibly cute. I get what you see in him."

The world might be watching him, and everyone will want a piece of him, but he's mine.

Mine. Mine. Mine.

At least, I think he is...

"I have something for you back at the house," she whispers, watching the melting pot of emotion pour out of me.

My brows narrow. "What is it?"

She bites her lip, looking suspicious. "Don't be mad at me... I really didn't think you would want to go."

I shake my head. "What are you talking about?"

"The town is finally hosting a wake for the deceased. They started planning it when Micah was declared dead." I heard about this—the lack of closure and open wounds. The town didn't feel it was right to hold one until Micah was found. I guess it's time to grieve.

"Your father sent me the invitation. London, with the way you've been acting, I didn't want to upset you."

Leave it to Micah Matei to return in time to crash his own funeral.

"What if he doesn't want to see me?" I ask as we settle into our seats, the weight and darkness of my thoughts returning.

That would be incredibly painful. And realistically, what should I expect? For him to sweep me off my feet and marry me like he promised? We were out of our minds when he asked me. That was then, and this is now. Everything is different.

I'm broken...

"He will, sweetie. I promise you that he will. You'll find a way back to each other."

"When is the wake?" I ask.

She swallows hard, studying me like I'm a fragile flower ready to crumble in the wind. "It's next weekend."

She's right. I wouldn't have gone. I'm not ready to face that town. I never believed Micah was dead, and I've already come to terms with Maison's death. In fact, I spent a good, solid month in therapy dealing with Maison. It's Micah that I can't seem to process.

"Let's go home and get packed."

CHAPTER TWENTY-SEVEN

LONDON

I learned this morning that the Matei family, despite their loss, were arrested for blackmail, embezzlement, and covering up murder. Both of Micah's parents are currently in prison until the trial.

The entirety of their estate, including the company, is in the possession of Micah. Ezra's parents want blood for what Micah did to him. However, they have no case because, despite all the hatred between them, Ezra is refusing to press charges.

The media is buzzing from this story. Between the death of Olivia, the plane crash, and Micah's miraculous resurrection, he is the most recognizable face on the planet right now.

He's become the face of tragedy and hope—a miracle. The world worships him as if they believe he is the modern-day incarnation of Christ.

My heart twists with every mile as we grow closer to New Ocean, my stomach coiling as if my phantom hunger pains have returned.

The trees. The trees here remind me of the Arctic. The same tall pines and gnarled branches that covered and surrounded us for miles. While in the depths of those trees, I simply couldn't see past them. In many ways, I'll be in their prison for the rest of my life. My body has not yet adjusted to life outside them.

I stare at my phone the entire five-hour drive to New Ocean, thinking I might miss a call or a text from Micah—which is silly because he doesn't even have my number, and I'm not sure he will be here. From what I gathered on the news, no one has seen him since he returned nearly a week ago. And if Micah was desperate enough to find me, he would find a way.

I can't imagine getting a text message from him—like we are normal. What would he even say?

My nerves are nearly shattered as we drive into the town I vowed never to return to. I almost ask my mom to turn around twice, and by the time she pulls into the circular driveway of my father's mansion, I'm nearly drowning in a pool of sweat.

One year. One year on this very day, I was lying on the beach, watching a careless group of teens enjoy their final days of summer. I didn't belong here then, and I don't belong here now.

I don't know why I thought I could do this.

Everyone else has told their story. They sat with that blonde reporter who chased them down, and she peppered them with questions about who turned on who, when it shifted for us, and why we did it. Each of them recounted their versions of the truth, as bullshit as most of it was. As if we might understand the *why* behind any of it.

She's relentless in her pursuit. She managed to find my phone number and location just fine, and when she came knocking on our door, my mom told her that if she came near me, she'd scratch her eyes out. Now I know where I get it from.

I hide in my father's house for the next five days while the media swarms the town, trying to pull any information out of anyone who will talk to them.

My phone doesn't ring.

I haven't put makeup on in over two years. Even when I started at New Ocean Prep, I didn't exactly want to be seen. I've spent the last hour readying myself to face the world and attend the first public event since our rescue. I'm ready to be seen and come out of hiding, but I still refuse to talk.

I'm clinging to whatever scraps of hope that Micah might show up for this event, but truly, I'm doing this for Maison. At least, that's what I'm telling myself.

I pull on a little black dress and frown as my boobs spill out of it. I adjust them as much as I can and apply some red lipstick. My mom had to help me with my hair because I still can't use my hand. She curled it in little ringlets and pinned it in a half-updo.

I hate how nervous I am. Micah always witnessed me in my lowest moments, yet now I find myself more concerned with Micah's perception of me when I am at my very best. It was the broken part of me he fell in love with, and no amount of lipstick will fix the shattered fragments of my being.

Even from the beginning, all I wanted was for him to *see* me.

"Oh honey, you look amazing," my mom says as I carefully step down the stairs in my awkward three-inch heels. My dad and stepmom pull up next to her. It's weird seeing my mom here, but she and my father have been communicating since the day the plane crashed, so it's weirder for me than it is for them.

My dad arches his eyebrows, likely from the amount of skin I'm showing. "Are you sure about this, London? We don't have to do this, and you can leave any time," he says.

My pulse kicks up a beat, and I work to steady it. "Yeah, I'm ready."

I'll never be *ready*, per se. But I owe it to the deceased to go and honor them. I just hope the world doesn't discover my secrets as if they were written on my face.

My dad drives us to the tennis club where the wake is being held. It took months for this town to come together. The grief bleeds everywhere. Every park, stone, planted tree, bench, and small shop is a memory for their loved ones lost. It took those months for everyone to come together and grieve while dealing with trials and investigations.

It's nothing but bricks and mortar for me.

The parking lot is already full by the time we arrive, and the local media is swarming. They aren't allowed inside, but they will be parked out here all night, so there is no avoiding them.

My heart rate spikes as my parents walk with me in the middle. My dad does his best to hide my face from the cameras, especially because of what I chose to wear, dressed like a pretty monster and hiding the ugliness inside me through designer clothes, frilly updos, and high heels.

The room is filled to capacity, nearly suffocating with the overwhelming crowd inside. Conversations pause, the room falling to a hushed whispers when I step inside.

My mom gives me a reassuring squeeze. "Any time you want to leave..." she reminds me.

Keeping my head held high, the click of my heels nearly echoes, even though there are at least three hundred people here. Slowly, the chatter continues, and I can breathe, no longer having the urge to run like hell. We take a seat at our assigned table, which, unfortunately, is near the front of the room.

Not every face is welcoming—some are curious, some are indifferent, and many stare with innate fascination as if I'm merely an act in a circus. They all think they know me—the new Olivia who captured the heart of their beloved twins.

"You have just as much of a right to be here as anyone else, London," my dad says as he ushers me to our table. Eventually, the whispers subside, and I nurse my water in front of me and try to catch a glimpse of anyone I recognize.

A certain twin...

I'm not surprised when I don't see him. His parents are in prison, his brother is dead, and he just came back a week ago after spending nearly a year in the wild. And if caught, everyone will want a piece of him, which I'm sure he hates.

I can honestly say I have no clue what his headspace is like after enduring what he has or what that isolation did to him. I only know what my headspace is like as darkness seeps in, infiltrating my thoughts at every corner.

After a few minutes, a shadow looms over me. I look up from staring down at my feet and see Jade smiling at me.

"It's nice to see you, London."

I can't help it. I lurch up and hug her.

I see a resemblance to her old self in her eyes, but a hardness lingers that will likely never go away. Her body is mostly covered. The scars are still evident, although I can only see them in a certain light. You have to know they are there to really notice them.

Thomas walks up beside her, and I hug him, too.

"You're still together," I say, not that I'm surprised. They were always a perfect match. They just needed the island to find each other.

The gleam in Jade's eye tells me everything. They are still very much in love, and a little wave of envy hits me at how easy it is for them. Thomas's unwavering presence by her side has obviously played a significant role in her healing journey.

James comes over next, followed by Serena, who gives me nothing but a weak smile. I hug him despite her. Secretly, I stayed in contact with James—mainly just text messages here and there. I also talk to Ezra, who writes letters to me all the time. With his upcoming trial, I doubt he will show up tonight. I can't help but feel the urge to watch out for him—a very unlikely friendship indeed.

Naomi is nowhere to be found.

James looks me up and down, his eyes lingering on my curves. "You look good, London. How are you holding up?"

I shrug. "As good as I can, I guess. California is nice, the weather is... warm." My facade is working. If everyone thinks I am okay based on my appearance, they will hopefully leave me alone.

"If you ever need anything, just call me, okay?" Serena's eyes flash at his comment.

He steps back with Serena, and I smile at the sight of his clean-cut appearance—the boy next door. James is all grown up now.

It looks like the rest of the survivors are doing much better than I am, still clinging to the ones they had during the winter.

However, the uncomfortable silence compels me to notice the haunted expression in Jade's eyes. As we lock gazes, the shadows within them sway, unveiling concealed layers of emotion.

She darts her eyes as quickly as she can when I notice it.

The fleeting moment with Jade has passed, but I saw it... She's as tormented as I am. "Where's Micah? Have you seen him?" I ask as if they know the answer.

Thomas's muscles flex underneath his shirt as he places a protective arm around Jade. "No one knows. He's here, though. He's staying at the mansion because the lights are on. The media is swarming the perimeter of the house, but no one has talked to or seen him."

That doesn't surprise me, either.

With the lights going down, a hush falls over the crowd, signaling the start of the formal program. "It's good to see you, London," James says as they dissipate back to their seats.

The presentation is mainly a slideshow of photos of the youth who lost their lives. Picture after picture of pretty girls and handsome athletes, none of them I recognize. As I watch it, vivid images of maggots crawling in their eyes and decaying bodies flood my mind. I recall their blood staining my clothes, and Nigel drinking the tainted water that embodied them.

To die in a plane crash is a statistically rare occurrence. It's considered a one in a billion event, though it does happen. I remember a story a few years ago where a plane disappeared over the South Pacific. All 280 passengers disappeared, and they never found the wreckage. I suppose we were luckier than they were. Or perhaps we weren't since they all died on impact, which would have been much more merciful.

Once the presentation ends, the celebration of life begins, and dinner is served—a six-course meal, which is still an overwhelming thought for me. The salad is served first, and the urge to devour it takes over. A low rumble develops in my belly as my mouth waters, and I have to remind myself to breathe.

All this food... All this waste.

I smile sweetly as cameras flash in my face, and I take a careful but *small* bite of food.

There is a different section in the program for Maison and Ollie. It's an unspoken understanding among all who are present. There is no photo or honor for Nigel.

The picture of Maison brings an unexpected twinge to my gut. He's with Micah, and they are fishing, of course. He looks happy; he always looks so happy. Except... I don't know which one is which because they are both smiling.

After course three, I can't take it anymore and excuse myself.

I drift outside to get a breath of fresh air just as I remember all the reporters hanging outside. I stop to hide in a dark corner before anyone notices me. My eyes dart to the ladies' bathroom, but not before powerful hands cover my mouth, and before I know it, I am being pulled into the shadows.

I recognize his smell, his hands, and his gripping fingers, which tickle the curves of my hips and pull me in close.

I close my eyes. "Micah," I whisper, "what are you doing?"

"Shh, sweetheart, be quiet. They'll hear you."

Sweetheart.

I'm surprised they *can't* hear my heart beating out of my chest.

I inhale his scent, which still reminds me of the Arctic—smoky, rustic, and woody. I part my lips to speak when a blonde reporter from the news emerges from the bathroom, muttering to herself about finding him, fully aware that he's here.

He tightens his grip, moving his hands around my waist, his body enveloping mine. My reaction is a mix of pure joy and extreme terror, and I flinch.

He softens his grip and rubs his knuckles up my arm, and I decide not to let Nigel ruin this moment for me. I enjoy the feeling of him—his safe hands, hard body, and muscled abs.

Fuck, I've missed him.

The reporter's heels click down the marble floor and eventually fade into the distance.

I'm shaking as he leans his mouth toward my ear. "You look fucking incredible," he whispers, his breath grazing my cheek.

I whip around, my eyes adjusting to the dimly lit hallway. He's wearing a black hoodie and jeans, shadows covering his face.

"Is it really you?" I whisper, nearly choking on the cry that escapes my lips. I can't help it; I run my fingers along his face. He shaved but kept his facial hair. His chestnut eyes blaze down on me.

With Micah's parents in jail, he is now the sole heir of the Matei fortune, and here he is, dressed like nothing more than a common criminal lurking in the shadows. I reach my hand up and pull his hood down so I can see him properly.

I can't help but gasp as he clasps his hands around my lower back, pulling me into him as a couple more reporters walk by, the blonde taking the lead. We stand curled into each other, hiding in plain sight.

When I look up at him, he's grinning at me. He's actually smiling. His hair is trimmed, too, back to the way it was when I first met him.

He still looks just as sexy—so incredibly dark and sexy.

"What are you doing out here, Micah?" I say when I'm certain we are alone.

He chews on his lip, his intense eyes on my cleavage. He's not even pretending he doesn't want to ravish me. "I came to get you out of here."

His voice. His voice is what dreams are made of.

My lips twitch into a small smile, my heart still beating against his. "Take me where?"

Where could we possibly go?

He runs his hands along my arms. "With me... You're mine, sweetheart. Or did you forget that?"

A rush of excitement causes my heart to flutter, and I look around before peering back up at him. "I haven't forgotten, Micah. I've been here waiting for you for so fucking long. You've been the one missing."

He keeps me locked tightly against him, his finger curling around one of my ringlets. "I'm back, London, and I'm not fucking going anywhere. But we have to leave now. Will you come with me?"

I scoff and push away from him. "How many times have you said that to me? And you've been back for what... a week? And suddenly, now, during your fucking funeral, it's imperative we leave immediately?"

Three. Three times, he has promised not to leave me again. At some point, expecting a different outcome is the precise definition of insanity.

It's how he is; he will come and go at his whim, and no amount of begging on my part will change that. There is no taming him, and if I want him, I have to accept all the dark parts of him. Dominant, angry, loving, and wild. All the reasons why I fell in love with him to begin with.

So, the question is... can I do it again?

"Let's get out here," I whisper.

There's a primal flicker in his eyes as he takes hold of my hand, swiftly leading me toward a nearby exit. "Come on. Follow me."

My heels barely stay on as I trip over my feet, so he pulls me into his arms like he's done so many times before. His fingers graze my bare ass cheeks as they hang out of my dress.

Wild. He's wild, like a child raised in a jungle. There is no going back to the way he was. He will never play by society's rules. He'll own me like he owns the woods, and now that he owns half this town, no one can really stop him.

My blood runs cold as voices echo in the hall behind us. I wrap my arms around his neck and shift myself into a more sensible position.

"Micah, this is Maison's wake. Maybe we shouldn't just leave. People will talk about it if they see us together."

He carries me like I'm nothing, even though I'm much heavier than I was before. He takes me to the back of the building and leads me through a side door that leads into the woods, where he has a car waiting—a silver Mercedes, of all things.

He sets me down, pressing me against the side of the car. "Maison would have hated this," he says.

He's probably not wrong.

He kisses me hard and fast and with such emotion that it takes my breath away.

I let out a moan, and he pulls his soft lips off mine and runs his fingers over my cheek. "I'm sorry," he says, out of breath. "I fucking missed you so much." His teeth scrape my lips as he bites them. "These fucking lips..." He runs his fingers down my bare chest, playing with the strap of my dress before tightening his fingers around it. "I missed your fucking skin."

I arch a brow and can't help but let out a weak smile. "My skin? Really, Micah?"

He smirks. "Yes, your fucking *skin*."

Voices carry from the front of the building, and Micah reaches behind and opens the door, gently nudging me into the passenger side.

The blonde reporter walks around the corner. "I think they are back here. Grab the camera and hurry."

Micah slams the door and jumps to the driver's side right as she and her cameraman come into view.

He peels out right past all the reporters and skids onto the road, leaving them in a cloud of dust. He peers at me, leans over, and pulls my seatbelt across my chest, clipping it in for me. "That bitch used to chase me around when Olivia died, too," he says. "I've gotten good at ditching her."

I catch my breath and dare to look at him, worried if I blink, he will disappear. That his voice is nothing but a hallucination, a dream I've had for months.

Despite how fast he's driving, Micah appears relaxed. In fact, everything about him is different. He's lighter, in a way. Not physically because he's still the strongest guy I know, but he has a calmness I've never seen in him before.

The complete opposite of me, as I'm still burdened by a heavy weight. I can't help but wonder if he can perceive that or sense that I haven't been able to truly put myself together despite my facade of hair, makeup, and strappy dresses.

With a soft touch, he runs his fingers along my bare thighs, guiding my legs up over him as he drives. He keeps his fingers on the skin he apparently misses so much. I close my eyes and let myself relax, loving the sensation of his body next to mine.

We pass through the sleepy town. He drives right through it in the dead of night, then turns on a long, windy road in the woods. The silence between us reminds me of how it used to be when we could just be together. A stillness in the dark that brought joy to my soul in an otherwise icy prison. My heart is racing, and I can tell he can sense my tension.

I shoot up. "Micah, my mom. I have to tell her I've left with you. She'll freak out if she finds me missing." I don't have anything with me, not even my purse, which I left at the table.

He squeezes me. "London, relax. I've taken care of it."

I have no clue what he means by that, but his response appeases me.

"I've taken care of it..." which means, "I'll take care of you."

"Micah, what were you doing out there all that time?" I ask him. "Why didn't you come back with us?" I crane my neck as the car crunches gravel. "And where are you taking me right now?"

What I'm really asking is, why did he not come back to me? Especially when he knew what I went through with Nigel.

His fingers grip my thigh, then he grabs my hand and squeezes it. "We're almost there, baby. Then I'll tell you everything."

I don't bother pushing him; I know he won't tell me where we are going. Instead, I rest my head on the side of the headrest and let him rub me as I enjoy the view of him.

Tiny explosions erupt in my stomach. A mix of excitement, hurt, anger, and every other emotion this man has made me feel since I met him and fell in love with him.

He finally slows the car, easing to a stop. "Close your eyes, London."

"Micah, what's going on? You can't just show up and steal me. We need to talk."

"Close them."

I let out a sigh and squeeze them shut as he exits the car and helps me out. I don't dare open them as he loops my arm with his, and I stumble with him over mud and rocks as I'm still in my three-inch heels.

I flinch and pull my hand away. I don't want him to know my hand is completely useless.

"Micah," I whisper, "it's still not better." Unfortunately, the doctors don't think it will ever be quite the same.

"I know," he says as if it doesn't surprise him. He interlaces his fingers with them anyway. "Open your eyes." He stands behind me, leaning his chin on the top of my head.

When I open them, I gasp. A two-story log cabin appears through the darkness, warm light spilling from the inside. Tall trees surround a veranda that wraps around the exterior.

My jaw drops from the mere size of it. "Micah..."

"It's yours, baby."

I look at him, narrowing my eyes. "What do you mean?"

"I want us to live here together if you still want me. Come on..."

I follow him inside, and the interior is just as gorgeous, with a large open kitchen and a spiral staircase leading into a nook above. Everything is mahogany, and it reminds me of our cabin, but much bigger and newer, but the feeling is the same. I walk into the kitchen, and he presses himself up behind me, wiping the hair from my neck before kissing it.

I tense... I wish I didn't, but he senses my unease and stops. I'm not sure how I will feel about being intimate again since I've not dealt with my assault.

I am fully aware of what Micah wants from me; I'm just not sure I can give it to him in this moment, or ever...

He moves my hair off my bare shoulders and presses his lips to my skin. "I know I hurt you," he whispers. "I know it will take a long time for you to trust me again."

I let out a little sob. He has no idea...

"But it doesn't change how I feel about you," he says.

I turn to face him, tears stinging my eyes, and he wipes the tears with his thumb as he peers down at me with more tenderness than I've ever seen from him.

"I still hear the laughter," I say in almost a whisper. "Every night, after I dream about you, he comes to me, and he's always laughing. I can't get rid of him, Micah. He's always in my head."

He pauses, a pained look on his face. I watch the bob of his throat as he processes my words.

"He's always in my head too, baby," he finally says. "Remember what I said to you when Maison died? That it's me and you, and we can kill him together?"

I nod, the memory of that night flashing back to me, and he leans his forehead against mine.

"We did that together, London. We killed him together, and now we can heal together, too."

The sob I've been holding back escapes me. I want to punch him, slap him, then kiss him for the rest of my life. "Where were you, Micah? I needed you, and you didn't come back."

He narrows his brows, so much emotion radiating from him. "I realized I needed to heal myself before I could help you. I'm sorry, London. It was a selfish thing to do, but I knew I would only end up hurting you even more. I was fucked up, and what I did to you was fucking wrong. I know that. I shouldn't have tied you up. I knew that then, too... I just didn't care. I wanted you so badly, and I was so terrified of losing you. And I was losing you; you were going to leave me."

"*Micah... I—*"

He gently presses his forehead against mine. "Shh, baby, please let me finish. I need to explain why I chose to stay on the island. You were better off without me, and I knew you were safe with the others. Giving you the space you wanted was the best decision for you, and I needed to heal. But please know, London, that all I want is to spend the rest of my life with you. There is no one else for me. I just hope it's not too late and you haven't moved on from me."

I can't help but bite my bottom lip as I gaze up at him, his face filled with anguish as he envisions a future without me. "There is no one else, Micah. How could I possibly be with anyone else?"

He grabs me by the hips and lifts me onto the low counter. I wrap my legs around him and let him continue.

He drops to his knees so he's at eye level with me. "I want you to experience me at my best for once. When I met you, too many fucked-up things had happened to me. You're the right person for me, baby; I just met you at the wrong time. You've seen the worst parts of me, London. I wouldn't blame you if you ran in the other direction."

And I still love him, despite those parts.

"And now?" I ask him. "How are you now?"

He smiles that new smile. "I'm better now. I've dealt with Maison, and I've dealt with Olivia. But I'm not ready for our story to be over, baby. The time I spent with you in that cabin was the happiest I've ever been. I know that's fucked up because I was hurting and controlling you, but I would have been happy never leaving that place. I wish I was still there."

I blow out a breath. "Then why are you back? Why not stay out there if it made you so happy?"

He licks his lips. "The only thing missing was you."

I lean my head forward. "Micah, I'm not healed. I'm a mess. I can't be around people. I can barely hold a conversation without feeling like I'm going to crumble. And I still hear laughter when I shouldn't."

"It's okay," he says, his lips gently touching my forehead. "We can work through it. Trust me, it can't be as bad as what I went through on the island the last few months. I hit rock bottom, London."

I look into his eyes—those dark eyes which seem so full of life now—full of hope.

"Are you healed, then? I can't imagine being all alone like that." How dark that must have been for him. I nearly lost my mind being alone for two days. Then again, I was tied up.

"As much as I can be, I think," he says. "I had to make some tough choices. Like if I wanted to continue living." He chuckles, a gleam twinkling in his eyes. "But I wasn't alone. Definitely not alone... although sometimes I wish I was. Maison was with me the whole time, baby. He got me through it."

I smile because I know exactly what he's talking about.

Tears form in his eyes. An emotion, I realize, I barely ever get out of him. My heart hurts for all he's been through, for everything he's lost.

He swallows hard. "I ran through every memory I had of him. I heard his voice clear as day every day I was there. I'm not perfect, London. I'm still me; I'm still an asshole. I can't promise I'll never hurt you again, but I'm way more confident I won't destroy you anymore."

I remember what the few days of solitude did to me, the laughter I heard, my hallucinations of Maison that ended up saving my life.

I slip my arms around him and lean my head into him fully. His heart is beating out of control. "What if we don't work in the real world? I don't even know how to function anymore, Micah. It's so hard."

He tilts his head, moving his hands to my hips. "We'll do it together. And we will always have this place to come back to. It's remote, so no one will be here but us. It's not the wilderness, but we can try to replicate the months when it was just you and me. The rest of the time, we can spend at my mansion."

His mansion...

"What about your parents?"

He shrugs. "I'll do my best to help them, but they made their bed. I'm not sure they can avoid prison time for what they did."

He leans in and kisses me, his hard body pressing against mine. He pulls my straps down one at a time, and I let him, but the nervous feeling returns, my heart racing. My breath hitches, causing him to pull back.

I *hate* feeling this way when he touches me. I *hate* that Nigel won in destroying us.

"I haven't told anyone what happened to me," I whisper, and he pauses. Only for a second, though, before continuing to pull the straps down, then pulling me to my feet. I let my dress fall to the floor, leaving me in just my bra and panties. I close my eyes tight as my nerves fire up, and I can feel his stare on my skin. My nipples tighten, and wetness builds like it always does when I'm this vulnerable.

"I'm not going to hurt you or touch you if you don't want me to," he whispers. "I just want to see you."

I nod, giving him permission. "You can touch me, Micah. Just go slow."

To my surprise, it's not my breasts he touches, although I am secretly craving it. Instead, he runs his hands from my shoulders and down my arms, grabbing both hands. I open my eyes, and he's peering down at me, smiling. "You're so fucking beautiful," he says. "And mine... I'm never going to let you go again."

"You said that the last time," I remind him.

He slips something onto my finger. I look down at the most obnoxious diamond ring I've ever seen.

My mouth falls open. "Jesus, Micah. It's beautiful." I'm speechless as I turn it and see it shimmer in the dim light.

I can't even fathom what this cost him.

He shrugs. "I can afford it."

"When did you buy this?"

"The same time I bought this house. Here, I have something else for you." He disappears for a moment, and he comes back out with something in his hand.

My leather-bound journal, along with the flower he carved for me when we were stranded. My stomach tightens, and my hand covers my mouth. All my thoughts, feelings, and fears when I was at my worst on that island are in there... so is the love I felt for the twins.

"You found it?" I whisper and peer up at him. "Did you... did you read it?"

"Yeah," he admits. "It kept me alive, baby. Your words saved my life. It was like having you there with me."

I run my hands over it, the soft brown leather and the memory of Nigel plopping it in front of me like the arrogant ass he was.

Can I re-live it?

He smiles and passes me something else.

I nearly scream when he hands me my wolf blanket. I rub the blanket over my face, enjoying the soft fur that brought me so much joy. This blanket was the one possession that meant the most to me and the only thing I acquired while I was there. That, and the flower. Somehow, I doubt he brought home my wooden spear.

I'm still admiring the diamond, this house, and everything he is giving me in abundance after spending months with him with absolutely nothing.

He pulls me into him, his eyes not leaving mine, despite my boobs being pressed up in the push-up bra I wore for him—in the hopes of seeing him again. This life he wants me to live sounds perfect, except—

"Micah, I can't live here. New Ocean isn't my home. No one wants me here."

He laughs darkly, that cocky demeanor as if he rules the word. "Don't worry about what people think of you in this town, baby. Because you are about to become the queen of it. You are about to become the richest woman in New Ocean and probably the richest woman in this entire state. That is if you still want to marry me."

I smile and look at him—his brooding face—then tug on his gray sweats. "Of course, I will marry you, Micah Matei."

He kisses me, and I savor the taste of him. "Good answer, baby," he murmurs against my lips.

Jesus, he sounds like Maison.

"What do we do now?" I ask him.

He kisses my lips, then my cheek, and finally moves to my neck before I stop him. "I'm going to keep you here," he whispers. "And worship every part of your mind and body until you start feeling better and trust me again. We can take everything slow, London; we are in absolutely no rush."

A voice deep inside me sings. It sings louder than the dark laughter and despair, easing the gripping panic that constantly plagues me.

A glimmer of hope... my medicine.

"Then what?" I breathe.

A slow smile spreads over his face. "I have a meeting next week, then I need to get back on the ice to train."

I narrow my eyes with confusion. "Who is your meeting with?"

"The farm team for the NHL. I called them as soon as I got home, and they said they would let me try out. It's time to get my life back." He never ceases to amaze me, and that doesn't surprise me at all. "And when you're ready, London, I want you to tell your story, but I want you to tell it your way."

I grip the leather-bound journal, the pages of which contain my story.

The story that's already written.

EPILOGUE

MICAH

A Year Later

Mornings are my favorite.

Fresh, crisp air, renewed energy, and the fact I can now sleep at night makes daytime much more sufferable. For the first time in my life, I'm at peace, and I'm lucky enough to wake up to the girl who was my literal dream for three months while I was in isolation. This girl who chooses to be with me every day despite every reason she shouldn't.

At the earliest hint of dawn, I wake up, brush a kiss over her ivory cheek, and slip out of bed. I head to my woodshop out back, suppressing the terror that I will blink and she'll be gone. I spent three months alone fighting my demons, and for at least a month of that time, I acted like she was with me. I spoke to her, and she answered. I cradled her and held her. In my mind, everything was as it should be.

It was heaven.

She was so real. It felt like I had slipped into an alternate reality where I had my happy ending with her and she never escaped my attempt at binding her.

Then, one day, after a long sleep, I woke up, reaching my hand out for her, and she wasn't there. Instead, I found my hand rested on the blood stain that still marred the spot where she tore through the skin on her hand. Reality smacked me in the face like an icy punch. That's when I knew I had to go home. I fought like hell after that to get my mind right. My existence took on a primitive form, spending weeks like a savage, ruthlessly hunting and obliterating everything within sight. I rage-hunted all the darkness out of me until it was... gone.

Now, every day, I fight to maintain control so I can help London find her light again.

The truth is that I wake up every day petrified that I'll turn back into that, and the morning solitude is what brings me back from the brink.

After a couple of hours in the wood shack and completing my morning run, I shower, dry myself off with a towel, and slip back into bed, where my sleeping beauty is still passed out.

My wife is not a morning person, despite the fresh rays of sunlight shining over her eyes, which are escaping through the tangled layer of trees and the enormous window in our bedroom. A familiarity that triggers torturous memories and blissful reminders of the place that started it all.

She's squinting her eyes, and she's curled up beside me, her arms and legs tucked into her body like a turtle, grasping her precious wolf blanket. She sleeps this way every night—careful, afraid, and exactly how I once left her.

She sleeps like that because memories still plague her. Nightmares of me...

I watch her silently while she sleeps. It's creepy as fuck, but I love the way she twitches her nose and grimaces in the cutest way. She also wore the sexiest fucking lace I had ever seen to bed last night, which is usually a signal she wants me close by when she wakes. Her skin is smooth and delicate, and the old me would have thought she was begging to be fucked with her ass in the air.

That was the old me, and London deserves better than the old me. So I lie and wait patiently for permission to ravish her.

I try not to wake her because she only sleeps in the morning; she usually stays up all night writing. This way, I can watch over her and wake her if the demons start to overwhelm her. The physical bruises on her body are long healed—mostly—and every day, I work tirelessly to heal her emotional scars.

While she won't admit it, she does the same for me at night when the story of what happened to us pours out of her. She handwrites in her journals. Pages of words she won't let me read, the story—our story—from her perspective.

After a few minutes, my hand falls to her cheek to gently wake her. Her eyes fly open in a startle, her initial panic giving way to immense relief when she catches sight of me.

I cup her chin as she scans my face. "I'm real, baby. This isn't a dream. You're at home." Sometimes, I have to remind her where we are. Reality still hasn't set in for her—that we're together. Even a year after our small wedding, I haven't left her side once. Even with my hockey schedule, she's always with me, facing plane ride after plane ride so she can be with me.

Her cherry lips part, and she closes her eyes with a smile that radiates out of her body.

She keeps her cheek planted on the silk pillow. "Micah, what time is it?"

I press my lips to hers, the heat from the sunlight warming her face. "Eleven," I murmur against her.

She stirs a bit more as I move my mouth to her earlobe and, ever so slightly, wipe the bit of drool dripping from the corner of her lips.

She nudges my hand away, still in a seemingly half-blissful daze. "Micah, don't get any ideas. We have to go soon." I pull off her and frown as a low tug hits my stomach.

The meeting with the mayor and his wife over lunch at the country club is in an hour.

Bleh.

I fucking hate the political shit in this town. London, however, is amazing at it. She's embraced her new position as the lady of New Ocean, even though the attention makes her uncomfortable. But she really, really enjoys giving away our money. She says it makes her feel good giving to local causes and that our money is tainted and would only burn our souls to hell if we held on to it all.

My mother wouldn't approve. She always played the game of philanthropy without actually being philanthropic. That's why I let London put the amount my parents stole from Ezra's family back to them—every fucking penny—and we put some in a trust fund for when Ezra gets out of prison, too.

I flip over and wrap my arm around her body, my fingers finding the sexy curves of her hips. "We still have an hour until lunch..."

I wait, as I always do, for her to tell me what she wants or needs from me in this moment. Because it's never the same from one day to the next.

She curls into me and settles her hips in me, heating my entire core. She arches her neck and smiles as I grab her chin and meet her lips for a soft kiss. I could easily spend an hour just making out with her if that's what she wants.

My dick, on the other hand, has other ideas.

She moans, and her entire body throbs under me, my erection pressing against her back.

"Micah," she warns. "I need to make sure I have enough time to get ready."

"We can be a few minutes late," I say, breezing my fingertips over the top of her ass cheeks. It's my favorite fucking part of her body whenever she gives me access to it.

Which is... sometimes. Usually, when I make her spaghetti.

Sometimes, it's the bruises she begs for, and I'm more than happy to oblige. And some days, she won't even let me close enough to touch her.

It always depends on how angry she is when she wakes up.

I snap the elastic band of her panties, and she reaches her hand down and wraps her fingers around my now painful erection. My thighs twitch, and my groin burns, my voice coming out as a low rumble. "London, don't tease me today."

She giggles, and I'll be damned if it's not the sweetest sound I've ever heard. She's had a few rough days, keeping her distance from me. Some new memories triggered her, and she needed time to cope with it.

She sits up and straddles me with a leg on either side of me, settling her hips over mine. Her bangs fall in front of her face, and the way the light shines down on her makes her look like an angel. She runs her hands through my hair, pressing herself down on me and moaning as she kisses me.

I cock my brow and arch my groin to meet hers. This is new... Usually, she likes me to take charge. "You better stop that, sweetheart, unless you're ready for me."

She's squeezing her thighs. "It's the mayor, Micah," she pants, "and I've been excited about this project, so quit trying to get out of it."

I can barely contain myself as she reaches down and pulls my cock out before sliding herself onto me.

Goddammit. This feeling never gets old. If I could spend an eternity inside her, I would.

I move my hands from her hips to her ass, and she grinds into me, slow and steady, taking her time, giving me a warning look. She holds all the power.

If she keeps clenching like that, I'm going to go *wild*.

"He's the one who wants our money to build the new rink," I remind her. "He can wait an extra twenty fucking minutes while I fuck my wife."

She tilts her head and frowns as I start to slide in and out of her, gripping her harder.

Harder.

She starts to ride me lazily. "Micah, it's for Maison. I know this is still hard for you, but with your travel schedule for hockey, it's the only time we can do it."

The Maison Matei Arena.

He'd love having that arena named after him. It's not hard for me to donate money to honor him. I'm so fucking proud of him, and I know he'd be proud of me, too.

I clutch her neck, drawing her closer and interrupting her train of thought. I quickly press my lips against hers, stealing another kiss, before pulling away and leaving her breathless.

She rolls off me and flips to her stomach on the other side of the bed, arching her back, but not before giving me a sweet, inviting smile.

Fuck yeah.

I waste no time as I position myself on top of her tight little body. I lean down and whisper in her ear, "Maison's going to have to wait for us, too."

NIGEL'S CAVE
CRASH SITE
HUNTING CABIN
MEETING SPOT
EZRA'S CAVE
CREEK SITE
N
W
E
S
HIDDEN COVE
Pretty Little Island
LAKE SITE

ABOUT THE AUTHOR

Rhea Ryan is a spicy writer of romance on the edge of dark and twisty. Her stories are a masterful exploration of the human heart, skillfully navigating the complex and often grey terrain of our inner lives. After writing in the corporate world for over a decade, she realized she had a desire and compulsion to write creatively. She lives in Western Canada with her husband, two young children and a fur baby. When she's not writing, she is usually carting her kids around to hockey arenas and swimming pools.

Pretty Little Island is her debut novel.

Follow her on Social Media

Instagram: https://www.instagram.com/rhearyanwrites/
Website: www.rhearyan.com
Goodreads: www.goodreads.com/rhearyan
Facebook Group: Rhea's Dark Hearts | Facebook
Newsletter: bit.ly/Rheasnewsletter
Email: rhearyanwrites@gmail.com
BookBub: Rhea Ryan Books - BookBub

ACKNOWLEDGEMENTS

Thank you to my readers for coming along this journey with Micah, Maison, and London.

Writing Wicked Little Island was a very different experience than writing Pretty Little Island. I felt every emotion while writing this and to be honest, I wasn't sure where the story was going to go when I finished the first book. Luckily for me, my characters talk to me constantly, and they knew the way forward even if it was a painful path to get there. I had the best time bringing this story to life and writing this book was life changing. I hope you enjoyed it as much as I loved writing it.

So many people were a part of this journey. I don't even know where to start.

Special thanks to my husband, Garreth and my kids. It's not always easy to be married to a writer. We are often distracted, thinking about our worlds, and needless to say, busy. My family allows me to carve out time to do this, and for that I am eternally grateful.

I can't even begin to express the appreciation I have for my street team. I formed my street team mainly from dedicated ARC readers who loved the first book. You make me smile every day and your daily enthusiasm keeps me going even on the days I don't feel like it.

Thank you to my editors Silvia and Noemie for helping to make this manuscript shine. And to my beta readers, Ellie, Veronica, Harley, and Legs, for your hilarious reactions and unwavering support. And of course Melissa, Amy and my sister Sarah who read an early draft of Wicked

Little Island and helped me shape the book. And of course, Shelbie for being the best PA ever.